W9-ARU-199

Also by Stephen King

STEPHEN
KING

THE
LANGOLIERS

SCRIBNER

New York   London   Toronto   Sydney   New Delhi

SCRIBNER
An Imprint of Simon & Schuster, Inc.
1230 Avenue of the Americas
New York, NY 10020

This book is a work of fiction. Any references to historical events, real people, or real places are used fictitiously. Other names, characters, places, and events are products of the author's imagination, and any resemblance to actual events or places or persons, living or dead, is entirely coincidental.

Copyright © 1990 by Stephen King

This story was previously published in *Four Past Midnight*

"Angel of the Morning" by Chip Taylor. Copyright © EMI Blackwood Music Inc., 1967. All rights reserved. International copyright secured. Used by permission.

All rights reserved, including the right to reproduce this book or portions thereof in any form whatsoever. For information, address Scribner Subsidiary Rights Department, 1230 Avenue of the Americas, New York, NY 10020.

First Scribner trade paperback edition November 2019

SCRIBNER and design are registered trademarks of The Gale Group, Inc., used under license by Simon & Schuster, Inc., the publisher of this work.

For information about special discounts for bulk purchases, please contact Simon & Schuster Special Sales at 1-866-506-1949 or business@simonandschuster.com.

The Simon & Schuster Speakers Bureau can bring authors to your live event. For more information or to book an event contact the Simon & Schuster Speakers Bureau at 1-866-248-3049 or visit our website at www.simonspeakers.com.

Manufactured in the United States of America

7   9   10   8

ISBN 978-1-9821-3605-5
ISBN 978-1-9821-3606-2 (ebook)

THIS IS FOR JOE,
ANOTHER WHITE-KNUCKLE FLIER

CONTENTS

CHAPTER ONE

BAD NEWS FOR CAPTAIN ENGLE.
THE LITTLE BLIND GIRL. THE LADY'S SCENT.
THE DALTON GANG ARRIVES IN TOMBSTONE.
THE STRANGE PLIGHT OF FLIGHT 29.

1

Brian Engle rolled the American Pride L1011 to a stop at Gate 22 and flicked off the FASTEN SEATBELT light at exactly 10:14 P.M. He let a long sigh hiss through his teeth and unfastened his shoulder harness.

He could not remember the last time he had been so relieved—and so tired—at the end of a flight. He had a nasty, pounding headache, and his plans for the evening were firmly set. No drink in the pilots' lounge, no dinner, not even a bath when he got back to Westwood. He intended to fall into bed and sleep for fourteen hours.

American Pride's Flight 7—Flagship Service from Tokyo to Los Angeles—had been delayed first by strong headwinds and then by typical congestion at LAX . . . which was, Engle thought, arguably America's worst airport, if you left out Logan in Boston. To make matters worse, a pressurization problem had developed during the latter part of the flight. Minor at first, it had gradually worsened until it was scary. It had almost gotten to the point where a blowout and explosive decompression could have occurred . . . and had mercifully grown no worse. Sometimes such problems suddenly and mysteriously stabilized themselves, and that was what had happened this

1

time. The passengers now disembarking just behind the control cabin had not the slightest idea how close they had come to being people *pâté* on tonight's flight from Tokyo, but Brian knew . . . and it had given him a whammer of a headache.

"This bitch goes right into diagnostic from here," he told his co-pilot. "They know it's coming and what the problem is, right?"

The co-pilot nodded. "They don't like it, but they know."

"I don't give a shit what they like and what they don't like, Danny. We came close tonight."

Danny Keene nodded. He knew they had.

Brian sighed and rubbed a hand up and down the back of his neck. His head ached like a bad tooth. "Maybe I'm getting too old for this business."

That was, of course, the sort of thing anyone said about his job from time to time, particularly at the end of a bad shift, and Brian knew damned well he wasn't too old for the job—at forty-three, he was just entering prime time for airline pilots. Nevertheless, tonight he almost believed it. God, he was tired.

There was a knock at the compartment door; Steve Searles, the navigator, turned in his seat and opened it without standing up. A man in a green American Pride blazer was standing there. He looked like a gate agent, but Brian knew he wasn't. It was John (or maybe it was James) Deegan, Deputy Chief of Operations for American Pride at LAX.

"Captain Engle?"

"Yes?" An internal set of defenses went up, and his headache flared. His first thought, born not of logic but of strain and weariness, was that they were going to try and pin responsibility for the leaky aircraft on him. Paranoid, of course, but he was in a paranoid frame of mind.

"I'm afraid I have some bad news for you, Captain."

"Is this about the leak?" Brian's voice was too sharp, and a few of the disembarking passengers glanced around, but it was too late to do anything about that now.

Deegan was shaking his head. "It's your wife, Captain Engle."

For a moment Brian didn't have the foggiest notion what the man was talking about and could only sit there, gaping at him and feeling exquisitely stupid. Then the penny dropped. He meant Anne, of course.

"She's my ex-wife. We were divorced eighteen months ago. What about her?"

"There's been an accident," Deegan said. "Perhaps you'd better come up to the office."

Brian looked at him curiously. After the last three long, tense hours, all of this seemed strangely unreal. He resisted an urge to tell Deegan that if this was some sort of *Candid Camera* bullshit, he could go fuck himself. But of course it wasn't. Airlines brass weren't into pranks and games, especially at the expense of pilots who had just come very close to having nasty midair mishaps.

"What about Anne?" Brian heard himself asking again, this time in a softer voice. He was aware that his co-pilot was looking at him with cautious sympathy. "Is she all right?"

Deegan looked down at his shiny shoes and Brian knew that the news was very bad indeed, that Anne was a lot more than not all right. Knew, but found it impossible to believe. Anne was only thirty-four, healthy, and careful in her habits. He had also thought on more than one occasion that she was the only completely sane driver in the city of Boston . . . perhaps in the whole state of Massachusetts.

Now he heard himself asking something else, and it was really like that—as if some stranger had stepped into his brain and was using his mouth as a loudspeaker. "Is she dead?"

John or James Deegan looked around, as if for support, but there was only a single flight attendant standing by the hatch, wishing the deplaning passengers a pleasant evening in Los Angeles and glancing anxiously toward the cockpit every now and then, probably worried about the same thing that had crossed Brian's mind—that the crew was for some reason to be blamed for the slow leak which had made the last few hours of the flight such a nightmare. Deegan was on his own. He looked at Brian again and nodded. "Yes—I'm afraid she is. Would you come with me, Captain Engle?"

2

At quarter past midnight, Brian Engle was settling into seat 5A of American Pride's Flight 29—Flagship Service from Los Angeles to Boston. In fifteen minutes or so, that flight known to transcontinental travelers as the red-eye would be airborne. He remembered thinking earlier that if LAX wasn't the most dangerous commercial airport in America, then Logan was. Through the most unpleasant of coincidences, he would now have a chance to experience both places within an eight-hour span of time: into LAX as the pilot, into Logan as a deadheading passenger.

His headache, now a good deal worse than it had been upon landing Flight 7, stepped up another notch.

A fire, he thought. *A goddamned fire. What happened to the smoke-detectors, for Christ's sake? It was a brand-new building!*

It occurred to him that he had hardly thought about Anne at all for the last four or five months. During the first year of the divorce, she was all he *had* thought about, it seemed— what she was doing, what she was wearing, and, of course, who she was seeing. When the healing finally began, it had happened very fast . . . as if he had been injected with some spirit-reviving antibiotic. He had read enough about divorce to know what that reviving agent usually was: not an antibiotic but another woman. The rebound effect, in other words.

There had been no other woman for Brian—at least not yet. A few dates and one cautious sexual encounter (he had come to believe that all sexual encounters outside of marriage in the

Age of AIDS were cautious), but no other woman. He had simply . . . healed.

Brian watched his fellow passengers come aboard. A young woman with blonde hair was walking with a little girl in dark glasses. The little girl's hand was on the blonde's elbow. The woman murmured to her charge, the girl looked immediately toward the sound of her voice, and Brian understood she was blind—it was something in the gesture of the head. Funny, he thought, how such small gestures could tell so much.

Anne, he thought. *Shouldn't you be thinking about Anne?*

But his tired mind kept trying to slip away from the subject of Anne—Anne, who had been his wife, Anne, who was the only woman he had ever struck in anger, Anne who was now dead.

He supposed he could go on a lecture tour; he would talk to groups of divorced men. Hell, divorced women as well, for that matter. His subject would be divorce and the art of forgetfulness.

Shortly after the fourth anniversary is the optimum time for divorce, he would tell them. *Take my case. I spent the following year in purgatory, wondering just how much of it was my fault and how much was hers, wondering how right or wrong it was to keep pushing her on the subject of kids—that was the big thing with us, nothing dramatic like drugs or adultery, just the old kids-versus-career thing—and then it was like there was an express elevator inside my head, and Anne was in it, and down it went.*

Yes. Down it had gone. And for the last several months, he hadn't really thought of Anne at all . . . not even when the monthly alimony check was due. It was a very reasonable, very civilized amount; Anne had been making eighty thousand a year on her own before taxes. His lawyer paid it, and it was just another item on the monthly statement Brian got, a little two-thousand-dollar item tucked between the electricity bill and the mortgage payment on the condo.

He watched a gangly teenaged boy with a violin case under his arm and a *yarmulke* on his head walk down the aisle. The boy looked both nervous and excited, his eyes full of the future. Brian envied him.

There had been a lot of bitterness and anger between the two of them during the last year of the marriage, and finally, about four months before the end, it had happened: his hand had said go before his brain could say no. He didn't like to remember that. She'd had too much to drink at a party, and she had really torn into him when they got home.

Leave me alone about it, Brian. Just leave me alone. No more talk about kids. If you want a sperm-test, go to a doctor. My job is advertising, not baby-making. I'm so tired of all your macho bullshit—

That was when he had slapped her, hard, across the mouth. The blow had clipped the last word off with brutal neatness. They had stood looking at each other in the apartment where she would later die, both of them more shocked and frightened than they would ever admit (except maybe now, sitting here in seat 5A and watching Flight 29's passengers come on board, he *was* admitting it, finally admitting it to himself). She had touched her mouth, which had started to bleed. She held out her fingers toward him.

You hit me, she said. It was not anger in her voice but wonder. He had an idea it might have been the first time anyone had ever laid an angry hand upon any part of Anne Quinlan Engle's body.

Yes, he had said. *You bet. And I'll do it again if you don't shut up. You're not going to whip me with that tongue of yours anymore, sweetheart. You better put a padlock on it. I'm telling you for your own good. Those days are over. If you want something to kick around the house, buy a dog.*

The marriage had crutched along for another few months, but it had really ended in that moment when Brian's palm made brisk contact with the side of Anne's mouth. He had been provoked—God knew he had been provoked—but he still would have given a great deal to take that one wretched second back.

As the last passengers began to trickle on board, he found himself also thinking, almost obsessively, about Anne's perfume. He could recall its fragrance exactly, but not the name. What had it been? Lissome? Lithesome? Lithium, for God's sake? It danced just beyond his grasp. It was maddening.

I miss her, he thought dully. *Now that she's gone forever, I miss her. Isn't that amazing?*

Lawnboy? Something stupid like that?

Oh stop it, he told his weary mind. *Put a cork in it.*

Okay, his mind agreed. *No problem; I can quit. I can quit anytime I want. Was it maybe Lifebuoy? No—that's soap. Sorry. Lovebite? Lovelorn?*

Brian snapped his seatbelt shut, leaned back, closed his eyes, and smelled a perfume he could not quite name.

That was when the flight attendant spoke to him. Of course: Brian Engle had a theory that they were taught— in a highly secret post-graduate course, perhaps called Teasing the Geese—to wait until the passenger closed his or her eyes before offering some not-quite-essential service. And, of course, they were to wait until they were reasonably sure the passenger was asleep before waking him to ask if he would like a blanket or a pillow.

"Pardon me . . ." she began, then stopped. Brian saw her eyes go from the epaulets on the shoulders of his black jacket to the hat, with its meaningless squiggle of scrambled eggs, on the empty seat beside him.

She rethought herself and started again.

"Pardon me, Captain, would you like coffee or orange juice?" Brian was faintly amused to see he had flustered her a little. She gestured toward the table at the front of the compartment, just below the small rectangular movie screen. There were two ice-buckets on the table. The slender green neck of a wine bottle poked out of each. "Of course, I also have champagne."

Engle considered
(Love Boy that's not it close but no cigar)
the champagne, but only briefly. "Nothing, thanks," he said. "And no in-flight service. I think I'll sleep all the way to Boston. How's the weather look?"

"Clouds at 20,000 feet from the Great Plains all the way to Boston, but no problem. We'll be at thirty-six. Oh, and we've had reports of the aurora borealis over the Mojave Desert. You might want to stay awake for that."

Brian raised his eyebrows. "You're kidding. The aurora borealis over California? And at this time of year?"

"That's what we've been told."

"Somebody's been taking too many cheap drugs," Brian said, and she laughed. "I think I'll just snooze, thanks."

"Very good, Captain." She hesitated a moment longer. "You're the captain who just lost his wife, aren't you?"

The headache pulsed and snarled, but he made himself smile. This woman—who was really no more than a girl—meant no harm. "She was my ex-wife, but otherwise, yes. I am."

"I'm awfully sorry for your loss."

"Thank you."

"Have I flown with you before, sir?"

His smile reappeared briefly. "I don't think so. I've been on overseas for the past four years or so." And because it seemed somehow necessary, he offered his hand. "Brian Engle."

She took it. "Melanie Trevor."

Engle smiled at her again, then leaned back and closed his eyes once more. He let himself drift, but not sleep—the pre-flight announcements, followed by the take-off roll, would only wake him up again. There would be time enough to sleep when they were in the air.

Flight 29, like most red-eye flights, left promptly—Brian reflected that was high on their meager list of attractions. The plane was a 767, a little over half full. There were half a dozen other passengers in first class. None of them looked drunk or rowdy to Brian. That was good. Maybe he really *would* sleep all the way to Boston.

He watched Melanie Trevor patiently as she pointed out the exit doors, demonstrated how to use the little gold cup if there was a pressure loss (a procedure Brian had been reviewing in his own mind, and with some urgency, not long ago), and how to inflate the life vest under the seat. When the plane was airborne, she came by his seat and asked him again if she could get him something to drink. Brian shook his head, thanked her, then pushed the button which caused his seat to recline. He closed his eyes and promptly fell asleep.

He never saw Melanie Trevor again.

3

About three hours after Flight 29 took off, a little girl named Dinah Bellman woke up and asked her Aunt Vicky if she could have a drink of water.

Aunt Vicky did not answer, so Dinah asked again. When there was still no answer, she reached over to touch her aunt's shoulder, but she was already quite sure that her hand would touch nothing but the back of an empty seat, and that was what happened. Dr. Feldman had told her that children who were blind from birth often developed a high sensitivity— almost a kind of radar—to the presence or absence of people in their immediate area, but Dinah hadn't really needed the information. She knew it was true. It didn't always work, but it usually did . . . especially if the person in question was her Sighted Person.

Well, she's gone to the bathroom and she'll be right back, Dinah thought, but she felt an odd, vague disquiet settle over her just the same. She hadn't come awake all at once; it had been a slow process, like a diver kicking her way to the surface of a lake. If Aunt Vicky, who had the window seat, had brushed by her to get to the aisle in the last two or three minutes, Dinah should have felt her.

So she went sooner, she told herself. *Probably she had to Number Two—it's really no big deal, Dinah. Or maybe she stopped to talk with somebody on her way back.*

Except Dinah couldn't hear *anyone* talking in the big airplane's main cabin; only the steady soft drone of the jet engines. Her feeling of disquiet grew.

The voice of Miss Lee, her therapist (except Dinah always thought of her as her blind teacher), spoke up in her head: *You mustn't be afraid to be afraid, Dinah—all children are afraid from time to time, especially in situations that are new to them. That goes double for children who are blind. Believe me, I know.* And Dinah did believe her, because, like Dinah herself, Miss Lee had been blind since birth. *Don't give up your fear . . . but don't give in to it, either. Sit still and try to reason things out. You'll be surprised how often it works.*

Especially in situations that are new to them.

Well, that certainly fit; this was the first time Dinah had ever flown in *anything,* let alone coast to coast in a huge transcontinental jetliner.

Try to reason it out.

Well, she had awakened in a strange place to find her Sighted Person gone. Of course that was scary, even if you knew the absence was only temporary—after all, your Sighted Person couldn't very well decide to pop off to the nearest Taco Bell because she had the munchies when she was shut up in an airplane flying at 37,000 feet. As for the strange silence in the cabin . . . well, this *was* the red-eye, after all. The other passengers were probably sleeping.

All of them? the worried part of her mind asked doubtfully. ALL *of them are sleeping? Can that be?*

Then the answer came to her: the movie. The ones who were awake were watching the in-flight movie. Of course.

A sense of almost palpable relief swept over her. Aunt Vicky had told her the movie was Billy Crystal and Meg Ryan in

When Harry Met Sally . . . , and said she planned to watch it herself . . . if she could stay awake, that was.

Dinah ran her hand lightly over her aunt's seat, feeling for her headphones, but they weren't there. Her fingers touched a paperback book instead. One of the romance novels Aunt Vicky liked to read, no doubt—tales of the days when men were men and women weren't, she called them.

Dinah's fingers went a little further and happened on something else—smooth, fine-grained leather. A moment later she felt a zipper, and a moment after that she felt the strap.

It was Aunt Vicky's purse.

Dinah's disquiet returned. The earphones weren't on Aunt Vicky's seat, but her purse was. All the traveller's checks, except for a twenty tucked deep into Dinah's own purse, were in there—Dinah knew, because she had heard Mom and Aunt Vicky discussing them before they left the house in Pasadena.

Would Aunt Vicky go off to the bathroom and leave her purse on the seat? Would she do that when her travelling companion was not only ten, not only asleep, but *blind*?

Dinah didn't think so.

Don't give up your fear . . . but don't give in to it, either. Sit still and try to reason things out.

But she didn't like that empty seat, and she didn't like the silence of the plane. It made perfect sense to her that most of the people would be asleep, and that the ones who were awake would be keeping as quiet as possible out of consideration for the rest, but she still didn't like it. An animal, one with extremely sharp teeth and claws, awakened and started to snarl inside of her head. She knew the name of that animal; it was panic, and if she didn't control it fast, she might do something which would embarrass both her and Aunt Vicky.

When I can see, when the doctors in Boston fix my eyes, I won't have to go through stupid stuff like this.

This was undoubtedly true, but it was absolutely no help to her right *now.*

Dinah suddenly remembered that, after they sat down, Aunt Vicky had taken her hand, folded all the fingers but the pointer under, and then guided that one finger to the side of her seat. The controls were there—only a few of them, simple, easy to remember. There were two little wheels you could use once you put on the headphones—one switched around to the different audio channels; the other controlled the volume. The small rectangular switch controlled the light over her seat. *You won't need that one,* Aunt Vicky said with a smile in her voice. *At least, not yet.* The last one was a square button—when you pushed that one, a flight attendant came.

Dinah's finger touched this button now, and skated over its slightly convex surface.

Do you really want to do this? she asked herself, and the answer came back at once. *Yeah, I do.*

She pushed the button and heard the soft chime. Then she waited.

No one came.

There was only the soft, seemingly eternal whisper of the jet engines. No one spoke. No one laughed (*Guess that movie isn't as funny as Aunt Vicky thought it would be,* Dinah thought). No one coughed. The seat beside her, Aunt Vicky's seat, was still empty, and no flight attendant bent over her in a comforting little envelope of perfume and shampoo and faint smells of make-up to ask Dinah if she could get her something—a snack, or maybe that drink of water.

Only the steady soft drone of the jet engines.

The panic animal was yammering louder than ever. To combat it, Dinah concentrated on focussing that radar gadget, making it into a kind of invisible cane she could jab out from her seat here in the middle of the main cabin. She was good at that; at times, when she concentrated *very* hard, she almost believed she could see through the eyes of others. If she thought about it hard enough, wanted to hard enough. Once she had told Miss Lee about this feeling, and Miss Lee's response had been uncharacteristically sharp. *Sight-sharing is a frequent fantasy of the blind,* she'd said. *Particularly of blind children. Don't ever make the mistake of relying on that feeling, Dinah, or you're apt to find yourself in traction after falling down a flight of stairs or stepping in front of a car.*

So she had put aside her efforts to "sight-share," as Miss Lee had called it, and on the few occasions when the sensation stole over her again—that she was seeing the world, shadowy, wavery, but *there*—through her mother's eyes or Aunt Vicky's eyes, she had tried to get rid of it . . . as a person who fears he is losing his mind will try to block out the murmur of phantom voices. But now she was afraid and so she felt for others, *sensed* for others, and did not find them.

Now the terror was very large in her, the yammering of the panic animal very loud. She felt a cry building up in her throat and clamped her teeth against it. Because it would not come out as a cry, or a yell; if she let it out, it would exit her mouth as a fireball scream.

I won't scream, she told herself fiercely. *I won't scream and embarrass Aunt Vicky. I won't scream and wake up all the ones who are asleep and scare all the ones who are awake and they'll all come running and say look at the scared little girl, look at the scared little blind girl.*

But now that radar sense—that part of her which evaluated all sorts of vague sensory input and which sometimes *did* seem to see through the eyes of others (no matter what Miss Lee said)—was adding to her fear rather than alleviating it.

Because that sense was telling her there was *nobody* within its circle of effectiveness.

Nobody at all.

4

Brian Engle was having a very bad dream. In it, he was once again piloting Flight 7 from Tokyo to L.A., but this time the leak was much worse. There was a palpable feeling of doom in the cockpit; Steve Searles was weeping as he ate a Danish pastry.

If you're so upset, how come you're eating? Brian asked. A shrill, teakettle whistling had begun to fill the cockpit—the sound of the pressure leak, he reckoned. This was silly, of course—leaks were almost always silent until the blowout occurred—but he supposed in dreams anything was possible.

Because I love these things, and I'm never going to get to eat another one, Steve said, sobbing harder than ever.

Then, suddenly, the shrill whistling sound stopped. A smiling, relieved flight attendant—it was, in fact, Melanie Trevor— appeared to tell him the leak had been found and plugged. Brian got up and followed her through the plane to the main cabin, where Anne Quinlan Engle, his ex-wife, was standing in a little alcove from which the seats had been removed. Written over the window beside her was the cryptic and somehow ominous phrase SHOOTING STARS ONLY. It was written in red, the color of danger.

Anne was dressed in the dark-green uniform of an American Pride flight attendant, which was strange—she was an advertising executive with a Boston agency, and had always looked down her narrow, aristocratic nose at the stews with whom her husband flew. Her hand was pressed against a crack in the fuselage.

See, darling? she said proudly. *It's all taken care of. It doesn't even matter that you hit me. I have forgiven you.*

Don't do that, Anne! he cried, but it was already too late. A fold appeared in the back of her hand, mimicking the shape of the crack in the fuselage. It grew deeper as the pressure differential sucked her hand relentlessly outward. Her middle finger went through first, then the ring finger, then the first finger and her pinky. There was a brisk popping sound, like a champagne cork being drawn by an overeager waiter, as her entire hand was pulled through the crack in the airplane.

Yet Anne went on smiling.

It's L'Envoi, darling, she said as her arm began to disappear. Her hair was escaping the clip which held it back and blowing around her face in a misty cloud. *It's what I've always worn, don't you remember?*

He did . . . now he did. But now it didn't matter.

Anne, come back! he screamed.

She went on smiling as her arm was sucked slowly into the emptiness outside the plane. *It doesn't hurt at all, Brian— believe me.*

The sleeve of her green American Pride blazer began to flutter, and Brian saw that her flesh was being pulled out through the crack in a thickish white ooze. It looked like Elmer's Glue.

L'Envoi, remember? Anne asked as she was sucked out through the crack, and now Brian could hear it again—that sound which the poet James Dickey once called "the vast beast-whistle of space." It grew steadily louder as the dream darkened, and at the same time it began to broaden. To become not the scream of wind but that of a human voice.

Brian's eyes snapped open. He was disoriented by the power of the dream for a moment, but only a moment—he was a professional in a high-risk, high-responsibility job, a job where one of the absolute prerequisites was fast reaction time. He was on Flight 29, not Flight 7, not Tokyo to Los Angeles but Los Angeles to Boston, where Anne was already dead—not the victim of a pressure leak but of a fire in her Atlantic Avenue condominium near the waterfront. But the sound was still there.

It was a little girl, screaming shrilly.

5

"Would somebody speak to me, please?" Dinah Bellman asked in a low, clear voice. "I'm sorry, but my aunt is gone and I'm blind."

No one answered her. Forty rows and two partitions forward, Captain Brian Engle was dreaming that his navigator was weeping and eating a Danish pastry.

There was only the continuing drone of the jet engines.

The panic overshadowed her mind again, and Dinah did the only thing she could think of to stave it off: she unbuckled her seatbelt, stood up, and edged into the aisle.

"Hello?" she asked in a louder voice. "Hello, *anybody*!"

There was still no answer. Dinah began to cry. She held onto herself grimly, nonetheless, and began walking forward slowly along the portside aisle. *Keep count, though,* part of her mind warned frantically. *Keep count of how many rows you pass, or you'll get lost and never find your way back again.*

She stopped at the row of portside seats just ahead of the row in which she and Aunt Vicky had been sitting and bent, arms outstretched, fingers splayed. She was steeled to touch the sleeping face of the man sitting there. She knew there *was* a man here, because Aunt Vicky had spoken to him only a minute or so before the plane took off. When he spoke back to her, his voice had come from the seat directly in front of Dinah's own. She knew that; marking the locations of voices was part of her life, an ordinary fact of existence like breathing. The sleeping man would jump when her outstretched fingers touched him, but Dinah was beyond caring.

Except the seat was empty.

Completely empty.

Dinah straightened up again, her cheeks wet, her head pounding with fright. They couldn't be in the bathroom *together*, could they? Of course not.

Perhaps there were two bathrooms. In a plane this big there *must* be two bathrooms.

Except that didn't matter, either.

Aunt Vicky wouldn't have left her purse, no matter what. Dinah was sure of it.

She began to walk slowly forward, stopping at each row of seats, reaching into the two closest her—first on the port side and then on the starboard.

She felt another purse in one, what felt like a briefcase in another, a pen and a pad of paper in a third. In two others she felt headphones. She touched something sticky on an earpiece of the second set. She rubbed her fingers together, then grimaced and wiped them on the mat which covered the headrest of the seat. That had been earwax. She was sure of it. It had its own unmistakable, yucky texture.

Dinah Bellman felt her slow way up the aisle, no longer taking pains to be gentle in her investigations. It didn't matter. She poked no eye, pinched no cheek, pulled no hair.

Every seat she investigated was empty.

This can't be, she thought wildly. *It just can't be! They were all around us when we got on! I heard them! I felt them! I smelled them! Where have they all gone?*

She didn't know, but they *were* gone: she was becoming steadily more sure of that.

At some point, while she slept, her aunt and everyone else on Flight 29 had disappeared.

No! The rational part of her mind clamored in the voice of Miss Lee. *No, that's impossible, Dinah! If everyone's gone, who is flying the plane?*

She began to move forward faster now, hands gripping the edges of the seats, her blind eyes wide open behind her dark glasses, the hem of her pink travelling dress fluttering. She had lost count, but in her greater distress over the continuing silence, this did not matter much to her.

She stopped again, and reached her groping hands into the seat on her right. This time she touched hair . . . but its location was all wrong. The hair was on the seat—how could that be?

Her hands closed around it . . . and lifted it. Realization, sudden and terrible, came to her.

It's hair, but the man it belongs to is gone. It's a scalp. I'm holding a dead man's scalp.

That was when Dinah Bellman opened her mouth and began to give voice to the shrieks which pulled Brian Engle from his dream.

6

Albert Kaussner was belly up to the bar, drinking Branding Iron Whiskey. The Earp brothers, Wyatt and Virgil, were on his right, and Doc Holliday was on his left. He was just lifting his glass to offer a toast when a man with a peg leg ran-hopped into the Sergio Leone Saloon.

"It's the Dalton Gang!" he screamed. *"The Daltons have just rid into Dodge!"*

Wyatt turned to face him calmly. His face was narrow, tanned, and handsome. He looked a great deal like Hugh O'Brian. "This here is Tombstone, Muffin," he said. "You got to get yore stinky ole shit together."

"Well, they're ridin in, wherever we are!" Muffin exclaimed. "And they look *maaad*, Wyatt! They look *reeely reeely maaaaaaad*!"

As if to prove this, guns began to fire in the street outside—the heavy thunder of Army .44s (probably stolen) mixed in with the higher whipcrack explosions of Garand rifles.

"Don't get your panties all up in a bunch, Muffy," Doc Holliday said, and tipped his hat back. Albert was not terribly surprised to see that Doc looked like Robert De Niro. He had always believed that if anyone was absolutely right to play the consumptive dentist, De Niro was the one.

"What do you say, boys?" Virgil Earp asked, looking around. Virgil didn't look like much of anyone.

"Let's go," Wyatt said. "I've had enough of these damned Clantons to last me a lifetime."

"It's the Daltons, Wyatt," Albert said quietly.

"I don't care if it's John Dillinger and Pretty Boy Floyd!" Wyatt exclaimed. "Are you with us or not, Ace?"

"I'm with you," Albert Kaussner said, speaking in the soft but menacing tones of the born killer. He dropped one hand to the butt of his long-barrelled Buntline Special and put the other to his head for a moment to make sure his *yarmulke* was on solidly. It was.

"Okay, boys," Doc said. "Let's go cut some Dalton butt."

They strode out together, four abreast through the batwing doors, just as the bell in the Tombstone Baptist Church began to toll high noon.

The Daltons were coming down Main Street at a full gallop, shooting holes in plate-glass windows and false fronts. They turned the waterbarrel in front of Duke's Mercantile and Reliable Gun Repair into a fountain.

Ike Dalton was the first to see the four men standing in the dusty street, their frock coats pulled back to free the handles of their guns. Ike reined his horse in savagely and it rose on its rear legs, squealing, foam splattering in thick curds around the bit. Ike Dalton looked quite a bit like Rutger Hauer.

"Look what we have got here," he sneered. "It is Wyatt Earp and his pansy brother, Virgil."

Emmett Dalton (who looked like Donald Sutherland after a month of hard nights) pulled up beside Ike. "And their faggot dentist friend, too," he snarled. "Who else wants—" Then he looked at Albert and paled. The thin sneer faltered on his lips.

Paw Dalton pulled up beside his two sons. Paw bore a strong resemblance to Slim Pickens.

"Christ," Paw whispered. "It's Ace Kaussner!"

Now Frank James pulled *his* mount into line next to Paw. His face was the color of dirty parchment. "What the hell, boys!" Frank cried. "I don't mind hoorawin a town or two on a dull day, but nobody told me The Arizona Jew was gonna be here!"

Albert "Ace" Kaussner, known from Sedalia to Steamboat

Springs as The Arizona Jew, took a step forward. His hand hovered over the butt of his Buntline. He spat a stream of tobacco to one side, never taking his chilly gray eyes from the hardcases mounted twenty feet in front of him.

"Go on and make your moves, boys," said The Arizona Jew. "By my count, hell ain't half full."

The Dalton Gang slapped leather just as the clock in the tower of the Tombstone Baptist Church beat the last stroke of noon into the hot desert air. Ace went for his own gun, his draw as fast as blue blazes, and as he began to fan the hammer with the flat of his left hand, sending a spray of .45-caliber death into the Dalton Gang, a little girl standing outside The Longhorn Hotel began to scream.

Somebody make that brat stop yowling, Ace thought. *What's the matter with her, anyway? I got this under control. They don't call me the fastest Hebrew west of the Mississippi for nothing.*

But the scream went on, ripping across the air, darkening it as it came, and everything began to break up.

For a moment Albert was nowhere at all—lost in a darkness through which fragments of his dream tumbled and spun in a whirlpool. The only constant was that terrible scream; it sounded like the shriek of an overloaded teakettle.

He opened his eyes and looked around. He was in his seat toward the front of Flight 29's main cabin. Coming up the aisle from the rear of the plane was a girl of about ten or twelve, wearing a pink dress and a pair of ditty-bop shades.

What is she, a movie star or something? he thought, but he was badly frightened, all the same. It was a bad way to exit his favorite dream.

"Hey!" he cried—but softly, so as not to wake the other passengers. "Hey, kid! What's the deal?"

The little girl whiplashed her head toward the sound of his voice. Her body turned a moment later, and she collided with one of the seats which ran down the center of the cabin in four-across rows. She struck it with her thighs, rebounded, and tumbled backward over the armrest of a portside seat. She fell into it with her legs up.

"Where is everybody?" she was screaming. *"Help me! Help me!"*

"Hey, stewardess!" Albert yelled, concerned, and unbuckled his seatbelt. He stood up, slipped out of his seat, turned toward the screaming little girl . . . and stopped. He was now facing fully toward the back of the plane, and what he saw froze him in place.

The first thought to cross his mind was, *I guess I don't have to worry about waking up the other passengers, after all.*

To Albert it looked like the entire main cabin of the 767 was empty.

7

Brian Engle was almost to the partition separating Flight 29's first-class and business-class sections when he realized that first class was now entirely empty. He stopped for just a moment, then got moving again. The others had left their seats to see what all the screaming was about, perhaps.

Of course he knew this was not the case; he had been flying passengers long enough to know a good bit about their group psychology. When a passenger freaked out, few if any of the others ever moved. Most air travellers meekly surrendered their option to take individual action when they entered the bird, sat down, and buckled their seatbelts around them. Once those few simple things were accomplished, all problem-solving tasks became the crew's responsibility. Airline personnel called them geese, but they were really sheep . . . an attitude most flight crews liked just fine. It made the nervous ones easier to handle.

But, since it was the only thing that made even remote sense, Brian ignored what he knew and plunged on. The rags of his own dream were still wrapped around him, and a part of his mind was convinced that it was Anne who was screaming, that he would find her halfway down the main cabin with her hand plastered against a crack in the body of the airliner, a crack located beneath a sign which read SHOOTING STARS ONLY.

There was only one passenger in the business section, an older man in a brown three-piece suit. His bald head gleamed mellowly in the glow thrown by his reading lamp. His arthritis-swollen hands were folded neatly over the buckle of his seatbelt. He was fast asleep and snoring loudly, ignoring the whole ruckus.

Brian burst through into the main cabin and there his forward motion was finally checked by utter stunned disbelief. He saw a teenaged boy standing near a little girl who had fallen into a seat on the port side about a quarter of the way down the cabin. The boy was not looking at her, however; he was staring toward the rear of the plane, with his jaw hanging almost all the way to the round collar of his Hard Rock Cafe tee-shirt.

Brian's first reaction was about the same as Albert Kaussner's: *My God, the whole plane is empty!*

Then he saw a woman on the starboard side of the airplane stand up and walk into the aisle to see what was happening. She had the dazed, puffy look of someone who has just been jerked out of a sound sleep. Halfway down, in the center aisle, a young man in a crew-necked jersey was craning his neck toward the little girl and staring with flat, incurious eyes. Another man, this one about sixty, got up from a seat close to Brian and stood there indecisively. He was dressed in a red flannel shirt and he looked utterly bewildered. His hair was fluffed up around his head in untidy mad-scientist corkscrews.

"Who's screaming?" he asked Brian. "Is the plane in trouble, mister? You don't think we're goin down, do you?"

The little girl stopped screaming. She struggled up from the seat she had fallen into, and then almost tumbled forward in the other direction. The kid caught her just in time; he was moving with dazed slowness.

Where have they gone? Brian thought. *My dear God, where have they all gone?*

But his feet were moving toward the teenager and the little girl now. As he went, he passed another passenger who was still sleeping, this one a girl of about seventeen. Her mouth was open in an unlovely yawp and she was breathing in long, dry inhalations.

He reached the teenager and the girl with the pink dress.

"Where are they, man?" Albert Kaussner asked. He had an arm around the shoulders of the sobbing child, but he wasn't looking at her; his eyes slipped relentlessly back and forth across the almost deserted main cabin. "Did we land someplace while I was asleep and let them off?"

"My aunt's gone!" the little girl sobbed. "My Aunt Vicky! I thought the plane was empty! I thought I was the only one! Where's my aunt, please? I want my aunt!"

Brian knelt beside her for a moment, so they were at approximately the same level. He noticed the sunglasses and remembered seeing her get on with the blonde woman.

"You're all right," he said. "You're all right, young lady. What's your name?"

"Dinah," she sobbed. "I can't find my aunt. I'm blind and I can't see her. I woke up and the seat was empty—"

"What's going on?" the young man in the crew-neck jersey asked. He was talking over Brian's head, ignoring both Brian and Dinah, speaking to the boy in the Hard Rock tee-shirt and the older man in the flannel shirt. "Where's everybody else?"

"You're all right, Dinah," Brian repeated. "There are other people here. Can you hear them?"

"Y-yes. I can hear them. But where's Aunt Vicky? And who's been killed?"

"Killed?" a woman asked sharply. It was the one from the starboard side. Brian glanced up briefly and saw she was young, dark-haired, pretty. "*Has* someone been killed? Have we been hijacked?"

"No one's been killed," Brian said. It was, at least, something to say. His mind felt weird: like a boat which has slipped its moorings. "Calm down, honey."

"I felt his hair!" Dinah insisted. "Someone cut off his HAIR!"

This was just too odd to deal with on top of everything else, and Brian dismissed it. Dinah's earlier thought suddenly struck home to him with chilly intensity—who the fuck was flying the plane?

He stood up and turned to the older man in the red shirt. "I have to go forward," he said. "Stay with the little girl."

"All right," the man in the red shirt said. "But what's happening?"

They were joined by a man of about thirty-five who was wearing pressed blue-jeans and an oxford shirt. Unlike the others, he looked utterly calm. He took a pair of horn-rimmed spectacles from his pocket, shook them out by one bow, and put them on. "We seem a few passengers short, don't we?" he said. His British accent was almost as crisp as his shirt. "What about crew? Anybody know?"

"That's what I'm going to find out," Brian said, and started forward again. At the head of the main cabin he turned back and counted quickly. Two more passengers had joined the huddle around the girl in the dark glasses. One was the teenaged girl who had been sleeping so heavily; she swayed on her feet as if she were either drunk or stoned. The other was an elderly gent in a fraying sport-coat. Eight people in all. To those he added himself and the guy in business class, who was, at least so far, sleeping through it all.

Ten people.

For the love of God, where are the rest of them?

But this was not the time to worry about it—there were bigger problems at hand. Brian hurried forward, barely glancing at the old bald fellow snoozing in business class.

8

The service area squeezed behind the movie screen and between the two first-class heads was empty. So was the galley, but there Brian saw something which was extremely troubling: the beverage trolley was parked kitty-corner by the starboard bathroom. There were a number of used glasses on its bottom shelf.

They were just getting ready to serve drinks, he thought. *When it happened—whatever "it" was—they'd just taken out the trolley. Those used glasses are the ones that were collected before the roll-out. So whatever happened must have happened within half an hour of take-off, maybe a little longer—weren't there turbulence reports over the desert? I think so. And that weird shit about the aurora borealis—*

For a moment Brian was almost convinced that last was a part of his dream—it was certainly odd enough—but further reflection convinced him that Melanie Trevor, the flight attendant, had actually said it.

Never mind that; what did *happen? In God's name,* what?

He didn't know, but he *did* know that looking at the abandoned drinks trolley put an enormous feeling of terror and superstitious dread into his guts. For just a moment he thought that this was what the first boarders of the *Mary Celeste* must have felt like, coming upon a totally abandoned ship where all the sail was neatly laid on, where the captain's table had been set for dinner, where all ropes were neatly coiled and some sailor's pipe was still smoldering away the last of its tobacco on the foredeck . . .

Brian shook these paralyzing thoughts off with a tremendous effort and went to the door between the service area and the cockpit. He knocked. As he had feared, there was no response. And although he knew it was useless to do so, he curled his fist up and hammered on it.

Nothing.

He tried the doorknob. It didn't move. That was SOP in the

age of unscheduled side-trips to Havana, Lebanon, and Tehran. Only the pilots could open it. Brian *could* fly this plane . . . but not from out here.

"Hey!" he shouted. "Hey, you guys! Open the door!"

Except he knew better. The flight attendants were gone; almost all the passengers were gone; Brian Engle was willing to bet the 767's two-man cockpit crew was also gone.

He believed Flight 29 was heading east on automatic pilot.

CHAPTER TWO

DARKNESS AND MOUNTAINS.
THE TREASURE TROVE. CREW-NECK'S NOSE.
THE SOUND OF NO DOGS BARKING. PANIC IS NOT
ALLOWED. A CHANGE OF DESTINATION.

1

Brian had asked the older man in the red shirt to look after Dinah, but as soon as Dinah heard the woman from the starboard side—the one with the pretty young voice—she imprinted on her with scary intensity, crowding next to her and reaching with a timid sort of determination for her hand. After the years spent with Miss Lee, Dinah knew a teacher's voice when she heard one. The dark-haired woman took her hand willingly enough.

"Did you say your name was Dinah, honey?"

"Yes," Dinah said. "I'm blind, but after my operation in Boston, I'll be able to see again. *Probably* be able to see. The doctors say there's a seventy percent chance I'll get some vision, and a forty per cent chance I'll get all of it. What's your name?"

"Laurel Stevenson," the dark-haired woman said. Her eyes were still conning the main cabin, and her face seemed unable to break out of its initial expression: dazed disbelief.

"Laurel, that's a flower, isn't it?" Dinah asked. She spoke with feverish vivacity.

"Uh-huh," Laurel said.

"Pardon me," the man with the horn-rimmed glasses and the British accent said. "I'm going forward to join our friend."

"I'll come along," the older man in the red shirt said.

"I want to know what's going on here!" the man in the crew-neck jersey exclaimed abruptly. His face was dead pale except for two spots of color, as bright as rouge, on his cheeks. "I want to know what's going on right *now*."

"Nor am I a bit surprised," the Brit said, and then began walking forward. The man in the red shirt trailed after him. The teenaged girl with the dopey look drifted along behind them for awhile and then stopped at the partition between the main cabin and the business section, as if unsure of where she was.

The elderly gent in the fraying sport-coat went to a portside window, leaned over, and peered out.

"What do you see?" Laurel Stevenson asked.

"Darkness and mountains," the man in the sport-coat said.

"The Rockies?" Albert asked.

The man in the frayed sport-coat nodded. "I believe so, young man."

Albert decided to go forward himself. He was seventeen, fiercely bright, and this evening's Bonus Mystery Question had also occurred to him: who was flying the plane?

Then he decided it didn't matter . . . at least for the moment. They were moving smoothly along, so presumably *someone* was, and even if some*one* turned out to be some*thing*—the autopilot, in other words—there wasn't a thing he could do about it. As Albert Kaussner he was a talented violinist—not quite a prodigy—on his way to study at The Berklee College of Music. As Ace Kaussner he was (in his dreams, at least) the fastest Hebrew west of the Mississippi, a bounty hunter who took it easy on Saturdays, was careful to keep his shoes off the bed, and always kept one eye out for the main chance and the other for a good kosher café somewhere along the dusty trail. Ace was, he supposed, his way of sheltering himself from loving parents who hadn't allowed him to play Little League baseball because he might damage his talented hands and who had believed, in their hearts, that every sniffle signalled the onset of pneumonia. He was a gunslinging violinist—an interesting combination—but he didn't know a thing about flying planes. And the little girl had said something which had simultaneously intrigued him and curdled his blood. *I felt his hair!* she had said. *Someone cut off his HAIR!*

He broke away from Dinah and Laurel (the man in the ratty sport-coat had moved to the starboard side of the plane to look out one of those windows, and the man in the crew-necked jersey was going forward to join the others, his eyes narrowed pugnaciously) and began to retrace Dinah's progress up the portside aisle.

Someone cut off his HAIR! she had said, and not too many rows down, Albert saw what she had been talking about.

2

"I am praying, sir," the Brit said, "that the pilot's cap I noticed in one of the first-class seats belongs to you."

Brian was standing in front of the locked door, head down, thinking furiously. When the Brit spoke up behind him, he jerked in surprise and whirled on his heels.

"Didn't mean to put your wind up," the Brit said mildly. "I'm Nick Hopewell." He stuck out his hand.

Brian shook it. As he did so, performing his half of the ancient ritual, it occurred to him that this must be a dream. The scary flight from Tokyo and finding out that Anne was dead had brought it on.

Part of his mind knew this was not so, just as part of his mind had known the little girl's scream had had nothing to do with the deserted first-class section, but he seized on this idea just as he had seized on that one. It helped, so why not? Everything else was nuts—so nutty that even attempting to think about it made his mind feel sick and feverish. Besides, there was really no time to think, simply no time, and he found that this was also something of a relief.

"Brian Engle," he said. "I'm pleased to meet you, although the circumstances are—". He shrugged helplessly. What *were* the circumstances, exactly? He could not think of an adjective which would adequately describe them.

"Bit bizarre, aren't they?" Hopewell agreed. "Best not to think of them right now, I suppose. Does the crew answer?"

"No," Brian said, and abruptly struck his fist against the door in frustration.

"Easy, easy," Hopewell soothed. "Tell me about the cap, Mr. Engle. You have no idea what satisfaction and relief it would give me to address you as Captain Engle."

Brian grinned in spite of himself. "I *am* Captain Engle," he said, "but under the circumstances, I guess you can call me Brian."

Nick Hopewell seized Brian's left hand and kissed it heartily. "I believe I'll call you Savior instead," he said. "Do you mind awfully?"

Brian threw his head back and began to laugh. Nick joined him. They were standing there in front of the locked door in the nearly empty plane, laughing wildly, when the man in the red shirt and the man in the crew-necked jersey arrived, looking at them as if they had both gone crazy.

3

Albert Kaussner held the hair in his right hand for several moments, looking at it thoughtfully. It was black and glossy in the overhead lights, a right proper pelt, and he wasn't at all surprised it had scared the hell out of the little girl. It would have scared Albert, too, if he hadn't been able to see it.

He tossed the wig back into the seat, glanced at the purse lying in the next seat, then looked more closely at what was lying next to the purse. It was a plain gold wedding ring. He picked it up, examined it, then put it back where it had been. He began walking slowly toward the back of the airplane. In less than a minute, Albert was so struck with wonder that he had forgotten all about who was flying the plane, or how the hell they were going to get down from here if it was the automatic pilot.

Flight 29's passengers were gone, but they had left a fabulous—and sometimes perplexing—treasure trove behind. Albert found jewelry on almost every seat: wedding rings, mostly, but there were also diamonds, emeralds, and rubies. There were earrings, most of them five-and-dime stuff but some which looked pretty expensive to Albert's eyes. His mom had a few good pieces, and some of this stuff made her best jewelry look like rummage-sale buys. There were studs, necklaces, cufflinks, ID bracelets. And watches, watches, watches. From Timex to Rolex, there seemed to be at least two hundred of them, lying on seats, lying on the floor between seats, lying in the aisles. They twinkled in the lights.

There were at least sixty pairs of spectacles. Wire-rimmed, horn-rimmed, gold-rimmed. There were prim glasses, punky glasses, and glasses with rhinestones set in the bows. There were Ray-Bans, Polaroids, and Foster Grants.

There were belt buckles and service pins and piles of pocket-change. No bills, but easily four hundred dollars in quarters, dimes, nickels, and pennies. There were wallets—not as many wallets as purses, but still a good dozen of them, from fine leather to plastic. There were pocket knives. There were at least a dozen hand-held calculators.

And odder things, as well. He picked up a flesh-colored plastic cylinder and examined it for almost thirty seconds before deciding it really *was* a dildo and putting it down again in a hurry. There was a small gold spoon on a fine gold chain. There were bright speckles of metal here and there on the seats and the floor, mostly silver but some gold. He picked up a couple of these to verify the judgment of his own wondering mind: some were dental caps, but most were fillings from human teeth. And, in one of the back rows, he picked up two tiny steel rods. He looked at these for several moments before realizing they were surgical pins, and that they belonged not on the floor of a nearly deserted airliner but in some passenger's knee or shoulder.

He discovered one more passenger, a young bearded man who was sprawled over two seats in the very last row, snoring loudly and smelling like a brewery.

Two seats away, he found a gadget that looked like a pacemaker implant.

Albert stood at the rear of the plane and looked forward along the large, empty tube of the fuselage.

"What in the fuck is going on here?" he asked in a soft, trembling voice.

4

"I demand to know just what is going on here!" the man in the crew-neck jersey said in a loud voice. He strode into the service area at the head of first class like a corporate raider mounting a hostile takeover.

"Currently? We're just about to break the lock on this door," Nick Hopewell said, fixing Crew-Neck with a bright gaze. "The flight crew appears to have abdicated along with everyone else, but we're in luck, just the same. My new acquaintance here is a pilot who just happened to be deadheading, and—"

"*Someone* around here is a deadhead, all right," Crew-Neck said, "and I intend to find out who, believe me." He pushed past Nick without a glance and stuck his face into Brian's, as aggressive as a ballplayer disputing an umpire's call. "Do you work for American Pride, friend?"

"Yes," Brian said, "but why don't we put that off for now, sir? It's important that—"

"*I'll* tell you what's important!" Crew-Neck shouted. A fine mist of spit settled on Brian's cheeks and he had to sit on a sudden and amazingly strong impulse to clamp his hands around this twerp's neck and see how far he could twist his head before something inside cracked. "I've got a meeting at the Prudential Center with representatives of Bankers International at nine o'clock this morning! *Promptly* at nine o'clock! I booked a seat on this conveyance in good faith, and I have no intention of being late for my appointment! I want to know three things: *who* authorized an unscheduled stop for this airliner while I was asleep, *where* that stop was made, and *why it was done!*"

"Have you ever watched *Star Trek?*" Nick Hopewell asked suddenly.

Crew-Neck's face, suffused with angry blood, swung around. His expression said that he believed the Englishman was clearly mad. "What in the hell are you talking about?"

"Marvellous American program," Nick said. "Science fiction. Exploring strange new worlds, like the one which apparently exists inside your head. And if you don't shut your gob at once, you bloody idiot, I'll be happy to demonstrate Mr. Spock's famous Vulcan sleeper-hold for you."

"You can't talk to me like that!" Crew-Neck snarled. "Do you know who I am?"

"Of course," Nick said. "You're a bloody-minded little bugger who has mistaken his airline boarding pass for credentials proclaiming him to be the Grand High Pooh-Bah of Creation. You're also badly frightened. No harm in that, but you *are* in the way."

Crew-Neck's face was now so clogged with blood that Brian began to be afraid his entire head would explode. He had once seen a movie where that happened. He did not want to see it in real life. "You can't talk to me like that! You're not even an American citizen!"

Nick Hopewell moved so fast that Brian barely saw what was happening. At one moment the man in the crew-neck jersey was yelling into Nick's face while Nick stood at ease beside Brian, his hands on the hips of his pressed jeans. A moment later, Crew-Neck's nose was caught firmly between the first and second fingers of Nick's right hand.

Crew-Neck tried to pull away. Nick's fingers tightened . . . and then his hand turned slightly, in the gesture of a man tightening a screw or winding an alarm clock. Crew-Neck bellowed.

"I can break it," Nick said softly. "Easiest thing in the world, believe me."

Crew-Neck tried to jerk backward. His hands beat ineffectually at Nick's arm. Nick twisted again and Crew-Neck bellowed again.

"I don't think you heard me. I can break it. Do you understand? Signify if you have understanding."

He twisted Crew-Neck's nose a third time.

Crew-Neck did not just bellow this time; he screamed.

"Oh, wow," the stoned-looking girl said from behind them. "A nose-hold."

"I don't have time to discuss your business appointments," Nick said softly to Crew-Neck. "Nor do I have time to deal with hysteria masquerading as aggression. We have a nasty, perplexing situation here. You, sir, are clearly not part of the solution, and I have no intention whatever of allowing you to become part of the problem. Therefore, I am going to send you back into the main cabin. This gentleman in the red shirt—"

"Don Gaffney," the gentleman in the red shirt said. He looked as vastly surprised as Brian felt.

"Thank you," Nick said. He still held Crew-Neck's nose in that amazing clamp, and Brian could now see a thread of blood lining one of the man's pinched nostrils.

Nick pulled him closer and spoke in a warm, confidential voice.

34

"Mr. Gaffney here will be your escort. Once you arrive in the main cabin, my buggardly friend, you will take a seat with your safety belt fixed firmly around your middle. Later, when the captain here has assured himself we are not going to fly into a mountain, a building, or another plane, we may be able to discuss our current situation at greater length. For the present, however, your input is not necessary. Do you understand all these things I have told you?"

Crew-Neck uttered a pained, outraged bellow.

"If you understand, please favor me with a thumbs-up."

Crew-Neck raised one thumb. The nail, Brian saw, was neatly manicured.

"Fine," Nick said. "One more thing. When I let go of your nose, you may feel vengeful. To *feel* that way is fine. To give vent to the feeling would be a terrible mistake. I want you to remember that what I have done to your nose I can just as easily do to your testicles. In fact, I can wind them up so far that when I let go of them, you may actually fly about the cabin like a child's airplane. I expect you to leave with Mr.—"

He looked questioningly at the man in the red shirt.

"Gaffney," the man in the red shirt repeated.

"Gaffney, right. Sorry. I expect you to leave with Mr. Gaffney. You will not remonstrate. You will not indulge in rebuttal. In fact, if you say so much as a single word, you will find yourself investigating hitherto unexplored realms of pain. Give me a thumbs-up if you understand *this*."

Crew-Neck waved his thumb so enthusiastically that for a moment he looked like a hitchhiker with diarrhea.

"Right, then!" Nick said, and let go of Crew-Neck's nose.

Crew-Neck stepped back, staring at Nick Hopewell with angry, perplexed eyes—he looked like a cat which had just been doused with a bucket of cold water. By itself, anger would have left Brian unmoved. It was the perplexity that made him feel a little sorry for Crew-Neck. He felt mightily perplexed himself.

Crew-Neck raised a hand to his nose, verifying that it was

still there. A narrow ribbon of blood, no wider than the pull-strip on a pack of cigarettes, ran from each nostril. The tips of his fingers came away bloody, and he looked at them unbelievingly. He opened his mouth.

"I wouldn't, mister," Don Gaffney said. "Guy means it. You better come along with me."

He took Crew-Neck's arm. For a moment Crew-Neck resisted Gaffney's gentle tug. He opened his mouth again.

"Bad idea," the girl who looked stoned told him.

Crew-Neck closed his mouth and allowed Gaffney to lead him back toward the rear of first class. He looked over his shoulder once, his eyes wide and stunned, and then dabbed his fingers under his nose again.

Nick, meanwhile, had lost all interest in the man. He was peering out one of the windows. "We appear to be over the Rockies," he said, "and we seem to be at a safe enough altitude."

Brian looked out himself for a moment. It was the Rockies, all right, and near the center of the range, by the look. He put their altitude at about 35,000 feet. Just about what Melanie Trevor had told him. So they were fine . . . at least, so far.

"Come on," he said. "Help me break down this door."

Nick joined him in front of the door. "Shall I captain this part of the operation, Brian? I have some experience."

"Be my guest." Brian found himself wondering exactly how Nick Hopewell had come by his experience in twisting noses and breaking down doors. He had an idea it was probably a long story.

"It would be helpful to know how strong the lock is," Nick said. "If we hit it too hard, we're apt to go catapulting straight into the cockpit. I wouldn't want to run into something that won't bear running into."

"I don't know," Brian said truthfully. "I don't think it's tremendously strong, though."

"All right," Nick said. "Turn and face me—your right shoulder pointing at the door, my left."

Brian did.

"I'll count off. We're going to shoulder it together on three. Dip your legs as we go in; we're more apt to pop the lock if we hit the door lower down. *Don't* hit it as hard as you can. About half. If that isn't enough, we can always go again. Got it?"

"I've got it."

The girl, who looked a little more awake and with it now, said: "I don't suppose they leave a key under the doormat or anything, huh?"

Nick looked at her, startled, then back at Brian. "*Do* they by any chance leave a key someplace?"

Brian shook his head. "I'm afraid not. It's an anti-terrorist precaution."

"Of course," Nick said. "Of course it is." He glanced at the girl and winked. "But that's using your head, just the same."

The girl smiled at him uncertainly.

Nick turned back to Brian. "Ready, then?"

"Ready."

"Right, then. One . . . two . . . *three!*"

They drove forward into the door, dipping down in perfect synchronicity just before they hit it, and the door popped open with absurd ease. There was a small lip—too short by at least three inches to be considered a step—between the service area and the cockpit. Brian struck this with the edge of his shoe and would have fallen sideways into the cockpit if Nick hadn't grabbed him by the shoulder. The man was as quick as a cat.

"Right, then," he said, more to himself than to Brian. "Let's just see what we're dealing with here, shall we?"

5

The cockpit was empty. Looking into it made Brian's arms and neck prickle with gooseflesh. It was all well and good to know that a 767 could fly thousands of miles on autopilot, using information which had been programmed into its inertial navigation system—God knew he had flown enough miles that way himself—but it was another to see the two empty seats. *That* was what chilled him. He had never seen an empty in-flight cockpit during his entire career.

He was seeing one now. The pilot's controls moved by themselves, making the infinitesimal corrections necessary to keep the plane on its plotted course to Boston. The board was green. The two small wings on the plane's attitude indicator were steady above the artificial horizon. Beyond the two small, slanted-forward windows, a billion stars twinkled in an early-morning sky.

"Oh, wow," the teenaged girl said softly.

"Coo-*eee*," Nick said at the same moment. "Look there, matey."

Nick was pointing at a half-empty cup of coffee on the service console beside the left arm of the pilot's seat. Next to the coffee was a Danish pastry with two bites gone. This brought Brian's dream back in a rush, and he shivered violently.

"It happened fast, whatever it was," Brian said. "And look there. And there."

He pointed first to the seat of the pilot's chair and then to the floor by the co-pilot's seat. Two wristwatches glimmered in the lights of the controls, one a pressure-proof Rolex, the other a digital Pulsar.

"If you want watches, you can take your pick," a voice said from behind them. "There's tons of them back there." Brian looked over his shoulder and saw Albert Kaussner, looking neat and very young in his small black skull-cap and his Hard Rock Cafe tee-shirt. Standing beside him was the elderly gent in the fraying sport-coat.

"Are there indeed?" Nick asked. For the first time he seemed to have lost his self-possession.

"Watches, jewelry, and glasses," Albert said. "Also purses. But the weirdest thing is . . . there's stuff I'm pretty sure came from *inside* people. Things like surgical pins and pacemakers."

Nick looked at Brian Engle. The Englishman had paled noticeably. "I had been going on roughly the same assumption as our rude and loquacious friend," he said. "That the plane set down someplace, for some reason, while I was asleep. That most of the passengers—and the crew—were somehow offloaded."

"I would have woken the minute descent started," Brian said. "It's habit." He found he could not take his eyes off the empty seats, the half-drunk cup of coffee, the half-eaten Danish.

"Ordinarily, I'd say the same," Nick agreed, "so I decided my drink had been doped."

I don't know what this guy does for a living, Brian thought, *but he sure doesn't sell used cars.*

"No one doped my drink," Brian said, "because I didn't have one."

"Neither did I," Albert said.

"In any case, there *couldn't* have been a landing and takeoff while we were sleeping," Brian told them. "You can *fly* a plane on autopilot, and the Concorde can *land* on autopilot, but you need a human being to take one up."

"We didn't land, then," Nick said.

"Nope."

"So where did they go, Brian?"

"I don't know," Brian said. He moved to the pilot's chair and sat down.

6

Flight 29 *was* flying at 36,000 feet, just as Melanie Trevor had told him, on heading 090. An hour or two from now that would change as the plane doglegged further north. Brian took the navigator's chart book, looked at the airspeed indicator, and made a series of rapid calculations. Then he put on the headset.

"Denver Center, this is American Pride Flight 29, over?"

He flicked the toggle . . . and heard nothing. Nothing at all. No static; no chatter; no ground control; no other planes. He checked the transponder setting: 7700, just as it should be. Then he flicked the toggle back to transmit again. "Denver Center, come in please, this is American Pride Flight 29, repeat, American Pride Heavy, and I have a problem, Denver, I have a problem."

Flicked back the toggle to receive. Listened.

Then Brian did something which made Albert "Ace" Kaussner's heart begin to bump faster with fear: he hit the control panel just below the radio equipment with the heel of his hand. The Boeing 767 was a high-tech, state-of-the-art passenger plane. One did not try to make the equipment on such a plane operate in such a fashion. What the pilot had just done was what you did when the old Philco radio you bought for a buck at the Kiwanis Auction wouldn't play after you got it home.

Brian tried Denver Center again. And got no response. No response at all.

7

To this moment, Brian had been dazed and terribly perplexed. Now he began to feel frightened—really frightened—as well. Up until now there had been no *time* to be scared. He wished that were still so . . . but it wasn't. He flicked the radio to the emergency band and tried again. There was no response. This was the equivalent of dialing 911 in Manhattan and getting a recording which said everyone had left for the weekend. When you called for help on the emergency band, you *always* got a prompt response.

Until now, at least, Brian thought.

He switched to UNICOM, where private pilots obtained

landing advisories at small airports. No response. He listened . . . and heard nothing at all. Which just couldn't be. Private pilots chattered like grackles on a telephone line. The gal in the Piper wanted to know the weather. The guy in the Cessna would just flop back dead in his seat if he couldn't get someone to call his wife and tell her he was bringing home three extra for dinner. The guys in the Lear wanted the girl on the desk at the Arvada Airport to tell their charter passengers that they were going to be fifteen minutes late and to hold their water, they would still make the baseball game in Chicago on time.

But none of that was there. All the grackles had flown, it seemed, and the telephone lines were bare.

He flicked back to the FAA emergency band. "Denver come in! Come in right now! *This is AP Flight 29, you answer me, goddammit!*"

Nick touched his shoulder. "Easy, mate."

"The dog won't bark!" Brian said frantically. "That's impossible, but that's what's happening! Christ, what did they do, have a fucking nuclear war?"

"*Easy*," Nick repeated. "Steady down, Brian, and tell me what you mean, the dog won't bark."

"I mean Denver Control!" Brian cried. "*That* dog! I mean FAA Emergency! *That* dog! UNICOM, that dog, too! I've never—"

He flicked another switch. "Here," he said, "this is the medium-shortwave band. They should be jumping all over each other like frogs on a hot sidewalk, but I can't pick up jack shit."

He flicked another switch, then looked up at Nick and Albert Kaussner, who had crowded in close. "There's no VOR beacon out of Denver," he said.

"Meaning?"

"Meaning I have no radio, I have no Denver navigation beacon, and my board says everything is just peachy keen. Which is crap. *Got* to be."

A terrible idea began to surface in his mind, coming up like a bloated corpse rising to the top of a river.

"Hey, kid—look out the window. Left side of the plane. Tell me what you see."

Albert Kaussner looked out. He looked out for a long time. "Nothing," he said. "Nothing at all. Just the last of the Rockies and the beginning of the plains."

"No lights?"

"No."

Brian got up on legs which felt weak and watery. He stood looking down for a long time.

At last Nick Hopewell said quietly, "Denver's gone, isn't it?"

Brian knew from the navigator's charts and his on-board navigational equipment that they should now be flying less than fifty miles south of Denver . . . but below them he saw only the dark, featureless landscape that marked the beginning of the Great Plains.

"Yes," he said. "Denver's gone."

8

There was a moment of utter silence in the cockpit, and then Nick Hopewell turned to the peanut gallery, currently consisting of Albert, the man in the ratty sport-coat, and the young girl. Nick clapped his hands together briskly, like a kindergarten teacher. He sounded like one, too, when he spoke. "All right, people! Back to your seats. I think we need a little quiet here."

"We *are* being quiet," the girl objected, and reasonably enough.

"I believe that what the gentleman actually means isn't quiet but a little privacy," the man in the ratty sport-coat said. He spoke in cultured tones, but his soft, worried eyes were fixed on Brian.

"That's *exactly* what I mean," Nick agreed. "Please?"

"Is he going to be all right?" the man in the ratty sport-coat asked in a low voice. "He looks rather upset."

Nick answered in the same confidential tone. "Yes," he said. "He'll be fine. I'll see to it."

"Come on, children," the man in the ratty sport-coat said. He put one arm around the girl's shoulders, the other around Albert's. "Let's go back and sit down. Our pilot has work to do."

They need not have lowered their voices even temporarily as far as Brian Engle was concerned. He might have been a fish feeding in a stream while a small flock of birds passes overhead. The sound may reach the fish, but he certainly attaches no significance to it. Brian was busy working his way through the radio bands and switching from one navigational touchpoint to another. It was useless. No Denver; no Colorado Springs; no Omaha. All gone.

He could feel sweat trickling down his cheeks like tears, could feel his shirt sticking to his back.

I must smell like a pig, he thought, *or a—*

Then inspiration struck. He switched to the military-aircraft band, although regulations expressly forbade his doing so. The Strategic Air Command practically owned Omaha. *They* would not be off the air. They might tell him to get the fuck off their frequency, would probably threaten to report him to the FAA, but Brian would accept all this cheerfully. Perhaps he would be the first to tell them that the city of Denver had apparently gone on vacation.

"Air Force Control, Air Force Control, this is American Pride Flight 29 and we have a problem here, a *big* problem here, do you read me? Over."

No dog barked there, either.

That was when Brian felt something—something like a bolt—starting to give way deep inside his mind. That was when he felt his entire structure of organized thought begin to slide slowly toward some dark abyss.

9

Nick Hopewell clamped a hand on him then, high up on his shoulder, near the neck. Brian jumped in his seat and almost cried out aloud. He turned his head and found Nick's face less than three inches from his own.

Now he'll grab my nose and start to twist it, Brian thought.

Nick did not grab his nose. He spoke with quiet intensity, his eyes fixed unflinchingly on Brian's. "I see a look in your eyes, my friend . . . but I didn't need to see your eyes to know it was there. I can hear it in your voice and see it in the way you're sitting in your seat. Now listen to me, and listen well: *panic is not allowed.*"

Brian stared at him, frozen by that blue gaze.

"Do you understand me?"

He spoke with great effort. "They don't let guys do what I do for a living if they panic, Nick."

"I know that," Nick said, "but this is a unique situation. You need to remember, however, that there are a dozen or more people on this plane, and your job is the same as it ever was: to bring them down in one piece."

"You don't need to tell me what my job is!" Brian snapped.

"I'm afraid I did," Nick said, "but you're looking a hundred per cent better now, I'm relieved to say."

Brian was doing more than looking better; he was starting to *feel* better again. Nick had stuck a pin into the most sensitive place—his sense of responsibility. *Just where he meant to stick me,* he thought.

"What do you do for a living, Nick?" he asked a trifle shakily.

Nick threw back his head and laughed. "Junior attaché, British embassy, old man."

"My aunt's hat."

Nick shrugged. "Well . . . that's what it says on my papers,

44

and I reckon that's good enough. If they said anything else, I suppose it would be Her Majesty's Mechanic. I fix things that need fixing. Right now that means you."

"Thank you," Brian said touchily, "but I'm fixed."

"All right, then—what do you mean to do? Can you navigate without those ground-beam thingies? Can you avoid other planes?"

"I can navigate just fine with on-board equipment," Brian said. "As for other planes—" He pointed at the radar screen. "This bastard says there *aren't* any other planes."

"Could be there are, though," Nick said softly. "Could be that radio and radar conditions are snafued, at least for the time being. You mentioned nuclear war, Brian. I think if there had been a nuclear exchange, we'd know. But that doesn't mean there hasn't been some sort of accident. Are you familiar with the phenomenon called the electromagnetic pulse?"

Brian thought briefly of Melanie Trevor. *Oh, and we've had reports of the aurora borealis over the Mojave Desert. You might want to stay awake for that.*

Could that be it? Some freakish weather phenomenon?

He supposed it was just possible. But, if so, how come he heard no static on the radio? How come there was no wave interference across the radar screen? Why just this dead blankness? And he didn't think the aurora borealis had been responsible for the disappearance of a hundred and fifty to two hundred passengers.

"Well?" Nick asked.

"You're some mechanic, Nick," Brian said at last, "but I don't think it's EMP. All on-board equipment—including the directional gear—seems to be working just fine." He pointed to the digital compass readout. "If we'd experienced an electromagnetic pulse, that baby would be all over the place. But it's holding dead steady."

"So. Do you intend to continue on to Boston?"

Do you intend . . . ?

And with that, the last of Brian's panic drained away. *That's right,* he thought. *I'm the captain of this ship now . . . and in the end, that's all it comes down to. You should have reminded me of that in the first place, my friend, and saved us both a lot of trouble.*

"Logan at dawn, with no idea what's going on in the country below us, or the rest of the world? No way."

"Then what *is* our destination? Or do you need time to consider the matter?"

Brian didn't. And now the other things he needed to do began to click into place.

"I know," he said. "And I think it's time to talk to the passengers. The few that are left, anyway."

He picked up the microphone, and that was when the bald man who had been sleeping in the business section poked his head into the cockpit. "Would one of you gentlemen be so kind as to tell me what's happened to all the service personnel on this craft?" he asked querulously. "I've had a very nice nap . . . but now I'd like my dinner."

10

Dinah Bellman felt much better. It was good to have other people around her, to feel their comforting presence. She was sitting in a small group with Albert Kaussner, Laurel Stevenson, and the man in the ratty sport-coat, who had introduced himself as Robert Jenkins. He was, he said, the author of more than forty mystery novels, and had been on his way to Boston to address a convention of mystery fans.

"Now," he said, "I find myself involved in a mystery a good deal more extravagant than any I would ever have dared to write."

These four were sitting in the center section, near the head of the main cabin. The man in the crew-neck jersey sat in the starboard aisle, several rows down, holding a handkerchief to his nose (which had actually stopped bleeding several minutes ago) and fuming in solitary splendor. Don Gaffney sat nearby, keeping an uneasy watch on him. Gaffney had only spoken once, to ask Crew-Neck what his name was. Crew-Neck had not replied. He simply fixed Gaffney with a gaze of baleful intensity over the crumpled bouquet of his handkerchief.

Gaffney had not asked again.

"Does anyone have the *slightest* idea of what's going on here?" Laurel almost pleaded. "I'm supposed to be starting my first real vacation in ten years tomorrow, and now *this* happens."

Albert happened to be looking directly at Miss Stevenson as she spoke. As she dropped the line about this being her first real vacation in ten years, he saw her eyes suddenly shift to the right and blink rapidly three or four times, as if a particle of dust had landed in one of them. An idea so strong it was a certainty rose in his mind: the lady was lying. For some reason, the lady was lying. He looked at her more closely and saw nothing really remarkable—a woman with a species of fading prettiness, a woman falling rapidly out of her twenties and toward middle age (and to Albert, thirty was definitely where middle age began), a woman who would soon become colorless and invisible. But she had color now; her cheeks flamed with it. He didn't know what the lie meant, but he could see that it had momentarily refreshed her prettiness and made her nearly beautiful.

There's a lady who should lie more often, Albert thought. Then, before he or anyone else could reply to her, Brian's voice came from the overhead speakers.

"Ladies and gentlemen, this is the captain."

"Captain my ass," Crew-Neck snarled.

"Shut up!" Gaffney exclaimed from across the aisle.

Crew-Neck looked at him, startled, and subsided.

"As you undoubtedly know, we have an extremely odd situation on our hands here," Brian continued. "You don't need me to explain it; you only have to look around yourselves to understand."

"I don't understand anything," Albert muttered.

"I know a few other things, as well. They won't exactly make your day, I'm afraid, but since we're in this together, I want to be as frank as I possibly can. I have no cockpit-to-ground communication. And about five minutes ago we should have been able to see the lights of Denver clearly from the airplane. We couldn't. The only conclusion I'm willing to draw right now is that somebody down there forgot to pay the electricity bill. And until we know a little more, I think that's the only conclusion *any* of us should draw."

He paused. Laurel was holding Dinah's hand. Albert produced a low, awed whistle. Robert Jenkins, the mystery writer, was staring dreamily into space with his hands resting on his thighs.

"All of that is the bad news," Brian went on. "The good news is this: the plane is undamaged, we have plenty of fuel, and I'm qualified to fly this make and model. Also to land it. I think we'll all agree that landing safely is our first priority. There isn't a thing we can do until we accomplish that, and I want you to rest assured that it will be done.

"The last thing I want to pass on to you is that our destination will now be Bangor, Maine."

Crew-Neck sat up with a jerk. "*Whaaat?*" he bellowed.

"Our in-flight navigation equipment is in five-by-five working order, but I can't say the same for the navigational beams—VOR—which we also use. Under these circumstances, I have elected not to enter Logan airspace. I haven't been able to raise anyone, in air or on ground, by radio. The aircraft's radio equipment appears to be working, but I don't feel I can depend on appearances in the current circumstances. Bangor International Airport has the following advantages: the short approach is over land rather than water; air traffic at our ETA, about 8:30 A.M., will be much lighter—assuming there's any at all; and BIA, which used to be Dow Air Force Base, has the longest commercial runway on the East Coast of the United States. Our British and French friends land the Concorde there when they can't get into New York."

Crew-Neck bawled: "*I have an important business meeting at the Pru this morning at nine o'clock AND I FORBID YOU TO FLY INTO SOME DIPSHIT MAINE AIRPORT!*"

Dinah jumped and then cringed away from the sound of Crew-Neck's voice, pressing her cheek against the side of Laurel Stevenson's breast. She was not crying—not yet, anyway—but Laurel felt her chest begin to hitch.

"*Do YOU HEAR ME?*" Crew-Neck was bellowing. "*I AM DUE IN BOSTON TO DISCUSS AN UNUSUALLY LARGE BOND TRANSACTION, AND I HAVE EVERY INTENTION OF ARRIVING AT THAT MEETING ON TIME!*" He unlatched his seatbelt and began to stand up. His cheeks were red, his brow waxy white. There was a blank look in his eyes which Laurel found extremely frightening. "*Do YOU UNDERSTA—*"

"Please," Laurel said. "Please, mister, you're scaring the little girl."

Crew-Neck turned his head and that unsettling blank gaze fell on her. Laurel could have waited. "*SCARING THE LITTLE GIRL? WE'RE DIVERTING TO SOME TINPOT, CHICKENSHIT AIRPORT IN THE MIDDLE OF NOWHERE, AND ALL YOU'VE GOT TO WORRY ABOUT IS—*"

"Sit down and shut up or I'll pop you one," Gaffney said, standing up. He had at least twenty years on Crew-Neck, but he was heavier and much broader through the chest. He had rolled the sleeves of his red flannel shirt to the elbows, and when he clenched his hands into fists, the muscles in his forearms bunched. He looked like a lumberjack just starting to soften into retirement.

Crew-Neck's upper lip pulled back from his teeth. This doglike grimace scared Laurel, because she didn't believe the man in the crew-neck jersey knew he was making a face. She was the first of them to wonder if this man might not be crazy.

"I don't think you could do it alone, pops," he said.

"He won't have to." It was the bald man from the business section. "I'll take a swing at you myself, if you don't shut up."

Albert Kaussner mustered all his courage and said, "So will I, you putz." Saying it was a great relief. He felt like one of the guys at the Alamo, stepping over the line Colonel Travis had drawn in the dirt.

Crew-Neck looked around. His lip rose and fell again in that queer, doglike snarl. "I see. I see. You're all against me. Fine." He sat down and stared at them truculently. "But if you knew anything about the market in South American bonds—" He didn't finish. There was a cocktail napkin sitting on the arm of the seat next to him. He picked it up, looked at it, and began to pluck at it.

"Doesn't have to be this way," Gaffney said. "I wasn't born a hardass, mister, and I ain't one by inclination, either." He was trying to sound pleasant, Laurel thought, but wariness showed through, perhaps anger as well. "You ought to just relax and take it easy. Look on the bright side! The airline'll probably refund your full ticket price on this trip."

Crew-Neck cut his eyes briefly in Don Gaffney's direction, then looked back at the cocktail napkin. He quit plucking it and began to tear it into long strips.

"Anyone here know how to run that little oven in the galley?" Baldy asked, as if nothing had happened. "I want my dinner."

No one answered.

"I didn't think so," the bald man said sadly. "This is the era of specialization. A shameful time to be alive." With this philosophical pronouncement, Baldy retreated once more to business class.

Laurel looked down and saw that, below the rims of the dark glasses with their jaunty red plastic frames, Dinah Bellman's cheeks were wet with tears. Laurel forgot some of her own fear and perplexity, at least temporarily, and hugged the little girl. "Don't cry, honey—that man was just upset. He's better now."

If you call sitting here and looking hypnotized while you tear a paper napkin into teeny shreds better, she thought.

"I'm scared," Dinah whispered. "We all look like monsters to that man."

"No, I don't think so," Laurel said, surprised and a little taken aback. "Why would you think a thing like that?"

"I don't know," Dinah said. She liked this woman—had liked her from the instant she heard her voice—but she had no intention of telling Laurel that for just a moment she had seen them all, herself included, looking back at the man with the loud voice. She had been *inside* the man with the loud voice— his name was Mr. Tooms or Mr. Tunney or something like that—and to him they looked like a bunch of evil, selfish trolls.

If she told Miss Lee something like that, Miss Lee would think she was crazy. Why would this woman, whom Dinah had just met, think any different?

So Dinah said nothing.

Laurel kissed the girl's cheek. The skin was hot beneath her lips. "Don't be scared, honey. We're going along just as smooth as can be—can't you feel it?—and in just a few hours we'll be safe on the ground again."

"That's good. I want my Aunt Vicky, though. Where is she, do you think?"

"I don't know, hon," Laurel said. "I wish I did."

Dinah thought again of the faces the yelling man saw: evil faces, cruel faces. She thought of her own face as he perceived it, a piggish baby face with the eyes hidden behind huge black lenses. Her courage broke then, and she began to weep in hoarse racking sobs that hurt Laurel's heart. She held the girl, because it was the only thing she could think of to do, and soon she was crying herself. They cried together for nearly five minutes, and then Dinah began to calm again. Laurel looked over at the slim young boy, whose name was either Albert or Alvin, she could not remember which, and saw that his eyes were also wet. He caught her looking and glanced hastily down at his hands.

Dinah fetched one final gasping sob and then just lay with

her head pillowed against Laurel's breast. "I guess crying won't help, huh?"

"No, I guess not," Laurel agreed. "Why don't you try going to sleep, Dinah?"

Dinah sighed—a watery, unhappy sound. "I don't think I can. I *was* asleep."

Tell me about it, Laurel thought. And Flight 29 continued east at 36,000 feet, flying at over five hundred miles an hour above the dark midsection of America.

CHAPTER THREE

THE DEDUCTIVE METHOD. ACCIDENTS AND
STATISTICS. SPECULATIVE POSSIBILITIES.
PRESSURE IN THE TRENCHES.
BETHANY'S PROBLEM. THE DESCENT BEGINS.

1

"That little girl said something interesting an hour or so ago," Robert Jenkins said suddenly.

The little girl in question had gone to sleep again in the meantime, despite her doubts about her ability to do so. Albert Kaussner had also been nodding, perchance to return once more to those mythic streets of Tombstone. He had taken his violin case down from the overhead compartment and was holding it across his lap.

"Huh!" he said, and straightened up.

"I'm sorry," Jenkins said. "Were you dozing?"

"Nope," Albert said. "Wide awake." He turned two large, bloodshot orbs on Jenkins to prove this. A darkish shadow lay under each. Jenkins thought he looked a little like a raccoon which has been startled while raiding garbage cans. "What did she say?"

"She told Miss Stevenson she didn't think she could get back to sleep because she *had* been sleeping. Earlier."

Albert gazed at Dinah for a moment. "Well, she's out now," he said.

"I see she is, but that is not the point, dear boy. Not the point at all."

Albert considered telling Mr. Jenkins that Ace Kaussner, the fastest Hebrew west of the Mississippi and the only Texan to survive the Battle of the Alamo, did not much cotton to being called dear boy, and decided to let it pass . . . at least for the time being. "Then what *is* the point?"

"I was also asleep. Corked off even before the captain—our *original* captain, I mean—turned off the NO SMOKING light. I've always been that way. Trains, busses, planes—I drift off like a baby the minute they turn on the motors. What about you, dear boy?"

"What about me what?"

"Were you asleep? You were, weren't you?"

"Well, yeah."

"We were *all* asleep. The people who disappeared were all awake."

Albert thought about this. "Well . . . maybe."

"Nonsense," Jenkins said almost jovially. "I write mysteries for a living. Deduction is my bread and butter, you might say. Don't you think that if someone had been awake when all those people were eliminated, that person would have screamed bloody murder, waking the rest of us?"

"I guess so," Albert agreed thoughtfully. "Except maybe for that guy all the way in the back. I don't think an air-raid siren would wake *that* guy up."

"All right; your exception is duly noted. But *no one* screamed, did they? And no one has offered to tell the rest of us what happened. So I deduce that only waking passengers were subtracted. Along with the flight crew, of course."

"Yeah. Maybe so."

"You look troubled, dear boy. Your expression says that, despite its charms, the idea does not scan perfectly for you. May I ask why not? Have I missed something?" Jenkins's expression said he didn't believe that was possible, but that his mother had raised him to be polite.

"I don't know," Albert said honestly. "How many of us are there? Eleven?"

"Yes. Counting the fellow in the back—the one who is comatose—we number eleven."

"If you're right, shouldn't there be more of us?"

"Why?"

But Albert fell silent, struck by a sudden, vivid image from his childhood. He had been raised in a theological twilight zone by parents who were not Orthodox but who were not agnostics, either. He and his brothers had grown up observing most of the dietary traditions (or laws, or whatever they were), they had had their Bar Mitzvahs, and they had been raised to know who they were, where they came from, and what that was supposed to mean. And the story Albert remembered most clearly from his childhood visits to temple was the story of the final plague which had been visited on Pharaoh—the gruesome tribute exacted by God's dark angel of the morning.

In his mind's eye he now saw that angel moving not over Egypt but through Flight 29, gathering most of the passengers to its terrible breast . . . not because they had neglected to daub their lintels (or their seat-backs, perhaps) with the blood of a lamb, but because . . .

Why? Because *why*?

Albert didn't know, but he shivered just the same. And wished that creepy old story had never occurred to him. *Let my Frequent Fliers go,* he thought. Except it wasn't funny.

"Albert?" Mr. Jenkins's voice seemed to come from a long way off. "Albert, are you all right?"

"Yes. Just thinking." He cleared his throat. "If *all* the sleeping passengers were, you know, passed over, there'd be at least sixty of us. Maybe more. I mean, this *is* the red-eye."

"Dear boy, have you ever . . ."

"Could you call me Albert, Mr. Jenkins? That's my name."

Jenkins patted Albert's shoulder. "I'm sorry. Really. I don't mean to be patronizing. I'm upset, and when I'm upset, I have a tendency to retreat . . . like a turtle pulling his head back into his shell. Only what I retreat into is fiction. I believe I was playing Philo Vance. He's a detective—a *great* detective—created by the late S. S. Van Dine. I suppose you've never read him. Hardly anyone does these days, which is a pity. At any rate, I apologize."

"It's okay," Albert said uncomfortably.

"Albert you are and Albert you shall be from now on," Robert Jenkins promised. "I started to ask you if you've ever taken the red-eye before."

"No. I've never even flown across the country before."

"Well, I have. Many times. On a few occasions I have even gone against my natural inclination and stayed awake for awhile. Mostly when I was a younger man and the flights were noisier. Having said that much, I may as well date myself outrageously by admitting that my first coast-to-coast trip was on a TWA prop-job that made two stops . . . to refuel.

"My observation is that very few people go to sleep on such flights during the first hour or so . . . and then just about *everyone* goes to sleep. During that first hour, people occupy themselves with looking at the scenery, talking with their spouses or their travelling companions, having a drink or two—"

"Settling in, you mean," Albert suggested. What Mr. Jenkins was saying made perfect sense to him, although he had done precious little settling in himself; he had been so excited about his coming journey and the new life which would be waiting for him that he had hardly slept at all during the last couple of nights. As a result, he had gone out like a light almost as soon as the 767 left the ground.

"Making little nests for themselves," Jenkins agreed. "Did you happen to notice the drinks trolley outside the cockpit, dea—Albert?"

"I saw it was there," Albert agreed.

Jenkins's eyes shone. "Yes indeed—it was either see it or fall over it. But did you really *notice* it?"

"I guess not, if you saw something I didn't."

"It's not the eye that notices, but the *mind,* Albert. The trained deductive mind. I'm no Sherlock Holmes, but I *did* notice that it had just been taken out of the small closet in which it is stored, and that the used glasses from the pre-flight service were still stacked on the bottom shelf. From this I deduce the following: the plane took off uneventfully, it climbed toward its cruising altitude, and the autopilot device was fortunately engaged. Then the captain turned off the seatbelt light. This would all be about thirty minutes into the flight, if I'm reading the signs correctly—about 1:00 A.M., PDT. When the seatbelt light was turned out, the stewardesses arose and began their first task—cocktails for about one hundred and fifty at about 24,000 feet and rising. The pilot, meanwhile, has programmed the autopilot to level the plane off at 36,000 feet and fly east on heading thus-and-such. A few passengers—eleven of us, in fact—have fallen asleep. Of the rest, some are dozing, perhaps (but not deeply enough to save them from whatever happened), and the rest are all wide awake."

"Building their nests," Albert said.

"Exactly! Building their nests!" Jenkins paused and then added, not without some melodrama: "And then it happened!"

"*What* happened, Mr. Jenkins?" Albert asked. "Do you have any ideas about that?"

Jenkins did not answer for a long time, and when he finally did, a lot of the fun had gone out of his voice. Listening to him, Albert understood for the first time that, beneath the slightly theatrical veneer, Robert Jenkins was as frightened as Albert was himself. He found he did not mind this; it made the elderly mystery writer in his running-to-seed sport-coat seem more real.

"The locked-room mystery is the tale of deduction at its most pure," Jenkins said. "I've written a few of them myself—more than a few, to be completely honest—but I never expected to be a part of one."

Albert looked at him and could think of no reply. He found himself remembering a Sherlock Holmes story called "The Speckled Band." In that story a poisonous snake had gotten into the famous locked room through a ventilating duct. The immortal Sherlock hadn't even had to wake up all his brain-cells to solve that one.

But even if the overhead luggage compartments of Flight 29 had been filled with poisonous snakes—*stuffed* with them—where were the bodies? *Where were the bodies?* Fear began to creep into him again, seeming to flow up his legs toward his vitals. He reflected that he had never felt less like that famous gunslinger Ace Kaussner in his whole life.

"If it were just the plane," Jenkins went on softly, "I suppose I could come up with a scenario—it is, after all, how I have been earning my daily bread for the last twenty-five years or so. Would you like to hear one such scenario?"

"Sure," Albert said.

"Very well. Let us say that some shadowy government organization like The Shop has decided to carry out an experiment, and we are the test subjects. The purpose of such an experiment, given the circumstances, might be to document the effects of severe mental and emotional stress on a number of average Americans. They, the scientists running the experiment, load the airplane's oxygen system with some sort of odorless hypnotic drug—"

"Are there such things?" Albert asked, fascinated.

"There are indeed," Jenkins said. "Diazaline, for one. Methoprominol, for another. I remember when readers who liked to think of themselves as 'serious-minded' laughed at Sax Rohmer's Fu Manchu novels. They called them panting melodrama at its most shameful." Jenkins shook his head slowly. "Now, thanks to biological research and the paranoia of alphabet agencies like the CIA and the DIA, we're living in a world that could be Sax Rohmer's worst nightmare.

"Diazaline, which is actually a nerve gas, would be best. It's supposed to be very fast. After it is released into the air, *everyone* falls asleep, except for the pilot, who is breathing uncontaminated air through a mask."

"But——" Albert began.

Jenkins smiled and raised a hand. "I know what your objection is, Albert, and I can explain it. Allow me?"

Albert nodded.

"The pilot lands the plane—at a secret airstrip in Nevada, let us say. The passengers who were awake when the gas was released—and the stewardesses, of course—are offloaded by sinister men wearing white *Andromeda Strain* suits. The passengers who were asleep—you and I among them, my young friend—simply go on sleeping, only a little more deeply than before. The pilot then returns Flight 29 to its proper altitude and heading. He engages the autopilot. As the plane reaches the Rockies, the effects of the gas begin to wear off. Diazaline is a so-called clear drug, one that leaves no appreciable aftereffects. No hangover, in other words. Over his intercom, the pilot can hear the little blind girl crying out for her aunt. He knows she will wake the others. The experiment is about to commence. So he gets up and leaves the cockpit, closing the door behind him."

"How could he do that? There's no knob on the outside."

Jenkins waved a dismissive hand. "Simplest thing in the world, Albert. He uses a strip of adhesive tape, sticky side out. Once the door latches from the inside, it's locked."

A smile of admiration began to overspread Albert's face—and then it froze. "In that case, the pilot would be one of us," he said.

"Yes and no. In my scenario, Albert, the pilot is the pilot. The pilot who just happened to be on board, supposedly deadheading to Boston. The pilot who was sitting in first class, less than thirty feet from the cockpit door, when the manure hit the fan."

"Captain Engle," Albert said in a low, horrified voice.

Jenkins replied in the pleased but complacent tone of a geometry professor who has just written QED below the proof of a particularly difficult theorem. "Captain Engle," he agreed.

Neither of them noticed Crew-Neck looking at them with glittering, feverish eyes. Now Crew-Neck took the in-flight magazine from the seat-pocket in front of him, pulled off the cover, and began to tear it in long, slow strips. He let them flutter to the floor, where they joined the shreds of the cocktail napkin around his brown loafers.

His lips were moving soundlessly.

2

Had Albert been a student of the New Testament, he would have understood how Saul, that most zealous persecutor of the early Christians, must have felt when the scales fell from his eyes on the road to Damascus. He stared at Robert Jenkins with shining enthusiasm, every vestige of sleepiness banished from his brain.

Of course, when you thought about it—or when somebody like Mr. Jenkins, who was clearly a real head, ratty sport-coat or no ratty sport-coat, thought about it for you—it was just too big and too obvious to miss. Almost the entire cast and crew of American Pride's Flight 29 had disappeared between the Mojave Desert and the Great Divide . . . but one of the few survivors just happened to be—surprise, surprise!—*another* American Pride pilot who was, in his own words, "qualified to fly this make and model—also to land it."

Jenkins had been watching Albert closely, and now he smiled. There wasn't much humor in that smile. "It's a tempting scenario," he said, "isn't it?"

"We'll have to capture him as soon as we land," Albert said, scraping one hand feverishly up the side of his face. "You, me, Mr. Gaffney, and that British guy. He looks tough. Only . . .

what if the Brit's in on it, too? He could be Captain Engle's, you know, bodyguard. Just in case someone figured things out the way you did."

Jenkins opened his mouth to reply, but Albert rushed on before he could.

"We'll just have to put the arm on them both. Somehow." He offered Mr. Jenkins a narrow smile—an Ace Kaussner smile. Cool, tight, dangerous. The smile of a man who is faster than blue blazes, and knows it. "I may not be the world's smartest guy, Mr. Jenkins, but I'm nobody's lab rat."

"But it doesn't stand up, you know," Jenkins said mildly.

Albert blinked. "What?"

"The scenario I just outlined for you. It doesn't stand up."

"But—you said—"

"I said *if it were just the plane,* I could come up with a scenario. And I did. A good one. If it was a book idea, I'll bet my agent could sell it. Unfortunately, it *isn't* just the plane. Denver might still have been down there, but all the lights were off if it was. I have been coordinating our route of travel with my wristwatch, and I can tell you now that it's not just Denver, either. Omaha, Des Moines—no sign of them down there in the dark, my boy. I have seen no lights at all, in fact. No farmhouses, no grain storage and shipping locations, no interstate turnpikes. Those things show up at night, you know—with the new high-intensity lighting, they show up very well, even when one is almost six miles up. The land is utterly dark. Now, I can believe that there *might* be a government agency unethical enough to drug us all in order to observe our reactions. Hypothetically, at least. What I cannot believe is that even The Shop could have persuaded everyone over our flight-path to turn off their lights in order to reinforce the illusion that we are all alone."

"Well . . . maybe it's all a fake," Albert suggested. "Maybe we're really still on the ground and everything we can see outside the windows is, you know, projected. I saw a movie something like that once."

Jenkins shook his head slowly, regretfully. "I'm sure it was an interesting film, but I don't believe it would work in real life. Unless our theoretical secret agency has perfected some sort of ultra-wide-screen 3-D projection, I think not. Whatever is happening is not just going on inside the plane, Albert, and that is where deduction breaks down."

"But the pilot!" Albert said wildly. "What about him just happening to be here at the right place and time?"

"Are you a baseball fan, Albert?"

"Huh? No. I mean, sometimes I watch the Dodgers on TV, but not really."

"Well, let me tell you what may be the most amazing statistic ever recorded in a game which thrives on statistics. In 1957, Ted Williams reached base on sixteen consecutive at-bats. This streak encompassed six baseball games. In 1941, Joe DiMaggio batted safely in fifty-six straight games, but the odds against what DiMaggio did pale next to the odds against Williams's accomplishment, which have been put somewhere in the neighborhood of two *billion* to one. Baseball fans like to say DiMaggio's streak will never be equaled. I disagree. But I'd be willing to bet that, if they're still playing baseball a thousand years from now, Williams's sixteen on-bases in a row will still stand."

"All of which means what?"

"It means that I believe Captain Engle's presence on board tonight is nothing more or less than an accident, like Ted Williams's sixteen consecutive on-bases. And, considering our circumstances, I'd say it's a very lucky accident indeed. If life was like a mystery novel, Albert, where coincidence is not allowed and the odds are never beaten for long, it would be a much tidier business. I've found, though, that in real life coincidence is not the exception but the rule."

"Then what *is* happening?" Albert whispered.

Jenkins uttered a long, uneasy sigh. "I'm the wrong person to ask, I'm afraid. It's too bad Larry Niven or John Varley isn't on board."

"Who are those guys?"

"Science-fiction writers," Jenkins said.

3

"I don't suppose you read science fiction, do you?" Nick Hopewell asked suddenly. Brian turned around to look at him. Nick had been sitting quietly in the navigator's seat since Brian had taken control of Flight 29, almost two hours ago now. He had listened wordlessly as Brian continued trying to reach someone—*anyone*—on the ground or in the air.

"I was crazy about it as a kid," Brian said. "You?"

Nick smiled. "Until I was eighteen or so, I firmly believed that the Holy Trinity consisted of Robert Heinlein, John Christopher, and John Wyndham. I've been sitting here and running all those old stories through my head, matey. And thinking about such exotic things as time-warps and space-warps and alien raiding parties."

Brian nodded. He felt relieved; it was good to know he wasn't the only one who was thinking crazy thoughts.

"I mean, we don't really have any way of knowing if *anything* is left down there, do we?"

"No," Brian said. "We don't."

Over Illinois, low-lying clouds had blotted out the dark bulk of the earth far below the plane. He was sure it still *was* the earth—the Rockies had looked reassuringly familiar, even from 36,000 feet—but beyond that he was sure of nothing. And the cloud cover might hold all the way to Bangor. With Air Traffic Control out of commission, he had no real way of knowing. Brian had been playing with a number of scenarios, and the most unpleasant of the lot was this: that they would come out of the clouds and discover that every sign of human life—including the airport where he hoped to land—was gone. Where would he put this bird down then?

"I've always found waiting the hardest part," Nick said.

The hardest part of what? Brian wondered, but he did not ask.

"Suppose you took us down to 5,000 feet or so?" Nick proposed suddenly. "Just for a quick look-see. Perhaps the sight of a few small towns and interstate highways will set our minds at rest."

Brian had already considered this idea. Had considered it with great longing. "It's tempting," he said, "but I can't do it."

"Why not?"

"The passengers are still my first responsibility, Nick. They'd probably panic, even if I explained what I was going to do in advance. I'm thinking of our loudmouth friend with the pressing appointment at the Pru in particular. The one whose nose you twisted."

"I can handle him," Nick replied. "Any others who cut up rough, as well."

"I'm sure you can," Brian said, "but I still see no need of scaring them unnecessarily. And we will find out, eventually. We can't stay up here forever, you know."

"Too true, matey," Nick said dryly.

"I might do it anyway, if I could be sure I could get under the cloud cover at 4,000 or 5,000 feet, but with no ATC and no other planes to talk to, I can't be sure. I don't even know for sure what the weather's like down there, and I'm not talking about normal stuff, either. You can laugh at me if you want to—".

"I'm not laughing, matey. I'm not even *close* to laughing. Believe me."

"Well, suppose we *have* gone through a time-warp, like in a science-fiction story? What if I took us down through the clouds and we got one quick look at a bunch of brontosauruses grazing in some Farmer John's field before we were torn apart by a cyclone or fried in an electrical storm?"

"Do you really think that's possible?" Nick asked. Brian looked at him closely to see if the question was sarcastic. It didn't appear to be, but it was hard to tell. The British were famous for their dry sense of humor, weren't they?

Brian started to tell him he had once seen something just like that on an old *Twilight Zone* episode and then decided it wouldn't help his credibility at all. "It's pretty unlikely, I suppose, but you get the idea—we just don't know what we're dealing with. We might hit a brand-new mountain in what used to be upstate New York. Or another plane. Hell—maybe even a rocket-shuttle. After all, if it's a time-warp, we could as easily be in the future as in the past."

Nick looked out through the window. "We seem to have the sky pretty much to ourselves."

"Up here, that's true. Down there, who knows? And who knows is a very dicey situation for an airline pilot. I intend to overfly Bangor when we get there, if these clouds still hold. I'll take us out over the Atlantic and drop under the ceiling as we head back. Our odds will be better if we make our initial descent over water."

"So for now, we just go on."

"Right."

"And wait."

"Right again."

Nick sighed. "Well, you're the captain."

Brian smiled. "That's three in a row."

4

Deep in the trenches carved into the floors of the Pacific and the Indian Oceans, there are fish which live and die without ever seeing or sensing the sun. These fabulous creatures cruise the depths like ghostly balloons, lit from within by their own radiance. Although they look delicate, they are actually marvels of biological design, built to withstand pressures that would squash a man as flat as a windowpane in the blink of an eye. Their great strength, however, is also their great weakness. Prisoners of their own alien bodies, they are locked forever in their dark depths. If they are captured and drawn toward the surface, toward the sun, they simply explode. It is not external pressure that destroys them, but its absence.

Craig Toomy had been raised in his own dark trench, had lived in his own atmosphere of high pressure. His father had been an executive in the Bank of America, away from home for long stretches of time, a caricature type-A overachiever. He drove his only child as furiously and as unforgivingly as he drove himself. The bedtime stories he told Craig in Craig's early years terrified the boy. Nor was this surprising, because terror was exactly the emotion Roger Toomy meant to awaken in the boy's breast. These tales concerned themselves, for the most part, with a race of monstrous beings called the langoliers.

Their job, their mission in life (in the world of Roger Toomy, *everything* had a job, *everything* had serious work to do), was to prey on lazy, time-wasting children. By the time he was seven, Craig was a dedicated type-A overachiever, just like Daddy. He had made up his mind: the langoliers were never going to get *him.*

A report card which did not contain all A's was an unacceptable report card. An A– was the subject of a lecture fraught with dire warnings of what life would be like digging ditches or emptying garbage cans, and a B resulted in punishment—most commonly confinement to his room for a week. During that week, Craig was allowed out only for school and for meals. There was no time off for good behavior. On the other hand, extraordinary achievement—the time Craig won the tri-school decathlon, for instance—warranted no corresponding praise. When Craig showed his father the medal which had been awarded him on that occasion—in an assembly before the entire student body—his father glanced at it, grunted once, and went back to his newspaper. Craig was nine years old when his father died of a heart attack. He was actually sort of relieved that the Bank of America's answer to General Patton was gone.

His mother was an alcoholic whose drinking had been controlled only by her fear of the man she had married. Once Roger Toomy was safely in the ground, where he could no longer search out her bottles and break them, or slap her and tell her to get hold of herself, for God's sake, Catherine Toomy began her life's work in earnest. She alternately smothered her son with affection and froze him with rejection, depending on how much gin was currently perking through her bloodstream. Her behavior was often odd and sometimes bizarre. On the day Craig turned ten, she placed a wooden kitchen match between two of his toes, lit it, and sang "Happy Birthday to You" while it burned slowly down toward his flesh. She told him that if he tried to shake it out or kick it loose, she would take him to THE ORPHAN'S HOME at once. The threat of THE ORPHAN'S HOME was a frequent one when Catherine Toomy was loaded. "I ought to, anyway," she told him as she lit the match which stuck up between her weeping son's toes like a skinny birthday candle. "You're just like your father. He didn't know how to have fun, and neither do you. You're a *bore*, Craiggy-weggy." She finished the song and blew out the match before the skin of Craig's second and third right toes was more than singed, but Craig never forgot the yellow flame, the curling, blackening stick of wood, and the growing heat as his mother warbled "Happy birthday, dear Craiggy-weggy, happy birthday to *yoooou*" in her droning, off-key drunk's voice.

Pressure.

Pressure in the trenches.

Craig Toomy continued to get all A's, and he continued to spend a lot of time in his room. The place which had been his Coventry had become his refuge. Mostly he studied there, but sometimes—when things were going badly, when he felt pressed to the wall—he would take one piece of notepaper after another and tear them into narrow strips. He would let them flutter around his feet in a growing drift while his eyes stared out blankly into space. But these blank periods were not frequent. Not then.

He graduated valedictorian from high school. His mother didn't come. She was drunk. He graduated ninth in his class from the UCLA Graduate School of Management. His mother didn't come. She was dead. In the dark trench which existed in the center of his own heart, Craig was quite sure that the langoliers had finally come for her.

Craig went to work for the Desert Sun Banking Corporation of California as part of the executive training program. He did very well, which was not surprising; Craig Toomy had been built, after all, to get all A's, built to thrive under the pressures which exist in the deep fathoms. And sometimes, following some small reverse at work (and in those days, only five short years ago, all the reverses had been small ones), he would go back to his apartment in Westwood, less than half a mile from the condo Brian Engle would occupy following his divorce, and tear small strips of paper for hours at a time. The paper-tearing episodes were gradually becoming more frequent.

During those five years, Craig ran the corporate fast track like a greyhound chasing a mechanical rabbit. Water-cooler gossips speculated that he might well become the youngest vice-president in Desert Sun's glorious forty-year history. But some fish are built to rise just so far and no farther; they explode if they transgress their built-in limits.

Eight months ago, Craig Toomy had been put in sole charge of his first big project—the corporate equivalent of a master's thesis. This project was created by the bonds department. Bonds—foreign bonds and junk bonds (they were frequently the same)—were Craig's specialty. This project proposed buying a limited number of questionable South American bonds—sometimes called Bad Debt Bonds—on a carefully set schedule. The theory behind these buys was sound enough, given the limited insurance on them that was available, and the much larger tax-breaks available on turn-overs resulting in a profit (Uncle Sam was practically falling all over himself to keep the complex structure of South American indebtedness from collapsing like a house of cards). It just had to be done carefully.

Craig Toomy had presented a daring plan which raised a good many eyebrows. It centered upon a large buy of various Argentinian bonds, generally considered to be the worst of a bad lot. Craig had argued forcefully and persuasively for his plan, producing facts, figures, and projections to prove his contention that Argentinian bonds were a good deal more solid than they looked. In one bold stroke, he argued, Desert Sun could become the most important—and *richest*—buyer of foreign bonds in the American West. The money they made, he said, would be a lot less important than the long-run credibility they would establish.

After a good deal of discussion—some of it hot—Craig's take on the project got a green light. Tom Holby, a senior vice-president, had drawn Craig aside after the meeting to offer congratulations . . . and a word of warning. "If this comes off the way you expect at the end of the fiscal year, you're going to be everyone's fair-haired boy. If it doesn't, you are going to find yourself in a very windy place, Craig. I'd suggest that the next few months might be a good time to build a storm-shelter."

"I won't need a storm-shelter, Mr. Holby," Craig said confidently. "After this, what I'll need is a hang-glider. This is going to be the bond-buy of the century—like finding diamonds at a barn-sale. Just wait and see."

He had gone home early that night, and as soon as his apartment door was closed and triple-locked behind him, the confident smile had slipped from his face. What replaced it was that unsettling look of blankness. He had bought the news magazines on the way home. He took them into the kitchen, squared them up neatly in front of him on the table, and began to rip them into long, narrow strips. He went on doing this for over six hours. He ripped until *Newsweek, Time,* and *U.S. News & World Report* lay in shreds on the floor all around him. His Gucci loafers were buried. He looked like the lone survivor of an explosion in a tickertape factory.

The bonds he had proposed buying—the Argentinian bonds in particular—were a much higher risk than he had let on. He had pushed his proposal through by exaggerating some facts, suppressing others . . . and even making some up out of whole cloth. Quite a few of these latter, actually. Then he had gone home, ripped strips of paper for hours, and wondered why he had done it. He did not know about the fish that exist in trenches, living their lives and dying their deaths without ever seeing the sun. He did not know that there are both fish and men whose *bête noire* is not pressure but the lack of it. He only knew that he had been under an unbreakable compulsion to buy those bonds, to paste a target on his own forehead.

Now he was due to meet with bond representatives of five large banking corporations at the Prudential Center in Boston. There would be much comparing of notes, much speculation about the future of the world bond market, much discussion about the buys of the last sixteen months and the result of those buys. And before the first day of the three-day conference was over, they would all know what Craig Toomy had known for the last ninety days: the bonds he had purchased were now worth less than six cents on the dollar. And not long after that, the top brass at Desert Sun would discover the rest of the truth: that he had bought more than three times as much as he had been empowered to buy. He had also invested every penny of his personal savings . . . not that they would care about *that.*

Who knows how the fish captured in one of those deep trenches and brought swiftly toward the surface—toward the light of a sun it has never suspected—may feel? Is it not at least possible that its final moments are filled with ecstasy rather than horror? That it senses the crushing reality of all that pressure only as it finally falls away? That it thinks—as far as fish may be supposed to think, that is—in a kind of joyous frenzy, *I am free of that weight at last!* in the seconds before it explodes? Probably not. Fish from those dark depths may not feel at all, at least not in any way we could recognize, and they certainly do not think . . . but people do.

Instead of feeling shame, Craig Toomy had been dominated by vast relief and a kind of hectic, horrified happiness as he boarded American Pride's Flight 29 to Boston. He was going to explode, and he found he didn't give a damn. In fact, he found himself looking forward to it. He could feel the pressure peeling away from all the surfaces of his skin as he rose toward the surface. For the first time in weeks, there had been no paper-ripping. He had fallen asleep before Flight 29 even left the gate, and he had slept like a baby until that blind little brat had begun to caterwaul.

And now they told him everything had changed, and that simply could not be allowed. It must not be allowed. He had been firmly caught in the net, had felt the dizzying rise and the stretch of his skin as it tried to compensate. They could not now change their minds and drop him back into the deeps.

Bangor?

Bangor, *Maine?*

Oh no. No indeed.

Craig Toomy was vaguely aware that most of the people on Flight 29 had disappeared, but he didn't care. They weren't the important thing. They weren't part of what his father had always liked to call THE BIG PICTURE. The meeting at the Pru *was* part of THE BIG PICTURE.

This crazy idea of diverting to Bangor, Maine . . . whose scheme, exactly, had *that* been?

It had been the pilot's idea, of course. Engle's idea. The so-called captain.

Engle, now . . . Engle might very well be part of THE BIG PICTURE. He might, in fact, be an AGENT OF THE ENEMY.

Craig had suspected this in his heart from the moment when Engle had begun to speak over the intercom, but in this case he hadn't needed to depend on his heart, had he? No indeed. He had been listening to the conversation between the skinny kid and the man in the fire-sale sport-coat. The man's taste in clothes was terrible, but what he had to say made perfect sense to Craig Toomy . . . at least, up to a point.

In that case, the pilot would be one of us, the kid had said.

Yes and no, the guy in the fire-sale sport-coat had said. *In my scenario, the pilot is the pilot. The pilot who just happened to be on board, supposedly deadheading to Boston, the pilot who just happened to be sitting less than thirty feet from the cockpit door.*

Engle, in other words.

And the other fellow, the one who had twisted Craig's nose, was clearly in on it with him, serving as a kind of sky-marshal to protect Engle from anyone who happened to catch on.

He hadn't eavesdropped on the conversation between the kid and the man in the fire-sale sport-coat much longer, because around that time the man in the fire-sale sport-coat stopped making sense and began babbling a lot of crazy shit about Denver and Des Moines and Omaha being gone. The idea that three large American cities could simply disappear was absolutely out to lunch . . . but that didn't mean *everything* the old guy had to say was out to lunch.

It *was* an experiment, of course. *That* idea wasn't silly, not a bit. But the old guy's idea that all of them were test subjects was just more crackpot stuff.

Me, Craig thought. *It's me. I'm the test subject.*

All his life Craig had felt himself a test subject in an experiment just like this one. *This is a question, gentlemen, of ratio: pressure to success. The right ratio produces some x-factor. What x-factor? That is what our test subject, Mr. Craig Toomy, will show us.*

But then Craig Toomy had done something they hadn't expected, something none of their cats and rats and guinea pigs had ever dared to do: he had told them he was pulling out.

But you can't do that! You'll explode!

Will I? Fine.

And now it had all become clear to him, so clear. These other people were either innocent bystanders or extras who had been hired to give this stupid little drama some badly needed verisimilitude. The whole thing had been rigged with one object in mind: to keep Craig Toomy away from Boston, to keep Craig Toomy from opting out of the experiment.

But I'll show them, Craig thought. He pulled another sheet from the in-flight magazine and looked at it. It showed a happy man, a man who had obviously never heard of the langoliers, who obviously did not know they were lurking everywhere, behind every bush and tree, in every shadow, just over the horizon. The happy man was driving down a country road behind the wheel of his Avis rental car. The ad said that when you showed your American Pride Frequent Flier Card at the Avis desk, they'd just about *give* you that rental car, and maybe a game-show hostess to drive it, as well. He began to tear a strip of paper from the side of the glossy ad. The long, slow ripping sound was at the same time excruciating and exquisitely calming.

I'll show them that when I say I'm getting out, I mean what I say.

He dropped the strip onto the floor and began on the next one. It was important to rip slowly. It was important that each strip should be as narrow as possible, but you couldn't make them *too* narrow or they got away from you and petered out before you got to the bottom of the page. Getting each one just right demanded sharp eyes and fearless hands. *And I've got them. You better believe it. You just better believe it.*

Rii-ip.

I might have to kill the pilot.

His hands stopped halfway down the page. He looked out the window and saw his own long, pallid face superimposed over the darkness.

I might have to kill the Englishman, too.

Craig Toomy had never killed anyone in his life. Could he

73

do it? With growing relief, he decided that he could. Not while they were still in the air, of course; the Englishman was very fast, very strong, and up here there were no weapons that were sure enough. But once they landed?

Yes. If I have to, yes.

After all, the conference at the Pru was scheduled to last for three days. It seemed now that his late arrival was unavoidable, but at least he would be able to explain: he had been drugged and taken hostage by a government agency. It would stun them. He could see their startled faces as he stood before them, the three hundred bankers from all over the country assembled to discuss bonds and indebtedness, bankers who would instead hear the dirty truth about what the government was up to. *My friends, I was abducted by—*

Rii-ip.

—and was able to escape only when I—

Rii-ip.

If I have to, I can kill them both. In fact, I can kill them all.

Craig Toomy's hands began to move again. He tore off the rest of the strip, dropped it on the floor, and began on the next one. There were a lot of pages in the magazine, there were a lot of strips to each page, and that meant a lot of work lay ahead before the plane landed. But he wasn't worried.

Craig Toomy was a can-do type of guy.

5

Laurel Stevenson didn't go back to sleep but she did slide into a light doze. Her thoughts—which became something close to dreams in this mentally untethered state—turned to why she had really been going to Boston.

I'm supposed to be starting my first real vacation in ten years, she had said, but that was a lie. It contained a small grain of truth, but she doubted if she had been very believable when she told it; she had not been raised to tell lies, and her technique was not very good. Not that any of the people left on Flight 29 would have cared much either way, she supposed. Not in this situation. The fact that you were going to Boston to meet—and almost certainly sleep with—a man you had never met paled next to the fact that you were heading east in an airplane from which most of the passengers and all of the crew had disappeared.

Dear Laurel,
   I am so much looking forward to meeting you. You won't even have to double-check my photo when you step out of the jetway. I'll have so many butterflies in my stomach that all you need to do is look for the guy who's floating somewhere near the ceiling . . .

His name was Darren Crosby.

She wouldn't need to look at his photograph; that much was true. She had memorized his face, just as she had memorized most of his letters. The question was *why*. And to that question she had no answer. Not even a clue. It was just another proof of J. R. R. Tolkien's observation: you must be careful each time you step out of your door, because your front walk is really a road, and the road leads ever onward. If you aren't careful, you're apt to find yourself . . . well . . . simply swept away, a stranger in a strange land with no clue as to how you got there.

Laurel had told everyone where she was going, but she had told no one *why* she was going or what she was doing. She was a graduate of the University of California with a master's degree in library science. Although she was no model, she was cleanly built and pleasant enough to look at. She had a small circle of good friends, and they would have been flabbergasted by what she was up to: heading off to Boston, planning to stay with a man she knew only through correspondence, a man she had met through the extensive personals column of a magazine called *Friends and Lovers*.

She was, in fact, flabbergasted herself.

Darren Crosby was six-feet-one, weighed one hundred and eighty pounds, and had dark-blue eyes. He preferred Scotch (although not to excess), he had a cat named Stanley, he was a dedicated heterosexual, he was a perfect gentleman (or so he claimed), and he thought Laurel was the most beautiful name he had ever heard. The pictures he had sent showed a man with a pleasant, open, intelligent face. She guessed he was the sort of man who would look sinister if he didn't shave twice a day. And that was really all she knew.

Laurel had corresponded with half a dozen men over half a dozen years—it was a hobby, she supposed—but she had never expected to take the next step . . . this step. She supposed that Darren's wry and self-deprecating sense of humor was part of the attraction, but she was dismally aware that her real reasons were not in him at all, but in herself. And wasn't the real attraction her own inability to understand this strong desire to step out of character? To just fly off into the unknown, hoping for the right kind of lightning to strike?

What are you doing? she asked herself again.

The plane ran through some light turbulence and back into smooth air again. Laurel stirred out of her doze and looked around. She saw the young teenaged girl had taken the seat across from her. She was looking out the window.

"What do you see?" Laurel asked. "Anything?"

"Well, the sun's up," the girl said, "but that's all."

"What about the ground?" Laurel didn't want to get up and look for herself. Dinah's head was still resting on her, and Laurel didn't want to wake her.

"Can't see it. It's all clouds down there." She looked around. Her eyes had cleared and a little color—not much, but a little—had come back into her face. "My name's Bethany Simms. What's yours?"

"Laurel Stevenson."

"Do you think we'll be all right?"

"I think so," Laurel said, and then added reluctantly: "I hope so."

"I'm scared about what might be under those clouds," Bethany said, "but I was scared anyway. About Boston. My mother all at once decided how it would be a great idea if I spent a couple of weeks with my Aunt Shawna, even though school starts again in ten days. I think the idea was for me to get off the plane, just like Mary's little lamb, and then Aunt Shawna pulls the string on me."

"What string?"

"Do not pass Go, do not collect two hundred dollars, go directly to the nearest rehab, and start drying out," Bethany said. She raked her hands through her short dark hair. "Things were already so weird that this seems like just more of the same." She looked Laurel over carefully and then added with perfect seriousness: "This *is* really happening, isn't it? I mean, I've already pinched myself. *Several* times. Nothing changed."

"It's real."

"It doesn't *seem* real," Bethany said. "It seems like one of those stupid disaster movies. *Airport 1990,* something like that. I keep looking around for a couple of old actors like Wilford Brimley and Olivia de Havilland. They're supposed to meet during the shitstorm and fall in love, you know?"

"I don't think they're on the plane," Laurel said gravely. They glanced into each other's eyes and for a moment they almost laughed together. It could have made them friends if it had happened . . . but it didn't. Not quite.

"What about you, Laurel? Do you have a disaster-movie problem?"

"I'm afraid not," Laurel replied . . . and then she *did* begin to laugh. Because the thought which shot across her mind in red neon was *Oh you liar!*

Bethany put a hand over her mouth and giggled.

"Jesus," she said after a minute. "I mean, this is the ultimate hairball, you know?"

Laurel nodded. "I know." She paused and then asked, "Do you need a rehab, Bethany?"

"I don't know." She turned to look out the window again. Her smile was gone and her voice was morose. "I guess I might. I used to think it was just party-time, but now I don't know. I guess it's out of control. But getting shipped off this way . . . I feel like a pig in a slaughterhouse chute."

"I'm sorry," Laurel said, but she was also sorry for herself. The blind girl had already adopted her; she did not need a second adoptee. Now that she was fully awake again she found herself scared—badly scared. She did not want to be behind this kid's dumpster if she was going to offload a big pile of disaster-movie angst. The thought made her grin again; she simply couldn't help it. It *was* the ultimate hairball. It really was.

"I'm sorry, too," Bethany said, "but I guess this is the wrong time to worry about it, huh?"

"I guess maybe it is," Laurel said.

"The pilot never disappeared in any of those *Airport* movies, did he?"

"Not that I remember."

"It's almost six o'clock. Two and a half hours to go."

"Yes."

"If only the world's still there," Bethany said, "that'll be enough for a start." She looked closely at Laurel again. "I don't suppose you've got any grass, do you?"

"I'm afraid not."

Bethany shrugged and offered Laurel a tired smile which was oddly winning. "Well," she said, "you're one ahead of me—I'm just afraid."

6

Some time later, Brian Engle rechecked his heading, his airspeed, his navigational figures, and his charts. Last of all he checked his wristwatch. It was two minutes past eight.

"Well," he said to Nick without looking around, "I think it's about that time. Shit or git."

He reached forward and flicked on the FASTEN SEATBELTS sign. The bell made its low, pleasant chime. Then he flicked the intercom toggle and picked up the mike.

"Hello, ladies and gentlemen. This is Captain Engle again. We're currently over the Atlantic Ocean, roughly thirty miles east of the Maine coast, and I'll be commencing our initial descent into the Bangor area very soon. Under ordinary circumstances I wouldn't turn on the seatbelt sign so early, but these circumstances aren't ordinary, and my mother always said prudence is the better part of valor. In that spirit, I want you to make sure your lap-belts are snug and secure. Conditions below us don't look especially threatening, but since I have no radio communication, the weather is going to be something of a surprise package for all of us. I kept hoping the clouds would break, and I did see a few small holes over Vermont, but I'm afraid they've closed up again. I can tell you from my experience as a pilot that the clouds you see below us don't suggest very bad weather to me. I think the weather in Bangor may be overcast, with some light rain. I'm beginning our descent now. Please be calm; my board is green across and all procedures here on the flight deck remain routine."

Brian had not bothered programming the autopilot for descent; he now began the process himself. He brought the plane around in a long, slow turn, and the seat beneath him canted slightly forward as the 767 began its slow slide down toward the clouds at 4,000 feet.

"Very comforting, that," Nick said. "You should have been a politician, matey."

"I doubt if they're feeling very comfortable right now," Brian said. "I know I'm not."

He was, in fact, more frightened than he had ever been while at the controls of an airplane. The pressure-leak on Flight 7 from Tokyo seemed like a minor glitch in comparison to this situation. His heart was beating slowly and heavily in his chest, like a funeral drum. He swallowed and heard a click in his throat. Flight 29 passed through 30,000 feet, still descending. The white, featureless clouds were closer now. They stretched from horizon to horizon like some strange ballroom floor.

"I'm scared shitless, mate," Nick Hopewell said in a strange, hoarse voice. "I saw men die in the Falklands, took a bullet in the leg there myself, got the Teflon knee to prove it, and I came within an ace of getting blown up by a truck bomb in Beirut—in '82, that was—but I've never been as scared as I am right now. Part of me would like to grab you and make you take us right back up. Just as far up as this bird will go."

"It wouldn't do any good," Brian replied. His own voice was no longer steady; he could hear his heartbeat in it, making it jig-jag up and down in minute variations. "Remember what I said before—we can't stay up here forever."

"I know it. But I'm afraid of what's under those clouds. Or *not* under them."

"Well, we'll all find out together."

"No help for it, is there, mate?"

"Not a bit."

The 767 passed through 25,000 feet, still descending.

7

All the passengers were in the main cabin; even the bald man, who had stuck stubbornly to his seat in business class for most of the flight, had joined them. And they were all awake, except for the bearded man at the very back of the plane. They could hear him snoring blithely away, and Albert Kaussner felt one moment of bitter jealousy, a wish that *he* could wake up after they were safely on the ground as the bearded man would most likely do, and say what the bearded man was most likely going to say: *Where the hell are we?*

The only other sound was the soft *rii-ip . . . rii-ip . . . rii-ip* of Craig Toomy dismembering the in-flight magazine. He sat with his shoes in a deep pile of paper strips.

"Would you mind stopping that?" Don Gaffney asked. His voice was tight and strained. "It's driving me up the wall, buddy."

Craig turned his head. Regarded Don Gaffney with a pair of wide, smooth, empty eyes. Turned his head back. Held up the page he was currently working on, which happened to be the eastern half of the American Pride route map.

Rii-ip.

Gaffney opened his mouth to say something, then closed it tight.

Laurel had her arm around Dinah's shoulders. Dinah was holding Laurel's free hand in both of hers.

Albert sat with Robert Jenkins, just ahead of Gaffney. Ahead of him was the girl with the short dark hair. She was looking out the window, her body held so stiffly upright it might have been wired together. And ahead of her sat Baldy from business class.

"Well, at least we'll be able to get some chow!" he said loudly.

No one answered. The main cabin seemed encased in a stiff shell of tension. Albert Kaussner felt each individual hair on his body standing at attention. He searched for the comforting cloak of Ace Kaussner, that duke of the desert, that baron of the Buntline, and could not find him. Ace had gone on vacation.

The clouds were much closer. They had lost their flat look;

Laurel could now see fluffy curves and mild crenellations filled with early-morning shadows. She wondered if Darren Crosby was still down there, patiently waiting for her at a Logan Airport arrivals gate somewhere along the American Pride concourse. She was not terribly surprised to find she didn't care much, one way or another. Her gaze was drawn back to the clouds, and she forgot all about Darren Crosby, who liked Scotch (although not to excess) and claimed to be a perfect gentleman.

She imagined a hand, a huge green hand, suddenly slamming its way up through those clouds and seizing the 767 the way an angry child might seize a toy. She imagined the hand *squeezing*, saw the jet-fuel exploding in orange licks of flame between the huge knuckles, and closed her eyes for a moment.

Don't go down there! she wanted to scream. *Oh please, don't go down there!*

But what choice had they? What choice?

"I'm very scared," Bethany Simms said in a blurred, watery voice. She moved to one of the seats in the center section, fastened her lap-belt, and pressed her hands tightly against her middle. "I think I'm going to pass out."

Craig Toomy glanced at her, and then began ripping a fresh strip from the route map. After a moment, Albert unbuckled his seatbelt, got up, sat down beside Bethany, and buckled up again. As soon as he had, she grasped his hands. Her skin was as cold as marble.

"It's going to be all right," he said, striving to sound tough and unafraid, striving to sound like the fastest Hebrew west of the Mississippi. Instead he only sounded like Albert Kaussner, a seventeen-year-old violin student who felt on the verge of pissing his pants.

"I hope——" she began, and then Flight 29 began to bounce. Bethany screamed.

"What's wrong?" Dinah asked Laurel in a thin, anxious voice. "Is something wrong with the plane? Are we going to crash?"

"I don't—"

Brian's voice came over the speakers. "This is ordinary light turbulence, folks," he said. "Please be calm. We're apt to hit some heavier bumps when we go into the clouds. Most of you have been through this before, so just settle down."

Rii-ip.

Don Gaffney looked toward the man in the crew-neck jersey again and felt a sudden, almost overmastering urge to rip the flight magazine out of the weird son of a bitch's hands and begin whacking him with it.

The clouds were very close now. Robert Jenkins could see the 767's black shape rushing across their white surfaces just below the plane. Shortly the plane would kiss its own shadow and disappear. He had never had a premonition in his life, but one came to him now, one which was sure and complete. *When we break through those clouds, we are going to see something no human being has ever seen before. It will be something which is utterly beyond belief . . . yet we will be forced to believe it. We will have no choice.*

His hands curled into tight knobs on the arms of his seat. A drop of sweat ran into one eye. Instead of raising a hand to wipe the eye clear, Jenkins tried to blink the sting away. His hands felt nailed to the arms of the seat.

"Is it going to be all right?" Dinah asked frantically. Her hands were locked over Laurel's. They were small, but they squeezed with almost painful force. "Is it really going to be all right?"

Laurel looked out the window. Now the 767 was skimming the tops of the clouds, and the first cotton-candy wisps drifted past her window. The plane ran through another series of jolts and she had to close her throat against a moan. For the first time in her life she felt physically ill with terror.

"I hope so, honey," she said. "I hope so, but I really don't know."

8

"What's on your radar, Brian?" Nick asked. "Anything unusual? Anything at all?"

"No," Brian said. "It says the world is down there, and that's all it says. We're—"

"Wait," Nick said. His voice had a tight, strangled sound, as if his throat had closed down to a bare pinhole. "Climb back up. Let's think this over. Wait for the clouds to break—"

"Not enough time and not enough fuel." Brian's eyes were locked on his instruments. The plane began to bounce again. He made the corrections automatically. "Hang on. We're going in."

He pushed the wheel forward. The altimeter needle began to move more swiftly beneath its glass circle. And Flight 29 slid into the clouds. For a moment its tail protruded, cutting through the fluffy surface like the fin of a shark. A moment later that was also gone and the sky was empty . . . as if no plane had ever been there at all.

CHAPTER FOUR

IN THE CLOUDS. WELCOME TO BANGOR.
A ROUND OF APPLAUSE. THE SLIDE AND
THE CONVEYOR BELT. THE SOUND OF
NO PHONES RINGING. CRAIG TOOMY MAKES
A SIDE-TRIP. THE LITTLE BLIND GIRL'S WARNING.

1

The main cabin went from bright sunlight to the gloom of late twilight and the plane began to buck harder. After one particularly hard washboard bump, Albert felt a pressure against his right shoulder. He looked around and saw Bethany's head lying there, as heavy as a ripe October pumpkin. The girl had fainted.

The plane leaped again and there was a heavy thud in first class. This time it was Dinah who shrieked, and Gaffney let out a yell: "What was that? *For God's sake what was that?*"

"The drinks trolley," Bob Jenkins said in a low, dry voice. He tried to speak louder so they would all hear him and found himself unable. "The drinks trolley was left out, remember? I think it must have rolled across—"

The plane took a dizzying rollercoaster leap, came down with a jarring smack, and the drinks trolley fell over with a bang. Glass shattered. Dinah screamed again.

"It's all right," Laurel said frantically. "Don't hold me so tight, Dinah, honey, it's okay—"

"Please, I don't want to die! I just don't want to *die*!"

"Normal turbulence, folks." Brian's voice, coming through

85

the speakers, sounded calm . . . but Bob Jenkins thought he heard barely controlled terror in that voice. "Just be—"

Another rocketing, twisting bump. Another crash as more glasses and mini-bottles fell out of the overturned drinks trolley.

"—calm," Brian finished.

From across the aisle on Don Gaffney's left: *rii-ip.*

Gaffney turned in that direction. "Quit it right now, motherfucker, or I'll stuff what's left of that magazine right down your throat."

Craig looked at him blandly. "Try it, you old jackass."

The plane bumped up and down again. Albert leaned over Bethany toward the window. Her breasts pressed softly against his arm as he did, and for the first time in the last five years that sensation did not immediately drive everything else out of his mind. He stared out the window, desperately looking for a break in the clouds, trying to *will* a break in the clouds.

There was nothing but shades of dark gray.

2

"How low is the ceiling, mate?" Nick asked. Now that they were actually in the clouds, he seemed calmer.

"I don't know," Brian said. "Lower than I'd hoped, I can tell you that."

"What happens if you run out of room?"

"If my instruments are off even a little, we'll go into the drink," he said flatly. "I doubt if they are, though. If I get down to five hundred feet and there's still no joy, I'll take us up again and fly down to Portland."

"Maybe you ought to just head that way now."

Brian shook his head. "The weather there is almost always worse than the weather here."

"What about Presque Isle? Isn't there a long-range SAC base there?"

Brian had just a moment to think that this guy really did know much more than he should. "It's out of our reach. We'd crash in the woods."

"Then Boston is out of reach, too."

"You bet."

"This is starting to look like being a bad decision, matey."

The plane struck another invisible current of turbulence, and the 767 shivered like a dog with a bad chill. Brian heard faint screams from the main cabin even as he made the necessary corrections and wished he could tell them all that this was nothing, that the 767 could ride out turbulence twenty times this bad. The real problem was the ceiling.

"We're not struck out yet," he said. The altimeter stood at 2,200 feet.

"But we *are* running out of room."

"We—" Brian broke off. A wave of relief rushed over him like a cooling hand. "Here we are," he said. "Coming through."

Ahead of the 767's black nose, the clouds were rapidly thinning. For the first time since they had overflown Vermont, Brian saw a gauzy rip in the whitish-gray blanket. Through it he saw the leaden color of the Atlantic Ocean.

Into the cabin microphone, Brian said: "We've reached the ceiling, ladies and gentlemen. I expect this minor turbulence to ease off once we pass through. In a few minutes, you're going to hear a thump from below. That will be the landing gear descending and locking into place. I am continuing our descent into the Bangor area."

He clicked off and turned briefly to the man in the navigator's seat.

"Wish me luck, Nick."

"Oh, I do, matey—I do."

3

Laurel looked out the window with her breath caught in her throat. The clouds were unravelling fast now. She saw the ocean in a series of brief winks: waves, whitecaps, then a large chunk of rock poking out of the water like the fang of a dead monster. She caught a glimpse of bright orange that might have been a buoy.

They passed over a small, tree-shrouded island, and by leaning and craning her neck, she could see the coast dead ahead. Thin wisps of smoky cloud obscured the view for an endless forty-five seconds. When they cleared, the 767 was over land again. They passed above a field; a patch of forest; what looked like a pond.

But where are the houses? Where are the roads and the cars and the buildings and the high-tension wires?

Then a cry burst from her throat.

"What is it?" Dinah nearly screamed. "What is it, Laurel? What's wrong?"

"Nothing!" she shouted triumphantly. Down below she could see a narrow road leading into a small seaside village. From up here, it looked like a toy town with tiny toy cars parked along the main street. She saw a church steeple, a town gravel pit, a Little League baseball field. "Nothing's wrong! *It's all there! It's all still there!*"

From behind her, Robert Jenkins spoke. His voice was calm, level, and deeply dismayed. "Madam," he said, "I'm afraid you are quite wrong."

4

A long white passenger jet cruised slowly above the ground thirty-five miles east of Bangor International Airport. 767 was printed on its tail in large, proud numerals. Along the fuselage, the words AMERICAN PRIDE were written in letters which had been raked backward to indicate speed. On both sides of the nose was the airline's trademark: a large red eagle. Its spread wings were spangled with blue stars; its talons were flexed and its head was slightly bent. Like the airliner it decorated, the eagle appeared to be coming in for a landing.

The plane printed no shadow on the ground below it as it flew toward the cluster of city ahead; there was no rain, but the morning was gray and sunless. Its belly slid open. The undercarriage dropped down and spread out. The wheels locked into place below the body of the plane and the cockpit area.

American Pride Flight 29 slipped down the chute toward Bangor. It banked slightly left as it went; Captain Engle was now able to correct his course visually, and he did so.

"I see it!" Nick cried. "I see the airport! My God, what a beautiful sight!"

"If you see it, you're out of your seat," Brian said. He spoke without turning around. There was no time to turn around now. "Buckle up and shut up."

But that single long runway *was* a beautiful sight.

Brian centered the plane's nose on it and continued down the slide, passing through 1,000 to 800. Below him, a seemingly endless pine forest passed beneath Flight 29's wings. This finally gave way to a sprawl of buildings—Brian's restless eyes automatically recorded the usual litter of motels, gas stations, and fast-food restaurants—and then they were passing over the Penobscot River and into Bangor airspace. Brian checked the board again, noted he had green lights on his flaps, and then tried the airport again . . . although he knew it was hopeless.

"Bangor tower, this is Flight 29," he said. "I am declaring an emergency. Repeat, *I am declaring an emergency.* If you have runway traffic, get it out of my way. I'm coming in."

He glanced at the airspeed indicator just in time to see it

drop below 140, the speed which theoretically committed him to landing. Below him, thinning trees gave way to a golf-course. He caught a quick glimpse of a green Holiday Inn sign and then the lights which marked the end of the runway—33 painted on it in big white numerals—were rushing toward him.

The lights were not red, not green.

They were simply dead.

No time to think about it. No time to think about what would happen to them if a Learjet or a fat little Doyka puddle-jumper suddenly trundled onto the runway ahead of them. No time to do anything now but land the bird.

They passed over a short strip of weeds and gravel and then concrete runway was unrolling thirty feet below the plane. They passed over the first set of white stripes and then the skidmarks—probably made by Air National Guard jets this far out—began just below them.

Brian babied the 767 down toward the runway. The second set of stripes flashed just below them . . . and a moment later there was a light bump as the main landing gear touched down. Now Flight 29 streaked along Runway 33 at a hundred and twenty miles an hour with its nose slightly up and its wings tilted at a mild angle. Brian applied full flaps and reversed the thrusters. There was another bump, even lighter than the first, as the nose came down.

Then the plane was slowing, from a hundred and twenty to a hundred, from a hundred to eighty, from eighty to forty, from forty to the speed at which a man might run.

It was done. They were down.

"Routine landing," Brian said. "Nothing to it." Then he let out a long, shuddery breath and brought the plane to a full stop still four hundred yards from the nearest taxiway. His slim body was suddenly twisted by a flock of shivers. When he raised his hand to his face, it wiped away a great warm handful of sweat. He looked at it and uttered a weak laugh.

A hand fell on his shoulder. "You all right, Brian?"

"Yes," he said, and picked up the intercom mike again. "Ladies and gentlemen," he said, "welcome to Bangor."

From behind him Brian heard a chorus of cheers and he laughed.

Nick Hopewell was not laughing. He was leaning over Brian's seat and peering out through the cockpit window. Nothing moved on the gridwork of runways; nothing moved on the taxiways. No trucks or security vehicles buzzed back and forth on the tarmac. He could see a few vehicles, he could see an Army transport plane—a C-12—parked on an outer taxiway and a Delta 727 parked at one of the jetways, but they were as still as statues.

"Thank you for the welcome, my friend," Nick said softly. "My deep appreciation stems from the fact that it appears you are the only one who is going to extend one. This place is utterly deserted."

5

In spite of the continued radio silence, Brian was reluctant to accept Nick's judgment . . . but by the time he had taxied to a point between two of the passenger terminal's jetways, he found it impossible to believe anything else. It was not just the absence of people; not just the lack of a single security car rushing out to see what was up with this unexpected 767; it was an air of utter lifelessness, as if Bangor International Airport had been deserted for a thousand years, or a hundred thousand. A Jeep-driven baggage train with a few scattered pieces of luggage on its flatties was parked beneath one wing of the Delta jet. It was to this that Brian's eyes kept returning as he brought Flight 29 as close to the terminal as he dared and parked it. The dozen or so bags looked as ancient as artifacts exhumed from the site of some fabulous ancient city. *I wonder if the guy who discovered King Tut's tomb felt the way I do now,* he thought.

He let the engines die and just sat there for a moment. Now there was no sound but the faint whisper of an auxiliary power unit—one of four—at the rear of the plane. Brian's hand moved toward a switch marked INTERNAL POWER and actually touched it before drawing his hand back. Suddenly he didn't want to shut down completely. There was no reason not to, but the voice of instinct was very strong.

Besides, he thought, *I don't think there's anyone around to bitch about wasting fuel . . . what little there is left to waste.*

Then he unbuckled his safety harness and got up.

"Now what, Brian?" Nick asked. He had also risen, and Brian noticed for the first time that Nick was a good four inches taller than he was. He thought: *I have been in charge. Ever since this weird thing happened—ever since we* discovered *it had happened, to be more accurate—I have been in charge. But I think that's going to change very shortly.*

He discovered he didn't care. Flying the 767 into the clouds had taken every ounce of courage he possessed, but he didn't expect any thanks for keeping his head and doing his job; courage was one of the things he got paid for. He remembered a pilot telling him once, "They pay us a hundred thousand dollars or more a year, Brian, and they really do it for just one reason. They know that in almost every pilot's career, there are thirty or forty seconds when he might actually make a difference. They pay us not to freeze when those seconds finally come."

It was all very well for your brain to tell you that you had to go down, clouds or no clouds, that there was simply no choice; your nerve-endings just went on screaming their old warning, telegraphing the old high-voltage terror of the unknown. Even Nick, whatever he was and whatever he did on the ground, had wanted to back away from the clouds when it came to the sticking point. He had needed Brian to do what needed to be done. He and all the others had needed Brian to be their guts. Now they were down and there were no monsters beneath the clouds; only this weird silence and one deserted luggage train sitting beneath the wing of a Delta 727.

So if you want to take over and be the captain, my nose-twisting friend, you have my blessing. I'll even let you wear my cap if you want to. But not until we're off the plane. Until you and the rest of the geese actually stand on the ground, you're my responsibility.

But Nick had asked him a question, and Brian supposed he deserved an answer.

"Now we get off the airplane and see what's what," he said, brushing past the Englishman.

Nick put a restraining hand on his shoulder. "Do you think—"

Brian felt a flash of uncharacteristic anger. He shook loose from Nick's hand. "I think we get off the plane," he said. "There's no one to extend a jetway or run us out a set of stairs, so I think we use the emergency slide. After that, *you* think. *Matey.*"

He pushed through into first class . . . and almost fell over the drinks trolley, which lay on its side. There was a lot of broken glass and an eye-watering stink of alcohol. He stepped over it. Nick caught up with him at the rear of the first-class compartment.

"Brian, if I said something to offend you, I'm sorry. You did a hell of a fine job."

"You didn't offend me," Brian said. "It's just that in the last ten hours or so I've had to cope with a pressure leak over the Pacific Ocean, finding out that my ex-wife died in a stupid apartment fire in Boston, and that the United States has been cancelled. I'm feeling a little zonked."

He walked through business class into the main cabin. For a moment there was utter silence; they only sat there, looking at him from their white faces with dumb incomprehension.

Then Albert Kaussner began to applaud.

After a moment, Bob Jenkins joined him . . . and Don

Gaffney . . . and Laurel Stevenson. The bald man looked around and also began to applaud.

"What is it?" Dinah asked Laurel. "What's happening?"

"It's the captain," Laurel said. She began to cry. "It's the captain who brought us down safe."

Then Dinah began to applaud, too.

Brian stared at them, dumbfounded. Standing behind him, Nick joined in. They unbuckled their belts and stood in front of their seats, applauding him. The only three who did not join in were Bethany, who had fainted, the bearded man, who was still snoring in the back row, and Craig Toomy, who panned them all with his strange lunar gaze and then began to rip a fresh strip from the airline magazine.

6

Brian felt his face flush—this was just too goony. He raised his hands but for a moment they went on, regardless.

"Ladies and gentlemen, please . . . please . . . I assure you, it was a very routine landing—"

"Shucks, ma'am—t'warn't nothin," Bob Jenkins said, doing a very passable Gary Cooper imitation, and Albert burst out laughing. Beside him, Bethany's eyes fluttered open and she looked around, dazed.

"We got down alive, didn't we?" she said. "My God! That's great! I thought we were all dead meat!"

"Please," Brian said. He raised his arms higher and now he felt weirdly like Richard Nixon, accepting his party's nomination for four more years. He had to struggle against sudden shrieks of laughter. He couldn't do that; the passengers wouldn't understand. They wanted a hero, and he was elected. He might as well accept the position . . . and use it. He still had to get them off the plane, after all. "If I could have your attention, please!"

They stopped applauding one by one and looked at him expectantly—all except Craig, who threw his magazine aside in a sudden resolute gesture. He unbuckled his seatbelt, rose, and stepped out into the aisle, kicking a drift of paper strips aside. He began to rummage around in the compartment above his seat, frowning with concentration as he did so.

"You've looked out the windows, so you know as much as I do," Brian said. "Most of the passengers and all of the crew on this flight disappeared while we were asleep. That's crazy enough, but now we appear to be faced with an even crazier proposition. It looks like a lot of other people have disappeared as well . . . but logic suggests that other people must be around *somewhere.* We survived whatever-it-was, so others must have survived it as well."

Bob Jenkins, the mystery writer, whispered something under his breath. Albert heard him but could not make out the words. He half-turned in Jenkins's direction just as the writer muttered the two words again. This time Albert caught them. They were *false logic.*

"The best way to deal with this, I think, is to take things one step at a time. Step one is exiting the plane."

"I bought a ticket to Boston," Craig Toomy said in a calm, rational voice. "Boston is where I want to go."

Nick stepped out from behind Brian's shoulder. Craig glanced at him and his eyes narrowed. For a moment he looked like a bad-tempered housecat again. Nick raised one hand with the fingers curled in against his palm and scissored two of his knuckles together in a nose-pinching gesture. Craig Toomy, who had once been forced to stand with a lit match between his toes while his mother sang "Happy Birthday," got the message at once. He had always been a quick study. And he could wait.

"We'll have to use the emergency slide," Brian said, "so I want to review the procedures with you. Listen carefully, then form a single-file line and follow me to the front of the aircraft."

7

Four minutes later, the forward entrance of American Pride's Flight 29 swung inward. Some murmured conversation drifted out of the opening and seemed to fall immediately dead on the cool, still air. There was a hissing sound and a large clump of orange fabric suddenly bloomed in the doorway. For a moment it looked like a strange hybrid sunflower. It grew and took shape as it fell, its surface inflating into a plump ribbed slide. As the foot of the slide struck the tarmac there was a low *pop!* and then it just leaned there, looking like a giant orange air mattress.

Brian and Nick stood at the head of the short line in the portside row of first class.

"There's something wrong with the air out there," Nick said in a low voice.

"What do you mean?" Brian asked. He pitched his voice even lower. "Poisoned?"

"No . . . at least I don't think so. But it has no smell, no taste."

"You're nuts," Brian said uneasily.

"No I'm not," Nick said. "This is an *airport,* mate, not a bloody hayfield, but can you smell oil or gas? I can't."

Brian sniffed. And there was nothing. If the air was poisoned— he didn't believe it was, but *if*—it was a slow-acting toxin. His lungs seemed to be processing it just fine. But Nick was right. There was no smell. And that other, more elusive, quality that the Brit had called taste . . . that wasn't there, either. The air outside the open door tasted utterly neutral. It tasted canned.

"Is something wrong?" Bethany Simms asked anxiously. "I mean, I'm not sure if I really want to know if there is, but—"

"There's nothing wrong," Brian said. He counted heads, came up with ten, and turned to Nick again. "That guy in the back is still asleep. Do you think we should wake him up?"

Nick thought for a moment, then shook his head. "Let's not. Haven't we got enough problems for now without having to play nursemaid to a bloke with a hangover?"

Brian grinned. They were his thoughts exactly. "Yes, I think we do. All right—you go down first, Nick. Hold the bottom of the slide. I'll help the rest off."

"Maybe *you'd* better go first. In case my loudmouthed friend decides to cut up rough about the unscheduled stop again." He pronounced *unscheduled* as *un-shed-youled.*

Brian glanced at the man in the crew-necked jersey. He was standing at the rear of the line, a slim monogrammed brief-case in one hand, staring blankly at the ceiling. His face had all the expression of a department-store dummy. "I'm not going to have any trouble with him," he said, "because I don't give a crap what he does. He can go or stay, it's all the same to me."

Nick grinned. "Good enough for me, too. Let the grand exodus begin."

"Shoes off?"

Nick held up a pair of black kidskin loafers.

"Okay—away you go." Brian turned to Bethany. "Watch closely, miss—you're next."

"Oh god—I *hate* shit like this."

Bethany nevertheless crowded up beside Brian and watched apprehensively as Nick Hopewell addressed the slide. He jumped, raising both legs at the same time so he looked like a man doing a seat-drop on a trampoline. He landed on his butt and slid to the bottom. It was neatly done; the foot of the slide barely moved. He hit the tarmac with his stocking feet, stood up, twirled around, and made a mock bow with his arms held out behind him.

"Easy as pie!" he called up. "Next customer!"

"That's you, miss," Brian said. "Is it Bethany?"

"Yes," she said nervously. "I don't think I can do this. I flunked gym all three semesters and they finally let me take home ec again instead."

"You'll do fine," Brian told her. He reflected that people used the slide with much less coaxing and a lot more enthusiasm when there was a threat they could see—a hole in the fuselage or a fire in one of the portside engines. "Shoes off?"

Bethany's shoes—actually a pair of old pink sneakers— were off, but she tried to withdraw from the doorway and the bright-orange slide just the same. "Maybe if I could just have a drink before—"

"Mr. Hopewell's holding the slide and you'll be fine," Brian coaxed, but he was beginning to be afraid he might have to push her. He didn't want to, but if she didn't jump soon, he would. You couldn't let them go to the end of the line until their courage returned; that was the big no-no when it came to the escape slide. If you did that, they *all* wanted to go to the end of the line.

"Go on, Bethany," Albert said suddenly. He had taken his violin case from the overhead compartment and held it tucked under one arm. "I'm scared to death of that thing, and if you go, I'll have to."

She looked at him, surprised. "Why?"

Albert's face was very red. "Because you're a girl," he said simply. "I know I'm a sexist rat, but that's it."

Bethany looked at him a moment longer, then laughed and turned to the slide. Brian had made up his mind to push her if she looked around or drew back again, but she didn't. "Boy, I wish I had some grass," she said, and jumped.

She had seen Nick's seat-drop maneuver and knew what to do, but at the last moment she lost her courage and tried to get her feet under her again. As a result, she skidded to one side when she came down on the slide's bouncy surface. Brian was sure she was going to tumble off, but Bethany herself saw the danger and managed to roll back. She shot down the slope on her right side, one hand over her head, her blouse rucking up almost to the nape of her neck. Then Nick caught her and she stepped off.

"Oh boy," she said breathlessly. "Just like being a kid again."

"Are you all right?" Nick asked.

"Yeah. I think I might have wet my pants a little, but I'm okay."

Nick smiled at her and turned back to the slide.

Albert looked apologetically at Brian and extended the violin case. "Would you mind holding this for me? I'm afraid if I fall off the slide, it might get broken. My folks'd kill me. It's a Gretch."

Brian took it. His face was calm and serious, but he was smiling inside. "Could I look? I used to play one of these about a thousand years ago."

"Sure," Albert said.

Brian's interest had a calming effect on the boy . . . which was exactly what he had hoped for. He unsnapped the three catches and opened the case. The violin inside was indeed a Gretch, and not from the bottom of that prestigious line, either. Brian guessed you could buy a compact car for the amount of money this had cost.

"Beautiful," he said, and plucked out four quick notes along the neck: *My dog has fleas.* They rang sweetly and beautifully. Brian closed and latched the case again. "I'll keep it safe. Promise."

"Thanks." Albert stood in the doorway, took a deep breath, then let it out again. "Geronimo," he said in a weak little voice and jumped. He tucked his hands into his armpits as he did so—protecting his hands in any situation where physical damage was possible was so ingrained in him that it had become a reflex. He seat-dropped onto the slide and shot neatly to the bottom.

"Well done!" Nick said.

"Nothing to it," Ace Kaussner drawled, stepped off, and then nearly tripped over his own feet.

"Albert!" Brian called down. "Catch!" He leaned out, placed the violin case on the center of the slide, and let it go. Albert caught it easily five feet from the bottom, tucked it under his arm, and stood back.

Jenkins shut his eyes as he leaped and came down aslant on one scrawny buttock. Nick stepped nimbly to the left side of the slide and caught the writer just as he fell off, saving him a nasty tumble to the concrete.

"Thank you, young man."

"Don't mention it, matey."

Gaffney followed; so did the bald man. Then Laurel and Dinah Bellman stood in the hatchway.

"I'm scared," Dinah said in a thin, wavery voice.

"You'll be fine, honey," Brian said. "You don't even have to jump." He put his hands on Dinah's shoulders and turned her so she was facing him with her back to the slide. "Give me your hands and I'll lower you onto the slide."

But Dinah put them behind her back. "Not you. I want Laurel to do it."

Brian looked at the youngish woman with the dark hair. "Would you?"

"Yes," she said. "If you tell me what to do."

"Dinah already knows. Lower her onto the slide by her hands. When she's lying on her tummy with her feet pointed straight, she can shoot right down."

Dinah's hands were cold in Laurel's. "I'm scared," she repeated.

"Honey, it'll be just like going down a playground slide," Brian said. "The man with the English accent is waiting at the bottom to catch you. He's got his hands up just like a catcher in a baseball game." Not, he reflected, that Dinah would know what *that* looked like.

Dinah looked at him as if he were being quite foolish. "Not of *that*. I'm scared of this *place*. It smells funny."

Laurel, who detected no smell but her own nervous sweat, looked helplessly at Brian.

"Honey," Brian said, dropping to one knee in front of the

little blind girl, "we have to get off the plane. You know that, don't you?"

The lenses of the dark glasses turned toward him. "*Why? Why* do we have to get off the plane? There's no one here."

Brian and Laurel exchanged a glance.

"Well," Brian said, "we won't really know that until we check, will we?"

"I know already," Dinah said. "There's nothing to smell and nothing to hear. But . . . but . . ."

"But what, Dinah?" Laurel asked.

Dinah hesitated. She wanted to make them understand that the way she had to leave the plane was really not what was bothering her. She had gone down slides before, and she trusted Laurel. Laurel would not let go of her hands if it was dangerous. Something was *wrong* here, *wrong,* and that was what she was afraid of—the wrong thing. It wasn't the quiet and it wasn't the emptiness. It might have to do with those things, but it was more than those things.

Something *wrong.*

But grownups did not believe children, especially not blind children, even more especially not blind *girl* children. She wanted to tell them they couldn't stay here, that it wasn't *safe* to stay here, that they had to start the plane up and get going again. But what would they say? Okay, sure, Dinah's right, everybody back on the plane? No *way.*

They'll see. They'll see that it's empty and then we'll get back on the airplane and go someplace else. Someplace where it doesn't feel wrong. There's still time.

I think.

"Never mind," she told Laurel. Her voice was low and resigned. "Lower me down."

Laurel lowered her carefully onto the slide. A moment later Dinah was looking up at her—*except she's not* really *looking,* Laurel thought, *she can't* really *look at all*—with her bare feet splayed out behind her on the orange slide.

"Okay, Dinah?" Laurel asked.

"No," Dinah said. "*Nothing's* okay here." And before Laurel could release her, Dinah unlocked her hands from Laurel's and released herself. She slid to the bottom, and Nick caught her.

Laurel went next, dropping neatly onto the slide and holding her skirt primly as she slid to the bottom. That left Brian, the snoozing drunk at the back of the plane, and that fun-loving paper-ripping party animal, Mr. Crew-Neck Jersey.

I'm not going to have any trouble with him, Brian had said, *because I don't give a crap what he does.* Now he discovered that was not really true. The man was not playing with a full deck. Brian suspected even the little girl knew that, and the little girl was blind. What if they left him behind and the guy decided to go on a rampage? What if, in the course of that rampage, he decided to trash the cockpit?

So what? You're not going anyplace. The tanks are almost dry.

Still, he didn't like the idea, and not just because the 767 was a multi-million-dollar piece of equipment, either. Perhaps what he felt was a vague echo of what he had seen in Dinah's face as she looked up from the slide. Things here seemed wrong, even wronger than they looked . . . and that was scary, because he didn't know how things could be wronger than that. The plane, however, was right. Even with its fuel tanks all but empty, it was a world he knew and understood.

"Your turn, friend," he said as civilly as he could.

"You know I'm going to report you for this, don't you?" Craig Toomy asked in a queerly gentle voice. "You know I plan to sue this entire airline for thirty million dollars, and that I plan to name you a primary respondent?"

"That's your privilege, Mr.——"

"Toomy. Craig Toomy."

"Mr. Toomy," Brian agreed. He hesitated. "Mr. Toomy, are you aware of what has happened to us?"

Craig looked out the open doorway for a moment—looked at the deserted tarmac and the wide, slightly polarized terminal windows on the second level, where no happy friends and relatives stood waiting to embrace arriving passengers, where no impatient travellers waited for their flights to be called.

Of course he knew. It was the langoliers. The langoliers had come for all the foolish, lazy people, just as his father had always said they would.

In that same gentle voice, Craig said: "In the Bond Department of the Desert Sun Banking Corporation, I am known as The Wheelhorse. Did you know that?" He paused for a moment, apparently waiting for Brian to make some response. When Brian didn't, Craig continued. "Of course you didn't. No more than you know how important this meeting at the Prudential Center in Boston is. No more than you care. But let me tell you something, Captain: the economic fate of nations may hinge upon the results of that meeting—that meeting from which I will be absent when the roll is taken."

"Mr. Toomy, all that's very interesting, but I really don't have time—"

"*Time!*" Craig screamed at him suddenly. "What in the hell do *you* know about time? Ask me! Ask me! I know about time! I know *all about* time! Time is short, sir! Time is *very fucking short*!"

Hell with it, I'm going to push the crazy son of a bitch, Brian thought, but before he could, Craig Toomy turned and leaped. He did a perfect seat-drop, holding his briefcase to his chest as he did so, and Brian was crazily reminded of that old Hertz ad on TV, the one where O. J. Simpson went flying through airports in a suit and a tie.

"*Time is short as hell!*" Craig shouted as he slid down, briefcase over his chest like a shield, pantslegs pulling up to reveal his knee-high dress-for-success black nylon socks.

Brian muttered: "Jesus, what a fucking weirdo." He paused at the head of the slide, looked around once more at the comforting, known world of his aircraft . . . and jumped.

8

Ten people stood in two small groups beneath the giant wing of the 767 with the red-and-blue eagle on the nose. In one group were Brian, Nick, the bald man, Bethany Simms, Albert Kaussner, Robert Jenkins, Dinah, Laurel, and Don Gaffney. Standing slightly apart from them and constituting his own group was Craig Toomy, a.k.a. The Wheelhorse. Craig bent and shook out the creases of his pants with fussy concentration, using his left hand to do it. The right was tightly locked around the handle of his briefcase. Then he simply stood and looked around with wide, disinterested eyes.

"What now, Captain?" Nick asked briskly.

"You tell me. Us."

Nick looked at him for a moment, one eyebrow slightly raised, as if to ask Brian if he really meant it. Brian inclined his head half an inch. It was enough.

"Well, inside the terminal will do for a start, I reckon," Nick said. "What would be the quickest way to get there? Any idea?"

Brian nodded toward a line of baggage trains parked beneath the overhang of the main terminal. "I'd guess the quickest way in without a jetway would be the luggage conveyor."

"All right; let's hike on over, ladies and gentlemen, shall we?"

It was a short walk, but Laurel, who walked hand-in-hand with Dinah, thought it was the strangest one she had ever taken in her life. She could see them as if from above, less than a dozen dots trundling slowly across a wide concrete plain. There was no breeze. No birds sang. No motors revved in the distance, and no human voice broke the unnatural quiet. Even their footfalls seemed wrong to her. She was wearing a pair of high heels, but instead of the brisk click she was used to, she seemed to hear only small, dull thuds.

Seemed, she thought. *That's the key word. Because the situation is so strange,* everything *begins to seem strange. It's the concrete, that's all. High heels sound different on concrete.*

But she had walked on concrete in high heels before. She didn't remember ever hearing a sound precisely like this. It was . . . pallid, somehow. Strengthless.

They reached the parked luggage trains. Nick wove between them, leading the line, and stopped at a dead conveyor belt which emerged from a hole lined with hanging strips of rubber. The conveyor made a wide circle on the apron where the handlers normally stood to unload the flatties, then reentered the terminal through another hole hung with rubber strips.

"What are those pieces of rubber for?" Bethany asked nervously.

"To keep out the draft in cold weather, I imagine," Nick said. "Just let me poke my head through and have a look. No fear; won't be a moment." And before anyone could reply, he had boosted himself onto the conveyor belt and was walking bent-over down to one of the holes cut into the building. When he got there, he dropped to his knees and poked his head through the rubber strips.

We're going to hear a whistle and then a thud, Albert thought wildly, *and when we pull him back, his head will be gone.*

There was no whistle, no thud. When Nick withdrew, his head was still firmly attached to his neck, and his face wore a thoughtful expression. "Coast's clear," he said, and to Albert his cheery tone now sounded manufactured. "Come on through, friends. When a body meet a body, and all that."

Bethany held back. "*Are* there bodies? Mister, are there dead people in there?"

"Not that I saw, miss," Nick said, and now he had dropped any attempt at lightness. "I was misquoting old Bobby Burns in an attempt to be funny. I'm afraid I achieved tastelessness instead of humor. The fact is, I didn't see anyone at all. But that's pretty much what we expected, isn't it?"

It was . . . but it struck heavily at their hearts just the same. Nick's as well, from his tone.

One after the other they climbed onto the conveyor belt and crawled after him through the hanging rubber strips.

Dinah paused just outside the entrance hole and turned her head back toward Laurel. Hazy light flashed across her dark glasses, turning them to momentary mirrors.

"It's really wrong here," she repeated, and pushed through to the other side.

9

One by one they emerged into the main terminal of Bangor International Airport, exotic baggage crawling along a stalled conveyor belt. Albert helped Dinah off and then they all stood there, looking around in silent wonder.

The shocked amazement at waking to a plane which had been magically emptied of people had worn off; now dislocation had taken the place of wonder. None of them had ever been in an airport terminal which was utterly empty. The rental-car stalls were deserted. The ARRIVALS/DEPARTURES monitors were dark and dead. No one stood at the bank of counters serving Delta, United, Northwest Air-Link, or Mid-Coast Airways. The huge tank in the middle of the floor with the BUY MAINE LOBSTERS banner stretched over it was full of water, but there were no lobsters in it. The overhead fluorescents were off, and the small amount of light entering through the doors on the far side of the large room petered out halfway across the floor, leaving the little group from Flight 29 huddled together in an unpleasant nest of shadows.

"Right, then," Nick said, trying for briskness and managing only unease. "Let's try the telephones, shall we?"

While he went to the bank of telephones, Albert wandered over to the Budget Rent A Car desk. In the slots on the rear wall he saw folders for BRIGGS, HANDLEFORD, MARCHANT, FENWICK and PESTLEMAN. There was, no doubt, a rental agreement inside each one, along with a map of the central Maine area, and on each map there would be an arrow with the legend YOU ARE HERE on it, pointing at the city of Bangor.

But where are we really? Albert wondered. *And where are Briggs, Handleford, Marchant, Fenwick, and Pestleman? Have they been transported to another dimension? Maybe it's the Grateful Dead. Maybe the Dead's playing somewhere downstate and everybody left for the show.*

There was a dry scratching noise just behind him. Albert nearly jumped out of his skin and whirled around fast, holding his violin case up like a cudgel. Bethany was standing there, just touching a match to the tip of her cigarette.

She raised her eyebrows. "Scare you?"

"A little," Albert said, lowering the case and offering her a small, embarrassed smile.

"Sorry." She shook out the match, dropped it on the floor, and drew deeply on her cigarette. "There. At least *that's* better. I didn't dare to on the plane. I was afraid something might blow up."

Bob Jenkins strolled over. "You know, I quit those about ten years ago."

"No lectures, please," Bethany said. "I've got a feeling that if we get out of this alive and sane, I'm in for about a month of lectures. Solid. Wall-to-wall."

Jenkins raised his eyebrows but didn't ask for an explanation. "Actually," he said, "I was going to ask you if I could have one. This seems like an excellent time to renew acquaintance with old habits."

Bethany smiled and offered him a Marlboro. Jenkins took it and she lit it for him. He inhaled, then coughed out a series of smoke-signal puffs.

"You *have* been away," she observed matter-of-factly.

Jenkins agreed. "But I'll get used to it again in a hurry.

That's the real horror of the habit, I'm afraid. Did you two notice the clock?"

"No," Albert said.

Jenkins pointed to the wall above the doors of the men's and women's bathrooms. The clock mounted there had stopped at 4:07.

"It fits," he said. "We knew we had been in the air for awhile when—let's call it The Event, for want of a better term—when The Event took place. 4:07 A.M. Eastern Daylight Time is 1:07 A.M. PDT. So now we know the when."

"Gee, that's great," Bethany said.

"Yes," Jenkins said, either not noticing or preferring to ignore the light overlay of sarcasm in her voice. "But there's something wrong with it. I only wish the sun was out. Then I could be sure."

"What do you mean?" Albert asked.

"The clocks—the electric ones, anyway—are no good. There's no juice. But if the sun was out, we could get at least a rough idea of what time it is by the length and direction of our shadows. My watch says it's going on quarter of nine, but I don't trust it. It feels later to me than that. I have no proof for it, and I can't explain it, but it does."

Albert thought about it. Looked around. Looked back at Jenkins. "You know," he said, "it *does*. It feels like it's almost lunchtime. Isn't that nuts?"

"It's not nuts," Bethany said, "it's just jetlag."

"I disagree," Jenkins said. "We travelled west to east, young lady. Any temporal dislocation west–east travellers feel goes the other way. They feel it's *earlier* than it should be."

"I want to ask you about something you said on the plane," Albert said. "When the captain told us that there must be *some* other people here, you said 'false logic.' In fact, you said it twice. But it seems straight enough to me. We were all asleep, and *we're* here. And if this thing happened at"—Albert glanced toward the clock—"at 4:07, Bangor time, almost everyone in *town* must have been asleep."

"Yes," Jenkins said blandly. "So where are they?"

Albert was nonplussed. "Well . . ."

There was a bang as Nick forcibly hung up one of the pay telephones. It was the last in a long line of them; he had tried every one. "It's a washout," he said. "They're all dead. The coin-fed ones as well as the direct-dials. You can add the sound of no phones ringing to that of no dogs barking, Brian."

"So what do we do now?" Laurel asked. She heard the forlorn sound of her own voice and it made her feel very small, very lost. Beside her, Dinah was turning in slow circles. She looked like a human radar dish.

"Let's go upstairs," Baldy proposed. "That's where the restaurant must be."

They all looked at him. Gaffney snorted. "You got a one-track mind, mister."

The bald man looked at him from beneath one raised eyebrow. "First, the name is Rudy Warwick, not mister," he replied. "Second, people think better when their stomachs are full." He shrugged. "It's just a law of nature."

"I think Mr. Warwick is quite right," Jenkins said. "We all *could* use something to eat . . . and if we go upstairs, we may find some other clues pointing toward what has happened. In fact, I rather think we will."

Nick shrugged. He looked suddenly tired and confused. "Why not?" he said. "I'm starting to feel like Mr. Robinson Bloody Crusoe."

They started toward the escalator, which was also dead, in a straggling little group. Albert, Bethany, and Bob Jenkins walked together, toward the rear.

"You know something, don't you?" Albert asked abruptly. "What is it?"

"I *might* know something," Jenkins corrected. "I might not.

For the time being I'm going to hold my peace . . . except for one suggestion."

"What?"

"It's not for you; it's for the young lady." He turned to Bethany. "Save your matches. That's my suggestion."

"What?" Bethany frowned at him.

"You heard me."

"Yeah, I guess I did, but I don't get what you mean. There's probably a newsstand upstairs, Mr. Jenkins. They'll have lots of matches. Cigarettes and disposable lighters, too."

"I agree," Jenkins said. "I still advise you to save your matches."

He's playing Philo Christie or whoever it was again, Albert thought.

He was about to point this out and ask Jenkins to please remember that this wasn't one of his novels when Brian Engle stopped at the foot of the escalator, so suddenly that Laurel had to jerk sharply on Dinah's hand to keep the blind girl from running into him.

"Watch where you're going, okay?" Laurel asked. "In case you didn't notice, the kid here can't see."

Brian ignored her. He was looking around at the little group of refugees. "Where's Mr. Toomy?"

"Who?" the bald man—Warwick—asked.

"The guy with the pressing appointment in Boston."

"Who cares?" Gaffney asked. "Good riddance to bad rubbish."

But Brian was uneasy. He didn't like the idea that Toomy had slipped away and gone off on his own. He didn't know why, but he didn't like that idea at all. He glanced at Nick. Nick shrugged, then shook his head. "Didn't see him go, mate. I was fooling with the phones. Sorry."

"*Toomy!*" Brian shouted. "*Craig Toomy! Where are you?*"

There was no response. Only that queer, oppressive silence. And Laurel noticed something then, something that made her skin cold. Brian had cupped his hands and shouted up the escalator. In a high-ceilinged place like this one, there should have been at least some echo.

But there had been none.

No echo at all.

10

While the others were occupied downstairs—the two teenagers and the old geezer standing by one of the car-rental desks, the others watching the British thug as he tried the phones— Craig Toomy had crept up the stalled escalator as quietly as a mouse. He knew exactly where he wanted to go; he knew exactly what to look for when he got there.

He strode briskly across the large waiting room with his briefcase swinging beside his right knee, ignoring both the empty chairs and an empty bar called The Red Baron. At the far end of the room was a sign hanging over the mouth of a wide, dark corridor. It read

GATE 5 INTERNATIONAL ARRIVALS
DUTY FREE SHOPS
U.S. CUSTOMS
AIRPORT SECURITY

He had almost reached the head of this corridor when he glanced out one of the wide windows at the tarmac again . . . and his pace faltered. He approached the glass slowly and looked out.

There was nothing to see but the empty concrete and the moveless white sky, but his eyes began to widen nonetheless and he felt fear begin to steal into his heart.

They're coming, a dead voice suddenly told him. It was the voice of his father, and it spoke from a small, haunted mausoleum tucked away in a gloomy corner of Craig Toomy's heart.

"No," he whispered, and the word spun a little blossom of fog on the window in front of his lips. "No one is coming."

You've been bad. Worse, you've been lazy.

"No!"

Yes. You had an appointment and you skipped it. You ran away. You ran away to Bangor, Maine, of all the silly places.

"It wasn't my fault," he muttered. He was gripping the handle of the briefcase with almost painful tightness now. "I was taken against my will. I . . . I was shanghaied!"

No reply from that interior voice. Only waves of disapproval. And once again Craig intuited the pressure he was under, the terrible never-ending pressure, the weight of the fathoms. The interior voice did not have to tell him there were no excuses; Craig knew that. He knew it of old.

THEY were here . . . and they will be back. You know that, don't you?

He knew. The langoliers would be back. They would be back for *him.* He could sense them. He had never seen them, but he knew how horrible they would be. And was he alone in his knowledge? He thought not.

He thought perhaps the little blind girl knew something about the langoliers as well.

But that didn't matter. The only thing which did was getting to Boston—getting to Boston before the langoliers could arrive in Bangor from their terrible, doomish lair to eat him alive and screaming. He had to get to that meeting at the Pru, had to let them know what he had done, and then he would be . . .

Free.

He would be free.

Craig pulled himself away from the window, away from the emptiness and the stillness, and plunged into the corridor beneath the sign. He passed the empty shops without a glance. Beyond them he came to the door he was looking for. There was a small rectangular plaque mounted on it, just above a bullseye peephole. AIRPORT SECURITY, it said.

He had to get in there. One way or another, he *had* to get in there.

All of this . . . this craziness . . . it doesn't have to belong to me. I don't have to own it. Not anymore.

Craig reached out and touched the doorknob of the Airport Security office. The blank look in his eyes had been replaced by an expression of clear determination.

I have been under stress for a long, a very long, time. Since I was seven? No—I think it started even before that. The fact is, I've been under stress for as long as I can remember. This latest piece of craziness is just a new variation. It's probably just what the man in the ratty sportcoat said it was: a test. Agents of some secret government agency or sinister foreign power running a test. But I choose not to participate in any more tests. I don't care if it's my father in charge, or my mother, or the dean of the Graduate School of Management, or the Desert Sun Banking Corporation's Board of Directors. I choose not to participate. I choose to escape. I choose to get to Boston and finish what I set out to do when I presented the Argentinian bond-buy in the first place. If I don't . . .

But he knew what would happen if he didn't.

He would go mad.

Craig tried the doorknob. It did not move beneath his hand, but when he gave it a small, frustrated push, the door swung open. Either it had been left slightly unlatched, or it had unlocked when the power went off and the security systems went dead. Craig didn't care which. The important thing was that he wouldn't need to muss his clothes trying to crawl through an air-conditioning duct or something. He still had every intention of showing up at his meeting before the end of the day, and he didn't want his clothes smeared with dirt and grease when he got there. One of the simple, unexceptioned truths of life was this: guys with dirt on their suits have no credibility.

He pushed the door open and went inside.

11

Brian and Nick reached the top of the escalator first, and the others gathered around them. This was BIA's central waiting room, a large square box filled with contour plastic seats (some with coin-op TVs bolted to the arms) and dominated by a wall of polarized floor-to-ceiling windows. To their immediate left was the airport newsstand and the security checkpoint which served Gate 1; to their right and all the way across the room were The Red Baron Bar and The Cloud Nine Restaurant. Beyond the restaurant was the corridor leading to the Airport Security office and the International Arrivals Annex.

"Come on——" Nick began, and Dinah said, "Wait."

She spoke in a strong, urgent voice and they all turned toward her curiously.

Dinah dropped Laurel's hand and raised both of her own. She cupped the thumbs behind her ears and splayed her fingers out like fans. Then she simply stood there, still as a post, in this odd and rather weird listening posture.

"What——" Brian began, and Dinah said "*Shhh!*" in an abrupt, inarguable sibilant.

She turned slightly to the left, paused, then turned in the other direction until the white light coming through the windows fell directly on her, turning her already pale face into something which was ghostlike and eerie. She took off her dark glasses. The eyes beneath were wide, brown, and not quite blank.

"There," she said in a low, dreaming voice, and Laurel felt terror begin to stroke at her heart with chilly fingers. Nor was she alone. Bethany was crowding close to her on one side, and Don Gaffney moved in against her other side. "There——I can feel the light. They said that's how they know I can see again. I can always feel the light. It's like heat inside my head."

"Dinah, what——" Brian began.

Nick elbowed him. The Englishman's face was long and drawn, his forehead ribbed with lines. "Be quiet, mate."

"The light is . . . here."

She walked slowly away from them, her hands still fanned out by her ears, her elbows held out before her to encounter any object which might stand in her way. She advanced until she was less than two feet from the window. Then she slowly reached out until her fingers touched the glass. They looked like black starfish outlined against the white sky. She let out a small, unhappy murmur.

"The glass is wrong, too," she said in that dreaming voice.

"Dinah——" Laurel began.

"Shhh . . ." she whispered without turning around. She stood at the window like a little girl waiting for her father to come home from work. "*I hear something.*"

These whispered words sent a wordless, thoughtless horror through Albert Kaussner's mind. He felt pressure on his shoulders and looked down to see he had crossed his arms across his chest and was clutching himself hard.

Brian listened with all his concentration. He heard his own breathing, and the breathing of the others . . . but he heard nothing else. *It's her imagination,* he thought. *That's all it is.*

But he wondered.

"What?" Laurel asked urgently. "What do you hear, Dinah?"

"I don't know," she said without turning from the window. "It's very faint. I thought I heard it when we got off the airplane, and then I decided it was just my imagination. Now I can hear it better. I can hear it even through the glass. It sounds . . . a little like Rice Krispies after you pour in the milk."

Brian turned to Nick and spoke in a low voice. "Do you hear anything?"

"Not a bloody thing," Nick said, matching Brian's tone. "But she's blind. She's used to making her ears do double duty."

"I think it's hysteria," Brian said. He was whispering now, his lips almost touching Nick's ear.

Dinah turned from the window.

" 'Do you hear anything?' " she mimicked. " 'Not a bloody thing. But she's blind. She's used to making her ears do double duty.' " She paused, then added: " 'I think it's hysteria.' "

"Dinah, what are you talking about?" Laurel asked, perplexed and frightened. She had not heard Brian and Nick's muttered conversation, although she had been standing much closer to them than Dinah was.

"Ask *them*," Dinah said. Her voice was trembling. "I'm not crazy! I'm blind, but I'm *not* crazy!"

"All right," Brian said, shaken. "All right, Dinah." And to Laurel he said: "I was talking to Nick. She heard us. From over there by the windows, she heard us."

"You've got great ears, hon," Bethany said.

"I hear what I hear," Dinah said. "And I hear something out there. In that direction." She pointed due east through the glass. Her unseeing eyes swept them. "And it's *bad*. It's an awful sound, a scary sound."

Don Gaffney said hesitantly: "If you knew what it was, little miss, that would help, maybe."

"I don't," Dinah said. "But I know that it's closer than it was." She put her dark glasses back on with a hand that was trembling. "We have to get out of here. And we have to get out soon. Because something is coming. The bad something making the cereal noise."

"Dinah," Brian said, "the plane we came in is almost out of fuel."

"*Then you have to put some more in it!*" Dinah screamed shrilly at him. "*It's coming*, don't you understand? It's *coming*, and if we haven't gone when it gets here, we're going to die! *We're all going to die!*"

Her voice cracked and she began to sob. She was not a sibyl or a medium but only a little girl forced to live her terror in a darkness which was almost complete. She staggered toward them, her self-possession utterly gone. Laurel grabbed her before she could stumble over one of the guide-ropes which marked the way to the security checkpoint and hugged her tight. She tried to soothe the girl, but those last words echoed and rang in Laurel's confused, shocked mind: *If we haven't gone when it gets here, we're going to die.*

We're all going to die.

12

Craig Toomy heard the brat begin to caterwaul back there someplace and ignored it. He had found what he was looking for in the third locker he opened, the one with the name MAR-KEY Dymotaped to the front. Mr. Markey's lunch—a sub sandwich poking out of a brown paper bag—was on the top shelf. Mr. Markey's street shoes were placed neatly side by side on the bottom shelf. Hanging in between, from the same hook, were a plain white shirt and a gunbelt. Protruding from the holster was the butt of Mr. Markey's service revolver.

Craig unsnapped the safety strap and took the gun out. He didn't know much about guns—this could have been a .32, a .38, or even a .45, for all of him—but he was not stupid, and after a few moments of fumbling he was able to roll the cylinder. All six chambers were loaded. He pushed the cylinder back in, nodding slightly when he heard it click home, and then inspected the hammer area and both sides of the grip. He was looking for a safety catch, but there didn't appear to be one. He put his finger on the trigger and tightened until he saw both the hammer and the cylinder move slightly. Craig nodded, satisfied.

He turned around and without warning the most intense loneliness of his adult life struck him. The gun seemed to take on weight and the hand holding it sagged. Now he stood with his shoulders slumped, the briefcase dangling from his right hand, the security guard's pistol dangling from his left. On his face was an expression of utter, abject misery. And suddenly a memory recurred to him, something he hadn't thought of in years: Craig Toomy, twelve years old, lying in bed and shivering as hot tears ran down his face. In the other room the stereo was turned up loud and his mother was singing along with Merrilee Rush in her droning off-key drunk's voice: "Just call me *angel* . . . of the *morn*-ing, *bay*-bee . . . just touch my cheek . . . before you leave me, *bay*-bee . . ."

Lying there in bed. Shaking. Crying. Not making a sound. And thinking: *Why can't you love me and leave me alone, Momma? Why can't you just love me and leave me alone?*

"I don't want to hurt anyone," Craig Toomy muttered through his tears. "I don't want to, but this . . . this is intolerable."

Across the room was a bank of TV monitors, all blank. For a moment, as he looked at them, the truth of what had happened, what was *still* happening, tried to crowd in on him. For a moment it almost broke through his complex system of neurotic shields and into the air-raid shelter where he lived his life.

Everyone is gone, Craiggy-weggy. The whole world is gone except for you and the people who were on that plane.

"No," he moaned, and collapsed into one of the chairs standing around the Formica-topped kitchen table in the center of the room. "No, that's not so. That's just not so. I refute that idea. I refute it *utterly.*"

The langoliers were here, and they will be back, his father said. It overrode the voice of his mother, as it always had. *You better be gone when they get here . . . or you know what will happen.*

He knew, all right. They would eat him. The langoliers would eat him up.

"But I don't want to hurt anyone," he repeated in a dreary, distraught voice. There was a mimeographed duty roster lying on the table. Craig let go of his briefcase and laid the gun on the table beside him. Then he picked up the duty roster, looked at it for a moment with unseeing eyes, and began to tear a long strip from the lefthand side.

Rii-ip.

Soon he was hypnotized as a pile of thin strips—maybe the thinnest ever!—began to flutter down onto the table. But even then the cold voice of his father would not entirely leave him:

Or you know what will happen.

CHAPTER FIVE

A BOOK OF MATCHES. THE ADVENTURE OF
THE SALAMI SANDWICH. ANOTHER EXAMPLE OF
THE DEDUCTIVE METHOD. THE ARIZONA JEW PLAYS
THE VIOLIN. THE ONLY SOUND IN TOWN.

1

The frozen silence following Dinah's warning was finally broken by Robert Jenkins. "We have some problems," he said in a dry lecture-hall voice. "If Dinah hears something—and following the remarkable demonstration she's just given us, I'm inclined to think she does—it would be helpful if we knew what it is. We don't. That's one problem. The plane's lack of fuel is another problem."

"There's a 727 out there," Nick said, "all cozied up to a jetway. Can you fly one of those, Brian?"

"Yes," Brian said.

Nick spread his hands in Bob's direction and shrugged, as if to say *There you are; one knot untied already.*

"Assuming we *do* take off again, where should we go?" Bob Jenkins went on. "A third problem."

"Away," Dinah said immediately. "Away from that sound. We *have* to get away from that sound, and what's making it."

"How long do you think we have?" Bob asked her gently. "How long before it gets here, Dinah? Do you have any idea at all?"

"No," she said from the safe circle of Laurel's arms. "I think it's still far. I think there's still time. But . . ."

"Then I suggest we do exactly as Mr. Warwick has suggested," Bob said. "Let's step over to the restaurant, have a bite to eat, and discuss what happens next. Food *does* have a beneficial effect on what Monsieur Poirot liked to call the little gray cells."

"We shouldn't *wait,*" Dinah said fretfully.

"Fifteen minutes," Bob said. "No more than that. And even at your age, Dinah, you should know that useful thinking must always precede useful action."

Albert suddenly realized that the mystery writer had his own reasons for wanting to go to the restaurant. Mr. Jenkins's little gray cells were all in apple-pie working order—or at least he *believed* they were—and following his eerily sharp assessment of their situation on board the plane, Albert was willing at least to give him the benefit of the doubt. *He wants to show us something, or prove something to us,* he thought.

"Surely we have fifteen minutes?" he coaxed.

"Well . . ." Dinah said unwillingly. "I guess so . . ."

"Fine," Bob said briskly. "It's decided." And he struck off across the room toward the restaurant, as if taking it for granted that the others would follow him.

Brian and Nick looked at each other.

"We better go along," Albert said quietly. "I think he knows stuff."

"What kind of stuff?" Brian asked.

"I don't know, exactly, but I think it might be stuff worth finding out."

Albert followed Bob; Bethany followed Albert; the others fell in behind them, Laurel leading Dinah by the hand. The little girl was very pale.

2

The Cloud Nine Restaurant was really a cafeteria with a cold-case full of drinks and sandwiches at the rear and a stainless-steel counter running beside a long, compartmentalized steam-table. All the compartments were empty, all sparkling clean. There wasn't a speck of grease on the grill. Glasses—those tough cafeteria glasses with the ripply sides—were stacked in neat pyramids on rear shelves, along with a wide selection of even tougher cafeteria crockery.

Robert Jenkins was standing by the cash register. As Albert and Bethany came in, he said: "May I have another cigarette, Bethany?"

"Gee, you're a real mooch," she said, but her tone was good-natured. She produced her box of Marlboros and shook one out. He took it, then touched her hand as she also produced her book of matches.

"I'll just use one of these, shall I?" There was a bowl filled with paper matches advertising LaSalle Business School by the cash register. FOR OUR MATCHLESS FRIENDS, a little sign beside the bowl read. Bob took a book of these matches, opened it, and pulled one of the matches free.

"Sure," Bethany said, "but why?"

"That's what we're going to find out," he said. He glanced at the others. They were standing around in a semicircle, watching—all except Rudy Warwick, who had drifted to the rear of the serving area and was closely inspecting the contents of the cold-case.

Bob struck the match. It left a little smear of white stuff on the striker, but didn't light. He struck it again with the same result. On the third try, the paper match bent. Most of the flammable head was gone, anyway.

"My, my," he said in an utterly unsurprised tone. "I suppose they must be wet. Let's try a book from the bottom, shall we? *They* should be dry."

He dug to the bottom of the bowl, spilling a number of matchbooks off the top and onto the counter as he did so. They all looked perfectly dry to Albert. Behind him, Nick and Brian exchanged another glance.

Bob fished out another book of matches, pulled one, and tried to strike it. It didn't light.

"Son of a bee," he said. "We seem to have discovered yet another problem. May I borrow your book of matches, Bethany?"

She handed it over without a word.

"Wait a minute," Nick said slowly. "What do you know, matey?"

"Only that this situation has even wider implications than we at first thought," Bob said. His eyes were calm enough, but the face from which they looked was haggard. "And I have an idea that we all may have made one *big* mistake. Understandable enough under the circumstances . . . but until we've rectified our thinking on this subject, I don't believe we can make any progress. An error of perspective, I'd call it."

Warwick was wandering back toward them. He had selected a wrapped sandwich and a bottle of beer. His acquisitions seemed to have cheered him considerably. "What's happening, folks?"

"I'll be damned if I know," Brian said, "but I don't like it much."

Bob Jenkins pulled one of the matches from Bethany's book and struck it. It lit on the first strike. "Ah," he said, and applied the flame to the tip of his cigarette. The smoke smelled incredibly pungent, incredibly sweet to Brian, and a moment's reflection suggested a reason why: it was the only thing, save for the faint tang of Nick Hopewell's shaving lotion and Laurel's perfume, that he *could* smell. Now that he thought about it, Brian realized that he could hardly even smell his travelling companions' sweat.

Bob still held the lit match in his hand. Now he bent back the top of the book he'd taken from the bowl, exposing all the matches, and touched the lit match to the heads of the others. For a long moment nothing happened. The writer slipped the flame back and forth along the heads of the matches, but they didn't light. The others watched, fascinated.

At last there was a sickly *phsssss* sound, and a few of the matches erupted into dull, momentary life. They did not really burn at all; there was a weak glow and they went out. A few tendrils of smoke drifted up . . . smoke which seemed to have no odor at all.

Bob looked around at them and smiled grimly. "Even that," he said, "is more than I expected."

"All right," Brian said. "Tell us about it. I know—"

At that moment, Rudy Warwick uttered a cry of disgust. Dinah gave a little shriek and pressed closer to Laurel. Albert felt his heart take a high skip in his chest.

Rudy had unwrapped his sandwich—it looked to Brian like salami and cheese—and had taken a large bite. Now he spat it out onto the floor with a grimace of disgust.

"It's spoiled!" Rudy cried. "Oh, goddam! I *hate* that!"

"Spoiled?" Bob Jenkins said swiftly. His eyes gleamed like blue electrical sparks. "Oh, I doubt that. Processed meats are so loaded with preservatives these days that it takes eight hours or more in the hot sun to send them over. And we know by the clocks that the power in that cold-case went out less than five hours ago."

"Maybe not," Albert spoke up. "You were the one who said it felt later than our wristwatches say."

"Yes, but I don't think . . . Was the case still cold, Mr. Warwick? When you opened it, was the case still cold?"

"Not *cold,* exactly, but cool," Rudy said. "That sandwich is all fucked up, though. Pardon me, ladies. Here." He held it out. "If you don't think it's spoiled, *you* try it."

Bob stared at the sandwich, appeared to screw up his courage, and then did just that, taking a small bite from the untouched half. Albert saw an expression of disgust pass over his face, but he did not get rid of the food immediately. He chewed once . . . twice . . . then turned and spat into his hand. He stuffed the half-chewed bite of sandwich into the trash-bin below the condiments shelf, and dropped the rest of the sand-wich in after it.

"Not spoiled," he said. "Tasteless. And not just that, either. It seemed to have no texture." His mouth drew down in an involuntary expression of disgust. "We talk about things being bland—unseasoned white rice, boiled potatoes—but even the blandest food has *some* taste, I think. That had none. It was like chewing paper. No wonder you thought it was spoiled."

"It *was* spoiled," the bald man reiterated stubbornly.

"Try your beer," Bob invited. "*That* shouldn't be spoiled. The cap is still on, and a capped bottle of beer shouldn't spoil even if it isn't refrigerated."

Rudy looked thoughtfully at the bottle of Budweiser in his hand, then shook his head and held it out to Bob. "I don't want it anymore," he said. He glanced at the cold-case. His gaze was baleful, as if he suspected Jenkins of having played an unfunny practical joke on him.

"I will if I have to," Bob said, "but I've already offered my body up to science once. Will somebody else try this beer? I think it's very important."

"Give it to me," Nick said.

"No." It was Don Gaffney. "Give it to me. I could use a beer, by God. I've drunk em warm before and they don't cross my eyes none."

He took the beer, twisted off the cap, and upended it. A moment later he whirled and sprayed the mouthful he had taken onto the floor.

"*Jesus!*" he cried. "Flat! Flat as a pancake!"

"Is it?" Bob asked brightly. "Good! Great! Something we can all see!" He was around the counter in a flash, and taking one of the glasses down from the shelf. Gaffney had set the bottle down beside the cash register, and Brian looked at it closely as Bob Jenkins picked it up. He could see no foam clinging to the inside of the bottleneck. *It might as well be water in there,* he thought.

What Bob poured out didn't look like water, however; it looked like beer. Flat beer. There was no head. A few small bubbles clung to the inside of the glass, but none of them came pinging up through the liquid to the surface.

"All right," Nick said slowly, "it's flat. Sometimes that happens. The cap doesn't get screwed on all the way at the factory and the gas escapes. Everyone's gotten a flat lager from time to time."

"But when you add in the tasteless salami sandwich, it's suggestive, isn't it?"

"Suggestive of *what?*" Brian exploded.

"In a moment," Bob said. "Let's take care of Mr. Hopewell's *caveat* first, shall we?" He turned, grabbed glasses with both hands (a couple of others fell off the shelf and shattered on the floor), then began to set them out along the counter with the agile speed of a bartender. "Bring me some more beer. And a couple of soft drinks, while you're at it."

Albert and Bethany went down to the cold-case and each took four or five bottles, picking at random.

"Is he nuts?" Bethany asked in a low voice.

"I don't think so," Albert said. He had a vague idea of what the writer was trying to show them . . . and he didn't like the shape it made in his mind. "Remember when he told you to save your matches? He knew something like this was going to happen. That's why he was so hot to get us to the restaurant. He wanted to show us."

3

The duty roster was ripped into three dozen narrow strips and the langoliers were closer now.

Craig could feel their approach at the back of his mind—more weight.

More insupportable weight.

It was time to go.

He picked up the gun and his briefcase, then stood up and left the security room. He walked slowly, rehearsing as he went: *I don't want to shoot you, but I will if I have to. Take me to Boston. I don't want to shoot you, but I will if I have to. Take me to Boston.*

"I will if I have to," Craig muttered as he walked back into the waiting room. "I will if I have to." His finger found the hammer of the gun and cocked it back.

Halfway across the room, his attention was once more snared by the pallid light which fell through the windows, and he turned in that direction. He could feel them out there. The langoliers. They had eaten all the useless, lazy people, and now they were returning for him. He *had* to get to Boston. It was the only way he knew to save the rest of himself . . . because *their* death would be horrible. Their death would be horrible indeed.

He walked slowly to the windows and looked out, ignoring— at least for the time being—the murmur of the other passengers behind him.

4

Bob Jenkins poured a little from each bottle into its own glass. The contents of each was as flat as the first beer had been. "Are you convinced?" he asked Nick.

"Yes," Nick said. "If you know what's going on here, mate, spill it. Please spill it."

"I have an idea," Bob said. "It's not . . . I'm afraid it's not very comforting, but I'm one of those people who believe that knowledge is always better—safer—in the long run than ignorance, no matter how dismayed one may feel when one first understands certain facts. Does that make any sense?"

"No," Gaffney said at once.

Bob shrugged and offered a small, wry smile. "Be that as it

may, I stand by my statement. And before I say anything else, I want to ask you all to look around this place and tell me what you see."

They looked around, concentrating so fiercely on the little clusters of tables and chairs that no one noticed Craig Toomy standing on the far side of the waiting room, his back to them, gazing out at the tarmac.

"Nothing," Laurel said at last. "I'm sorry, but I don't see anything. Your eyes must be sharper than mine, Mr. Jenkins."

"Not a bit. I see what you see: nothing. But airports are open twenty-four hours a day. When this thing—this Event—happened, it was probably at the dead low tide of its twenty-four-hour cycle, but I find it difficult to believe there weren't at least a few people in here, drinking coffee and perhaps eating early breakfasts. Aircraft maintenance men. Airport personnel. Perhaps a handful of connecting passengers who elected to save money by spending the hours between midnight and six or seven o'clock in the terminal instead of in a nearby motel. When I first got off that baggage conveyor and looked around, I felt utterly dislocated. Why? Because airports are *never* completely deserted, just as police and fire stations are never completely deserted. Now look around again, and ask yourself this: where are the half-eaten meals, the half-empty glasses? Remember the drinks trolley on the airplane with the dirty glasses on the lower shelf? Remember the half-eaten pastry and the half-drunk cup of coffee beside the pilot's seat in the cockpit? There's nothing like that here. *Where is the least sign that there were people here at all when this Event occurred?*"

Albert looked around again and then said slowly, "There's no pipe on the foredeck, is there?"

Bob looked at him closely. "What? What do you say, Albert?"

"When we were on the plane," Albert said slowly, "I was thinking of this sailing ship I read about once. It was called the *Mary Celeste,* and someone spotted it, just floating aimlessly along. Well . . . not really *floating,* I guess, because the book said the sails were set, but when the people who found it boarded her, everyone on the *Mary Celeste* was gone. Their stuff was still there, though, and there was food cooking on the stove. Someone even found a pipe on the foredeck. It was still lit."

"Bravo!" Bob cried, almost feverishly. They were all looking at him now, and no one saw Craig Toomy walking slowly toward them. The gun he had found was no longer pointed at the floor.

"Bravo, Albert! You've put your finger on it! And there was another famous disappearance—an entire colony of settlers at a place called Roanoke Island . . . off the coast of North Carolina, I believe. All gone, but they had left remains of campfires, cluttered houses, and trash middens behind. Now, Albert, take this a step further. How else does this terminal differ from our airplane?"

For a moment Albert looked entirely blank, and then understanding dawned in his eyes. "The rings!" he shouted. "The purses! The wallets! The money! The surgical pins! None of that stuff is here!"

"Correct," Bob said softly. "One hundred per cent correct. As you say, none of that stuff is here. But it was on the airplane when we survivors woke up, wasn't it? There were even a cup of coffee and a half-eaten Danish in the cockpit. The equivalent of a smoking pipe on the foredeck."

"You think we've flown into another dimension, don't you?" Albert said. His voice was awed. "Just like in a science-fiction story."

Dinah's head cocked to one side, and for a moment she looked strikingly like Nipper, the dog on the old RCA Victor labels.

"No," Bob said. "I think—"

"Watch out!" Dinah cried sharply. "I hear some—"

She was too late. Once Craig Toomy broke the paralysis which had held him and he started to move, he moved fast. Before Nick or Brian could do more than begin to turn around, he had locked one forearm around Bethany's throat and was dragging her backward. He pointed the gun at her temple. The girl uttered a desperate, terrorized squawk.

"I don't want to shoot her, but I will if I have to," Craig panted. "Take me to Boston." His eyes were no longer blank; they shot glances full of terrified, paranoid intelligence in every direction. "Do you hear me? Take me to Boston!"

Brian started toward him, and Nick placed a hand against his chest without shifting his eyes away from Craig. "Steady down, mate," he said in a low voice. "It wouldn't be safe. Our friend here is quite bonkers."

Bethany was squirming under Craig's restraining forearm. "You're choking me! Please stop *choking* me!"

"What's happening?" Dinah cried. "What is it?"

"Stop that!" Craig shouted at Bethany. "Stop moving around! You're going to force me to do something I don't want to do!" He pressed the muzzle of the gun against the side of her head. She continued to struggle, and Albert suddenly realized she didn't know he had a gun—even with it pressed against her skull she didn't know.

"Quit it, girl!" Nick said sharply. "Quit fighting!"

For the first time in his waking life, Albert found himself not just thinking like The Arizona Jew but possibly called upon to *act* like that fabled character. Without taking his eyes off the lunatic in the crew-neck jersey, he slowly began to raise his violin case. He switched his grip from the handle and settled both hands around the neck of the case. Toomy was not looking at him; his eyes were shuttling rapidly back and forth between Brian and Nick, and he had his hands full—quite literally—holding onto Bethany.

"I don't want to shoot her—" Craig was beginning again, and then his arm slipped upward as the girl bucked against him, socking her behind into his crotch. Bethany immediately sank her teeth into his wrist. "*Ow!*" Craig screamed. "*owwww!*"

His grip loosened. Bethany ducked under it. Albert leaped forward, raising the violin case, as Toomy pointed the gun at Bethany. Toomy's face was screwed into a grimace of pain and anger.

"*No, Albert!*" Nick bawled.

Craig Toomy saw Albert coming and shifted the muzzle toward him. For one moment Albert looked straight into it, and it was like none of his dreams or fantasies. Looking into the muzzle was like looking into an open grave.

I might have made a mistake here, he thought, and then Craig pulled the trigger.

5

Instead of an explosion there was a small pop—the sound of an old Daisy air rifle, no more. Albert felt something thump against the chest of his Hard Rock Cafe tee-shirt, had time to realize he had been shot, and then he brought the violin case down on Craig's head. There was a solid thud which ran all the way up his arms, and the indignant voice of his father suddenly spoke up in his mind: *What's the matter with you, Albert? That's no way to treat an expensive musical instrument!*

There was a startled *broink!* from inside the case as the violin jumped. One of the brass latches dug into Toomy's forehead and blood splashed outward in an amazing spray. Then the man's knees came unhinged and he went down in front of Albert like an express elevator. Albert saw his eyes roll up to whites, and then Craig Toomy was lying at his feet, unconscious.

A crazy but somehow wonderful thought filled Albert's mind for a moment: *By God, I never played better in my life!* And then he realized that he was no longer able to get his breath. He turned to the others, the corners of his mouth turning up in a thin-lipped, slightly confused smile. "I think I have been plugged," Ace Kaussner said, and then the world bleached out to shades of gray and his own knees came unhinged. He crumpled to the floor on top of his violin case.

6

He was out for less than thirty seconds. When he came around, Brian was slapping his cheeks lightly and looking anxious. Bethany was on her knees beside him, looking at Albert with shining my-hero eyes. Behind her, Dinah Bellman was still crying within the circle of Laurel's arms. Albert looked back at Bethany and felt his heart—apparently still whole—expand in his chest. "The Arizona Jew rides again," he muttered.

"What, Albert?" she asked, and stroked his cheek. Her hand was wonderfully soft, wonderfully cool. Albert decided he was in love.

"Nothing," he said, and then the pilot whacked him across the face again.

"Are you all right, kid?" Brian was asking. "Are you all right?"

"I think so," Albert said. "Stop doing that, okay? And the name is Albert. Ace, to my friends. How bad am I hit? I can't feel anything yet. Were you able to stop the bleeding?"

Nick Hopewell squatted beside Bethany. His face wore a bemused, unbelieving smile. "I think you'll live, matey. I never saw anything like that in my life . . . and I've seen a lot. You Americans are too foolish not to love. Hold out your hand and I'll give you a souvenir."

Albert held out a hand which shook uncontrollably with reaction, and Nick dropped something into it. Albert held it up to his eyes and saw it was a bullet.

"I picked it up off the floor," Nick said. "Not even misshapen. It must have hit you square in the chest—there's a little powder mark on your shirt—and then bounced off. It was a misfire. God must like you, mate."

"I was thinking of the matches," Albert said weakly. "I sort of thought it wouldn't fire at all."

"That was very brave and very foolish, my boy," Bob Jenkins said. His face was dead white and he looked as if he might pass out himself in another few moments. "Never believe a writer. Listen to them, by all means, but never *believe* them. My God, what if I'd been wrong?"

"You almost were," Brian said. He helped Albert to his feet. "It was like when you lit the other matches—the ones from the bowl. There was just enough pop to drive the bullet out of the muzzle. A little more pop and Albert would have had a bullet in his lung."

Another wave of dizziness washed over Albert. He swayed on his feet, and Bethany immediately slipped an arm around his waist. "I thought it was really brave," she said, looking up at him with eyes which suggested she believed Albert Kaussner must shit diamonds from a platinum asshole. "I mean *incredible.*"

"Thanks," Ace said, smiling coolly (if a trifle woozily). "It wasn't much." The fastest Hebrew west of the Mississippi was aware that there was a great deal of girl pressed tightly against him, and that the girl smelled almost unbearably good. Suddenly *he* felt good. In fact, he believed he had never felt better in his life. Then he remembered his violin, bent down, and picked up the case. There was a deep dent in one side, and one of the catches had been sprung. There was blood and hair on it, and Albert felt his stomach turn over lazily. He opened the case and looked in. The instrument looked all right, and he let out a little sigh.

Then he thought of Craig Toomy, and alarm replaced relief.

"Say, I didn't kill that guy, did I? I hit him pretty hard." He looked toward Craig, who was lying near the restaurant door with Don Gaffney kneeling beside him. Albert suddenly felt like passing out again. There was a great deal of blood on Craig's face and forehead.

"He's alive," Don said, "but he's out like a light."

Albert, who had blown away more hardcases than The Man with No Name in his dreams, felt his gorge rise. "Jesus, there's so much *blood*!"

"Doesn't mean a thing," Nick said. "Scalp wounds tend to bleed a lot." He joined Don, picked up Craig's wrist, and felt for a pulse. "You want to remember he had a gun to that girl's head, matey. If he'd pulled the trigger at point-blank range, he might well have done for her. Remember the actor who killed himself with a blank round a few years ago? Mr. Toomy brought this on himself; he owns it completely. Don't take on."

Nick dropped Craig's wrist and stood up.

"Besides," he said, pulling a large swatch of paper napkins from the dispenser on one of the tables, "his pulse is strong and regular. I think he'll wake up in a few minutes with nothing but a bad headache. I also think it might be prudent to take a few precautions against that happy event. Mr. Gaffney, the tables in yonder watering hole actually appear to be equipped with tablecloths—strange but true. I wonder if you'd get a couple? We might be wise to bind old Mr. I've-Got-to-Get-to-Boston's hands behind him."

"Do you really have to do that?" Laurel asked quietly. "The man is unconscious, after all, and bleeding."

Nick pressed his makeshift napkin compress against Craig Toomy's head-wound and looked up at her. "You're Laurel, right?"

"Right."

"Well, Laurel, let's not paint it fine. This man is a lunatic. I don't know if our current adventure did that to him or if he just growed that way, like Topsy, but I *do* know he's dangerous. He would have grabbed Dinah instead of Bethany if she had been closer. If we leave him untied, he might do just that next time."

Craig groaned and waved his hands feebly. Bob Jenkins stepped away from him the moment he began to move, even though the revolver was now safely tucked into the waistband of Brian Engle's pants, and Laurel did the same, pulling Dinah with her.

"Is anybody dead?" Dinah asked nervously. "No one is, are they?"

"No, honey."

"I should have heard him sooner, but I was listening to the man who sounds like a teacher."

"It's okay," Laurel said. "It turned out all right, Dinah." Then she looked out at the empty terminal and her own words mocked her. *Nothing* was all right here. Nothing at all.

Don returned with a red-and-white-checked tablecloth in each fist.

"Marvellous," Nick said. He took one of them and spun it quickly and expertly into a rope. He put the center of it in his mouth, clamping his teeth on it to keep it from unwinding, and used his hands to flip Craig over like a human omelette.

Craig cried out and his eyelids fluttered.

"Do you have to be so *rough*?" Laurel asked sharply.

Nick gazed at her for a moment, and she dropped her eyes at once. She could not help comparing Nick Hopewell's eyes with the eyes in the pictures which Darren Crosby had sent her. Widely spaced, clear eyes in a good-looking—if unremarkable—face. But the eyes had also been rather unremarkable, hadn't they? And didn't Darren's eyes have something, perhaps even a great deal, to do with why she had made this trip in the first place? Hadn't she decided, after a great deal of close study, that they were the eyes of a man who would behave himself? A man who would back off if you told him to back off?

She had boarded Flight 29 telling herself that this was her great adventure, her one extravagant tango with romance—an impulsive transcontinental dash into the arms of the tall, dark stranger. But sometimes you found yourself in one of those tiresome situations where the truth could no longer be avoided, and Laurel reckoned the truth to be this: she had chosen Darren Crosby because his pictures and letters had told her he wasn't much different from the placid boys and men she had been dating ever since she was fifteen or so, boys and men who would learn quickly to wipe their feet on the mat before they came in on rainy nights, boys and men who would grab a towel and help with the dishes without being asked, boys and men who would let you go if you told them to do it in a sharp enough tone of voice.

Would she have been on Flight 29 tonight if the photos had shown Nick Hopewell's dark-blue eyes instead of Darren's mild brown ones? She didn't think so. She thought she would have written him a kind but rather impersonal note—*Thank you for your reply and your picture, Mr. Hopewell, but I somehow don't think we would be right for each other*—and gone on looking for a man like Darren. And, of course, she doubted very much if men like Mr. Hopewell even read the lonely-hearts magazines, let alone placed ads in their personals columns. All the same, she was here with him now, in this weird situation.

Well . . . she had wanted to have an adventure, just one adventure, before middle-age settled in for keeps. Wasn't that true? Yes. And here she was, proving Tolkien right—she had stepped out of her own door last evening, just the same as always, and look where she had ended up: a strange and dreary version of Fantasyland. But it was an adventure, all right. Emergency landings . . . deserted airports . . . a lunatic with a gun. Of course it was an adventure. Something she had read years ago suddenly popped into Laurel's mind. *Be careful what you pray for, because you just might get it.*

How true.

And how confusing.

There was no confusion in Nick Hopewell's eyes . . . but there was no mercy in them, either. They made Laurel feel shivery, and there was nothing romantic in the feeling.

Are you sure? a voice whispered, and Laurel shut it up at once.

Nick pulled Craig's hands out from under him, then brought his wrists together at the small of his back. Craig groaned again, louder this time, and began to struggle weakly.

"Easy now, my good old mate," Nick said soothingly. He wrapped the tablecloth rope twice around Craig's lower forearms and knotted it tightly. Craig's elbows flapped and he uttered a strange weak scream. "There!" Nick said, standing up. "Trussed as neatly as Father John's Christmas turkey. We've even got a spare if that one looks like not holding." He sat on the edge of one of the tables and looked at Bob Jenkins. "Now, what were you saying when we were so rudely interrupted?"

Bob looked at him, dazed and unbelieving. "What?"

"Go on," Nick said. He might have been an interested lecturegoer instead of a man sitting on a table in a deserted airport restaurant with his feet planted beside a bound man lying in a pool of his own blood. "You had just got to the part about Flight 29 being like the *Mary Celeste*. Interesting concept, that."

"And you want me to . . . to just go on?" Bob asked incredulously. "As if nothing had happened?"

"Let me *up!*" Craig shouted. His words were slightly muffled by the tough industrial carpet on the restaurant floor, but he still sounded remarkably lively for a man who had been coldcocked with a violin case not five minutes previous. "Let me up right *now*! I demand that you—"

Then Nick did something that shocked all of them, even those who had seen the Englishman twist Craig's nose like the handle of a bathtub faucet. He drove a short, hard kick into Craig's ribs. He pulled it at the last instant . . . but not much. Craig uttered a pained grunt and shut up.

"Start again, mate, and I'll stave them in," Nick said grimly. "My patience with you has run out."

"Hey!" Gaffney cried, bewildered. "What did you do that f—"

"Listen to me!" Nick said, and looked around. His urbane

surface was entirely gone for the first time; his voice vibrated with anger and urgency. "You need waking up, fellows and girls, and I haven't the time to do it gently. That little girl—Dinah—says we are in bad trouble here, and I believe her. She says she hears something, something which may be coming our way, and I rather believe that, too. I don't hear a bloody thing, but my nerves are jumping like grease on a hot griddle, and I'm used to paying attention when they do that. I think something *is* coming, and I don't believe it's going to try and sell us vacuum-cleaner attachments or the latest insurance scheme when it gets here. Now we can make all the correct civilized noises over this bloody madman or we can try to understand what has happened to us. Understanding may not save our lives, but I'm rapidly becoming convinced that the lack of it may end them, and soon." His eyes shifted to Dinah. "Tell me I'm wrong if you believe I am, Dinah. I'll listen to *you,* and gladly."

"I don't want you to hurt Mr. Toomy, but I don't think you're wrong, either," Dinah said in a small, wavery voice.

"All right," Nick said. "Fair enough. I'll try my very best not to hurt him again . . . but I make no promises. Let's begin with a very simple concept. This fellow I've trussed up—"

"Toomy," Brian said. "His name is Craig Toomy."

"All right. Mr. Toomy is mad. Perhaps if we find our way back to our proper place, or if we find the place where all the people have gone, we can get some help for him. But for now, we can only help him by putting him out of commission—which I have done, with the generous if foolhardy assistance of Albert there—and getting back to our current business. Does anyone hold a view which runs counter to this?"

There was no reply. The other passengers who had been aboard Flight 29 looked at Nick uneasily.

"All right," Nick said. "Please go on, Mr. Jenkins."

"I . . . I'm not used to . . ." Bob made a visible effort to collect himself. "In books, I suppose I've killed enough people to fill every seat in the plane that brought us here, but what just happened is the first act of violence I've ever personally witnessed. I'm sorry if I've . . . er . . . behaved badly."

"I think you're doing great, Mr. Jenkins," Dinah said. "And I like listening to you, too. It makes me feel better."

Bob looked at her gratefully and smiled. "Thank you, Dinah." He stuffed his hands in his pockets, cast a troubled glance at Craig Toomy, then looked beyond them, across the empty waiting room.

"I think I mentioned a central fallacy in our thinking," he said at last. "It is this: we all assumed, when we began to grasp the dimensions of this Event, that something had happened to *the rest of the world.* That assumption is easy enough to understand, since we are all fine and everyone else—including those other passengers with whom we boarded at Los Angeles International—seems to have disappeared. But the evidence before us doesn't bear the assumption out. What has happened has happened to us and us alone. I am convinced that the world as we have always known it is ticking along just as it always has.

"It's us—the missing passengers and the eleven survivors of Flight 29—who are lost."

7

"Maybe I'm dumb, but I don't understand what you're getting at," Rudy Warwick said after a moment.

"Neither do I," Laurel added.

"We've mentioned two famous disappearances," Bob said quietly. Now even Craig Toomy seemed to be listening . . . he had stopped struggling, at any rate. "One, the case of the *Mary Celeste,* took place at sea. The second, the case of Roanoke Island, took place *near* the sea. They are not the only ones, either. I can think of at least two others which involved aircraft: the disappearance of the aviatrix Amelia Earhart over the Pacific Ocean, and the disappearance of several Navy planes over that part of the Atlantic known as the Bermuda Triangle. That happened in 1945 or 1946, I believe. There was some sort of garbled transmission from the lead aircraft's pilot, and rescue planes were sent out at once from an airbase in Florida, but no trace of the planes or their crews was ever found."

"I've heard of the case," Nick said. "It's the basis for the Triangle's infamous reputation, I think."

"No, there have been *lots* of ships and planes lost there," Albert put in. "I read the book about it by Charles Berlitz. Really interesting." He glanced around. "I just never thought I'd be *in* it, if you know what I mean."

Jenkins said, "I don't know if an aircraft has ever disappeared over the continental United States before, but—"

"It's happened lots of times with small planes," Brian said, "and once, about thirty-five years ago, it happened with a commercial passenger plane. There were over a hundred people aboard. 1955 or '56, this was. The carrier was either TWA or Monarch, I can't remember which. The plane was bound for Denver out of San Francisco. The pilot made radio contact with the Reno tower—absolutely routine—and the plane was never heard from again. There was a search, of course, but . . . nothing."

Brian saw they were all looking at him with a species of dreadful fascination, and he laughed uncomfortably.

"Pilot ghost stories," he said with a note of apology in his voice. "It sounds like a caption for a Gary Larson cartoon."

"I'll bet they all went through," the writer muttered. He had begun to scrub the side of his face with his hand again. He looked distressed—almost horrified. "Unless they found bodies . . . ?"

"Please tell us what you know, or what you think you know," Laurel said. "The effect of this . . . this thing . . . seems to pile up on a person. If I don't get some answers soon, I think you can tie me up and put me down next to Mr. Toomy."

"Don't flatter yourself," Craig said, speaking clearly if rather obscurely.

Bob favored him with another uncomfortable glance and then appeared to muster his thoughts. "There's no mess here, but there's a mess on the plane. There's no electricity here, but there's electricity on the plane. That isn't conclusive, of course—the plane has its own self-contained power supply, while the electricity here comes from a power plant somewhere. But then consider the matches. Bethany was on the plane, and her matches work fine. The matches I took from the bowl in here wouldn't strike. The gun which Mr. Toomy took—from the Security office, I imagine—barely fired. I think that, if you tried a battery-powered flashlight, you'd find *that* wouldn't work, either. Or, if it did work, it wouldn't work for long."

"You're right," Nick said. "And we don't need to find a flashlight in order to test your theory." He pointed upward. There was an emergency light mounted on the wall behind the kitchen grill. It was as dead as the overhead lights. "That's battery-powered," Nick went on. "A light-sensitive solenoid turns it on when the power fails. It's dim enough in here for that thing to have gone into operation, but it didn't do so. Which means that either the solenoid's circuit failed or the battery is dead."

"I suspect it's both," Bob Jenkins said. He walked slowly toward the restaurant door and looked out. "We find ourselves in a world which appears to be whole, but it is also a world which seems almost exhausted. The carbonated drinks are flat. The food is tasteless. The air is odorless. *We* still give off scents—I can smell Laurel's perfume and the captain's after-shave lotion, for instance—but everything else seems to have lost its smell."

Albert picked up one of the glasses with beer in it and sniffed deeply. There *was* a smell, he decided, but it was very, very faint. A flower-petal pressed for many years between the pages of a book might give off the same distant memory of scent.

"The same is true for sounds," Bob went on. "They are flat, one-dimensional, utterly without resonance."

Laurel thought of the listless *clup-clup* sound of her high heels on the cement, and the lack of echo when Captain Engle cupped his hands around his mouth and called up the escalator for Mr. Toomy.

"Albert, could I ask you to play something on your violin?" Bob asked.

Albert glanced at Bethany. She smiled and nodded.

"All right. Sure. In fact, I'm sort of curious about how it sounds after . . ." He glanced at Craig Toomy. "You know."

He opened the case, grimacing as his fingers touched the latch which had opened the wound in Craig Toomy's forehead, and drew out his violin. He caressed it briefly, then took the bow in his right hand and tucked the violin under his chin. He stood like that for a moment, thinking. What was the proper sort of music for this strange new world where no phones rang and no dogs barked? Ralph Vaughan Williams? Stravinsky? Mozart? Dvořák, perhaps? No. None of them were right. Then inspiration struck, and he began to play "Someone's in the Kitchen with Dinah."

Halfway through the tune the bow faltered to a stop.

"I guess you must have hurt your fiddle after all when you bopped that guy with it," Don Gaffney said. "It sounds like it's stuffed full of cotton batting."

"No," Albert said slowly. "My violin is perfectly okay. I can tell just by the way it feels, and the action of the strings under my fingers . . . but there's something else as well. Come on over here, Mr. Gaffney." Gaffney came over and stood beside Albert. "Now get as close to my violin as you can. No . . . not that close; I'd put out your eye with the bow. There. Just right. Listen again."

Albert began to play, singing along in his mind, as he almost always did when he played this corny but endlessly cheerful shitkicking music:

Singing fee-fi-fiddly-I-oh,
Fee-fi-fiddly-I-oh-oh-oh-oh,
Fee-fi-fiddly-I-oh,
Strummin' on the old banjo.

"Did you hear the difference?" he asked when he had finished.

"It sounds a lot better close up, if that's what you mean," Gaffney said. He was looking at Albert with real respect. "You play good, kid."

Albert smiled at Gaffney, but it was really Bethany Simms he was talking to. "Sometimes, when I'm sure my music teacher isn't around, I play old Led Zeppelin songs," he said. "That stuff *really* cooks on the violin. You'd be surprised." He looked at Bob. "Anyway, it fits right in with what you were saying. The closer you get, the better the violin sounds. It's the *air* that's wrong, not the instrument. It's not conducting the sounds the way it should, and so what comes out sounds the way the beer tasted."

"Flat," Brian said.

Albert nodded.

"Thank you, Albert," Bob said.

"Sure. Can I put it away now?"

"Of course." Bob continued as Albert replaced his violin in its case, and then used a napkin to clean off the fouled latch and his own fingers. "Taste and sound are not the only off-key elements of the situation in which we find ourselves. Take the clouds, for instance."

"What about them?" Rudy Warwick asked.

"They haven't moved since we arrived, and I don't think they're *going* to move. I think the weather patterns we're all used to living with have either stopped or are running down like an old pocket-watch."

Bob paused for a moment. He suddenly looked old and helpless and frightened.

"As Mr. Hopewell would say, let's not draw it fine. *Every-*

thing here feels wrong. Dinah, whose senses—including that odd, vague one we call the sixth sense—are more developed than ours, has perhaps felt it the most strongly, but I think we've all felt it to some degree. Things here are just *wrong*.

"And now we come to the very hub of the matter."

He turned to face them.

"I said not fifteen minutes ago that it felt like lunchtime. It now feels much later than that to me. Three in the afternoon, perhaps four. It isn't breakfast my stomach is grumbling for right now; it wants high tea. I have a terrible feeling that it may start to get dark outside before our watches tell us it's quarter to ten in the morning."

"Get to it, mate," Nick said.

"I think it's about time," Bob said quietly. "Not about dimension, as Albert suggested, but *time.* Suppose that, every now and then, a hole appears in the time stream? Not a time-*warp,* but a time-*rip.* A rip in the temporal fabric."

"That's the craziest shit I ever heard!" Don Gaffney exclaimed.

"Amen!" Craig Toomy seconded from the floor.

"No," Bob replied sharply. "If you want crazy shit, think about how Albert's violin sounded when you were standing six feet away from it. Or look around you, Mr. Gaffney. Just look around you. What's happening to us . . . what we're *in* . . . *that's* crazy shit."

Don frowned and stuffed his hands deep in his pockets.

"Go on," Brian said.

"All right. I'm not saying that I've got this right; I'm just offering a hypothesis that fits the situation in which we have found ourselves. Let us say that such rips in the fabric of time appear every now and then, but mostly over unpopulated areas . . . by which I mean the ocean, of course. I can't say why that would be, but it's still a logical assumption to make, since that's where most of these disappearances seem to occur."

"Weather patterns over water are almost always different

from weather patterns over large land-masses," Brian said. "That could be it."

Bob nodded. "Right or wrong, it's a good way to think of it, because it puts it in a context we're all familiar with. This could be similar to rare weather phenomena which are sometimes reported: upside-down tornadoes, circular rainbows, daytime starlight. These time-rips may appear and disappear at random, or they may move, the way fronts and pressure systems move, but they very rarely appear over land.

"But a statistician will tell you that sooner or later whatever can happen will happen, so let us say that last night one *did* appear over land . . . and we had the bad luck to fly into it. And we know something else. Some unknown rule or property of this fabulous meteorological freak makes it impossible for any living being to travel through unless he or she is fast asleep."

"Aw, this is a fairy tale," Gaffney said.

"I agree completely," Craig said from the floor.

"Shut your cake-hole," Gaffney growled at him. Craig blinked, then lifted his upper lip in a feeble sneer.

"It feels right," Bethany said in a low voice. "It feels as if we're out of step with . . . with everything."

"What happened to the crew and the passengers?" Albert asked. He sounded sick. "If the plane came through, and *we* came through, what happened to the rest of them?"

His imagination provided him with an answer in the form of a sudden indelible image: hundreds of people falling out of the sky, ties and trousers rippling, dresses skating up to reveal garter-belts and underwear, shoes falling off, pens (the ones which weren't back on the plane, that was) shooting out of pockets; people waving their arms and legs and trying to scream in the thin air; people who had left wallets, purses, pocket-change, and, in at least one case, a pacemaker implant, behind. He saw them hitting the ground like dud bombs, squashing bushes flat, kicking up small clouds of stony dust, imprinting the desert floor with the shapes of their bodies.

"My guess is that they were vaporized," Bob said. "Utterly discorporated."

Dinah didn't understand at first; then she thought of Aunt Vicky's purse with the traveller's checks still inside and began to cry softly. Laurel crossed her arms over the little blind girl's shoulders and hugged her. Albert, meanwhile, was fervently thanking God that his mother had changed her mind at the last moment, deciding not to accompany him east after all.

"In many cases their things went with them," the writer went on. "Those who left wallets and purses may have had them out at the time of The . . . The Event. It's hard to say, though. What was taken and what was left behind—I suppose I'm thinking of the wig more than anything else—doesn't seem to have a lot of rhyme or reason to it."

"You got that right," Albert said. "The surgical pins, for instance. I doubt if the guy they belonged to took them out of his shoulder or knee to play with because he got bored."

"I agree," Rudy Warwick said. "It was too early in the flight to get *that* bored."

Bethany looked at him, startled, then burst out laughing.

"I'm originally from Kansas," Bob said, "and the element of caprice makes me think of the twisters we used to sometimes get in the summer. They'd totally obliterate a farmhouse and leave the privy standing, or they'd rip away a barn without pulling so much as a shingle from the silo standing right next to it."

"Get to the bottom line, mate," Nick said. "Whatever time it is we're in, I can't help feeling that it's very late in the day."

Brian thought of Craig Toomy, Old Mr. I've-Got-to-Get-to-Boston, standing at the head of the emergency slide and screaming: *Time is short! Time is very fucking short!*

"All right," Bob said. "The bottom line. Let's suppose there *are* such things as time-rips, and we've gone through one. I think we've gone into the past and discovered the unlovely truth of time-travel: you can't appear in the Texas State School Book Depository on November 22, 1963, and put a stop to the Kennedy assassination; you can't watch the building of the pyramids or the sack of Rome; you can't investigate the Age of the Dinosaurs at first hand."

He raised his arms, hands outstretched, as if to encompass the whole silent world in which they found themselves.

"Take a good look around you, fellow time-travellers. This is the past. It is empty; it is silent. It is a world—perhaps a *universe*—with all the sense and meaning of a discarded paint-can. I believe we may have hopped an absurdly short distance in time, perhaps as little as fifteen minutes—at least initially. But the world is clearly unwinding around us. Sensory input is disappearing. Electricity has already disappeared. The weather is what the weather was when we made the jump into the past. But it seems to me that as the world winds down, time itself is winding up in a kind of spiral . . . crowding in on itself."

"Couldn't this be the future?" Albert asked cautiously.

Bob Jenkins shrugged. He suddenly looked very tired. "I don't know for sure, of course—how could I?—but I don't think so. This place we're in feels old and stupid and feeble and meaningless. It feels . . . I don't know . . ."

Dinah spoke then. They all looked toward her.

"It feels *over*," she said softly.

"Yes," Bob said. "Thank you, dear. That's the word I was looking for."

"Mr. Jenkins?"

"Yes?"

"The sound I told you about before? I can hear it again." She paused. "It's getting closer."

8

They all fell silent, their faces long and listening. Brian thought he heard something, then decided it was the sound of his own heart. Or simply imagination.

"I want to go out by the windows again," Nick said abruptly. He stepped over Craig's prone body without so much as a glance down and strode from the restaurant without another word.

"Hey!" Bethany cried. "Hey, I want to come, too!"

Albert followed her; most of the others trailed after. "What about you two?" Brian asked Laurel and Dinah.

"I don't want to go," Dinah said. "I can hear it as well as I want to from here." She paused and added: "But I'm going to hear it better, I think, if we don't get out of here soon."

Brian glanced at Laurel Stevenson.

"I'll stay here with Dinah," she said quietly.

"All right," Brian said. "Keep away from Mr. Toomy."

"'Keep away from Mr. Toomy,'" Craig mimicked savagely from his place on the floor. He turned his head with an effort and rolled his eyes in their sockets to look at Brian. "You really can't get away with this, Captain Engle. I don't know what game you and your Limey friend think you're playing, but you can't get away with it. Your next piloting job will probably be running cocaine in from Colombia after dark. At least you won't be lying when you tell your friends all about what a crack pilot you are."

Brian started to reply, then thought better of it. Nick said this man was at least temporarily insane, and Brian thought Nick was right. Trying to reason with a madman was both useless and time-consuming.

"We'll keep our distance, don't worry," Laurel said. She drew Dinah over to one of the small tables and sat down with her. "And we'll be fine."

"All right," Brian said. "Yell if he starts trying to get loose."

Laurel smiled wanly. "You can count on it."

Brian bent, checked the tablecloth with which Nick had bound Craig's hands, then walked across the waiting room to join the others, who were standing in a line at the floor-to-ceiling windows.

9

He began to hear it before he was halfway across the waiting room and by the time he had joined the others, it was impossible to believe it was an auditory hallucination.

That girl's hearing is really remarkable, Brian thought.

The sound was very faint—to him, at least—but it was there, and it *did* seem to be coming from the east. Dinah had said it sounded like Rice Krispies after you poured milk over them. To Brian it sounded more like radio static—the exceptionally rough static you got sometimes during periods of high sunspot activity. He agreed with Dinah about one thing, though; it sounded *bad.*

He could feel the hairs on the nape of his neck stiffening in response to that sound. He looked at the others and saw identical expressions of frightened dismay on every face. Nick was controlling himself the best, and the young girl who had almost balked at using the slide—Bethany—looked the most deeply scared, but they all heard the same thing in the sound.

Bad.

Something bad on the way. *Hurrying.*

Nick turned toward him. "What do you make of it, Brian? Any ideas?"

"No," Brian said. "Not even a little one. All I know is that it's the only sound in town."

"It's not in town yet," Don said, "but it's going to be, I think. I only wish I knew how long it was going to take."

They were quiet again, listening to the steady hissing crackle from the east. And Brian thought: *I almost know that sound, I think. Not cereal in milk, not radio static, but . . . what? If only it wasn't so faint . . .*

But he didn't want to know. He suddenly realized that, and very strongly. He didn't want to know at all. The sound filled him with a bone-deep loathing.

"We *do* have to get out of here!" Bethany said. Her voice was loud and wavery. Albert put an arm around her waist and she gripped his hand in both of hers. Gripped it with panicky tightness. "We have to get out of here *right now!*"

"Yes," Bob Jenkins said. "She's right. That sound—I don't know what it is, but it's *awful.* We have to get out of here."

They were all looking at Brian and he thought, *It looks like I'm the captain again. But not for long.* Because they didn't understand. Not even Jenkins understood, sharp as some of his other deductions might have been, that they weren't going anywhere.

Whatever was making that sound was on its way, and it didn't matter, because they would still be here when it arrived. There was no way out of that. He understood the reason why it was so, even if none of the others did . . . and Brian Engle suddenly understood how an animal caught in a trap must feel as it hears the steady thud of the hunter's approaching boots.

CHAPTER SIX

STRANDED. BETHANY'S MATCHES.
TWO-WAY TRAFFIC AHEAD. ALBERT'S EXPERIMENT.
NIGHTFALL. THE DARK AND THE BLADE.

1

Brian turned to look at the writer. "You say we have to get out of here, right?"

"Yes. I think we must do that just as soon as we possibly—"

"And where do you suggest we go? Atlantic City? Miami Beach? Club Med?"

"You are suggesting, Captain Engle, that there's no place we *can* go. I think—I *hope*—that you're wrong about that. I have an idea."

"Which is?"

"In a moment. First, answer one question for me. Can you refuel the airplane? Can you do that even if there's no power?"

"I think so, yes. Let's say that, with the help of a few able-bodied men, I could. Then what?"

"Then we take off again," Bob said. Little beads of sweat stood out on his deeply lined face. They looked like droplets of clear oil. "That sound—that crunchy sound—is coming from the east. The time-rip was several thousand miles west of here. If we retraced our original course . . . could you do that?"

"Yes," Brian said. He had left the auxiliary power units running, and that meant the INS computer's program was still intact. That program was an exact log of the trip they had just made, from the moment Flight 29 had left the ground in southern California until the moment it had set down in central Maine. One touch of a button would instruct the computer to simply reverse that course; the touch of another button, once in the air, would put the autopilot to work flying it. The Teledyne inertial navigation system would re-create the trip down to the smallest degree deviations. "I could do that, but why?"

"Because the rip may still be there. Don't you see? *We might be able to fly back through it.*"

Nick looked at Bob in sudden startled concentration, then turned to Brian. "He might have something there, mate. He just might."

Albert Kaussner's mind was diverted onto an irrelevant but fascinating side-track: if the rip were still there, and if Flight 29 had been on a frequently used altitude and heading—a kind of east-west avenue in the sky—then perhaps other planes had gone through it between 1:07 this morning and now (whenever *now* was). Perhaps there were other planes landing or landed at other deserted American airports, other crews and passengers wandering around, stunned . . .

No, he thought. *We happened to have a pilot on board. What are the chances of that happening twice?*

He thought of what Mr. Jenkins had said about Ted Williams's sixteen consecutive on-bases and shivered.

"He might or he might not," Brian said. "It doesn't really matter, because we're not going anyplace in that plane."

"Why not?" Rudy asked. "If you could refuel it, I don't see . . ."

"Remember the matches? The ones from the bowl in the restaurant? The ones that wouldn't light?"

Rudy looked blank, but an expression of huge dismay dawned on Bob Jenkins's face. He put his hand to his forehead and took a step backward. He actually seemed to shrink before them.

"What?" Don asked. He was looking at Brian from beneath drawn-together brows. It was a look which conveyed both confusion and suspicion. "What does that have to—"

But Nick knew.

"Don't you see?" he asked quietly. "Don't you see, mate? If batteries don't work, if matches don't light—"

"—then jet-fuel won't burn," Brian finished. "It will be as used up and worn out as everything else in this world." He looked at each one of them in turn. "I might as well fill up the fuel tanks with molasses."

2

"Have either of you fine young ladies ever heard of the langoliers?" Craig asked suddenly. His tone was light, almost vivacious.

Laurel jumped and looked nervously toward the others, who were still standing by the windows and talking. Dinah only turned toward Craig's voice, apparently not surprised at all.

"No," she said calmly. "What are those?"

"Don't talk to him, Dinah," Laurel whispered.

"I heard that," Craig said in the same pleasant tone of voice. "Dinah's not the only one with sharp ears, you know."

Laurel felt her face grow warm.

"I wouldn't hurt the child, anyway," Craig went on. "No more than I would have hurt that girl. I'm just frightened. Aren't you?"

"Yes," Laurel snapped, "but I don't take hostages and then try to shoot teenage boys when I'm frightened."

"*You* didn't have what looked like the whole front line of the Los Angeles Rams caving in on you at once," Craig said. "And that English fellow . . ." He laughed. The sound of his laughter in this quiet place was disturbingly merry, disturbingly *normal.* "Well, all I can say is that if you think *I'm* crazy, you haven't been watching *him* at all. That man's got a chain-saw for a mind."

Laurel didn't know what to say. She knew it hadn't been the way Craig Toomy was presenting it, but when he spoke it seemed as though it *should* have been that way . . . and what he said about the Englishman was too close to the truth. The man's eyes . . . and the kick he had chopped into Mr. Toomy's ribs after he had been tied up . . . Laurel shivered.

"What are the langoliers, Mr. Toomy?" Dinah asked.

"Well, I always used to think they were just make-believe," Craig said in that same good-humored voice. "Now I'm beginning to wonder . . . because I hear it, too, young lady. Yes I do."

"The sound?" Dinah asked softly. "That sound is the langoliers?"

Laurel put one hand on Dinah's shoulder. "I really wish you wouldn't talk to him anymore, honey. He makes me nervous."

"Why? He's tied up, isn't he?"

"Yes, but—"

"And you could always call for the others, couldn't you?"

"Well, I think—"

"I want to know about the langoliers."

With some effort, Craig turned his head to look at them . . . and now Laurel felt some of the charm and force of personality which had kept Craig firmly on the fast track as he worked out the high-pressure script his parents had written for him. She felt this even though he was lying on the floor with his hands tied behind him and his own blood drying on his forehead and left cheek.

"My father said the langoliers were little creatures that lived in closets and sewers and other dark places."

"Like elves?" Dinah wanted to know.

Craig laughed and shook his head. "Nothing so pleasant, I'm afraid. He said that all they really were was hair and teeth and fast little legs—their little legs were fast, he said, so they could catch up with bad boys and girls no matter how quickly they scampered."

"Stop it," Laurel said coldly. "You're scaring the child."

"No, he's not," Dinah said. "I know make-believe when I hear it. It's interesting, that's all." Her face said it was something more than interesting, however. She was intent, fascinated.

"It *is,* isn't it?" Craig said, apparently pleased by her interest. "I think what Laurel means is that I'm scaring *her.* Do I win the cigar, Laurel? If so, I'd like an El Producto, please. None of those cheap White Owls for me." He laughed again.

Laurel didn't reply, and after a moment Craig resumed.

"My dad said there were thousands of langoliers. He said there had to be, because there were *millions* of bad boys and girls scampering about the world. That's how he always put it. My father never saw a child run in his entire life. They always scampered. I think he liked that word because it implies senseless, directionless, nonproductive motion. But the langoliers . . . *they* ran. *They* have purpose. In fact, you could say that the langoliers are purpose personified."

"What did the kids do that was so bad?" Dinah asked. "What did they do that was so bad the langoliers had to run after them?"

"You know, I'm glad you asked that question," Craig said. "Because when my father said someone was bad, Dinah, what he meant was lazy. A lazy person couldn't be part of THE BIG PICTURE. No way. In my house, you were either part of THE BIG PICTURE or you were LYING DOWN ON THE JOB, and that was the worst kind of bad you could be. Throat-cutting was a venial sin compared to LYING DOWN ON THE JOB. He said that if you weren't part of THE BIG PICTURE, the langoliers would come and take you out of the picture completely. He said you'd be in your bed one night and then you'd hear them coming . . . crunching and smacking their way toward you . . . and even if you tried to scamper off, they'd get you. Because of their fast little—"

"*That's enough,*" Laurel said. Her voice was flat and dry.

"The sound *is* out there, though," Craig said. His eyes regarded her brightly, almost roguishly. "You can't deny that. The sound really is out th—"

"Stop it or I'll hit you with something myself."

"Okay," Craig said. He rolled over on his back, grimaced, and then rolled further, onto his other side and away from them. "A man gets tired of being hit when he's down and hog-tied."

Laurel's face grew not just warm but hot this time. She bit her lip and said nothing. She felt like crying. How was she supposed to handle someone like this? *How?* First the man seemed as crazy as a bedbug, and then he seemed as sane as could be. And meanwhile, the whole world—Mr. Toomy's BIG PICTURE—had gone to hell.

"I bet you were scared of your dad, weren't you, Mr. Toomy?"

Craig looked back over his shoulder at Dinah, startled. He smiled again, but this smile was different. It was a rueful, hurt smile with no public relations in it. "This time *you* win the cigar, miss," he said. "I was terrified of him."

"Is he dead?"

"Yes."

"Was he LYING DOWN ON THE JOB? Did the langoliers get him?"

Craig thought for a long time. He remembered being told that his father had had his heart attack while in his office. When his secretary buzzed him for his ten o'clock staff meeting and there was no answer, she had come in to find him dead on the carpet, eyes bulging, foam drying on his mouth.

Did someone tell you that? he wondered suddenly. *That his eyes were bugging out, that there was foam on his mouth? Did someone actually tell you that—Mother, perhaps, when she was drunk—or was it just wishful thinking?*

"Mr. Toomy? Did they?"

"Yes," Craig said thoughtfully. "I guess he was, and I guess they did."

"Mr. Toomy?"

"What?"

"I'm not the way you see me. I'm not ugly. None of us are."

He looked at her, startled. "How would you know how you look to me, little blind miss?"

"You might be surprised," Dinah said.

Laurel turned toward her, suddenly more uneasy than ever . . . but of course there was nothing to see. Dinah's dark glasses defeated curiosity.

3

The other passengers stood on the far side of the waiting room, listening to that low rattling sound and saying nothing. It seemed there was nothing left to say.

"What do we do now?" Don asked. He seemed to have wilted inside his red lumberjack's shirt. Albert thought the shirt itself had lost some of its cheerfully macho vibrancy.

"I don't know," Brian said. He felt a horrible impotence toiling away in his belly. He looked out at the plane, which had been *his* plane for a little while, and was struck by its clean lines and smooth beauty. The Delta 727 sitting to its left at the jetway looked like a dowdy matron by comparison. *It looks good to you because it's never going to fly again, that's all. It's like glimpsing a beautiful woman for just a moment in the back seat of a limousine—she looks even more beautiful than she really is because you know she's not yours, can never be yours.*

"How much fuel is left, Brian?" Nick asked suddenly. "Maybe the burn-rate isn't the same over here. Maybe there's more than you realize."

"All the gauges are in apple-pie working order," Brian said. "When we landed, I had less than 600 pounds. To get back to where this happened, we'd need at least 50,000."

Bethany took out her cigarettes and offered the pack to Bob.

157

He shook his head. She stuck one in her mouth, took out her matches, and struck one.

It didn't light.

"Oh-oh," she said.

Albert glanced over. She struck the match again . . . and again . . . and again. There was nothing. She looked at him, frightened.

"Here," Albert said. "Let me."

He took the matches from her hand and tore another one loose. He struck it across the strip on the back. There was nothing.

"Whatever it is, it seems to be catching," Rudy Warwick observed.

Bethany burst into tears, and Bob offered her his handkerchief.

"Wait a minute," Albert said, and struck the match again. This time it lit . . . but the flame was low, guttering, unenthusiastic. He applied it to the quivering tip of Bethany's cigarette and a clear image suddenly filled his mind: a sign he had passed as he rode his ten-speed to Pasadena High School every day for the last three years. CAUTION, this sign said. TWO-WAY TRAFFIC AHEAD.

What in the hell does that mean?

He didn't know . . . at least not yet. All he knew for sure was that some idea wanted out but was, at least for the time being, stuck in the gears.

Albert shook the match out. It didn't take much shaking.

Bethany drew on her cigarette, then grimaced. "Blick! It tastes like a Carlton, or something."

"Blow smoke in my face," Albert said.

"What?"

"You heard me. Blow some in my face."

She did as he asked, and Albert sniffed at the smoke. Its former sweet fragrance was now muted. *Whatever it is, it seems to be catching.*

CAUTION: TWO-WAY TRAFFIC AHEAD.

"I'm going back to the restaurant," Nick said. He looked depressed. "Yon Cassius has a lean and slippery feel. I don't like leaving him with the ladies for too long."

Brian started after him and the others followed. Albert thought there was something a little amusing about these tidal flows—they were behaving like cows which sense thunder in the air.

"Come on," Bethany said. "Let's go." She dropped her half-smoked cigarette into an ashtray and used Bob's handkerchief to wipe her eyes. Then she took Albert's hand.

They were halfway across the waiting room and Albert was looking at the back of Mr. Gaffney's red shirt when it struck him again, more forcibly this time: *TWO-WAY TRAFFIC AHEAD.*

"Wait a minute!" he yelled. He suddenly slipped an arm around Bethany's waist, pulled her to him, put his face into the hollow of her throat, and breathed in deeply.

"Oh my! We hardly know each other!" Bethany cried. Then she began to giggle helplessly and put her arms around Albert's neck. Albert, a boy whose natural shyness usually disappeared only in his daydreams, paid no notice. He took another deep breath through his nose. The smells of her hair, sweat, and perfume were still there, but they were faint; very faint.

They all looked around, but Albert had already let Bethany go and was hurrying back to the windows.

"Wow!" Bethany said. She was still giggling a little, and blushing brightly. "Strange dude!"

Albert looked at Flight 29 and saw what Brian had noticed a few minutes earlier: it was clean and smooth and almost impossibly white. It seemed to vibrate in the dull stillness outside.

Suddenly the idea came up for him. It seemed to burst behind his eyes like a firework. The central concept was a bright, burning ball; implications radiated out from it like fiery spangles and for a moment he quite literally forgot to breathe.

"Albert?" Bob asked. "Albert, what's wro—"

"*Captain Engle!*" Albert screamed. In the restaurant, Laurel sat bolt upright and Dinah clasped her arm with hands like talons. Craig Toomy craned his neck to look. "*Captain Engle, come here!*"

4

Outside, the sound was louder.

To Brian it was the sound of radio static. Nick Hopewell thought it sounded like a strong wind rattling dry tropical grasses. Albert, who had worked at McDonald's the summer before, was reminded of the sound of french fries in a deep-fat fryer, and to Bob Jenkins it was the sound of paper being crumpled in a distant room.

The four of them crawled through the hanging rubber strips and then stepped down into the luggage-unloading area, listening to the sound of what Craig Toomy called the langoliers.

"How much closer is it?" Brian asked Nick.

"Can't tell. It *sounds* closer, but of course we were inside before."

"Come on," Albert said impatiently. "How do we get back aboard? Climb the slide?"

"Won't be necessary," Brian said, and pointed. A rolling stairway stood on the far side of Gate 2. They walked toward it, their shoes clopping listlessly on the concrete.

"You know what a long shot this is, don't you, Albert?" Brian asked as they walked.

"Yes, but—"

"Long shots are better than no shots at all," Nick finished for him.

"I just don't want him to be too disappointed if it doesn't pan out."

"Don't worry," Bob said softly. "I will be disappointed

160

enough for all of us. The lad's idea makes good logical sense. It *should* prove out . . . although, Albert, you do realize there may be factors here which we haven't discovered, don't you?"

"Yes."

They reached the rolling ladder, and Brian kicked up the foot-brakes on the wheels. Nick took a position on the grip which jutted from the left railing, and Brian laid hold of the one on the right.

"I hope it still rolls," Brian said.

"It should," Bob Jenkins answered. "Some—perhaps even most—of the ordinary physical and chemical components of life seem to remain in operation; our bodies are able to process the air, doors open and close—"

"Don't forget gravity," Albert put in. "The earth still sucks."

"Let's quit talking about it and just try it," Nick said.

The stairway rolled easily. The two men trundled it across the tarmac toward the 767 with Albert and Bob walking behind them. One of the wheels squeaked rhythmically. The only other sound was that low, constant crunch-rattle-crunch from somewhere over the eastern horizon.

"Look at it," Albert said as they neared the 767. "Just *look* at it. Can't you see? Can't you see how much more *there* it is than anything else?"

There was no need to answer, and no one did. They could all see it. And reluctantly, almost against his will, Brian began to think the kid might have something.

They set the stairway at an angle between the escape slide and the fuselage of the plane, with the top step only a long stride away from the open door. "I'll go first," Brian said. "After I pull the slide in, Nick, you and Albert roll the stairs into better position."

"Aye, aye, Captain," Nick said, and clipped off a smart little salute, the knuckles of his first and second fingers touching his forehead.

Brian snorted. "Junior attaché," he said, and then ran fleetly up the stairs. A few moments later he had used the escape slide's lanyard to pull it back inside. Then he leaned out to watch as Nick and Albert carefully maneuvered the rolling staircase into position with its top step just below the 767's forward entrance.

5

Rudy Warwick and Don Gaffney were now babysitting Craig. Bethany, Dinah, and Laurel were lined up at the waiting-room windows, looking out. "What are they doing?" Dinah asked.

"They've taken away the slide and put a stairway by the door," Laurel said. "Now they're going up." She looked at Bethany. "You're sure you don't know what they're up to?"

Bethany shook her head. "All I know is that Ace—Albert, I mean—almost went nuts. I'd like to think it was this mad sexual attraction, but I don't think it was." She paused, smiled, and added: "At least, not yet. He said something about the plane being more *there*. And my perfume being *less* there, which probably wouldn't please Coco Chanel or whatever her name is. And two-way traffic. I didn't get it. He was really jabbering."

"I bet I know," Dinah said.

"What's your guess, hon?"

Dinah only shook her head. "I just hope they hurry up. Because poor Mr. Toomy is right. The langoliers are coming."

"Dinah, that's just something his father made up."

"Maybe once it was make-believe," Dinah said, turning her sightless eyes back to the windows, "but not anymore."

6

"All right, Ace," Nick said. "On with the show."

Albert's heart was thudding and his hands shook as he set

162

the four elements of his experiment out on the shelf in first class, where, a thousand years ago and on the other side of the continent, a woman named Melanie Trevor had supervised a carton of orange juice and two bottles of champagne.

Brian watched closely as Albert put down a book of matches, a bottle of Budweiser, a can of Pepsi, and a peanut-butter-and-jelly sandwich from the restaurant cold-case. The sandwich had been sealed in plastic wrap.

"Okay," Albert said, and took a deep breath. "Let's see what we got here."

7

Don left the restaurant and walked over to the windows. "What's happening?"

"We don't know," Bethany said. She had managed to coax a flame from another of her matches and was smoking again. When she removed the cigarette from her mouth, Laurel saw she had torn off the filter. "They went inside the plane; they're still inside the plane; end of story."

Don gazed out for several seconds. "It looks different outside. I can't say just why, but it does."

"The light's going," Dinah said. "That's what's different." Her voice was calm enough, but her small face was an imprint of loneliness and fear. "I can feel it going."

"She's right," Laurel agreed. "It's only been daylight for two or three hours, but it's already getting dark again."

"I keep thinking this is a dream, you know," Don said. "I keep thinking it's the worst nightmare I ever had but I'll wake up soon."

Laurel nodded. "How is Mr. Toomy?"

Don laughed without much humor. "You won't believe it."

"Won't believe what?" Bethany asked.

"He's gone to sleep."

8

Craig Toomy, of course, was not sleeping. People who fell asleep at critical moments, like that fellow who was supposed to have been keeping an eye out while Jesus prayed in the Garden of Gethsemane, were most definitely not part of THE BIG PICTURE.

He had watched the two men carefully through eyes which were not quite shut and willed one or both of them to go away. Eventually the one in the red shirt *did* go away. Warwick, the bald man with the big false teeth, walked over to Craig and bent down. Craig let his eyes close all the way.

"Hey," Warwick said. "Hey, you 'wake?"

Craig lay still, eyes closed, breathing regularly. He considered manufacturing a small snore and thought better of it.

Warwick poked him in the side.

Craig kept his eyes shut and went on breathing regularly.

Baldy straightened up, stepped over him, and went to the restaurant door to watch the others. Craig cracked his eyelids and made sure Warwick's back was turned. Then, very quietly and very carefully, he began to work his wrists up and down inside the tight figure-eight of cloth which bound them. The tablecloth rope felt looser already.

He moved his wrists in short strokes, watching Warwick's back, ready to cease movement and close his eyes again the instant Warwick showed signs of turning around. He willed Warwick *not* to turn around. He wanted to be free before the assholes came back from the plane. Especially the English asshole, the one who had hurt his nose and then kicked him while he was down. The English asshole had tied him up pretty well; thank God it was only a tablecloth instead of a length of nylon line. Then he would have been out of luck, but as it was—

One of the knots loosened, and now Craig began to rotate

his wrists from side to side. He could hear the langoliers approaching. He intended to be out of here and on his way to Boston before they arrived. In Boston he would be safe. When you were in a boardroom filled with bankers, no scampering was allowed.

And God help anyone—man, woman, or child—who tried to get in his way.

9

Albert picked up the book of matches he had taken from the bowl in the restaurant. "Exhibit A," he said. "Here goes."

He tore a match from the book and struck it. His unsteady hands betrayed him and he struck the match a full two inches above the rough strip which ran along the bottom of the paper folder. The match bent.

"Shit!" Albert cried.

"Would you like me to—" Bob began.

"Let him alone," Brian said. "It's Albert's show."

"Steady on, Albert," Nick said.

Albert tore another match from the book, offered them a sickly smile, and struck it. The match didn't light. He struck it again. The match didn't light.

"I guess that does it," Brian said. "There's nothing—"

"I *smelled* it," Nick said. "I smelled the sulphur! Try another one, Ace!"

Instead, Albert snapped the same match across the rough strip a third time . . . and this time it flared alight. It did not just burn the flammable head and then gutter out; it stood up in the familiar little teardrop shape, blue at its base, yellow at its tip, and began to burn the paper stick.

Albert looked up, a wild grin on his face. "You see?" he said. "*You see?*"

He shook the match out, dropped it, and pulled another.

This one lit on the first strike. He bent back the cover of the matchbook and touched the lit flame to the other matches, just as Bob Jenkins had done in the restaurant. This time they all flared alight with a dry *fsss!* sound. Albert blew them out like a birthday candle. It took two puffs of air to do the job.

"You see?" he asked. "You see what it means? Two-way traffic! *We brought our own time with us!* There's the past out there . . . and everywhere, I guess, east of the hole we came through . . . but the present is still in here! *Still caught inside this airplane!*"

"I don't know," Brian said, but suddenly everything seemed possible again. He felt a wild, almost unrestrainable urge to pull Albert into his arms and pound him on the back.

"Bravo, Albert!" Bob said. "The beer! Try the beer!"

Albert spun the cap off the beer while Nick fished an unbroken glass from the wreckage around the drinks trolley.

"Where's the smoke?" Brian asked.

"Smoke?" Bob asked, puzzled.

"Well, I guess it's not smoke, exactly, but when you open a beer there's usually something that looks like smoke around the mouth of the bottle."

Albert sniffed, then tipped the beer toward Brian. "Smell."

Brian did, and began to grin. He couldn't help it. "By God, it sure *smells* like beer, smoke or no smoke."

Nick held out the glass, and Albert was pleased to see that the Englishman's hand was not quite steady, either. "Pour it," he said. "Hurry up, mate—my sawbones says suspense is bad for the old ticker."

Albert poured the beer and their smiles faded.

The beer was flat. Utterly flat. It simply sat in the whiskey glass Nick had found, looking like a urine sample.

10

"Christ almighty, it's getting dark!"

The people standing at the windows looked around as Rudy Warwick joined them.

"You're supposed to be watching the nut," Don said.

Rudy gestured impatiently. "He's out like a light. I think that whack on the head rattled his furniture a little more than we thought at first. What's going on out there? And why is it getting dark so fast?"

"We don't know," Bethany said. "It just *is*. Do you think that weird dude is going into a coma, or something like that?"

"I don't know," Rudy said. "But if he is, we won't have to worry about him anymore, will we? Christ, is that sound *creepy*! It sounds like a bunch of coked-up termites in a balsa-wood glider." For the first time, Rudy seemed to have forgotten his stomach.

Dinah looked up at Laurel. "I think we better check on Mr. Toomy," she said. "I'm worried about him. I bet he's scared."

"If he's unconscious, Dinah, there isn't anything we can—"

"I don't think he's unconscious," Dinah said quietly. "I don't think he's even asleep."

Laurel looked down at the child thoughtfully for a moment and then took her hand. "All right," she said. "Let's have a look."

11

The knot Nick Hopewell had tied against Craig's right wrist finally loosened enough for him to pull his hand free. He used it to push down the loop holding his left hand. He got quickly to his feet. A bolt of pain shot through his head, and for a moment he swayed. Flocks of black dots chased across his field of vision and then slowly cleared away. He became aware that the terminal was being swallowed in gloom. Premature night was falling. He could hear the chew-crunch-chew sound of the langoliers much more clearly now, perhaps because his ears had become attuned to them, perhaps because they were closer.

On the far side of the terminal he saw two silhouettes, one tall and one short, break away from the others and start back toward the restaurant. The woman with the bitchy voice and the little blind girl with the ugly, pouty face. He couldn't let them raise the alarm. That would be very bad.

Craig backed away from the bloody patch of carpet where he had been lying, never taking his eyes from the approaching figures. He could not get over how rapidly the light was failing.

There were pots of eating utensils set into a counter to the left of the cash register, but it was all plastic crap, no good to him. Craig ducked around the cash register and saw something better: a butcher knife lying on the counter next to the grill. He took it and crouched behind the cash register to watch them approach. He watched the little girl with a particular anxious interest. The little girl knew a lot . . . too much, maybe. The question was, where had she come by her knowledge?

That was a very interesting question indeed.

Wasn't it?

12

Nick looked from Albert to Bob. "So," he said. "The matches work but the lager doesn't." He turned to set the glass of beer on the counter. "What does that mea—"

All at once a small mushroom cloud of bubbles burst from nowhere in the bottom of the glass. They rose rapidly, spread, and burst into a thin head at the top. Nick's eyes widened.

"Apparently," Bob said dryly, "it takes a moment or two for things to catch up." He took the glass, drank it off and smacked his lips. "Excellent," he said. They all looked at the complicated lace of white foam on the inside of the glass. "I can say without doubt that it's the best glass of beer I ever drank in my life."

Albert poured more beer into the glass. This time it came out foaming; the head overspilled the rim and ran down the outside. Brian picked it up.

"Are you sure you want to do that, matey?" Nick asked, grinning. "Don't you fellows like to say 'twenty-four hours from bottle to throttle'?"

"In cases of time-travel, the rule is suspended," Brian said. "You could look it up." He tilted the glass, drank, then laughed out loud. "You're right," he said to Bob. "It's the best goddam beer there ever was. Try the Pepsi, Albert."

Albert opened the can and they all heard the familiar *pop-hisss* of carbonation, mainstay of a hundred soft-drink commercials. He took a deep drink. When he lowered the can he was grinning . . . but there were tears in his eyes.

"Gentlemen, the Pepsi-Cola is also very good today," he said in plummy headwaiter's tones, and they all began to laugh.

13

Don Gaffney caught up with Laurel and Dinah just as they entered the restaurant. "I thought I'd better—" he began, and then stopped. He looked around. "Oh, shit. Where is he?"

"I don't—" Laurel began, and then, from beside her, Dinah Bellman said, *"Be quiet."*

Her head turned slowly, like the lamp of a dead searchlight. For a moment there was no sound at all in the restaurant . . . at least no sound Laurel could hear.

"There," Dinah said at last, and pointed toward the cash register. "He's hiding over there. Behind something."

"How do you know that?" Don asked in a dry, nervous voice. "I don't hear—"

"*I* do," Dinah said calmly. "I hear his fingernails on metal. And I hear his heart. It's beating very fast and very hard. He's scared to death. I feel so sorry for him." She suddenly disengaged her hand from Laurel's and stepped forward.

"*Dinah, no!*" Laurel screamed.

Dinah took no notice. She walked toward the cash register, arms out, fingers seeking possible obstacles. The shadows seemed to reach for her and enfold her.

"Mr. Toomy? Please come out. We don't want to hurt you. Please don't be afraid—"

A sound began to arise from behind the cash register. It was a high, keening scream. It was a word, or something which was trying to *be* a word, but there was no sanity in it.

"*Youuuuuuuuuuu—*"

Craig arose from his hiding place, eyes blazing, butcher knife upraised, suddenly understanding that it was *her,* she was one of *them,* behind those dark glasses she was one of *them,* she was not only a langolier but the *head* langolier, the one who was calling the others, calling them with her dead blind eyes.

"*Youuuuuuuuuuu—*"

He rushed at her, shrieking. Don Gaffney shoved Laurel out of his way, almost knocking her to the floor, and leaped forward. He was fast, but not fast enough. Craig Toomy was crazy, and he moved with the speed of a langolier himself. He approached Dinah at a dead-out run. No scampering for him.

Dinah made no effort to draw away. She looked up from her darkness and into his, and now she held her arms out, as if to enfold him and comfort him.

"*—ooooouuuuuuuu—*"

"It's all right, Mr. Toomy," she said. "Don't be afr—" And

then Craig buried the butcher knife in her chest and ran past Laurel into the terminal, still shrieking.

Dinah stood where she was for a moment. Her hands found the wooden handle jutting out of the front of her dress and her fingers fluttered over it, exploring it. Then she sank slowly, gracefully, to the floor, becoming just another shadow in the growing darkness.

CHAPTER SEVEN

DINAH IN THE VALLEY OF THE SHADOW.
THE FASTEST TOASTER EAST OF THE MISSISSIPPI.
RACING AGAINST TIME. NICK MAKES A DECISION.

1

Albert, Brian, Bob, and Nick passed the peanut-butter-and-jelly sandwich around. They each got two bites and then it was gone . . . but while it lasted, Albert thought he had never sunk his teeth into such wonderful chow in his life. His belly awakened and immediately began clamoring for more.

"I think our bald friend Mr. Warwick is going to like this part best," Nick said, swallowing. He looked at Albert. "You're a genius, Ace. You know that, don't you? Nothing but a pure genius."

Albert flushed happily. "It wasn't much," he said. "Just a little of what Mr. Jenkins calls the deductive method. If two streams flowing in different directions come together, they mix and make a whirlpool. I saw what was happening with Bethany's matches and thought something like that might be happening here. And there was Mr. Gaffney's bright-red shirt. It started to lose its color. So I thought, well, if stuff starts to fade when it's not on the plane anymore, maybe if you brought faded stuff *onto* the plane, it would—"

"I hate to interrupt," Bob said softly, "but I think that if we intend to try and get back, we should start the process as soon as possible. The sounds we are hearing worry me, but there's something else that worries me more. This airplane is not a

172

closed system. I think there's a good chance that before long it will begin to lose its . . . its . . ."

"Its temporal integrity?" Albert suggested.

"Yes. Well put. Any fuel we load into its tanks now may burn . . . but a few hours from now, it may not."

An unpleasant idea occurred to Brian: that the fuel might stop burning halfway across the country, with the 767 at 36,000 feet. He opened his mouth to tell them this . . . and then closed it again. What good would it do to put the idea in their minds, when they could do nothing about it?

"How do we start, Brian?" Nick asked in clipped, business-like tones.

Brian ran the process over in his mind. It would be a little awkward, especially working with men whose only experience with aircraft probably began and ended with model planes, but he thought it could be done.

"We start by turning on the engines and taxiing as close to that Delta 727 as we can get," he said. "When we get there, I'll kill the starboard engine and leave the portside engine turning over. We're lucky. This 767 is equipped with wet-wing fuel tanks and an APU system that—"

A shrill, panicked scream drifted up to them, cutting across the low rattling background noise like a fork drawn across a slate blackboard. It was followed by running footfalls on the ladder. Nick turned in that direction and his hands came up in a gesture Albert recognized at once; he had seen some of the martial-arts freaks at school back home practicing the move. It was the classic Tae Kwan Do defensive position. A moment later Bethany's pallid, terrified face appeared in the doorway and Nick let his hands relax.

"*Come!*" Bethany screamed. "You've got to *come!*" She was panting, out of breath, and she reeled backward on the plat-form of the ladder. For a moment Albert and Brian were sure she was going to tumble back down the steep steps, breaking her neck on the way. Then Nick leaped forward, cupped a hand on the nape of her neck, and pulled her into the plane. Bethany did not even seem to realize she had had a close call. Her dark eyes blazed at them from the white circle of her face. "Please come! He's stabbed her! I think she's dying!"

Nick put his hands on her shoulders and lowered his face toward hers as if he intended to kiss her. "Who has stabbed whom?" he asked very quietly. "Who is dying?"

"I . . . she . . . Mr. T-T-Toomy—"

"Bethany, say teacup."

She looked at him, eyes shocked and uncomprehending. Brian was looking at Nick as though he had gone insane.

Nick gave the girl's shoulders a little shake.

"Say teacup. Right now."

"T-T-Teacup."

"Teacup and saucer. Say it, Bethany."

"Teacup and saucer."

"All right. Better?"

She nodded. "Yes."

"Good. If you feel yourself losing control again, say teacup at once and you'll come back. Now—who's been stabbed?"

"The blind girl. Dinah."

"Bloody *shit*. All right, Bethany. Just—" Nick raised his voice sharply as he saw Brian move behind Bethany, headed for the ladder, with Albert right behind him. "*No!*" he shouted in a bright, hard tone that stopped both of them. "Stay fucking *put*!"

Brian, who had served two tours in Vietnam and knew the sound of unquestionable command when he heard it, stopped so suddenly that Albert ran face-first into the middle of his back. *I knew it,* he thought. *I knew he'd take over. It was just a matter of time and circumstance.*

"Do you know how this happened or where our wretched travelling companion is now?" Nick asked Bethany.

"The guy . . . the guy in the red shirt said—"

"All right. Never mind." He glanced briefly up at Brian.

His eyes were red with anger. "The bloody fools left him alone. I'd wager my pension on it. Well, it won't happen again. Our Mr. Toomy has cut his last caper."

He looked back at the girl. Her head drooped; her hair hung dejectedly in her face; she was breathing in great, watery swoops of breath.

"Is she alive, Bethany?" he asked gently.

"I . . . I . . . I . . ."

"Teacup, Bethany."

"*Teacup!*" Bethany shouted, and looked up at him from teary, red-rimmed eyes. "I don't know. She was alive when I . . . you know, came for you. She might be dead now. He really got her. Jesus, why did we have to get stuck with a fucking psycho? Weren't things bad enough without that?"

"And none of you who were supposed to be minding this fellow have the slightest idea where he went following the attack, is that right?"

Bethany put her hands over her face and began to sob. It was all the answer any of them needed.

"Don't be so hard on her," Albert said quietly, and slipped an arm around Bethany's waist. She put her head on his shoulder and began to sob more strenuously.

Nick moved the two of them gently aside. "If I was inclined to be hard on someone, it would be myself, Ace. I should have stayed behind."

He turned to Brian.

"I'm going back into the terminal. You're not. Mr. Jenkins here is almost certainly right; our time here is short. I don't like to think just *how* short. Start the engines but don't move the aircraft yet. If the girl is alive, we'll need the stairs to bring her up. Bob, bottom of the stairs. Keep an eye out for that bugger Toomy. Albert, you come with me."

Then he said something which chilled them all.

"I almost hope she's dead, God help me. It will save time if she is."

2

Dinah was not dead, not even unconscious. Laurel had taken off her sunglasses to wipe away the sweat which had sprung up on the girl's face, and Dinah's eyes, deep brown and very wide, looked up unseeingly into Laurel's blue-green ones. Behind her, Don and Rudy stood shoulder to shoulder, looking down anxiously.

"I'm sorry," Rudy said for the fifth time. "I really thought he was out. Out *cold.*"

Laurel ignored him. "How are you, Dinah?" she asked softly. She didn't want to look at the wooden handle growing out of the girl's dress, but couldn't take her eyes from it. There was very little blood, at least so far; a circle the size of a demitasse cup around the place where the blade had gone in, and that was all.

So far.

"It hurts," Dinah said in a faint voice. "It's hard to breathe. And it's *hot.*"

"You're going to be all right," Laurel said, but her eyes were drawn relentlessly back to the handle of the knife. The girl was very small, and she couldn't understand why the blade hadn't gone all the way through her. Couldn't understand why she wasn't dead already.

". . . out of here," Dinah said. She grimaced, and a thick, slow curdle of blood escaped from the corner of her mouth and ran down her cheek.

"Don't try to talk, honey," Laurel said, and brushed damp curls back from Dinah's forehead.

"You have to get *out* of here," Dinah insisted. Her voice was little more than a whisper. "And you shouldn't blame Mr. Toomy. He's . . . he's scared, that's all. Of *them.*"

Don looked around balefully. "If I find that bastard, *I'll* scare him," he said, and curled both hands into fists. A lodge ring gleamed above one knuckle in the growing gloom. "I'll make him wish he was born dead."

Nick came into the restaurant then, followed by Albert. He pushed past Rudy Warwick without a word of apology and knelt next to Dinah. His bright gaze fixed upon the handle of the knife for a moment, then moved to the child's face.

"Hello, love." He spoke cheerily, but his eyes had darkened. "I see you've been air-conditioned. Not to worry; you'll be right as a trivet in no time flat."

Dinah smiled a little. "What's a trivet?" she whispered. More blood ran out of her mouth as she spoke, and Laurel could see it on her teeth. Laurel's stomach did a slow, lazy roll.

"I don't know, but I'm sure it's something nice," Nick replied. "I'm going to turn your head to one side. Be as still as you can."

"Okay."

Nick moved her head, very gently, until her cheek was almost resting on the carpet. "Hurt?"

"Yes," Dinah whispered. "Hot. Hurts to . . . breathe." Her whispery voice had taken on a hoarse, cracked quality. A thin stream of blood ran from her mouth and pooled on the carpet less than ten feet from the place where Craig Toomy's blood was drying.

From outside came the sudden high-pressure whine of aircraft engines starting. Don, Rudy, and Albert looked in that direction. Nick never looked away from the girl. He spoke gently. "Do you feel like coughing, Dinah?"

"Yes . . . no . . . don't know."

"It's better if you don't," he said. "If you get that tickly feeling, try to ignore it. And don't talk anymore, right?"

"Don't . . . hurt . . . Mr. Toomy." Her words, whispered though they were, conveyed great emphasis, great urgency.

"No, love, wouldn't think of it. Take it from me."

". . . don't . . . trust . . . you . . ."

He bent, kissed her cheek, and whispered in her ear: "But

you *can,* you know—trust me, I mean. For now, all you've got to do is lie still and let us take care of things."

He looked at Laurel.

"You didn't try to remove the knife?"

"I . . . no." Laurel swallowed. There was a hot, harsh lump in her throat. The swallow didn't move it. "Should I have?"

"If you had, there wouldn't be much chance. Do you have any nursing experience?"

"No."

"All right, I'm going to tell you what to do . . . but first I need to know if the sight of blood—quite a bit of it—is going to make you pass out. And I need the truth."

Laurel said, "I haven't really *seen* a lot of blood since my sister ran into a door and knocked out two of her teeth while we were playing hide-and-seek. But I didn't faint then."

"Good. And you're not going to faint now. Mr. Warwick, bring me half a dozen tablecloths from that grotty little pub around the corner." He smiled down at the girl. "Give me a minute or two, Dinah, and I think you'll feel much better. Young Dr. Hopewell is ever so gentle with the ladies—especially the ones who are young and pretty."

Laurel felt a sudden and absolutely absurd desire to reach out and touch Nick's hair.

What's the matter with you? This little girl is probably dying, and you're wondering what his hair feels like! Quit it! How stupid can you be?

Well, let's see . . . Stupid enough to have been flying across the country to meet a man I first contacted through the personals column of a so-called friendship magazine. Stupid enough to have been planning to sleep with him if he turned out to be reasonably presentable . . . and if he didn't have bad breath, of course.

Oh, quit it! Quit it, Laurel!

Yes, the other voice in her mind agreed. *You're absolutely right, it's crazy to be thinking things like that at a time like this, and I* will *quit it . . . but I wonder what Young Dr. Hopewell would be like in bed? I wonder if he would be gentle, or—*

Laurel shivered and wondered if this was the way your average nervous breakdown started.

"They're closer," Dinah said. "You really . . ." She coughed, and a large bubble of blood appeared between her lips. It popped, splattering her cheeks. Don Gaffney muttered and turned away. ". . . really have to hurry," she finished.

Nick's cheery smile didn't change a bit. "I know," he said.

3

Craig dashed across the terminal, nimbly vaulted the escalator's handrail, and ran down the frozen metal steps with panic roaring and beating in his head like the sound of the ocean in a storm; it even drowned out that other sound, the relentless chewing, crunching sound of the langoliers. No one saw him go. He sprinted across the lower lobby toward the exit doors . . . and crashed into them. He had forgotten everything, including the fact that the electric-eye door-openers wouldn't work with the power out.

He rebounded, the breath knocked out of him, and fell to the floor, gasping like a netted fish. He lay there for a moment, groping for whatever remained of his mind, and found himself gazing at his right hand. It was only a white blob in the growing darkness, but he could see the black splatters on it, and he knew what they were: the little girl's blood.

Except she wasn't a little girl, not really. She just looked *like a little girl. She was the head langolier, and with her gone the others won't be able to . . . won't be able to . . . to . . .*

To what?

To find him?

But he could still hear the hungry sound of their approach:

that maddening chewing sound, as if somewhere to the east a tribe of huge, hungry insects was on the march.

His mind whirled. Oh, he was so confused.

Craig saw a smaller door leading outside, got up, and started in that direction. Then he stopped. There was a road out there, and the road undoubtedly led to the town of Bangor, but so what? He didn't care about *Bangor;* Bangor was most definitely not part of that fabled BIG PICTURE. It was *Boston* that he had to get to. If he could get there, everything would be all right. And what did that mean? His father would have known. It meant he had to STOP SCAMPERING AROUND and GET WITH THE PROGRAM.

His mind seized on this idea the way a shipwreck victim seizes upon a piece of wreckage—anything that still floats, even if it's only the shithouse door, is a prize to be cherished. If he could get to Boston, this whole experience would be . . . would be . . .

"Set aside," he muttered.

At the words, a bright beam of rational light seemed to shaft through the darkness inside his head, and a voice (it might have been his father's) cried out *YES!!* in affirmation.

But how was he to do that? Boston was too far to walk and the others wouldn't let him back on board the only plane that still worked. Not after what he had done to their little blind mascot.

"But they don't know," Craig whispered. "They don't know I did them a favor, because they don't know what she is." He nodded his head sagely. His eyes, huge and wet in the dark, gleamed.

Stow away, his father's voice whispered to him. *Stow away on the plane.*

Yes! his mother's voice added. *Stow away! That's the ticket, Craiggy-weggy! Only if you do that, you won't* need *a ticket, will you?*

Craig looked doubtfully toward the luggage conveyor belt.

He could use it to get to the tarmac, but suppose they had posted a guard by the plane? The pilot wouldn't think of it— once out of his cockpit, the man was obviously an imbecile— but the Englishman almost surely would.

So what was he supposed to do?

If the Bangor side of the terminal was no good, and the runway side of the terminal was *also* no good, what was he supposed to do and where was he supposed to go?

Craig looked nervously at the dead escalator. They would be hunting him soon—the Englishman undoubtedly leading the pack—and here he stood in the middle of the floor, as exposed as a stripper who has just tossed her pasties and g-string into the audience.

I have to hide, at least for awhile.

He had heard the jet engines start up outside, but this did not worry him; he knew a little about planes and understood that Engle couldn't go anywhere until he had refuelled. And refuelling would take time. He didn't have to worry about them leaving without him.

Not yet, anyway.

Hide, Craiggy-weggy. That's what you have to do right now. You have to hide before they come for you.

He turned slowly, looking for the best place, squinting into the growing dark. And this time he saw a sign on a door tucked between the Avis desk and the Bangor Travel Agency.

AIRPORT SERVICES,

it read. A sign which could mean almost anything.

Craig hurried across to the door, casting nervous looks back over his shoulder as he went, and tried it. As with the door to Airport Security, the knob would not turn but the door opened when he pushed on it. Craig took one final look over his shoulder, saw no one, and closed the door behind him.

Utter, total dark swallowed him; in here, he was as blind as the little girl he had stabbed. Craig didn't mind. He was not afraid of the dark; in fact, he rather liked it. Unless you were with a woman, no one expected you to do anything significant in the dark. In the dark, performance ceased to be a factor.

Even better, the chewing sound of the langoliers was muffled.

Craig felt his way slowly forward, hands outstretched, feet shuffling. After three of these shuffling steps, his thigh came in contact with a hard object that felt like the edge of a desk. He reached forward and down. Yes. A desk. He let his hands flutter over it for a moment, taking comfort in the familiar accoutrements of white-collar America: a stack of paper, an IN/OUT basket, the edge of a blotter, a caddy filled with paper-clips, a pencil-and-pen set. He worked his way around the desk to the far side, where his hip bumped the arm of a chair. Craig maneuvered himself between the chair and the desk and then sat down. Being behind a desk made him feel better still. It made him feel like himself—calm, in control. He fumbled for the top drawer and pulled it open. Felt inside for a weapon—something sharp. His hand happened almost immediately upon a letter-opener.

He took it out, shut the drawer, and put it on the desk by his right hand.

He just sat there for a moment, listening to the muffled *whisk-thud* of his heartbeat and the dim sound of the jet engines, then sent his hands fluttering delicately over the surface of the desk again until they re-encountered the stack of papers. He took the top sheet and brought it toward him, but there wasn't a glimmer of white . . . not even when he held it right in front of his eyes.

That's all right, Craiggy-weggy. You just sit here in the dark. Sit here and wait until it's time to move. When the time comes—

I'll tell you, his father finished grimly.

"That's right," Craig said. His fingers spidered up the unseen sheet of paper to the righthand corner. He tore smoothly downward.

Riii-ip.

Calm filled his mind like cool blue water. He dropped the unseen strip on the unseen desk and returned his fingers to the top of the sheet. Everything was going to be fine. Just fine. He began to sing under his breath in a tuneless little whisper.

"Just call me angel . . . of the *morn*-ing, *ba*-by . . ."

Riii-ip.

"Just touch my cheek before you leave me . . . *ba*-by . . ."

Calm now, at peace, Craig sat and waited for his father to tell him what he should do next, just as he had done so many times as a child.

4

"Listen carefully, Albert," Nick said. "We have to take her on board the plane, but we'll need a litter to do it. There won't be one on board, but there must be one in here. Where?"

"Gee, Mr. Hopewell, Captain Engle would know better than—"

"But Captain Engle isn't here," Nick said patiently. "We shall have to manage on our own."

Albert frowned . . . then thought of a sign he had seen on the lower level. "Airport Services?" he asked. "Does that sound right?"

"It bloody well does," Nick said. "Where did you see that?"

"On the lower level. Next to the rent-a-car counters."

"All right," Nick said. "Here's how we're going to handle this. You and Mr. Gaffney are designated litter-finders and litter-bearers. Mr. Gaffney, I suggest you check by the grill behind the counter. I expect you'll find some sharp knives. I'm sure that's where our unpleasant friend found his. Get one for you and one for Albert."

Don went behind the counter without a word. Rudy Warwick returned from The Red Baron Bar with an armload of red-and-white-checked tablecloths.

183

"I'm really sorry—" he began again, but Nick cut him off. He was still looking at Albert, his face now only a circle of white above the deeper shadow of Dinah's small body. The dark had almost arrived.

"You probably won't see Mr. Toomy; my guess is that he left here unarmed, in a panic. I imagine he's either found a bolthole by now or has left the terminal. If you *do* see him, I advise you very strongly not to engage him unless he makes it necessary." He swung his head to look at Don as Don returned with a pair of butcher knives. "Keep your priorities straight, you two. Your mission isn't to recapture Mr. Toomy and bring him to justice. Your job is to get a stretcher and bring it here as quick as you can. We have to get out of here."

Don offered Albert one of the knives, but Albert shook his head and looked at Rudy Warwick. "Could I have one of those tablecloths instead?"

Don looked at him as if Albert had gone crazy. "A tablecloth? What in God's name for?"

"I'll show you."

Albert had been kneeling by Dinah. Now he got up and went behind the counter. He peered around, not sure exactly what he was looking for, but positive he would know it when he saw it. And so he did. There was an old-fashioned two-slice toaster sitting well back on the counter. He picked it up, jerking the plug out of the wall, and wrapped the cord tightly around it as he came back to where the others were. He took one of the tablecloths, spread it, and placed the toaster in one corner. Then he turned it over twice, wrapping the toaster in the end of the tablecloth like a Christmas present. He fashioned tight rabbit's-ear knots in the corners to make a pocket. When he gripped the loose end of the tablecloth and stood up, the wrapped toaster had become a rock in a makeshift sling.

"When I was a kid, we used to play Indiana Jones," Albert said apologetically. "I made something like this and pretended it was my whip. I almost broke my brother David's arm once. I loaded an old blanket with a sashweight I found in the garage. Pretty stupid, I guess. I didn't know how hard it would hit. I got a hell of a spanking for it. It looks stupid, I guess, but it actually works pretty well. It always did, at least."

Nick looked at Albert's makeshift weapon dubiously but said nothing. If a toaster wrapped in a tablecloth made Albert feel more comfortable about going downstairs in the dark, so be it.

"Good enough, then. Now go find a stretcher and bring it back. If there isn't one in the Airport Services office, try some-place else. If you don't find anything in fifteen minutes—no, make that ten—just come back and we'll carry her."

"You can't do that!" Laurel cried softly. "If there's internal bleeding—"

Nick looked up at her. "There's internal bleeding already. And ten minutes is all the time I think we can spare."

Laurel opened her mouth to answer, to *argue,* but Dinah's husky whisper stopped her. "He's right."

Don slipped the blade of his knife into his belt. "Come on, son," he said. They crossed the terminal together and started down the escalator to the first floor. Albert wrapped the end of his loaded tablecloth around his hand as they went.

5

Nick turned his attention back to the girl on the floor. "How are you feeling, Dinah?"

"Hurts bad," Dinah said faintly.

"Yes, of course it does," Nick said. "And I'm afraid that what I'm about to do is going to make it hurt a good deal more, for a few seconds, at least. But the knife is in your lung, and it's got to come out. You know that, don't you?"

"Yes." Her dark, unseeing eyes looked up at him. "Scared."

"So am I, Dinah. So am I. But it has to be done. Are you game?"

"Yes."

"Good girl." Nick bent and planted a soft kiss on her cheek. "That's a good, brave girl. It won't take long, and that's a promise. I want you to lie just as still as you can, Dinah, and try not to cough. Do you understand me? It's very important. *Try not to cough.*"

"I'll try."

"There may be a moment or two when you feel that you can't breathe. You may even feel that you're leaking, like a tire with a puncture. That's a scary feeling, love, and it may make you want to move around, or cry out. You mustn't do it. *And you mustn't cough.*"

Dinah made a reply none of them could hear.

Nick swallowed, armed sweat off his forehead in a quick gesture, and turned to Laurel. "Fold two of those tablecloths into square pads. Thick as you can. Kneel beside me. Close as you can get. Warwick, take off your belt."

Rudy began to comply at once.

Nick looked back at Laurel. She was again struck, and not unpleasantly this time, by the power of his gaze. "I'm going to grasp the handle of the knife and draw it out. If it's not caught on one of her ribs—and judging from its position, I don't think it is—the blade should come out in one slow, smooth pull. The moment it's out, I will draw back, giving you clear access to the girl's chest area. You will place one of your pads over the wound and press. Press *hard.* You're not to worry about hurting her, or compressing her chest so much she can't breathe. She's got at least one perforation in her lung, and I'm betting there's a pair of them. Those are what we've got to worry about. Do you understand?"

"Yes."

"When you've placed the pad, I'm going to lift her against the pressure you're putting on. Mr. Warwick here will then slip the other pad beneath her if we see blood on the back of her dress. Then we're going to tie the compresses in place with Mr. Warwick's belt." He glanced up at Rudy. "When I call for it, my friend, give it to me. Don't make me ask you twice."

"I won't."

"Can you see well enough to do this, Nick?" Laurel asked.

"I think so," Nick replied. "I hope so." He looked at Dinah again. "Ready?"

Dinah muttered something.

"All right," Nick said. He drew in a long breath and then let it out. "Jesus help me."

He wrapped his slim, long-fingered hands around the handle of the knife like a man gripping a baseball bat. He pulled. Dinah shrieked. A great gout of blood spewed from her mouth. Laurel had been leaning tensely forward, and her face was suddenly bathed in Dinah's blood. She recoiled.

"No!" Nick spat at her without looking around. "Don't you *dare* go weak-sister on me! Don't you *dare*!"

Laurel leaned forward again, gagging and shuddering. The blade, a dully gleaming triangle of silver in the deep gloom, emerged from Dinah's chest and glimmered in the air. The little blind girl's chest heaved and there was a high, unearthly whistling sound as the wound sucked inward.

"*Now!*" Nick grunted. "Press down! Hard as you can!"

Laurel leaned forward. For just a moment she saw blood pouring out of the hole in Dinah's chest, and then the wound was covered. The tablecloth pad grew warm and wet under her hands almost immediately.

"Harder!" Nick snarled at her. "Press harder! Seal it! Seal the wound!"

Laurel now understood what people meant when they talked about coming completely unstrung, because she felt on the verge of it herself. "I can't! I'll break her ribs if—"

"*Fuck her ribs!* You *have* to make a seal!"

Laurel rocked forward on her knees and brought her entire

weight down on her hands. Now she could feel liquid seeping slowly between her fingers, although she had folded the table-cloth thick.

The Englishman tossed the knife aside and leaned forward until his face was almost touching Dinah's. Her eyes were closed. He rolled one of the lids. "I think she's finally out," he said. "Can't tell for sure because her eyes are so odd, but I hope to heaven she is." Hair had fallen over his brow. He tossed it back impatiently with a jerk of his head and looked at Laurel. "You're doing well. Stay with it, all right? I'm rolling her now. Keep the pressure on as I do."

"There's so much blood," Laurel groaned. "Will she drown?"

"I don't know. Keep the pressure on. Ready, Mr. Warwick?"

"Oh Christ I guess so," Rudy Warwick croaked.

"Right. Here we go." Nick slipped his hands beneath Dinah's right shoulderblade and grimaced. "It's worse than I thought," he muttered. "Far worse. She's *soaked*." He began to pull Dinah slowly upward against the pressure Laurel was putting on. Dinah uttered a thick, croaking moan. A gout of half-congealed blood flew from her mouth and spattered across the floor. And now Laurel could hear a rain of blood pattering down on the carpet from beneath the girl.

Suddenly the world began to swim away from her.

"Keep that pressure on!" Nick cried. "Don't let up!"

But she was fainting.

It was her understanding of what Nick Hopewell would think of her if she *did* faint which caused her to do what she did next. Laurel stuck her tongue out between her teeth like a child making a face and bit down on it as hard as she could. The pain was bright and exquisite, the salty taste of her own blood immediately filled her mouth . . . but that sensation that the world was swimming away from her like a big lazy fish in an aquarium passed. She was *here* again.

Downstairs, there was a sudden shriek of pain and surprise.

It was followed by a hoarse shout. On the heels of the shout came a loud, drilling scream.

Rudy and Laurel both turned in that direction. "The boy!" Rudy said. "Him and Gaffney! They——"

"They've found Mr. Toomy after all," Nick said. His face was a complicated mask of effort. The tendons on his neck stood out like steel pulleys. "We'll just have to hope——"

There was a thud from downstairs, followed by a terrible howl of agony. Then a whole series of muffled thumps.

"——that they're on top of the situation. We can't do anything about it now. If we stop in the middle of what we're doing, this little girl is going to die for sure."

"But that sounded like the *kid*!"

"Can't be helped, can it? Slide the pad under her, Warwick. Do it right now, or I'll kick your bloody arse square."

6

Don led the way down the escalator, then stopped briefly at the bottom to fumble in his pocket. He brought out a square object that gleamed faintly in the dark. "It's my Zippo," he said. "Do you think it'll still work?"

"I don't know," Albert said. "It might . . . for awhile. You better not try it until you have to. I sure hope it does. We won't be able to see a thing without it."

"Where's this Airport Services place?"

Albert pointed to the door Craig Toomy had gone through less than five minutes before. "Right over there."

"Do you think it's unlocked?"

"Well," Albert said, "there's only one way to find out."

They crossed the terminal, Don still leading the way with his lighter in his right hand.

7

Craig heard them coming—more servants of the langoliers, no doubt. But he wasn't worried. He had taken care of the thing which had been masquerading as a little girl, and he would take care of these other things, as well. He curled his hand around the letter-opener, got up, and sidled back around the desk.

"Do you think it's unlocked?"

"Well, there's only one way to find out."

You're going to find out something, *anyway,* Craig thought. He reached the wall beside the door. It was lined with paper-stacked shelves. He reached out and felt doorhinges. Good. The opening door would block him off from them . . . not that they were likely to see him, anyway. It was as black as an elephant's asshole in here. He raised the letter-opener to shoulder height.

"The knob doesn't move." Craig relaxed . . . but only for a moment.

"Try pushing it." That was the smart-ass kid.

The door began to open.

8

Don stepped in, blinking at the gloom. He thumbed the cover of his lighter back, held it up, and flicked the wheel. There was a spark and the wick caught at once, producing a low flame. They saw what was apparently a combined office and storeroom. There was an untidy stack of luggage in one corner and a Xerox machine in another. The back wall was lined with shelves and the shelves were stacked with what looked like forms of various kinds.

Don stepped further into the office, lifting his lighter like a spelunker holding up a guttering candle in a dark cave. He pointed to the right wall. "Hey, kid! Ace! Look!"

A poster mounted there showed a tipsy guy in a business suit staggering out of a bar and looking at his watch. WORK IS THE CURSE OF THE DRINKING CLASS, the poster advised. Mounted on the wall beside it was a white plastic box with a large red cross on it. And leaning below it was a folded stretcher . . . the kind with wheels.

Albert wasn't looking at the poster or the first-aid kit or the stretcher, however. His eyes were fixed on the desk in the center of the room.

On it he saw a heaped tangle of paper strips.

"Look out!" he shouted. *"Look out, he's in h—"*

Craig Toomy stepped out from behind the door and struck.

9

"Belt," Nick said.

Rudy didn't move or reply. His head was turned toward the door of the restaurant. The sounds from downstairs had ceased. There was only the rattling noise and the steady, throbbing rumble of the jet engine in the dark outside.

Nick kicked backward like a mule, connecting with Rudy's shin.

"Ow!"

"Belt! *Now!"*

Rudy dropped clumsily to his knees and moved next to Nick, who was holding Dinah up with one hand and pressing a second tablecloth pad against her back with the other.

"Slip it under the pad," Nick said. He was panting, and sweat was running down his face in wide streams. "Quick! I can't hold her up forever!"

Rudy slid the belt under the pad. Nick lowered Dinah, reached across the girl's small body, and lifted her left shoulder long enough to pull the belt out the other side. Then he looped it over her chest and cinched it tight. He put the belt's free end in Laurel's hand. "Keep the pressure on," he said, standing up. "You can't use the buckle—she's much too small."

"Are you going downstairs?" Laurel asked.

"Yes. That seems indicated."

"Be careful. Please be careful."

He grinned at her, and all those white teeth suddenly shining out in the gloom were startling . . . but not frightening, she discovered. Quite the opposite.

"Of course. It's how I get along." He reached down and squeezed her shoulder. His hand was warm, and at his touch a little shiver chased through her. "You did very well, Laurel. Thank you."

He began to turn away, and then a small hand groped out and caught the cuff of his blue-jeans. He looked down and saw that Dinah's blind eyes were open again.

"Don't . . ." she began, and then a choked sneezing fit shook her. Blood flew from her nose in a spray of fine droplets.

"Dinah, you mustn't—"

"Don't . . . you . . . kill him!" she said, and even in the dark Laurel could sense the fantastic effort she was making to speak at all.

Nick looked down at her thoughtfully. "The bugger stabbed you, you know. Why are you so insistent on keeping him whole?"

Her narrow chest strained against the belt. The blood-stained tablecloth pad heaved. She struggled and managed to say one thing more. They all heard it; Dinah was at great pains to speak clearly. "All . . . I know . . . is that we need him," she whispered, and then her eyes closed again.

10

Craig buried the letter-opener fist-deep in the nape of Don Gaffney's neck. Don screamed and dropped the lighter. It struck the floor and lay there, guttering sickishly. Albert shouted in surprise as he saw Craig step toward Don, who was now staggering in the direction of the desk and clawing weakly behind him for the protruding object.

Craig grabbed the opener with one hand and planted his other against Don's back. As he simultaneously pushed and pulled, Albert heard the sound of a hungry man pulling a drumstick off a well-done turkey. Don screamed again, louder this time, and went sprawling over the desk. His arms flew out ahead of him, knocking to the floor an IN/OUT box and the stack of lost-luggage forms Craig had been ripping.

Craig turned toward Albert, flicking a spray of blood-droplets from the blade of the letter-opener as he did so. "You're one of them, too," he breathed. "Well, fuck you. I'm going to Boston and you can't stop me. *None* of you can stop me." Then the lighter on the floor went out and they were in darkness.

Albert took a step backward and felt a warm swoop of air in his face as Craig swung the blade through the spot where he had been only a second before. He flailed behind him with his free hand, terrified of backing into a corner where Craig could use the knife (in the Zippo's pallid, fading light, that was what he had thought it was) on him at will and his own weapon would be useless as well as stupid. His fingers found only empty space, and he backed through the door into the lobby. He did not feel cool; he did not feel like the fastest Hebrew on *any* side of the Mississippi; he did not feel faster than blue blazes. He felt like a scared kid who had foolishly chosen a childhood playtoy instead of a real weapon because he had been unable to believe—really, really believe—that it could come to this in spite of what the lunatic asshole had done to the little girl upstairs. He could smell himself. Even in the dead air he could smell himself. It was the rancid monkeypiss aroma of fear.

Craig came gliding out through the door with the letter-opener raised. He moved like a dancing shadow in the dark. "I see you, sonny," he breathed. "I see you just like a cat."

He began to slide forward. Albert backed away from him. At the same time he began to pendulum the toaster back and forth, reminding himself that he would have only one good shot before Toomy moved in and planted the blade in his throat or chest.

And if the toaster goes flying out of the goddam pocket before it hits him, I'm a goner.

11

Craig closed in, weaving the top half of his body from side to side like a snake coming out of a basket. An absent little smile touched the corners of his lips and made small dimples there. *That's right,* Craig's father said grimly from his undying stronghold inside Craig's head. *If you have to pick them off one by one, you can do that. EPO, Craig, remember? EPO. Effort Pays Off.*

That's right, Craiggy-weggy, his mother chimed in. *You can do it, and you* have *to do it.*

"I'm sorry," Craig murmured to the white-faced boy through his smile. "I'm really, really sorry, but I have to do it. If you could see things from my perspective, you'd understand."

12

Albert shot a quick glance behind him and saw he was backing toward the United Airlines ticket desk. If he retreated much further, the backward arc of his swing would be restricted. It had to be soon. He began to pendulum the toaster more rapidly, his sweaty hand clutching the twist of tablecloth.

Craig caught the movement in the dark, but couldn't tell what it was the kid was swinging. It didn't matter. He couldn't *let* it matter. He gathered himself, then sprang forward.

"I'M GOING TO BOSTON!" he shrieked. *"I'M GOING TO—"*

Albert's eyes were adjusting to the dark, and he saw Craig make his move. The toaster was on the rearward half of its arc. Instead of snapping his wrist forward to reverse its direction, Albert let his arm go with the weight of the toaster, swinging it up and over his head in an exaggerated pitching gesture. At the same time he stepped to the left. The lump at the end of the tablecloth made a short, hard circlet in the air, held firmly in its pocket by centripetal force. Craig cooperated by stepping forward into the toaster's descending arc. It met his forehead and the bridge of his nose with a hard, toneless crunch.

Craig wailed with agony and dropped the letter-opener. His hands went to his face and he staggered backward. Blood from his broken nose poured between his fingers like water from a busted hydrant. Albert was terrified of what he had done but even more terrified of letting up now that Toomy was hurt. Albert took another step to the left and swung the tablecloth sidearm. It whipped through the air and smashed into the center of Craig's chest with a hard thump. Craig fell over backward, still howling.

For Albert "Ace" Kaussner, only one thought remained; all else was a tumbling, fragmented swirl of color, image, and emotion.

I have to make him stop moving or he'll get up and kill me. I have to make him stop moving or he'll get up and kill me.

At least Toomy had dropped his weapon; it lay glinting on the lobby carpet. Albert planted one of his loafers on it and unloaded with the toaster again. As it came down, Albert bowed from the waist like an old-fashioned butler greeting a member of the royal family. The lump at the end of the table-cloth smashed into Craig Toomy's gasping mouth. There was a sound like glass being crushed inside of a handkerchief.

Oh God, Albert thought. *That was his teeth.*

Craig flopped and squirmed on the floor. It was terrible to watch him, perhaps more terrible because of the poor light. There was something monstrous and unkillable and insectile about his horrible vitality.

His hand closed upon Albert's loafer. Albert stepped away from the letter-opener with a little cry of revulsion, and Craig tried to grasp it when he did. Between his eyes, his nose was a burst bulb of flesh. He could hardly see Albert at all; his vision was eaten up by a vast white corona of light. A steady high keening note rang in his head, the sound of a TV test-pattern turned up to full volume.

He was beyond doing any damage, but Albert didn't know it. In a panic, he brought the toaster down on Craig's head again. There was a metallic crunch-rattle as the heating ele-ments inside it broke free.

Craig stopped moving.

Albert stood over him, sobbing for breath, the weighted tablecloth dangling from one hand. Then he took two long, shambling steps toward the escalator, bowed deeply again, and vomited on the floor.

13

Brian crossed himself as he thumbed back the black plastic shield which covered the screen of the 767's INS video-display terminal, half-expecting it to be smooth and blank. He looked at it closely . . . and let out a deep sigh of relief.

LAST PROGRAM COMPLETE

it informed him in cool blue-green letters, and below that:

NEW PROGRAM? Y N

Brian typed Y, then:

REVERSE AP 29: LAX/LOGAN

The screen went dark for a moment. Then:

INCLUDE DIVERSION IN REVERSE PROGRAM AP
29?
Y N

Brian typed Y.

COMPUTING REVERSE

the screen informed him, and less than five seconds later:

PROGRAM COMPLETE

"Captain Engle?"

He turned around. Bethany was standing in the cockpit doorway. She looked pale and haggard in the cabin lights.

"I'm a little busy right now, Bethany."

"Why aren't they back?"

"I can't say."

"I asked Bob—Mr. Jenkins—if he could see anyone moving inside the terminal, and he said he couldn't. What if they're all dead?"

"I'm sure they're not. If it will make you feel better, why don't you join him at the bottom of the ladder? I've got some more work to do here." *At least I hope I do.*

"Are you scared?" she asked.

"Yes. I sure am."

She smiled a little. "I'm sort of glad. It's bad to be scared all by yourself—totally bogus. I'll leave you alone now."

"Thanks. I'm sure they'll be out soon."

She left. Brian turned back to the INS monitor and typed:

```
ARE THERE PROBLEMS WITH THIS PROGRAM?
```

He hit execute.

```
NO PROBLEMS. THANK YOU FOR FLYING
            AMERICAN PRIDE.
```

"You're welcome, I'm sure," Brian murmured, and wiped his forehead with his sleeve.

Now, he thought, *if only the fuel will burn.*

14

Bob heard footsteps on the ladder and turned quickly. It was only Bethany, descending slowly and carefully, but he still felt jumpy. The sound coming out of the east was gradually growing louder.

Closer.

"Hi, Bethany. May I borrow another of your cigarettes?"

She offered the depleted pack to him, then took one herself. She had tucked Albert's book of experimental matches into the cellophane covering the pack, and when she tried one it lit easily.

"Any sign of them?"

"Well, it all depends on what you mean by 'any sign,' I guess," Bob said cautiously. "I think I heard some shouting just before you came down." What he had heard actually sounded like screaming—*shrieking,* not to put too fine a point on it—but he saw no reason to tell the girl that. She looked as frightened as Bob felt, and he had an idea she'd taken a liking to Albert.

"I hope Dinah's going to be all right," she said, "but I don't know. He cut her really bad."

"Did you see the captain?"

Bethany nodded. "He sort of kicked me out. I guess he's programming his instruments, or something."

Bob Jenkins nodded soberly. "I hope so."

Conversation lapsed. They both looked east. A new and even more ominous sound now underlay the crunching, chewing noise: a high, inanimate screaming. It was a strangely mechanical sound, one that made Bob think of an automatic transmission low on fluid.

"It's a lot closer now, isn't it?"

Bob nodded reluctantly. He drew on his cigarette and the glowing ember momentarily illuminated a pair of tired, terrified eyes.

"What do you suppose it is, Mr. Jenkins?"

He shook his head slowly. "Dear girl, I hope we never have to find out."

15

Halfway down the escalator, Nick saw a bent-over figure standing in front of the useless bank of pay telephones. It was impossible to tell if it was Albert or Craig Toomy. The Englishman reached into his right front pocket, holding his left hand against it to prevent any jingling, and by touch selected a pair of quarters from his change. He closed his right hand into a fist and slipped the quarters between his fingers, creating a makeshift set of brass knuckles. Then he continued down to the lobby.

The figure by the telephones looked up as Nick approached. It was Albert. "Don't step in the puke," he said dully.

Nick dropped the quarters back into his pocket and hurried to where the boy was standing with his hands propped above his knees like an old man who has badly overestimated his capacity for exercise. He could smell the high, sour stench of vomit. That and the sweaty stink of fear coming off the boy were smells with which he was all too familiar. He knew them from the Falklands, and even more intimately from Northern Ireland. He put his left arm around the boy's shoulders and Albert straightened very slowly.

"Where are they, Ace?" Nick asked quietly. "Gaffney and Toomy—where are they?"

"Mr. Toomy's there." He pointed toward a crumpled shape on the floor. "Mr. Gaffney's in the Airport Services office. I think they're both dead. Mr. Toomy was in the Airport Services office. Behind the door, I guess. He killed Mr. Gaffney because Mr. Gaffney walked in first. If I'd walked in first, he would have killed me instead."

Albert swallowed hard.

"Then I killed Mr. Toomy. I had to. He came after me, see? He found another knife someplace and he came after me." He spoke in a tone which could have been mistaken for indifference, but Nick knew better. And it was not indifference he saw on the white blur of Albert's face.

"Can you get hold of yourself, Ace?" Nick asked.

"I don't know. I never k-k-killed anyone before, and—" Albert uttered a strangled, miserable sob.

"I know," Nick said. "It's a horrible thing, but it can be gotten over. I know. And you must get over it, Ace. We have miles to go before we sleep, and there's no time for therapy. The sound is louder."

He left Albert and went over to the crumpled form on the floor. Craig Toomy was lying on his side with one upraised arm partially obscuring his face. Nick rolled him onto his back, looked, whistled softly. Toomy was still alive—he could hear the harsh rasp of his breath—but Nick would have bet his bank account that the man was not shamming this time. His nose hadn't just been broken; it looked vaporized. His mouth was a bloody socket ringed with the shattered remains of his teeth. And the deep, troubled dent in the center of Toomy's forehead suggested that Albert had done some creative retooling of the man's skull-plate.

"He did all this with a *toaster*?" Nick muttered. "Jesus and Mary, Tom, Dick, and Harry." He got up and raised his voice. "He's not dead, Ace."

Albert had bent over again when Nick left him. Now he straightened slowly and took a step toward him. "He's not?"

"Listen for yourself. Out for the count, but still in the game." *Not for long, though; not by the sound of him.* "Let's check on Mr. Gaffney—maybe he got off lucky, too. And what about the stretcher?"

"Huh?" Albert looked at Nick as though he had spoken in a foreign language.

"The stretcher," Nick repeated patiently as they walked toward the open Airport Services door.

"We found it," Albert said.

"Did you? Super!"

Albert stopped just inside the door. "Wait a minute," he muttered, then squatted and felt around for Don's lighter. He found it after a moment or two. It was still warm. He stood up again. "Mr. Gaffney's on the other side of the desk, I think."

They walked around, stepping over the tumbled stacks of paper and the IN/OUT basket. Albert held out the lighter and flicked the wheel. On the fifth try the wick caught and burned feebly for three or four seconds. It was enough. Nick had actually seen enough in the spark-flashes the lighter's wheel had struck, but he hadn't liked to say so to Albert. Don Gaffney lay sprawled on his back, eyes open, a look of terrible surprise still fixed on his face. He hadn't gotten off lucky after all.

"How was it that Toomy didn't get you as well?" Nick asked after a moment.

"I knew he was in here," Albert said. "Even before he stuck Mr. Gaffney, I knew." His voice was still dry and shaky, but he felt a little better. Now that he had actually faced poor Mr. Gaffney—looked him in the eye, so to speak—he felt a little better.

"Did you hear him?"

"No—I saw those. On the desk." Albert pointed to the little heap of torn strips.

"Lucky you did." Nick put his hand on Albert's shoulder in the dark. "You deserve to be alive, mate. You earned the privilege. All right?"

"I'll try," Albert said.

"You do that, old son. It saves a lot of nightmares. You're looking at a man who knows."

Albert nodded.

"Keep it together, Ace. That's all there is to it—just keep things together and you'll be fine."

"Mr. Hopewell?"

"Yes?"

"Would you mind not calling me that? I—" His voice clogged, and Albert cleared his throat violently. "I don't think I like it anymore."

16

They emerged from the dark cave which was Airport Services thirty seconds later, Nick carrying the folded stretcher by the handle. When they reached the bank of phones, Nick handed the stretcher to Albert, who accepted it wordlessly. The table-cloth lay on the floor about five feet away from Toomy, who was snoring now in great rhythmless snatches of air.

Time was short, time was very fucking short, but Nick had to see this. He *had* to.

He picked up the tablecloth and pulled the toaster out. One

of the heating elements caught in a bread slot; the other tumbled out onto the floor. The timer-dial and the handle you used to push the bread down fell off. One corner of the toaster was crumpled inward. The left side was bashed into a deep circular dent.

That's the part that collided with Friend Toomy's sniffer, Nick thought. *Amazing.* He shook the toaster and listened to the loose rattle of broken parts inside.

"A toaster," he marvelled. "I have friends, Albert— *professional* friends—who wouldn't believe it. I hardly believe it myself. I mean . . . a *toaster.*"

Albert had turned his head. "Throw it away," he said hoarsely. "I don't want to look at it."

Nick did as the boy asked, then clapped him on the shoulder. "Take the stretcher upstairs. I'll join you directly."

"What are you going to do?"

"I want to see if there's anything else we can use in that office."

Albert looked at him for a moment, but he couldn't make out Nick's features in the dark. At last he said, "I don't believe you."

"Nor do you have to," Nick said in an oddly gentle voice. "Go on, Ace . . . Albert, I mean. I'll join you soon. And don't look back."

Albert stared at him a moment longer, then began to trudge up the frozen escalator, his head down, the stretcher dangling like a suitcase from his right hand. He didn't look back.

17

Nick waited until the boy had disappeared into the gloom. Then he walked back over to where Craig Toomy lay and squatted beside him. Toomy was still out, but his breathing seemed a little more regular. Nick supposed it was not impossible, given a week or two of constant-care treatment in hospital, that Toomy might recover. He had proved at least one thing: he had an awesomely hard head.

Shame the brains underneath are so soft, mate, Nick thought. He reached out, meaning to put one hand over Toomy's mouth and the other over his nose—or what remained of it. It would take less than a minute, and they would not have to worry about Mr. Craig Toomy anymore. The others would have recoiled in horror at the act—would have called it coldblooded murder—but Nick saw it as an insurance policy, no more and no less. Toomy had arisen once from what appeared to be total unconsciousness and now one of their number was dead and another was badly, perhaps mortally, wounded. There was no sense taking the same chance again.

And there was something else. If he left Toomy alive, what, exactly, would he be leaving him alive *for*? A short, haunted existence in a dead world? A chance to breathe dying air under a moveless sky in which all weather patterns appeared to have ceased? An opportunity to meet whatever was approaching from the east . . . approaching with a sound like that of a colony of giant, marauding ants?

No. Best to see him out of it. It would be painless, and that would have to be good enough.

"Better than the bastard deserves," Nick said, but still he hesitated.

He remembered the little girl looking up at him with her dark, unseeing eyes.

Don't you kill him! Not a plea; that had been a command. She had summoned up a little strength from some hidden last reserve in order to give him that command. *All I know is that we need him.*

Why is she so bloody protective of him?

He squatted a moment longer, looking into Craig Toomy's ruined face. And when Rudy Warwick spoke from the head of the escalator, he jumped as if it had been the devil himself.

"Mr. Hopewell? Nick? Are you coming?"

"In a jiffy!" he called back over his shoulder. He reached toward Toomy's face again and stopped again, remembering her dark eyes.

We need him.

Abruptly he stood up, leaving Craig Toomy to his tortured struggle for breath. "Coming now," he called, and ran lightly up the escalator.

CHAPTER EIGHT

REFUELLING. DAWN'S EARLY LIGHT.
THE APPROACH OF THE LANGOLIERS.
ANGEL OF THE MORNING. THE TIME-KEEPERS
OF ETERNITY. TAKE-OFF.

1

Bethany had cast away her almost tasteless cigarette and was halfway up the ladder again when Bob Jenkins shouted: "I think they're coming out!"

She turned and ran back down the stairs. A series of dark blobs was emerging from the luggage bay and crawling along the conveyor belt. Bob and Bethany ran to meet them.

Dinah was strapped to the stretcher. Rudy had one end, Nick the other. They were walking on their knees, and Bethany could hear the bald man breathing in harsh, out-of-breath gasps.

"Let me help," she told him, and Rudy gave up his end of the stretcher willingly.

"Try not to jiggle her," Nick said, swinging his legs off the conveyor belt. "Albert, get on Bethany's end and help us take her up the stairs. We want this thing to stay as level as possible."

"How bad is she?" Bethany asked Albert.

"Not good," he said grimly. "Unconscious but still alive. That's all I know."

"Where are Gaffney and Toomy?" Bob asked as they crossed to the plane. He had to raise his voice slightly to be heard; the crunching sound was louder now, and that shrieking wounded-transmission undertone was becoming a dominant, maddening note.

"Gaffney's dead and Toomy might as well be," Nick said. "We'll discuss it later, if you like. Right now there's no time." He halted at the foot of the stairs. "Mind you keep your end up, you two."

They moved the stretcher slowly and carefully up the stairs, Nick walking backward and bent over the forward end, Albert and Bethany holding the stretcher up at forehead level and jostling hips on the narrow stairway at the rear. Bob, Rudy, and Laurel followed behind. Laurel had spoken only once since Albert and Nick had returned, to ask if Toomy was dead. When Nick told her he wasn't, she had looked at him closely and then nodded her head with relief.

Brian was standing at the cockpit door when Nick reached the top of the ladder and eased his end of the stretcher inside.

"I want to put her in first class," Nick said, "with this end of the stretcher raised so her head is up. Can I do that?"

"No problem. Secure the stretcher by looping a couple of seatbelts through the head-frame. Do you see where?"

"Yes." And to Albert and Bethany: "Come on up. You're doing fine."

In the cabin lights, the blood smeared on Dinah's cheeks and chin stood out starkly against her yellow-white skin. Her eyes were closed; her lids were a delicate shade of lavender. Under the belt (in which Nick had punched a new hole, high above the others), the makeshift compress was dark red. Brian could hear her breathing. It sounded like a straw dragging wind at the bottom of an almost empty glass.

"It's bad, isn't it?" Brian asked in a low voice.

"Well, it's her lung and not her heart, and she's not filling up anywhere near as fast as I was afraid she might . . . but it's bad, yes."

"Will she live until we get back?"

"How in hell should I know?" Nick shouted at him suddenly. "I'm a soldier, not a bloody sawbones!"

The other froze, looking at him with cautious eyes. Laurel felt her skin prickle again.

"I'm sorry," Nick muttered. "Time travel plays the very devil with one's nerves, doesn't it? I'm very sorry."

"No need to apologize," Laurel said, and touched his arm. "We're all under strain."

He gave her a tired smile and touched her hair. "You're a sweetheart, Laurel, and no mistake. Come on—let's strap her in and see what we can do about getting the hell out of here."

2

Five minutes later Dinah's stretcher had been secured in an inclined position to a pair of first-class seats, her head up, her feet down. The rest of the passengers were gathered in a tight little knot around Brian in the first-class serving area.

"We need to refuel the plane," Brian said. "I'm going to start the other engine now and pull over as close as I can to that 727-400 at the jetway." He pointed to the Delta plane, which was just a gray lump in the dark. "Because our aircraft sits higher, I'll be able to lay our right wing right over the Delta's left wing. While I do that, four of you are going to bring over a hose cart—there's one sitting by the other jetway. I saw it before it got dark."

"Maybe we better wake Sleeping Beauty at the back of the plane and get him to lend a hand," Bob said.

Brian thought it over briefly and then shook his head. "The last thing we need right now is another scared, disoriented passenger on our hands . . . and one with a killer hangover to boot. And we won't need him—two strong men can push a hose cart in a pinch. I've seen it done. Just check the transmission lever to make sure it's in neutral. It wants to end up directly beneath the overlapping wings. Got it?"

They all nodded. Brian looked them over and decided that Rudy and Bethany were still too blown from wrestling the stretcher to be of much help. "Nick, Bob, and Albert. You push. Laurel, you steer. Okay?"

They nodded.

"Go on and do it, then. Bethany? Mr. Warwick? Go down with them. Pull the ladder away from the plane, and when I've got the plane repositioned, place it next to the overlapping wings. The wings, not the door. Got it?"

They nodded. Looking around at them, Brian saw that their eyes looked clear and bright for the first time since they had landed. *Of course,* he thought. *They have something to do now. And so do I, thank God.*

3

As they approached the hose cart sitting off to the left of the unoccupied jetway, Laurel realized she could actually *see* it. "My God," she said. "It's coming daylight again already. How long has it been since it got dark?"

"Less than forty minutes, by my watch," Bob said, "but I have a feeling that my watch doesn't keep very accurate time when we're outside the plane. I've also got a feeling time doesn't matter much here, anyway."

"What's going to happen to Mr. Toomy?" Laurel asked.

They had reached the cart. It was a small vehicle with a tank on the back, an open-air cab, and thick black hoses coiled on either side. Nick put an arm around her waist and turned her toward him. For a moment she had the crazy idea that he meant to kiss her, and she felt her heart speed up.

"I don't know what's going to happen to him," he said. "All I know is that when the chips were down, I chose to do what

Dinah wanted. I left him lying unconscious on the floor. All right?"

"No," she said in a slightly unsteady voice, "but I guess it will have to do."

He smiled a little, nodded, and gave her waist a brief squeeze. "Would you like to go to dinner with me when and if we make it back to L.A.?"

"Yes," she said at once. "That would be something to look forward to."

He nodded again. "For me, too. But unless we can get this airplane refuelled, we're not going anywhere." He looked at the open cab of the hose cart. "Can you find neutral, do you think?"

Laurel eyed the stick-shift jutting up from the floor of the cab. "I'm afraid I only drive an automatic."

"I'll do it." Albert jumped into the cab, depressed the clutch, then peered at the diagram on the knob of the shift lever. Behind him, the 767's second engine whined into life and both engines began to throb harder as Brian powered up. The noise was very loud, but Laurel found she didn't mind it at all. It blotted out that other sound, at least temporarily. And she kept wanting to look at Nick. Had he actually invited her out to dinner? Already it seemed hard to believe.

Albert changed gears, then waggled the shift lever. "Got it," he said, and jumped down. "Up you go, Laurel. Once we get it rolling, you'll have to hang a hard right and bring it around in a circle."

"All right."

She looked back nervously as the three men lined themselves up along the rear of the hose cart with Nick in the middle.

"Ready, you lot?" he asked.

Albert and Bob nodded.

"Right, then—all together."

Bob had been braced to push as hard as he could, and damn the low back pain which had plagued him for the last ten years, but the hose cart rolled with absurd ease. Laurel hauled the stiff, balky steering wheel around with all her might. The yellow cart described a small circle on the gray tarmac and began to roll back toward the 767, which was trundling slowly into position on the righthand side of the parked Delta jet.

"The difference between the two aircraft is incredible," Bob said.

"Yes," Nick agreed. "You were right, Albert. We may have wandered away from the present, but in some strange way, that airplane is still a part of it."

"So are *we*," Albert said. "At least, so far."

The 767's turbines died, leaving only the steady low rumble of the APUs—Brian was now running all four of them. They were not loud enough to cover the sound in the east. Before, that sound had had a kind of massive uniformity, but as it neared it was fragmenting; there seemed to be sounds within sounds, and the sum total began to seem horribly familiar.

Animals at feeding time, Laurel thought, and shivered. *That's what it sounds like—the sound of feeding animals, sent through an amplifier and blown up to grotesque proportions.*

She shivered violently and felt panic begin to nibble at her thoughts, an elemental force she could control no more than she could control whatever was making that sound.

"Maybe if we could see it, we could deal with it," Bob said as they began to push the fuel cart again.

Albert glanced at him briefly and said, "I don't think so."

4

Brian appeared in the forward door of the 767 and motioned Bethany and Rudy to roll the ladder over to him. When they did, he stepped onto the platform at the top and pointed to the overlapping wings. As they rolled him in that direction, he listened to the approaching noise and found himself remembering a movie he had seen on the late show a long time ago.

In it, Charlton Heston had owned a big plantation in South America. The plantation had been attacked by a vast moving carpet of soldier ants, ants which ate everything in their path—trees, grass, buildings, cows, men. What had that movie been called? Brian couldn't remember. He only remembered that Charlton had kept trying increasingly desperate tricks to stop the ants, or at least delay them. Had he beaten them in the end? Brian couldn't remember, but a fragment of his dream suddenly recurred, disturbing in its lack of association to anything: an ominous red sign which read SHOOTING STARS ONLY.

"Hold it!" he shouted down to Rudy and Bethany.

They ceased pushing, and Brian carefully climbed down the ladder until his head was on a level with the underside of the Delta jet's wing. Both the 767 and 727 were equipped with single-point fuelling ports in the left wing. He was now looking at a small square hatch with the words FUEL TANK ACCESS and CHECK SHUT-OFF VALVE BEFORE REFUELLING stencilled across it. And some wit had pasted a round yellow happy-face sticker to the fuel hatch. It was the final surreal touch.

Albert, Bob, and Nick had pushed the hose cart into position below him and were now looking up, their faces dirty gray circles in the brightening gloom. Brian leaned over and shouted down to Nick.

"There are two hoses, one on each side of the cart! I want the short one!"

Nick pulled it free and handed it up. Holding both the ladder and the nozzle of the hose with one hand, Brian leaned under the wing and opened the refuelling hatch. Inside was a male connector with a steel prong poking out like a finger. Brian leaned further out . . . and slipped. He grabbed the railing of the ladder.

"Hold on, mate," Nick said, mounting the ladder. "Help is on the way." He stopped three rungs below Brian and seized his belt. "Do me a favor, all right?"

"What's that?"

"Don't fart."

"I'll try, but no promises."

He leaned out again and looked down at the others. Rudy and Bethany had joined Bob and Albert below the wing. "Move away, unless you want a jet-fuel shower!" he called. "I can't control the Delta's shut-off valve, and it may leak!" As he waited for them to back away he thought, *Of course, it may not. For all I know, the tanks on this thing are as dry as a goddam bone.*

He leaned out again, using both hands now that Nick had him firmly anchored, and slammed the nozzle into the fuel port. There was a brief, spattering shower of jet-fuel—a very welcome shower, under the circumstances—and then a hard metallic click. Brian twisted the nozzle a quarter-turn to the right, locking it in place, and listened with satisfaction as jet-fuel ran down the hose to the cart, where a closed valve would dam its flow.

"Okay," he sighed, pulling himself back to the ladder. "So far, so good."

"What now, mate? How do we make that cart run? Do we jump-start it from the plane, or what?"

"I doubt if we could do that even if someone had remembered to bring the jumper cables," Brian said. "Luckily, it doesn't *have* to run. Essentially, the cart is just a gadget to filter and transfer fuel. I'm going to use the auxiliary power units on our plane to suck the fuel out of the 727 the way you'd use a straw to suck lemonade out of a glass."

"How long is it going to take?"

"Under optimum conditions—which would mean pumping with ground power—we could load 2,000 pounds of fuel a minute. Doing it like this makes it harder to figure. I've never had to use the APUs to pump fuel before. At least an hour. Maybe two."

Nick gazed anxiously eastward for a moment, and when he spoke again his voice was low. "Do me a favor, mate—don't tell the others that."

"Why not?"

"Because I don't think we *have* two hours. We may not even have one."

5

Alone in first class, Dinah Catherine Bellman opened her eyes.
And *saw.*
"Craig," she whispered.

6

Craig.

But he didn't want to hear his name again. When people called his name, something bad always happened. *Always.*

Craig! Get up, Craig!

No. He *wouldn't* get up. His head had become a vast chambered hive; pain roared and raved in each irregular room and crooked corridor. Bees had come. The bees had thought he was dead. They had invaded his head and turned his skull into a honeycomb. And now . . . now . . .

They sense my thoughts and are trying to sting them to death, he thought, and uttered a thick, agonized groan. His blood-streaked hands opened and closed slowly on the industrial carpet which covered the lower-lobby floor. *Let me die, oh please just let me die.*

Craig, you have to get up! Now!

It was his father's voice, the one voice he had never been able to refuse or shut out. But he would refuse it now. He would shut it out now.

"Go away," he croaked. "I hate you. Go away."

Pain blared through his head in a golden shriek of trumpets. Clouds of bees, furious and stinging, flew from the bells as they blew.

214

Oh let me die, he thought. *Oh let me die. This is hell. I am in a hell of bees and big-band horns.*

Get up, Craiggy-weggy. It's your birthday, and guess what? As soon as you get up, someone's going to hand you a beer and hit you over the head . . . because THIS *thud's for you!*

"No," he said. "No more hitting." His hands shuffled on the carpet. He made an effort to open his eyes, but a glue of drying blood had stuck them shut. "You're dead. Both of you are dead. You can't hit me, and you can't make me do things. Both of you are dead, and I want to be dead, too."

But he wasn't dead. Somewhere beyond these phantom voices he could hear the whine of jet engines . . . and that other sound. The sound of the langoliers on the march. On the *run.*

Craig, get up. You have to get up.

He realized that it wasn't the voice of his father, or of his mother, either. That had only been his poor, wounded mind trying to fool itself. This was a voice from . . . from

(above?)

some other place, some high bright place where pain was a myth and pressure was a dream.

Craig, they've come to you—all the people you wanted to see. They left Boston and came here. That's how important you are to them. You can still do it, Craig. You can still pull the pin. There's still time to hand in your papers and fall out of your father's army . . . if you're man enough to do it, that is.

If you're man enough to do it.

"Man enough?" he croaked. "*Man* enough? Whoever you are, you've *got* to be shitting me."

He tried again to open his eyes. The tacky blood holding them shut gave a little but would not let go. He managed to work one hand up to his face. It brushed the remains of his nose and he gave voice to a low, tired scream of pain. Inside his head the trumpets blared and the bees swarmed. He waited until the worst of the pain had subsided, then poked out two fingers and used them to pull his own eyelids up.

That corona of light was still there. It made a vaguely evocative shape in the gloom.

Slowly, a little at a time, Craig raised his head.

And saw *her.*

She stood within the corona of light.

It was the little girl, but her dark glasses were gone and she was looking at him, and her eyes were kind.

Come on, Craig. Get up. I know it's hard, but you have to get up— you have to. Because they are all here, they are all waiting . . . but they won't wait forever. The langoliers will see to that.

She was not standing on the floor, he saw. Her shoes appeared to float an inch or two above it, and the bright light was all around her. She was outlined in spectral radiance.

Come, Craig. Get up.

He started struggling to his feet. It was very hard. His sense of balance was almost gone, and it was hard to hold his head up—because, of course, it was full of angry honeybees. Twice he fell back, but each time he began again, mesmerized and entranced by the glowing girl with her kind eyes and her promise of ultimate release.

They are all waiting, Craig. For you.

They are waiting for you.

7

Dinah lay on the stretcher, watching with her blind eyes as Craig Toomy got to one knee, fell over on his side, then began trying to rise once more. Her heart was suffused with a terrible stern pity for this hurt and broken man, this murdering fish that only wanted to explode. On his ruined, bloody face she saw a terrible mixture of emotions: fear, hope, and a kind of merciless determination.

I'm sorry, Mr. Toomy, she thought. *In spite of what you did, I'm sorry. But we need you.*

Then called to him again, called with her own dying con-
sciousness:

Get up, Craig! Hurry! It's almost too late!

And she sensed that it was.

8

Once the longer of the two hoses was looped under the belly
of the 767 and attached to its fuel port, Brian returned to the
cockpit, cycled up the APUs, and went to work sucking the
727-400's fuel tanks dry. As he watched the LED readout on
his right tank slowly climb toward 24,000 pounds, he waited
tensely for the APUs to start chugging and lugging, trying to
eat fuel which would not burn.

The right tank had reached the 8,000-pound mark when he
heard the note of the small jet engines at the rear of the plane
change—they grew rough and labored.

"What's happening, mate?" Nick asked. He was sitting in
the co-pilot's chair again. His hair was disarrayed, and there
were wide streaks of grease and blood across his formerly natty
button-down shirt.

"The APU engines are getting a taste of the 727's fuel and
they don't like it," Brian said. "I hope Albert's magic works,
Nick, but I don't know."

Just before the LED reached 9,000 pounds in the right
tank, the first APU cut out. A red ENGINE SHUTDOWN light
appeared on Brian's board. He flicked the APU off.

"What can you do about it?" Nick asked, getting up and
coming to look over Brian's shoulder.

"Use the other three APUs to keep the pumps running and
hope," Brian said.

The second APU cut out thirty seconds later, and while
Brian was moving his hand to shut it down, the third went.
The cockpit lights went with it; now there was only the irreg-

217

ular chug of the hydraulic pumps and the lights on Brian's board, which were flickering. The last APU was roaring choppily, cycling up and down, shaking the plane.

"I'm shutting down completely," Brian said. He sounded harsh and strained to himself, a man who was way out of his depth and tiring fast in the undertow. "We'll have to wait for the Delta's fuel to join our plane's time-stream, or time-frame, or whatever the fuck it is. We can't go on like this. A strong power-surge before the last APU cuts out could wipe the INS clean. Maybe even fry it."

But as Brian reached for the switch, the engine's choppy note suddenly began to smooth out. He turned and stared at Nick unbelievingly. Nick looked back, and a big, slow grin lit his face.

"We might have lucked out, mate."

Brian raised his hands, crossed both sets of fingers, and shook them in the air. "I hope so," he said, and swung back to the boards. He flicked the switches marked APU 1,3, and 4. They kicked in smoothly. The cockpit lights flashed back on. The cabin bells binged. Nick whooped and clapped Brian on the back.

Bethany appeared in the doorway behind them. "What's happening? Is everything all right?"

"I think," Brian said without turning, "that we might just have a shot at this thing."

9

Craig finally managed to stand upright. The glowing girl now stood with her feet just above the luggage conveyor belt. She looked at him with a supernatural sweetness and something else . . . something he had longed for his whole life. What was it?

He groped for it, and at last it came to him.

It was compassion.

Compassion and understanding.

He looked around and saw that the darkness was draining away. That meant he had been out all night, didn't it? He didn't know. And it didn't matter. All that mattered was that the glowing girl had brought *them* to *him*—the investment bankers, the bond specialists, the commission-brokers, and the stock-rollers. They were here, they would want an explanation of just what young Mr. Craiggy-Weggy Toomy-Woomy had been up to, and here was the ecstatic truth: *monkey-business!* That was what he had been up to—yards and yards of monkey-business—*miles* of monkey-business. And when he told them that . . .

"They'll have to let me go . . . won't they?"

Yes, she said. *But you have to hurry, Craig. You have to hurry before they decide you're not coming and leave.*

Craig began to make his slow way forward. The girl's feet did not move, but as he approached her she floated backward like a mirage, toward the rubber strips which hung between the luggage-retrieval area and the loading dock outside.

And . . . oh, glorious: she was *smiling*.

10

They were all back on the plane now, all except Bob and Albert, who were sitting on the stairs and listening to the sound roll toward them in a slow, broken wave.

Laurel Stevenson was standing at the open forward door and looking at the terminal, still wondering what they were going to do about Mr. Toomy, when Bethany tugged the back of her blouse.

"Dinah is talking in her sleep, or something. I think she might be delirious. Can you come?"

Laurel came. Rudy Warwick was sitting across from Dinah, holding one of her hands and looking at her anxiously.

"I dunno," he said worriedly. "I dunno, but I think she might be going."

Laurel felt the girl's forehead. It was dry and very hot. The bleeding had either slowed down or stopped entirely, but the girl's respiration came in a series of pitiful whistling sounds. Blood was crusted around her mouth like strawberry sauce.

Laurel began, "I think—" and then Dinah said, quite clearly, "You have to hurry before they decide you're not coming and leave."

Laurel and Bethany exchanged puzzled, frightened glances.

"I think she's dreaming about that guy Toomy," Rudy told Laurel. "She said his name once."

"Yes," Dinah said. Her eyes were closed, but her head moved slightly and she appeared to listen. "Yes I will be," she said. "If you want me to, I will. But hurry. I know it hurts, but you have to hurry."

"She *is* delirious, isn't she?" Bethany whispered.

"No," Laurel said. "I don't think so. I think she might be . . . dreaming."

But that was not what she thought at all. What she really thought was that Dinah might be

(seeing)

doing something else. She didn't think she wanted to know what that something might be, although an idea whirled and danced far back in her mind. Laurel knew she could summon that idea if she wanted to, but she didn't. Because something creepy was going on here, *extremely* creepy, and she could not escape the idea that it *did* have something to do with

(don't kill him . . . we need him)

Mr. Toomy.

"Leave her alone," she said in a dry, abrupt tone of voice. "Leave her alone and let her

(do what she has to do to him)

sleep."

"God, I hope we take off soon," Bethany said miserably, and Rudy put a comforting arm around her shoulders.

11

Craig reached the conveyor belt and fell onto it. A white sheet of agony ripped through his head, his neck, his chest. He tried to remember what had happened to him and couldn't. He had run down the stalled escalator, he had hidden in a little room, he had sat tearing strips of paper in the dark . . . and that was where memory stopped.

He raised his head, hair hanging in his eyes, and looked at the glowing girl, who now sat cross-legged in front of the rubber strips, an inch off the conveyor belt. She was the most beautiful thing he had ever seen in his life; how could he ever have thought she was one of *them*?

"Are you an angel?" he croaked.

Yes, the glowing girl replied, and Craig felt his pain overwhelmed with joy. His vision blurred and then tears—the first ones he had ever cried as an adult—began to run slowly down his cheeks. Suddenly he found himself remembering his mother's sweet, droning, drunken voice as she sang that old song.

"Are you an angel of the morning? Will you be *my* angel of the morning?"

Yes—I will be. If you want me to, I will. But hurry. I know it hurts, Mr. Toomy, but you have to hurry.

"Yes," Craig sobbed, and began to crawl eagerly along the luggage conveyor belt toward her. Every movement sent fresh pain jig-jagging through him on irregular courses; blood dripped from his smashed nose and shattered mouth. Yet he still hurried as much as he could. Ahead of him, the little girl faded back through the hanging rubber strips, somehow not disturbing them at all as she went.

"Just touch my cheek before you leave me, baby," Craig said. He hawked up a spongy mat of blood, spat it on the wall where it clung like a dead spider, and tried to crawl faster.

12

To the east of the airport, a large cracking, rending sound filled the freakish morning. Bob and Albert got to their feet, faces pallid and filled with dreadful questions.

"What was that?" Albert asked.

"I think it was a tree," Bob replied, and licked his lips.

"But there's no wind!"

"No," Bob agreed. "There's no wind."

The noise had now become a moving barricade of splintered sound. Parts of it would seem to come into focus . . . and then drop back again just before identification was possible. At one moment Albert could swear he heard something barking, and then the barks . . . or yaps . . . or whatever they were . . . would be swallowed up by a brief sour humming sound like evil electricity. The only constants were the crunching and the steady drilling whine.

"What's happening?" Bethany called shrilly from behind them.

"Noth—" Albert began, and then Bob seized his shoulder and pointed.

"*Look!*" he shouted. "*Look over there!*"

Far to the east of them, on the horizon, a series of power pylons marched north and south across a high wooded ridge. As Albert looked, one of the pylons tottered like a toy and then fell over, pulling a snarl of power cables after it. A moment later another pylon went, and another, and another.

"That's not all, either," Albert said numbly. "Look at the trees. The trees over there are shaking like shrubs."

But they were not just shaking. As Albert and the others looked, the trees began to fall over, to disappear.

Crunch, smack, crunch, thud, BARK!

Crunch, smack, BARK!, thump, crunch.

"We have to get out of here," Bob said. He gripped Albert with both hands. His eyes were huge, avid with a kind of idiotic terror. The expression stood in sick, jagged contrast to his narrow, intelligent face. "I believe we have to get out of here *right now.*"

On the horizon, perhaps ten miles distant, the tall gantry of a radio tower trembled, rolled outward, and crashed down to disappear into the quaking trees. Now they could feel the very earth beginning to vibrate; it ran up the ladder and shook their feet in their shoes.

"Make it stop!" Bethany suddenly screamed from the doorway above them. She clapped her hands to her ears. "*Oh please make it STOP!*"

But the sound-wave rolled on toward them—the crunching, smacking, eating sound of the langoliers.

13

"I don't like to tease, Brian, but how much longer?" Nick's voice was taut. "There's a river about four miles east of here—I saw it when we were coming down—and I reckon whatever's coming is just now on the other side of it."

Brian glanced at his fuel readouts. 24,000 pounds in the right wing; 16,000 pounds in the left. It was going faster now that he didn't have to pump the Delta's fuel overwing to the other side.

"Fifteen minutes," he said. He could feel sweat standing out on his brow in big drops. "We've got to have more fuel, Nick, or we'll come down dead in the Mojave Desert. Another ten minutes to unhook, button up, and taxi out."

"You can't cut that? You're sure you can't cut that?"
Brian shook his head and turned back to his gauges.

14

Craig crawled slowly through the rubber strips, feeling them slide down his back like limp fingers. He emerged in the white, dead light of a new—and vastly shortened—day. The sound was terrible, overwhelming, the sound of an invading cannibal army. Even the sky seemed to shake with it, and for a moment fear froze him in place.

Look, his angel of the morning said, and pointed.

Craig looked . . . and forgot his fear. Beyond the American Pride 767, in a triangle of dead grass bounded by two taxiways and a runway, there was a long mahogany boardroom table. It gleamed brightly in the listless light. At each place were a yellow legal pad, a pitcher of ice water, and a Waterford glass. Sitting around the table were two dozen men in sober bankers' suits, and now they were all turning to look at him.

Suddenly they began to clap their hands. They stood and faced him, applauding his arrival. Craig felt a huge, grateful grin begin to stretch his face.

15

Dinah had been left alone in first class. Her breathing had become very labored now, and her voice was a strangled choke.

"Run to them, Craig! Quick! Quick!"

16

Craig tumbled off the conveyor, struck the concrete with a bone-rattling thump, and flailed to his feet. The pain no longer mattered. The angel had brought them! Of *course* she had brought them! Angels were like the ghosts in that story about Mr. Scrooge—they could do anything they wanted! The corona around her had begun to dim and she was fading out, but it didn't matter. She had brought his salvation: a net in which he was finally, blessedly caught.

Run to them, Craig! Run around the plane! Run away from the plane! Run to them now!

Craig began to run—a shambling stride that quickly became a crippled sprint. As he ran his head nodded up and down like a sunflower on a broken stalk. He ran toward humorless, unforgiving men who were his salvation, men who might have been fisher-folk standing in a boat beyond an unsuspected silver sky, retrieving their net to see what fabulous thing they had caught.

17

The LED readout for the left tank began to slow down when it reached 21,000 pounds, and by the time it topped 22,000 it had almost stopped. Brian understood what was happening and quickly flicked two switches, shutting down the hydraulic pumps. The 727-400 had given them what she had to give: a little over 46,000 pounds of jet-fuel. It would have to be enough.

"All right," he said, standing up.

"All right what?" Nick asked, also standing.

"We're uncoupling and getting the fuck out of here."

The approaching noise had reached deafening levels. Mixed

into the crunching smacking sound and the transmission squeal were falling trees and the dull crump of collapsing buildings. Just before shutting the pumps down he had heard a number of crackling thuds followed by a series of deep splashes. A bridge falling into the river Nick had seen, he imagined.

"Mr. Toomy!" Bethany screamed suddenly. "*It's Mr. Toomy!*"

Nick beat Brian out the door and into first class, but they were both in time to see Craig go shambling and lurching across the taxiway. He ignored the plane completely. His destination appeared to be an empty triangle of grass bounded by a pair of crisscrossing taxiways.

"What's he doing?" Rudy breathed.

"Never mind him," Brian said. "We're all out of time. Nick? Go down the ladder ahead of me. Hold me while I uncouple the hose." Brian felt like a man standing naked on a beach as a tidal wave humps up on the horizon and rushes toward the shore.

Nick followed him down and laid hold of Brian's belt again as Brian leaned out and twisted the nozzle of the hose, unlocking it. A moment later he yanked the hose free and dropped it to the cement, where the nozzle-ring clanged dully. Brian slammed the fuel-port door shut.

"Come on," he said after Nick had pulled him back. His face was dirty gray. "Let's get out of here."

But Nick did not move. He was frozen in place, staring to the east. His skin had gone the color of paper. On his face was an expression of dreamlike horror. His upper lip trembled, and in that moment he looked like a dog that is too frightened to snarl.

Brian turned his head slowly in that direction, hearing the tendons in his neck creak like a rusty spring on an old screen door as he did so. He turned his head and watched as the langoliers finally entered stage left.

18

"So you see," Craig said, approaching the empty chair at the head of the table and standing before the men seated around it, "the brokers with whom I did business were not only unscrupulous; many of them were actually CIA plants whose job it was to contact and fake out just such bankers as myself—men looking to fill up skinny portfolios in a hurry. As far as they are concerned, the end—keeping communism out of South America—justifies any available means."

"What procedures did you follow to check these fellows out?" a fat man in an expensive blue suit asked. "Did you use a bond-insurance company, or does your bank retain a specific investigation firm in such cases?" Blue Suit's round, jowly face was perfectly shaved; his cheeks glowed with either good health or forty years of Scotch and sodas; his eyes were merciless chips of blue ice. They were wonderful eyes; they were father-eyes.

Somewhere, far away from this boardroom two floors below the top of the Prudential Center, Craig could hear a hell of a racket going on. Road construction, he supposed. There was always road construction going on in Boston, and he suspected that most of it was unnecessary, that in most cases it was just the old, old story—the unscrupulous taking cheerful advantage of the unwary. It had nothing to do with him. Nothing whatever. His job was to deal with the man in the blue suit, and he couldn't wait to get started.

"We're waiting, Craig," the president of his own banking institution said. Craig felt momentary surprise—Mr. Parker hadn't been scheduled to attend this meeting—and then the feeling was overwhelmed by happiness.

"*No procedures at all!*" he screamed joyfully into their shocked faces. "*I just bought and bought and bought! I followed* NO . . . *PROCEDURES . . . AT ALL!*"

He was about to go on, to elaborate on this theme, to really *expound* on it, when a sound stopped him. *This* sound was not miles away; this sound was close, very close, perhaps in the boardroom itself.

A whickering chopping sound, like dry hungry teeth.

Suddenly Craig felt a deep need to tear some paper—any paper would do. He reached for the legal pad in front of his place at the table, but the pad was gone. So was the table. So were the bankers. So was *Boston*.

"Where *am* I?" he asked in a small, perplexed voice, and looked around. Suddenly he realized . . . and suddenly he saw *them*.

The langoliers had come.

They had come for *him*.

Craig Toomy began to scream.

19

Brian could see them, but could not understand what it was he was seeing. In some strange way they seemed to *defy* seeing, and he sensed his frantic, overstressed mind trying to change the incoming information, to make the shapes which had begun to appear at the east end of Runway 21 into something it could understand.

At first there were only two shapes, one black, one a dark tomato red.

Are they balls? his mind asked doubtfully. *Could they be balls?*

Something actually seemed to *click* in the center of his head and they *were* balls, sort of like beachballs, but balls which rippled and contracted and then expanded again, as if he was seeing them through a heat-haze. They came bowling out of the high dead grass at the end of Runway 21, leaving cut swaths of blackness behind them. They were somehow cutting the grass—

228

No, his mind reluctantly denied. *They are not just cutting the grass, and you know it. They are cutting a lot more than the grass.*

What they left behind were narrow lines of perfect blackness. And now, as they raced playfully down the white concrete at the end of the runway, they were *still* leaving narrow dark tracks behind. They glistened like tar.

No, his mind reluctantly denied. *Not tar. You know what that blackness is. It's nothing. Nothing at all. They are eating a lot more than the surface of the runway.*

There was something malignantly joyful about their behavior. They crisscrossed each other's paths, leaving a wavery black X on the outer taxiway. They bounced high in the air, did an exuberant, crisscrossing maneuver, and then raced straight for the plane.

As they did, Brian screamed and Nick screamed beside him. *Faces* lurked below the surfaces of the racing balls—monstrous, alien faces. They shimmered and twitched and wavered like faces made of glowing swamp-gas. The eyes were only rudimentary indentations, but the mouths were huge: semicircular caves lined with gnashing, blurring teeth.

They ate as they came, rolling up narrow strips of the world.

A Texaco fuel truck was parked on the outer taxiway. The langoliers pounced upon it, high-speed teeth whirring and crunching and bulging out of their blurred bodies. They went through it without pause. One of them burrowed a path directly through the rear tires, and for a moment, before the tires collapsed, Brian could see the shape it had cut—a shape like a cartoon mouse-hole in a cartoon baseboard.

The other leaped high, disappeared for a moment behind the Texaco truck's boxy tank, and then blasted straight through, leaving a metal-ringed hole from which av-gas sprayed in a dull amber flood. They struck the ground, bounced as if on springs, crisscrossed again, and raced on toward the airplane. Reality peeled away in narrow strips beneath them, peeled away wherever and whatever they touched, and as they neared, Brian realized that they were unzipping more than the world—they were opening all the depths of forever.

They reached the edge of the tarmac and paused. They jittered uncertainly in place for a moment, looking like the bouncing balls that hopped over the words in old movie-house sing-alongs.

Then they turned and zipped off in a new direction.

Zipped off in the direction of Craig Toomy, who stood watching them and screaming into the white day.

With a huge effort, Brian snapped the paralysis which held him. He elbowed Nick, who was still frozen below him. "Come on!" Nick didn't move and Brian drove his elbow back harder this time, connecting solidly with Nick's forehead. "Come on, I said! Move your ass! *We're getting out of here!*"

Now more black and red balls were appearing at the edge of the airport. They bounced, danced, circled . . . and then raced toward them.

20

You can't get away from them, his father had said, *because of their legs. Their fast little legs.*

Craig tried, nevertheless.

He turned and ran for the terminal, casting horrified, grimacing looks behind him as he did. His shoes rattled on the pavement. He ignored the American Pride 767, which was now cycling up again, and ran for the luggage area instead.

No, Craig, his father said. *You may* THINK *you're running, but you're not. You know what you're really doing—you're* SCAMPERING!

Behind him the two ball-shapes sped up, closing the gap with effortless, happy speed. They crisscrossed twice, just a pair of daffy showoffs in a dead world, leaving spiky lines of blackness behind them. They rolled after Craig about seven inches apart, creating what looked like negative ski-tracks behind their weird, shimmering bodies. They caught him twenty feet from the luggage conveyor belt and chewed off his feet in a millisecond. At one moment his briskly scampering feet were there. At the next, Craig was three inches shorter; his feet, along with his expensive Bally loafers, had simply ceased to exist. There was no blood; the wounds were cauterized instantly in the langoliers' scorching passage.

Craig didn't know his feet had ceased to exist. He scampered on the stumps of his ankles, and as the first pain began to sizzle up his legs, the langoliers banked in a tight turn and came back, rolling up the pavement side by side. Their trails crossed twice this time, creating a crescent of cement bordered in black, like a depiction of the moon in a child's coloring book. Only this crescent began to *sink,* not into the earth—for there appeared to be no earth beneath the surface—but into nowhere at all.

This time the langoliers bounced upward in perfect tandem and clipped Craig off at the knees. He came down, still trying to run, and then fell sprawling, waving his stumps. His scampering days were over.

"*No!*" he screamed. "*No, Daddy! No! I'll be good! Please make them go away! I'll be good, I SWEAR I'LL BE GOOD FROM NOW ON IF YOU JUST MAKE THEM GO AW—*"

Then they rushed at him again, gibbering yammering buzzing whining, and he saw the frozen machine blur of their gnashing teeth and felt the hot bellows of their frantic, blind vitality in the half-instant before they began to cut him apart in random chunks.

His last thought was: *How can their little legs be fast? They* have *no le*

21

Scores of the black things had now appeared, and Laurel understood that soon there would be hundreds, thousands, millions, billions. Even with the jet engines screaming through the open forward door as Brian pulled the 767 away from the ladder and the wing of the Delta jet, she could hear their yammering, inhuman cry.

Great looping coils of blackness crisscrossed the end of Runway 21—and then the tracks narrowed toward the terminal, converging as the balls making them rushed toward Craig Toomy.

I guess they don't get live meat very often, she thought, and suddenly felt like vomiting.

Nick Hopewell slammed the forward door after one final, unbelieving glance and dogged it shut. He began to stagger back down the aisle, swaying from side to side like a drunk as he came. His eyes seemed to fill his whole face. Blood streamed down his chin; he had bitten his lower lip deeply. He put his arms around Laurel and buried his burning face in the hollow where her neck met her shoulder. She put her arms around him and held him tight.

22

In the cockpit, Brian powered up as fast as he dared, and sent the 767 charging along the taxiway at a suicidal rate of speed. The eastern edge of the airport was now black with the invading balls; the end of Runway 21 had completely disappeared and the world beyond it was going. In that direction the white, unmoving sky now arched down over a world of scrawled black lines and fallen trees.

As the plane neared the end of the taxiway, Brian grabbed the microphone and shouted: "Belt in! Belt in! If you're not belted in, hold on!"

He slowed marginally, then slewed the 767 onto Runway 33. As he did so he saw something which made his mind cringe and wail: huge sections of the world which lay to the east of the runway, huge irregular pieces of *reality itself,* were falling into the ground like freight elevators, leaving big senseless chunks of emptiness behind.

They are eating the world, he thought. *My God, my dear God, they are eating the world.*

Then the entire airfield was turning in front of him and Flight 29 was pointed west again, with Runway 33 lying open and long and deserted before it.

23

Overhead compartments burst open when the 767 swerved onto the runway, spraying carry-on luggage across the main cabin in a deadly hail. Bethany, who hadn't had time to fasten her seatbelt, was hurled into Albert Kaussner's lap. Albert noticed neither his lapful of warm girl nor the attaché case that caromed off the curved wall three feet in front of his nose. He saw only the dark, speeding shapes rushing across Runway 21 to the left of them, and the glistening dark tracks they left behind. These tracks converged in a giant well of blackness where the luggage-unloading area had been.

They are being drawn to Mr. Toomy, he thought, *or to where Mr. Toomy was. If he hadn't come out of the terminal, they would have chosen the airplane instead. They would have eaten it—and us inside it—from the wheels up.*

Behind him, Bob Jenkins spoke in a trembling, awed voice. "Now we know, don't we?"

"*What?*" Laurel screamed in an odd, breathless voice she did not recognize as her own. A duffel-bag landed in her lap; Nick raised his head, let go of her, and batted it absently into the aisle. "*What do we know?*"

"Why, what happens to today when it becomes yesterday, what happens to the present when it becomes the past. It waits—dead and empty and deserted. It waits for *them.* It waits for the time-keepers of eternity, always running along behind, cleaning up the mess in the most efficient way possible . . . by eating it."

"Mr. Toomy knew about them," Dinah said in a clear, dreaming voice. "Mr. Toomy says they are the langoliers." Then the jet engines cycled up to full power and the plane charged down Runway 33.

24

Brian saw two of the balls zip across the runway ahead of him, peeling back the surface of reality in a pair of parallel tracks which gleamed like polished ebony. It was too late to stop. The 767 shuddered like a dog with a chill as it raced over the empty places, but he was able to hold it on the runway. He shoved his throttles forward, burying them, and watched his ground-speed indicator rise toward the commit point.

Even now he could hear those manic chewing, gobbling sounds . . . although he did not know if they were in his ears or only his reeling mind. And did not care.

25

Leaning over Laurel to look out the window, Nick saw the Bangor International terminal sliced, diced, chopped, and channelled. It tottered in its various jigsaw pieces and then began to tumble into loony chasms of darkness.

Bethany Simms screamed. A black track was speeding along next to the 767, chewing up the edge of the runway. Suddenly it jagged to the right and disappeared underneath the plane.

There was another terrific bump.

"Did it get us?" Nick shouted. *"Did it get us?"*

No one answered him. Their pale, terrified faces stared out

the windows and no one answered him. Trees rushed by in a gray-green blur. In the cockpit, Brian sat tensely forward in his seat, waiting for one of those balls to bounce up in front of the cockpit window and bullet through. None did.

On his board, the last red lights turned green. Brian hauled back on the yoke and the 767 was airborne again.

26

In the main cabin, a black-bearded man with bloodshot eyes staggered forward, blinking owlishly at his fellow travellers. "Are we almost in Boston yet?" he inquired at large. "I hope so, because I want to go back to bed. I've got one *bastard* of a headache."

CHAPTER NINE

GOODBYE TO BANGOR. HEADING WEST
THROUGH DAYS AND NIGHTS. SEEING THROUGH
THE EYES OF OTHERS. THE ENDLESS GULF. THE RIP.
THE WARNING. BRIAN'S DECISION. THE LANDING.
SHOOTING STARS ONLY.

1

The plane banked heavily east, throwing the man with the black beard into a row of empty seats three-quarters of the way up the main cabin. He looked around at all the other empty seats with a wide, frightened gaze, and squeezed his eyes shut. "Jesus," he muttered. "DTs. Fucking DTs. This is the worst they've ever been." He looked around fearfully. "The bugs come next . . . where's the motherfuckin bugs?"

No bugs, Albert thought, *but wait till you see the balls. You're going to love those.*

"Buckle yourself in, mate," Nick said, "and shut u—"

He broke off, staring down incredulously at the airport . . . or where the airport had been. The main buildings were gone, and the National Guard base at the west end was going. Flight 29 overflew a growing abyss of darkness, an eternal cistern that seemed to have no end.

"Oh dear Jesus, Nick," Laurel said unsteadily, and suddenly put her hands over her eyes.

As they overflew Runway 33 at 1,500 feet, Nick saw sixty or a hundred parallel lines racing up the concrete, cutting the runway into long strips that sank into emptiness. The strips reminded him of Craig Toomy:

Rii-ip.

On the other side of the aisle, Bethany pulled down the windowshade beside Albert's seat with a bang.

"Don't you dare open that!" she told him in a scolding, hysterical voice.

"Don't worry," Albert said, and suddenly remembered that he had left his violin down there. Well . . . it was undoubtedly gone now. He abruptly put his hands over his own face.

2

Before Brian began to turn west again, he saw what lay east of Bangor. It was nothing. Nothing at all. A titanic river of blackness lay in a still sweep from horizon to horizon under the white dome of the sky. The trees were gone, the city was gone, the earth itself was gone.

This is what it must be like to fly in outer space, he thought, and he felt his rationality slip a cog, as it had on the trip east. He held onto himself desperately and made himself concentrate on flying the plane.

He brought them up quickly, wanting to be in the clouds, wanting that hellish vision to be blotted out. Then Flight 29 was pointed west again. In the moments before they entered the clouds, he saw the hills and woods and lakes which stretched to the west of the city, saw them being cut ruthlessly apart by thousands of black spiderweb lines. He saw huge swatches of reality go sliding soundlessly into the growing mouth of the abyss, and Brian did something he had never done before while in the cockpit of an airplane.

He closed his eyes. When he opened them again they were in the clouds.

3

There was almost no turbulence this time; as Bob Jenkins had suggested, the weather patterns appeared to be running down like an old clock. Ten minutes after entering the clouds, Flight 29 emerged into the bright-blue world which began at 18,000 feet. The remaining passengers looked around at each other nervously, then at the speakers as Brian came on the intercom.

"We're up," he said simply. "You all know what happens now: we go back exactly the way we came, and hope that whatever doorway we came through is still there. If it is, we'll try going through."

He paused for a moment, then resumed.

"Our return flight is going to take somewhere between four and a half and six hours. I'd like to be more exact, but I can't. Under ordinary circumstances, the flight west usually takes longer than the flight east, because of prevailing wind conditions, but so far as I can tell from my cockpit instruments, there *is* no wind." Brian paused for a moment and then added, "There's nothing moving up here but us." For a moment the intercom stayed on, as if Brian meant to add something else, and then it clicked off.

4

"What in God's name is going on here?" the man with the black beard asked shakily.

Albert looked at him for a moment and then said, "I don't think you want to know."

"Am I in the hospital again?" The man with the black beard blinked at Albert fearfully, and Albert felt sudden sympathy for him.

"Well, why don't you believe you are, if it will help?"

The man with the black beard continued to stare at him for a moment in dreadful fascination and then announced, "I'm going back to sleep. Right now." He reclined his seat and closed his eyes. In less than a minute his chest was moving up and down with deep regularity and he was snoring under his breath.

Albert envied him.

5

Nick gave Laurel a brief hug, then unbuckled his seatbelt and stood up. "I'm going forward," he said. "Want to come?"

Laurel shook her head and pointed across the aisle at Dinah. "I'll stay with her."

"There's nothing you can do, you know," Nick said. "It's in God's hands now, I'm afraid."

"I do know that," she said, "but I want to stay."

"All right, Laurel." He brushed at her hair gently with the palm of his hand. "It's such a pretty name. You deserve it."

She glanced up at him and smiled. "Thank you."

"We have a dinner date—you haven't forgotten, have you?"

"No," she said, still smiling. "I haven't and I won't."

He bent down and brushed a kiss lightly across her mouth. "Good," he said. "Neither will I."

He went forward and she pressed her fingers lightly against her mouth, as if to hold his kiss there, where it belonged. Dinner with Nick Hopewell—a dark, mysterious stranger. Maybe with candles and a good bottle of wine. More kisses afterward—real kisses. It all seemed like something which might happen in one of the Harlequin romances she sometimes read. So what? They were pleasant stories, full of sweet and harmless dreams. It didn't hurt to dream a little, did it?

Of course not. But why did she feel the dream was so unlikely to come true?

239

She unbuckled her own seatbelt, crossed the aisle, and put her hand on the girl's forehead. The hectic heat she had felt before was gone; Dinah's skin was now waxy-cool.

I think she's going, Rudy had said shortly before they started their headlong take-off charge. Now the words recurred to Laurel and rang in her head with sickening validity. Dinah was taking air in shallow sips, her chest barely rising and falling beneath the strap which cinched the tablecloth pad tight over her wound.

Laurel brushed the girl's hair off her forehead with infinite tenderness and thought of that strange moment in the restaurant, when Dinah had reached out and grasped the cuff of Nick's jeans. *Don't you kill him . . . we need him.*

Did you save us, Dinah? Did you do something to Mr. Toomy that saved us? Did you make him somehow trade his life for ours?

She thought that perhaps something like that had happened . . . and reflected that, if it was true, this little girl, blind and badly wounded, had made a dreadful decision inside her darkness.

She leaned forward and kissed each of Dinah's cool, closed lids. "Hold on," she whispered. "Please hold on, Dinah."

6

Bethany turned to Albert, grasped both of his hands in hers, and asked: "What happens if the fuel goes bad?"

Albert looked at her seriously and kindly. "You know the answer to that, Bethany."

"You can call me Beth, if you want."

"Okay."

She fumbled out her cigarettes, looked up at the NO SMOK-ING light, and put them away again. "Yeah," she said. "I know. We crash. End of story. And do you know what?"

He shook his head, smiling a little.

"If we can't find that hole again, I hope Captain Engle won't even try to land the plane. I hope he just picks out a nice high mountain and crashes us into the top of it. Did you see what happened to that crazy guy? I don't want that to happen to me."

She shuddered, and Albert put an arm around her. She looked up at him frankly. "Would you like to kiss me?"

"Yes," Albert said.

"Well, you better go ahead, then. The later it gets, the later it gets."

Albert went ahead. It was only the third time in his life that the fastest Hebrew west of the Mississippi had kissed a girl, and it was great. He could spend the whole trip back in a lip-lock with this girl and never worry about a thing.

"Thank you," she said, and put her head on his shoulder. "I needed that."

"Well, if you need it again, just ask," Albert said.

She looked up at him, amused. "Do you *need* me to ask, Albert?"

"I reckon not," drawled The Arizona Jew, and went back to work.

7

Nick had stopped on his way to the cockpit to speak to Bob Jenkins—an extremely nasty idea had occurred to him, and he wanted to ask the writer about it.

"Do you think there could be any of those things up here?"

Bob thought it over for a moment. "Judging from what we saw back at Bangor, I would think not. But it's hard to tell, isn't it? In a thing like this, all bets are off."

"Yes. I suppose so. All bets are off." Nick thought this over for a moment. "What about this time-rip of yours? Would you like to give odds on us finding it again?"

Bob Jenkins slowly shook his head.

Rudy Warwick spoke up from behind them, startling them both. "You didn't ask me, but I'll give you my opinion just the same. I put them at one in a thousand."

Nick thought this over. After a moment a rare, radiant smile burst across his face. "Not bad odds at all," he said. "Not when you consider the alternative."

8

Less than forty minutes later, the blue sky through which Flight 29 moved began to deepen in color. It cycled slowly to indigo, and then to deep purple. Sitting in the cockpit, monitoring his instruments and wishing for a cup of coffee, Brian thought of an old song: *When the deep purple falls . . . over sleepy garden walls . . .*

No garden walls up here, but he could see the first ice-chip stars gleaming in the firmament. There was something reassuring and calming about the old constellations appearing, one by one, in their old places. He did not know how they could be the same when so many other things were so badly out of joint, but he was very glad they were.

"It's going faster, isn't it?" Nick said from behind him.

Brian turned in his seat to face him. "Yes. It is. After awhile the 'days' and 'nights' will be passing as fast as a camera shutter can click, I think."

Nick sighed. "And now we do the hardest thing of all, don't we? We wait to see what happens. And pray a little bit, I suppose."

"It couldn't hurt." Brian took a long, measuring look at Nick Hopewell. "I was on my way to Boston because my ex-wife died in a stupid fire. Dinah was going because a bunch of doctors promised her a new pair of eyes. Bob was going to a convention, Albert to music school, Laurel on vacation. Why were you going to Boston, Nick? 'Fess up. The hour groweth late."

Nick looked at him thoughtfully for a long time and then laughed. "Well, why not?" he asked, but Brian was not so foolish as to believe this question was directed at him. "What does a Most Secret classification mean when you've just seen a bunch of killer fuzzballs rolling up the world like an old rug?"

He laughed again.

"The United States hasn't exactly cornered the market on dirty tricks and covert operations," he told Brian. "We Limeys have forgotten more nasty mischief than you johnnies ever knew. We've cut capers in India, South Africa, China, and the part of Palestine which became Israel. We certainly got into a pissing contest with the wrong fellows that time, didn't we? Nevertheless, we British are great believers in cloak and dagger, and the fabled MI5 isn't where it ends but only where it begins. I spent eighteen years in the armed services, Brian—the last five of them in Special Operations. Since then I've done various odd jobs, some innocuous, some fabulously nasty."

It was full dark outside now, the stars gleaming like spangles on a woman's formal evening gown.

"I was in Los Angeles—on vacation, actually—when I was contacted and told to fly to Boston. Extremely short notice, this was, and after four days spent backpacking in the San Gabriels, I was falling-down tired. That's why I happened to be sound asleep when Mr. Jenkins's Event happened.

"There's a man in Boston, you see . . . or was . . . or will be (time-travel plays hell on the old verb tenses, doesn't it?) . . . who is a politician of some note. The sort of fellow who moves and shakes with great vigor behind the scenes. This man—I'll call him Mr. O'Banion, for the sake of conversation—is very rich, Brian, and he is an enthusiastic supporter of the Irish Republican Army. He has channelled millions of dollars into what some like to call Boston's favorite charity, and there is a good deal of blood on his hands. Not just British soldiers but children in schoolyards, women in laundrettes, and babies blown out of their prams in pieces. He is an idealist of the most dangerous sort: one who never has to view the carnage at first hand, one who has never had to look at a severed leg lying in the gutter and been forced to reconsider his actions in light of that experience."

"You were supposed to kill this man O'Banion?"

"Not unless I had to," Nick said calmly. "He's very wealthy, but that's not the only problem. He's the total politician, you see, and he's got more fingers than the one he uses to stir the pot in Ireland. He has a great many powerful American friends, and some of his friends are our friends . . . that's the nature of politics; a cat's cradle woven by men who for the most part belong in rooms with rubber walls. Killing Mr. O'Banion would be a great political risk. But he keeps a little bit of fluff on the side. *She* was the one I was supposed to kill."

"As a warning," Brian said in a low, fascinated voice.

"Yes. As a warning."

Almost a full minute passed as the two men sat in the cockpit, looking at each other. The only sound was the sleepy drone of the jet engines. Brian's eyes were shocked and somehow very young. Nick only looked weary.

"If we get out of this," Brian said at last, "if we get back, will you carry through with it?"

Nick shook his head. He did this slowly, but with great finality. "I believe I've had what the Adventist blokes like to call a soul conversion, old mate of mine. No more midnight creeps or extreme-prejudice jobs for Mrs. Hopewell's boy Nicholas. If we get out of this—a proposition I find rather shaky just now—I believe I'll retire."

"And do what?"

Nick looked at him thoughtfully for a moment or two and then said, "Well . . . I suppose I could take flying lessons."

Brian burst out laughing. After a moment, Mrs. Hopewell's boy Nicholas joined him.

9

Thirty-five minutes later, daylight began to seep back into the main cabin of Flight 29. Three minutes later it might have been mid-morning; fifteen minutes after that it might have been noon.

Laurel looked around and saw that Dinah's sightless eyes were open.

Yet were they *entirely* sightless? There was something in them, something just beyond definition, which made Laurel wonder. She felt a sense of unknown awe creep into her, a feeling which almost touched upon fear.

She reached out and gently grasped one of Dinah's hands. "Don't try to talk," she said quietly. "If you're awake, Dinah, don't try to talk—just listen. We're in the air. We're going back, and you're going to be all right—I promise you that."

Dinah's hand tightened on hers, and after a moment Laurel realized the little girl was tugging her forward. She leaned over the secured stretcher. Dinah spoke in a tiny voice that seemed to Laurel a perfect scale model of her former voice.

"Don't worry about me, Laurel. I got . . . what I wanted."

"Dinah, you shouldn't—"

The unseeing brown eyes moved toward the sound of Laurel's voice. A little smile touched Dinah's bloody mouth. "I *saw*," that tiny voice, frail as a glass reed, told her. "I saw through Mr. Toomy's eyes. At the beginning, and then again at the end. It was better at the end. At the start, everything looked mean and nasty to him. It was better at the end."

Laurel looked at her with helpless wonder.

The girl's hand let go of Laurel's and rose waveringly to touch her cheek. "He wasn't such a bad guy, you know." She coughed. Small flecks of blood flew from her mouth.

"Please, Dinah," Laurel said. She had a sudden sensation that she could almost see through the little blind girl, and this

245

brought a feeling of stifling, directionless panic. "Please don't try to talk anymore."

Dinah smiled. "I saw *you,*" she said. "You are beautiful, Laurel. *Everything* was beautiful . . . even the things that were dead. It was so wonderful to . . . you know . . . just to *see.*"

She drew in one of her tiny sips of air, let it out, and simply didn't take the next one. Her sightless eyes now seemed to be looking far beyond Laurel Stevenson.

"Please breathe, Dinah," Laurel said. She took the girl's hands in hers and began to kiss them repeatedly, as if she could kiss life back into that which was now beyond it. It was not fair for Dinah to die after she had saved them all; no God could demand such a sacrifice, not even for people who had somehow stepped outside of time itself. "Please breathe, please, please, please breathe."

But Dinah did not breathe. After a long time, Laurel returned the girl's hands to her lap and looked fixedly into her pale, still face. Laurel waited for her own eyes to fill up with tears, but no tears came. Yet her heart ached with fierce sorrow and her mind beat with its own deep and outraged protest: *Oh, no! Oh, not fair! This is not fair! Take it back, God! Take it back, damn you, take it back, you just take it BACK!*

But God did not take it back. The jet engines throbbed steadily, the sun shone on the bloody sleeve of Dinah's good travelling dress in a bright oblong, and God did not take it back. Laurel looked across the aisle and saw Albert and Bethany kissing. Albert was touching one of the girl's breasts through her tee-shirt, lightly, delicately, almost religiously. They seemed to make a ritual shape, a symbolic representation of life and that stubborn, intangible spark which carries life on in the face of the most dreadful reversals and ludicrous turns of fate. Laurel looked hopefully from them to Dinah . . . and God had not taken it back.

God had not taken it back.

Laurel kissed the still slope of Dinah's cheek and then raised her hand to the little girl's face. Her fingers stopped only an inch from her eyelids.

I saw through Mr. Toomy's eyes. Everything was beautiful . . . even the things that were dead. It was so wonderful to see.

"Yes," Laurel said. "I can live with that."

She left Dinah's eyes open.

10

American Pride 29 flew west through the days and nights, going from light to darkness and light to darkness as if flying through a great, lazily shifting parade of fat clouds. Each cycle came slightly faster than the one before.

A little over three hours into the flight, the clouds below them ceased, and over exactly the same spot where they had begun on the flight east. Brian was willing to bet the front had not moved so much as a single foot. The Great Plains lay below them in a silent roan-colored expanse of land.

"No sign of them over here," Rudy Warwick said. He did not have to specify what he was talking about.

"No," Bob Jenkins agreed. "We seem to have outrun them, either in space or in time."

"Or in both," Albert put in.

"Yes—or both."

But they had not. As Flight 29 crossed the Rockies, they began to see the black lines below them again, thin as threads from this height. They shot up and down the rough, slabbed slopes and drew not-quite-meaningless patterns in the blue-gray carpet of trees. Nick stood at the forward door, looking out of the bullet porthole set into it. This porthole had a queer magnifying effect, and he soon discovered he could see better than he really wanted to. As he watched, two of the black lines split, raced around a jagged, snow-tipped peak, met on the far side, crossed, and raced down the other slope in diverg-

247

ing directions. Behind them the entire top of the mountain fell into itself, leaving something which looked like a volcano with a vast dead caldera at its truncated top.

"Jumping Jiminy Jesus," Nick muttered, and passed a quivering hand over his brow.

As they crossed the Western Slope toward Utah, the dark began to come down again. The setting sun threw an orange-red glare over a fragmented hellscape that none of them could look at for long; one by one, they followed Bethany's example and pulled their windowshades. Nick went back to his seat on unsteady legs and dropped his forehead into one cold, clutching hand. After a moment or two he turned toward Laurel and she took him wordlessly in her arms.

Brian was forced to look at it. There were no shades in the cockpit.

Western Colorado and eastern Utah fell into the pit of eternity piece by jagged piece below him and ahead of him. Mountains, buttes, mesas, and cols one by one ceased to exist as the crisscrossing langoliers cut them adrift from the rotting fabric of this dead past, cut them loose and sent them tumbling into sunless endless gulfs of forever. There was no sound up here, and somehow that was the most horrible thing of all. The land below them disappeared as silently as dust-motes.

Then darkness came like an act of mercy and for a little while he could concentrate on the stars. He clung to them with the fierceness of panic, the only real things left in this horrible world: Orion the hunter; Pegasus, the great shimmering horse of midnight; Cassiopeia in her starry chair.

11

Half an hour later the sun rose again, and Brian felt his sanity give a deep shudder and slide closer to the edge of its own abyss. The world below was gone; utterly and finally gone.

The deepening blue sky was a dome over a cyclopean ocean of deepest, purest ebony.

The world had been torn from beneath Flight 29.

Bethany's thought had also crossed Brian's mind; if push came to shove, if worse came to worst, he had thought, he could put the 767 into a dive and crash them into a mountain, ending it for good and all. But now there were no mountains to crash into.

Now there was no *earth* to crash into.

What will happen to us if we can't find the rip again? he wondered. *What will happen if we run out of fuel? Don't try to tell me we'll crash, because I simply don't believe it—you can't crash into nothing. I think we'll simply fall . . . and fall . . . and fall. For how long? And how far? How far can you fall into nothing?*

Don't think about it.

But how, exactly, did one do that? How did one refuse to think about nothing?

He turned deliberately back to his sheet of calculations. He worked on them, referring frequently to the INS readout, until the light had begun to fade out of the sky again. He now put the elapsed time between sunrise and sunset at about twenty-eight minutes.

He reached for the switch that controlled the cabin intercom and opened the circuit.

"Nick? Can you come up front?"

Nick appeared in the cockpit doorway less than thirty seconds later.

"Have they got their shades pulled back there?" Brian asked him before he could come all the way in.

"You better believe it," Nick said.

"Very wise of them. I'm going to ask you not to look down yet, if you can help it. I'll *want* you to look out in a few minutes, and once you look out I don't suppose you'll be able to help looking down, but I advise you to put it off as long as possible. It's not . . . very nice."

"Gone, is it?"

"Yes. Everything."

"The little girl is gone, too. Dinah. Laurel was with her at the end. She's taking it very well. She liked that girl. So did I."

Brian nodded. He was not surprised—the girl's wound was the sort that demanded immediate treatment in an emergency room, and even then the prognosis would undoubtedly be cloudy—but it still rolled a stone against his heart. He had also liked Dinah, and he believed what Laurel believed—that the girl was somehow more responsible for their continued survival than anyone else. She had done something to Mr. Toomy, had used him in some strange way . . . and Brian had an idea that, somewhere inside, Toomy would not have minded being used in such a fashion. So, if her death was an omen, it was one of the worst sort.

"She never got her operation," he said.

"No."

"But Laurel is okay?"

"More or less."

"You like her, don't you?"

"Yes," Nick said. "I have mates who would laugh at that, but I do like her. She's a bit dewy-eyed, but she's got grit."

Brian nodded. "Well, if we get back, I wish you the best of luck."

"Thanks." Nick sat down in the co-pilot's seat again. "I've been thinking about the question you asked me before. About what I'll do when and if we get out of this mess . . . besides taking the lovely Laurel to dinner, that is. I suppose I might end up going after Mr. O'Banion after all. As I see it, he's not all that much different from our friend Toomy."

"Dinah asked you to spare Mr. Toomy," Brian pointed out. "Maybe that's something you should add into the equation."

Nick nodded. He did this as if his head had grown too heavy for his neck. "Maybe it is."

"Listen, Nick. I called you up front because if Bob's time-rip actually exists, we've got to be getting close to the place where we went through it. We're going to man the crow's nest together, you and I. You take the starboard side and right center; I'll take port and left center. If you see anything that looks like a time-rip, sing out."

Nick gazed at Brian with wide, innocent eyes. "Are we looking for a thingumabob-type time-rip, or do you think it'll be one of the more or less fuckadelic variety, mate?"

"Very funny." Brian felt a grin touch his lips in spite of himself. "I don't have the slightest idea what it's going to look like or even if we'll be able to see it at all. If we can't, we're going to be in a hell of a jam if it's drifted to one side, or if its altitude has changed. Finding a needle in a haystack would be child's play in comparison."

"What about radar?"

Brian pointed to the RCA/TL color radar monitor. "Nothing, as you can see. But that's not surprising. If the original crew had acquired the damned thing on radar, they never would have gone through it in the first place."

"They wouldn't have gone through it if they'd seen it, either," Nick pointed out gloomily.

"That's not necessarily true. They might have seen it too late to avoid it. Jetliners move fast, and airplane crews don't spend the entire flight searching the sky for bogies. They don't have to; that's what ground control is for. Thirty or thirty-five minutes into the flight, the crew's major outbound tasks are completed. The bird is up, it's out of L.A. airspace, the anti-collision honker is on and beeping every ninety seconds to show it's working. The INS is all programmed—that happens before the bird ever leaves the ground—and it is telling the autopilot just what to do. From the look of the cockpit, the pilot and co-pilot were on their coffee break. They could have been sitting here, facing each other, talking about the last movie they saw or how much they dropped at Hollywood Park. If there had been a flight attendant up front just before

The Event took place, there would at least have been one more set of eyes, but we know there wasn't. The male crew had their coffee and Danish; the flight attendants were getting ready to serve drinks to the passengers when it happened."

"That's an extremely detailed scenario," Nick said. "Are you trying to convince me or yourself?"

"At this point, I'll settle for convincing anyone at all."

Nick smiled and stepped to the starboard cockpit window. His eyes dropped involuntarily downward, toward the place where the ground belonged, and his smile first froze, then dropped off his face. His knees buckled, and he gripped the bulkhead with one hand to steady himself.

"Shit on toast," he said in a tiny dismayed voice.

"Not very nice, is it?"

Nick looked around at Brian. His eyes seemed to float in his pallid face. "All my life," he said, "I've thought of Australia when I heard people talk about the great bugger-all, but it's not. *That's* the great bugger-all, right down there."

Brian checked the INS and the charts again, quickly. He had made a small red circle on one of the charts; they were now on the verge of entering the airspace that circle represented. "Can you do what I asked? If you can't, say so. Pride is a luxury we can't—"

"Of course I can," Nick murmured. He had torn his eyes away from the huge black socket below the plane and was scanning the sky. "I only wish I knew what I was looking *for.*"

"I think you'll know it when you see it," Brian said. He paused and then added, "If you see it."

12

Bob Jenkins sat with his arms folded tightly across his chest, as if he were cold. Part of him *was* cold, but this was not a physical coldness. The chill was coming out of his head.

Something was wrong.

He did not know what it was, but something was wrong. Something was out of place . . . or lost . . . or forgotten. Either a mistake had been made or was going to be made. The feeling nagged at him like some pain not quite localized enough to be identified. That sense of wrongness would almost crystallize into a thought . . . and then it would skitter away again like some small, not-quite-tame animal.

Something wrong.

Or out of place. Or lost.

Or forgotten.

Ahead of him, Albert and Bethany were spooning contentedly. Behind him, Rudy Warwick was sitting with his eyes closed and his lips moving. The beads of a rosary were clamped in one fist. Across the aisle, Laurel Stevenson sat beside Dinah, holding one of her hands and stroking it gently.

Wrong.

Bob eased up the shade beside his seat, peeked out, and slammed it down again. Looking at *that* would not aid rational thought but erase it. What lay below the plane was utter madness.

I must warn them. I have to. They are going forward on my hypothesis, but if my hypothesis is somehow mistaken—and dangerous—then I must warn them.

Warn them of what?

Again it almost came into the light of his focussed thoughts, then slipped away, becoming just a shadow among shadows . . . but one with shiny feral eyes.

He abruptly unbuckled his seatbelt and stood up.

Albert looked around. "Where are you going?"

"Cleveland," Bob said grumpily, and began to walk down the aisle toward the tail of the aircraft, still trying to track the source of that interior alarm bell.

13

Brian tore his eyes away from the sky—which was already showing signs of light again—long enough to take a quick glance first at the INS readout and then at the circle on his chart. They were approaching the far side of the circle now. If the time-rip was still here, they should see it soon. If they didn't, he supposed he would have to take over the controls and send them circling back for another pass at a slightly different altitude and on a slightly different heading. It would play hell on their fuel situation, which was already tight, but since the whole thing was probably hopeless anyway, it didn't matter very—

"Brian?" Nick's voice was unsteady. "Brian? I think I see something."

14

Bob Jenkins reached the rear of the plane, made an about-face, and started slowly back up the aisle again, passing row after row of empty seats. He looked at the objects that lay in them and on the floor in front of them as he passed: purses . . . pairs of eyeglasses . . . wristwatches . . . a pocket-watch . . . two worn, crescent-shaped pieces of metal that were probably heel-taps . . . dental fillings . . . wedding rings . . .

Something is wrong.

Yes? Was that really so, or was it only his overworked mind nagging fiercely over nothing? The mental equivalent of a tired muscle which will not stop twitching?

Leave it, he advised himself, but he couldn't.

If something really is amiss, why can't you see it? Didn't you tell the boy that deduction is your meat and drink? Haven't you written forty mystery novels, and weren't a dozen of those actually quite good?

Didn't Newgate Callendar call The Sleeping Madonna *"a master-piece of logic" when he—*

Bob Jenkins came to a dead stop, his eyes widening. They fixed on a portside seat near the front of the cabin. In it, the man with the black beard was out cold again, snoring lustily. Inside Bob's head, the shy animal at last began to creep fearfully into the light. Only it wasn't small, as he had thought. That had been his mistake. Sometimes you couldn't see things because they were too small, but sometimes you ignored things because they were too big, too obvious.

The Sleeping Madonna.

The sleeping man.

He opened his mouth and tried to scream, but no sound came out. His throat was locked. Terror sat on his chest like an ape. He tried again to scream and managed no more than a breathless squeak.

Sleeping madonna, sleeping man.

They, the survivors, had all been asleep.

Now, with the exception of the bearded man, none *of them were asleep.*

Bob opened his mouth once more, tried once more to scream, and once more nothing came out.

15

"Holy Christ in the morning," Brian whispered.

The time-rip lay about ninety miles ahead, off to the starboard side of the 767's nose by no more than seven or eight degrees. If it had drifted, it had not drifted much; Brian's guess was that the slight differential was the result of a minor navigational error.

It was a lozenge-shaped hole in reality, but not a black void. It cycled with a dim pink-purple light, like the aurora borealis. Brian could see the stars beyond it, but they were also rippling. A wide white ribbon of vapor was slowly streaming either into or out of the shape which hung in the sky. It looked like some strange, ethereal highway.

We can follow it right in, Brian thought excitedly. *It's better than an ILS beacon!*

"We're in business!" he said, laughed idiotically, and shook his clenched fists in the air.

"It must be two miles across," Nick whispered. "My God, Brian, how many other planes do you suppose went through?"

"I don't know," Brian said, "but I'll bet you my gun and dog that we're the only one with a shot at getting back."

He opened the intercom.

"Ladies and gentlemen, we've found what we were look-ing for." His voice crackled with triumph and relief. "I don't know exactly what happens next, or how, or why, but we have sighted what appears to be an extremely large trapdoor in the sky. I'm going to take us straight through the middle of it. We'll find out what's on the other side together. Right now I'd like you all to fasten your seatbelts and—"

That was when Bob Jenkins came pelting madly up the aisle, screaming at the top of his lungs. *"No! No! We'll all die if you go into it! Turn back! You've got to turn back!"*

Brian swung around in his seat and exchanged a puzzled look with Nick.

Nick unbuckled his belt and stood up. "That's Bob Jen-kins," he said. "Sounds like he's worked himself up to a good set of nerves. Carry on, Brian. I'll handle him."

"Okay," Brian said. "Just keep him away from me. I'd hate to have him grab me at the wrong second and send us into the edge of that thing."

He turned off the autopilot and took control of the 767 himself. The floor tilted gently to the right as he banked toward the long, glowing slot ahead of them. It seemed to slide across the sky until it was centered in front of the 767's nose. Now he could hear a sound mixing with the drone of the jet engines—a deep throbbing noise, like a huge diesel idling. As they approached the river of vapor—it was flowing into the hole, he now saw, not out of it—he began to pick up flashes of color travelling within it: green, blue, violet, red, candy pink. *It's the first real color I've seen in this world,* he thought.

Behind him, Bob Jenkins sprinted through the first-class section, up the narrow aisle which led to the service area . . . and right into Nick's waiting arms.

"Easy, mate," Nick soothed. "Everything's going to be all right now."

"No!" Bob struggled wildly, but Nick held him as easily as a man might hold a struggling kitten. "No, you don't understand! He's got to turn back! He's got to turn back before it's too late!"

Nick pulled the writer away from the cockpit door and back into first class. "We'll just sit down here and belt up tight, shall we?" he said in that same soothing, chummy voice. "It may be a trifle bumpy."

To Brian, Nick's voice was only a faint blur of sound. As he entered the wide flow of vapor streaming into the time-rip, he felt a large and immensely powerful hand seize the plane, dragging it eagerly forward. He found himself thinking of the leak on the flight from Tokyo to L.A., and of how fast air rushed out of a hole in a pressurized environment.

It's as if this whole world—or what is left of it—is leaking through that hole, he thought, and then that queer and ominous phrase from his dream recurred again: SHOOTING STARS ONLY.

The rip lay dead ahead of the 767's nose now, growing rapidly. *We're going in,* he thought. *God help us, we're really going in.*

16

Bob continued to struggle as Nick pinned him in one of the first-class seats with one hand and worked to fasten his seatbelt with the other. Bob was a small, skinny man, surely no more than a hundred and forty pounds soaking wet, but panic had animated him and he was making it extremely hard for Nick.

"We're really going to be all right, matey," Nick said. He finally managed to click Bob's seatbelt shut. "We were when we came through, weren't we?"

"*We were all asleep when we came through, you damned fool!*" Bob shrieked into his face. "*Don't you understand? WE WERE ASLEEP! You've got to stop him!*"

Nick froze in the act of reaching for his own belt. What Bob was saying—what he had been trying to say all along—suddenly struck him like a dropped load of bricks.

"Oh dear God," he whispered. "Dear God, what were we thinking of?"

He leaped out of his seat and dashed for the cockpit.

"Brian, stop! Turn back! *Turn back!*"

17

Brian had been staring into the rip, nearly hypnotized, as they approached. There was no turbulence, but that sense of tremendous power, of air rushing into the hole like a mighty river, had increased. He looked down at his instruments and saw the 767's airspeed was increasing rapidly. Then Nick began to shout, and a moment later the Englishman was behind him, gripping his shoulders, staring at the rip as it swelled in front of the jet's nose, its play of deepening colors racing across his cheeks and brow, making him look like a man staring at a stained-glass window on a sunny day. The steady thrumming sound had become dark thunder.

"*Turn back, Brian, you have to turn back!*"

Did Nick have a reason for what he was saying, or had Bob's

258

panic been infectious? There was no time to make a decision on any rational basis; only a split-second to consult the silent tickings of instinct.

Brain Engle grabbed the steering yoke and hauled it hard over to port.

18

Nick was thrown across the cockpit and into a bulkhead; there was a sickening crack as his arm broke. In the main cabin, the luggage which had fallen from the overhead compartments when Brian swerved onto the runway at BIA now flew once more, striking the curved walls and thudding off the windows in a vicious hail. The man with the black beard was thrown out of his seat like a Cabbage Patch Kid and had time to utter one bleary squawk before his head collided with the arm of a seat and he fell into the aisle in an untidy tangle of limbs. Bethany screamed and Albert hugged her tight against him. Two rows behind, Rudy Warwick closed his eyes tighter, clutched his rosary harder, and prayed faster as his seat tilted away beneath him.

Now there was turbulence; Flight 29 became a surfboard with wings, rocking and twisting and thumping through the unsteady air. Brian's hands were momentarily thrown off the yoke and then he grabbed it again. At the same time he opened the throttle all the way to the stop and the plane's turbos responded with a deep snarl of power rarely heard outside of the airline's diagnostic hangars. The turbulence increased; the plane slammed viciously up and down, and from somewhere came the deadly shriek of overstressed metal.

In first class, Bob Jenkins clutched at the arms of his seat, numbly grateful that the Englishman had managed to belt him in. He felt as if he had been strapped to some madman's jet-powered pogo stick. The plane took another great leap, rocked up almost to the vertical on its portside wing, and his false teeth shot from his mouth.

Are we going in? Dear Jesus, are we?

He didn't know. He only knew that the world was a thumping, bucking nightmare . . . but he was still in it.

For the time being, at least, he was still in it.

19

The turbulence continued to increase as Brian drove the 767 across the wide stream of vapor feeding into the rip. Ahead of him, the hole continued to swell in front of the plane's nose even as it continued sliding off to starboard. Then, after one particularly vicious jolt, they came out of the rapids and into smoother air. The time-rip disappeared to starboard. They had missed it . . . by how little Brian did not like to think.

He continued to bank the plane, but at a less drastic angle. "Nick!" he shouted without turning around. "Nick, are you all right?"

Nick got slowly to his feet, holding his right arm against his belly with his left hand. His face was very white and his teeth were set in a grimace of pain. Small trickles of blood ran from his nostrils. "I've been better, mate. Broke my arm, I think. Not the first time for this poor old fellow, either. We missed it, didn't we?"

"We missed it," Brian agreed. He continued to bring the plane back in a big, slow circle. "And in just a minute you're going to tell me *why* we missed it, when we came all this way to find it. And it better be good, broken arm or no broken arm."

He reached for the intercom toggle.

20

Laurel opened her eyes as Brian began to speak and discovered that Dinah's head was in her lap. She stroked her hair gently and then readjusted her position on the stretcher.

"This is Captain Engle, folks. I'm sorry about that. It was pretty damned hairy, but we're okay; I've got a green board. Let me repeat that we've found what we were looking for, but—"

He clicked off suddenly.

The others waited. Bethany Simms was sobbing against Albert's chest. Behind them, Rudy was still saying his rosary.

21

Brian had broken his transmission when he realized that Bob Jenkins was standing beside him. The writer was shaking, there was a wet patch on his slacks, his mouth had an odd, sunken look Brian hadn't noticed before . . . but he seemed in charge of himself. Behind him, Nick sat heavily in the co-pilot's chair, wincing as he did so and still cradling his arm. It had begun to swell.

"What the hell is this all about?" Brian asked Bob sternly. "A little more turbulence and this bitch would have broken into about ten thousand pieces."

"Can I talk through that thing?" Bob asked, pointing to the switch marked INTERCOM.

"Yes, but—"

"Then let me do it."

Brian started to protest, then thought better of it. He flicked the switch. "Go ahead; you're on." Then he repeated: "And it better be good."

"Listen to me, all of you!" Bob shouted.

From behind them came a protesting whine of feedback. "We—"

"Just talk in your normal tone of voice," Brian said. "You'll blow their goddam eardrums out."

Bob made a visible effort to compose himself, then went on in a lower tone of voice. "We had to turn back, and we did. The captain has made it clear to me that we only just managed to do it. We have been extremely lucky . . . and extremely stupid, as well. We forgot the most elementary thing, you see, although it was right in front of us all the time. When we went through the time-rip in the first place, *everyone on the plane who was awake disappeared.*"

Brian jerked in his seat. He felt as if someone had slugged him. Ahead of the 767's nose, about thirty miles distant, the faintly glowing lozenge shape had appeared again in the sky, looking like some gigantic semi-precious stone. It seemed to mock him.

"We are all awake," Bob said. (In the main cabin, Albert looked at the man with the black beard lying out cold in the aisle and thought, *With one exception.*) "Logic suggests that if we try to go through that way, *we* will disappear." He thought about this and then said, "That is all."

Brian flicked the intercom link closed without thinking about it. Behind him, Nick voiced a painful, incredulous laugh.

"That is all? That is bloody *all*? What do we *do* about it?"

Brian looked at him and didn't answer. Neither did Bob Jenkins.

22

Bethany raised her head and looked into Albert's strained, bewildered face. "We have to go to sleep? How do we do *that*? I never felt less like sleeping in my whole *life*!"

"I don't know." He looked hopefully across the aisle at Laurel. She was already shaking her head. She wished she *could* go to sleep, just go to sleep and make this whole crazy nightmare *gone*—but, like Bethany, she had never felt less like it in her entire life.

23

Bob took a step forward and gazed out through the cockpit window in silent fascination. After a long moment he said in a soft, awed voice: "So that's what it looks like."

A line from some rock-and-roll song popped into Brian's head: *You can look but you better not touch.* He glanced down at the LED fuel indicators. What he saw there didn't ease his mind any, and he raised his eyes helplessly to Nick's. Like the others, he had never felt so wide awake in his life.

"I don't know what we do now," he said, "but if we're going to try that hole, it has to be soon. The fuel we've got will carry us for an hour, maybe a little more. After that, forget it. Got any ideas?"

Nick lowered his head, still cradling his swelling arm. After a moment or two he looked up again. "Yes," he said. "As a matter of fact, I do. People who fly rarely stick their prescription medicine in their checked baggage—they like to have it with them in case their luggage ends up on the other side of the world and takes a few days to get back to them. If we go through the hand-carry bags, we're sure to find scads of sedatives. We won't even have to take the bags out of the bins. Judging from the sounds, most of them are already lying on the floor . . . what? What's the matter with it?"

This last was directed at Bob Jenkins, who had begun shaking his head as soon as the phrase "prescription medicines" popped out of Nick's mouth.

"Do you know anything about prescription sedatives?" he asked Nick.

"A little," Nick said, but he sounded defensive. "A little, yeah."

"Well, I know a lot," Bob said dryly. "I've researched them exhaustively—from All-Nite to Xanax. Murder by sleeping potion has always been a great favorite in my field, you understand. Even if you happened to find one of the more potent medications in the very first bag you checked—unlikely in itself—you couldn't administer a safe dose which would act quickly enough."

"Why bloody *not*?"

"Because it would take at least forty minutes for the stuff to work . . . and I strongly doubt it *would* work on everyone. The natural reaction of minds under stress to such medication is to fight—to try to refuse it. There is absolutely no way to combat such a reaction, Nick . . . you might as well try to legislate your own heartbeat. What you'd do, always supposing you found a supply of medication large enough to allow it, would be to administer a series of lethal overdoses and turn the plane into Jonestown. We might all come through, but we'd be dead."

"Forty minutes," Nick said. "Christ. Are you sure? Are you absolutely *sure*?"

"Yes," Bob said unflinchingly.

Brian looked out at the glowing lozenge shape in the sky. He had put Flight 29 into a circling pattern and the rip was on the verge of disappearing again. It would be back shortly . . . but they would be no closer to it.

"I can't believe it," Nick said heavily. "To go through the things we've gone through . . . to have taken off successfully and come all this way . . . to have actually *found* the bloody thing . . . and then we find out we can't go through it and back to our own time just because we can't go to *sleep*?"

"We don't have forty minutes, anyway," Brian said quietly. "If we waited that long, this plane would crash sixty miles east of the airport."

"Surely there are other fields—"

"There are, but none big enough to handle an airplane of this size."

"If we went through and then turned back east again?"

"Vegas. But Vegas is going to be out of reach in . . ." Brian glanced at his instruments. ". . . less than eight minutes. I think it has to be LAX. I'll need at least thirty-five minutes to get there. That's cutting it extremely fine even if they clear everything out of our way and vector us straight in. That gives us . . ." He looked at the chronometer again. ". . . twenty minutes at most to figure this thing out and get through the hole."

Bob was looking thoughtfully at Nick. "What about you?" he asked.

"What do you mean, what about me?"

"I think you're a soldier . . . but I don't think you're an ordinary one. Might you be SAS, perhaps?"

Nick's face tightened. "And if I was that or something like it, mate?"

"Maybe *you* could put us to sleep," Bob said. "Don't they teach you Special Forces men tricks like that?"

Brian's mind flashed back to Nick's first confrontation with Craig Toomy. *Have you ever watched* Star Trek? he had asked Craig. *Marvellous American program . . . And if you don't shut your gob at once, you bloody idiot, I'll be happy to demonstrate Mr. Spock's famous Vulcan sleeper-hold for you.*

"What about it, Nick?" he said softly. "If we ever needed the famous Vulcan sleeper-hold, it's now."

Nick looked unbelievingly from Bob to Brian and then back to Bob again. "Please don't make me laugh, gents—it makes my arm hurt worse."

"What does that mean?" Bob asked.

"I've got my sedatives all wrong, have I? Well, let me tell you both that you've got it all wrong about me. I am *not* James Bond. There never *was* a James Bond in the real world. I suppose I might be able to kill you with a neck-chop, Bob, but

I'd more likely just leave you paralyzed for life. Might not even knock you out. And then there's this." Nick held up his rapidly swelling right arm with a little wince. "My smart hand happens to be attached to my recently re-broken arm. I could perhaps defend myself with my left hand—against an unschooled opponent—but the kind of thing you're talking about? No. No way."

"You're all forgetting the most important thing of all," a new voice said.

They turned. Laurel Stevenson, white and haggard, was standing in the cockpit door. She had folded her arms across her breasts as if she was cold and was cupping her elbows in her hands.

"If we're all knocked out, who is going to fly the plane?" she asked. "Who is going to fly the plane into L.A.?"

The three men gaped at her wordlessly. Behind them, unnoticed, the large semi-precious stone that was the time-rip glided into view again.

"We're fucked," Nick said quietly. "Do you know that? We are absolutely dead-out fucked." He laughed a little, then winced as his stomach jogged his broken arm.

"Maybe not," Albert said. He and Bethany had appeared behind Laurel; Albert had his arm around the girl's waist. His hair was plastered against his forehead in sweaty ringlets, but his dark eyes were clear and intent. They were focussed on Brian. "I think *you* can put us to sleep," he said, "and I think *you* can land us."

"What are you talking about?" Brian asked roughly.

Albert replied: "Pressure. I'm talking about pressure."

24

Brian's dream recurred to him then, recurred with such terrible force that he might have been reliving it: Anne with her hand plastered over the crack in the body of the plane, the crack with the words SHOOTING STARS ONLY printed over it in red.

Pressure.

See, darling? It's all taken care of.

"What does he mean, Brian?" Nick asked. "I can see he's got *something*—your face says so. What is it?"

Brian ignored him. He looked steadily at the seventeen-year-old music student who might just have thought of a way out of the box they were in.

"What about after?" he asked. "What about after we come through? How do I wake up again so I can land the plane?"

"Will somebody please explain this?" Laurel pleaded. She had gone to Nick, who put his good arm around her waist.

"Albert is suggesting that I use this"—Brian tapped a rheostat on the control board, a rheostat marked CABIN PRESSURE—"to knock us all out cold."

"Can you do that, mate? Can you really do that?"

"Yes," Brian said. "I've known pilots—charter pilots . . . who *have* done it, when passengers who've had too much to drink started cutting up and endangering either themselves or the crew. Knocking out a drunk by lowering the air pressure isn't that difficult. To knock out everyone, all I have to do is lower it some more . . . to half sea-level pressure, say. It's like ascending to a height of two miles without an oxygen mask. Boom! You're out cold."

"If you can really do that, why hasn't it been used on terrorists?" Bob asked.

"Because there *are* oxygen masks, right?" Albert asked.

"Yes," Brian said. "The cabin crew demonstrates them at the start of every commercial jet-flight—put the gold cup over your mouth and nose and breathe normally, right? They drop automatically when cabin pressure falls below twelve psi. If a hostage pilot tried to knock out a terrorist by lowering the air pressure, all the terrorist would have to do is grab a mask, put it on, and start shooting. On smaller jets, like the Lear, that isn't the case. If the cabin loses pressure, the passenger has to open the overhead compartment himself."

Nick looked at the chronometer. Their window was now only fourteen minutes wide.

"I think we better stop talking about it and just do it," he said. "Time is getting very short."

"Not yet," Brian said, and looked at Albert again. "I can bring us back in line with the rip, Albert, and start decreasing pressure as we head toward it. I can control the cabin pressure pretty accurately, and I'm pretty sure I can put us all out before we go through. But that leaves Laurel's question: who flies the airplane if we're all knocked out?"

Albert opened his mouth; closed it again and shook his head.

Bob Jenkins spoke up then. His voice was dry and toneless, the voice of a judge pronouncing doom. "I think *you* can fly us home, Brian. But someone else will have to die in order for you to do it."

"Explain," Nick said crisply.

Bob did so. It didn't take long. By the time he finished, Rudy Warwick had joined the little group standing in the cockpit door.

"Would it work, Brian?" Nick asked.

"Yes," Brian said absently. "No reason why not." He looked at the chronometer again. Eleven minutes now. Eleven minutes to get across to the other side of the rip. It would take almost that long to line the plane up, program the autopilot, and move them along the forty-mile approach. "But who's going to do it? Do the rest of you draw straws, or what?"

"No need for that," Nick said. He spoke lightly, almost casually. "I'll do it."

"No!" Laurel said. Her eyes were very wide and very dark. "Why you? Why does it have to be you?"

"Shut up!" Bethany hissed at her. "If he wants to, let him!"

Albert glanced unhappily at Bethany, at Laurel, and then

back at Nick. A voice—not a very strong one—was whispering that *he* should have volunteered, that this was a job for a tough Alamo survivor like The Arizona Jew. But most of him was only aware that he loved life very much . . . and did not want it to end just yet. So he opened his mouth and then closed it again without speaking.

"Why you?" Laurel asked again, urgently. "Why *shouldn't* we draw straws? Why not Bob? Or Rudy? Why not me?"

Nick took her arm. "Come with me a moment," he said.

"Nick, there's not much time," Brian said. He tried to keep his tone of voice even, but he could hear desperation—perhaps even panic—bleeding through.

"I know. Start doing the things you have to do."

Nick drew Laurel through the door.

25

She resisted for a moment, then came along. He stopped in the small galley alcove and faced her. In that moment, with his face less than four inches from hers, she realized a dismal truth—he was the man she had been hoping to find in Boston. He had been on the plane all the time. There was nothing at all romantic about this discovery; it was horrible.

"I think we might have had something, you and me," he said. "Do you think I could be right about that? If you do, say so—there's no time to dance. Absolutely none."

"Yes," she said. Her voice was dry, uneven. "I think that's right."

"But we don't know. We *can't* know. It all comes back to time, doesn't it? Time . . . and sleep . . . and not knowing. But I have to be the one, Laurel. I have tried to keep some reasonable account of myself, and all my books are deeply in the red. This is my chance to balance them, and I mean to take it."

"I don't understand what you mea—"

"No—but I do." He spoke fast, almost rapping his words. Now he reached out and took her forearm and drew her even closer to him. "You were on an adventure of some sort, weren't you, Laurel?"

"I don't know what you're—"

He gave her a brisk shake. "I told you—there's no time to dance! *Were* you on an adventure?"

"I . . . yes."

"Nick!" Brian called from the cockpit.

Nick looked rapidly in that direction. "Coming!" he shouted, and then looked back at Laurel. "I'm going to send you on another one. If you get out of this, that is, and if you agree to go."

She only looked at him, her lips trembling. She had no idea of what to say. Her mind was tumbling helplessly. His grip on her arm was very tight, but she would not be aware of that until later, when she saw the bruises left by his fingers; at that moment, the grip of his eyes was much stronger.

"Listen. Listen carefully." He paused and then spoke with peculiar, measured emphasis: "I was going to quit it. I'd made up my mind."

"Quit what?" she asked in a small, quivery voice.

Nick shook his head impatiently. "Doesn't matter. What matters is whether or not you believe me. Do you?"

"Yes," she said. "I don't know what you're talking about, but I believe you mean it."

"*Nick!*" Brian warned from the cockpit. "*We're heading toward it!*"

He shot a glance toward the cockpit again, his eyes narrow and gleaming. "Coming just now!" he called. When he looked at her again, Laurel thought she had never in her life been the focus of such ferocious, focussed intensity. "My father lives in the village of Fluting, south of London," he said. "Ask for him in any shop along the High Street. Mr. Hopewell. The older ones still call him the gaffer. Go to him and tell him I'd made up my mind to quit it. You'll need to be persistent; he tends to turn away and curse loudly when he hears my name. The old I-have-no-son bit. Can you be persistent?"

"Yes."

He nodded and smiled grimly. "Good! Repeat what I've told you, and tell him you believed me. Tell him I tried my best to atone for the day behind the church in Belfast."

"In Belfast."

"Right. And if you can't get him to listen any other way, tell him he *must* listen. Because of the daisies. The time I brought the daisies. Can you remember that, as well?"

"Because once you brought him daisies."

Nick seemed to almost laugh—but she had never seen a face filled with such sadness and bitterness. "No—not to him, but it'll do. That's your adventure. Will you do it?"

"Yes . . . but . . ."

"Good. Laurel, thank you." He put his left hand against the nape of her neck, pulled her face to his, and kissed her. His mouth was cold, and she tasted fear on his breath.

A moment later he was gone.

26

"Are we going to feel like we're—you know, choking?" Bethany asked. "Suffocating?"

"No," Brian said. He had gotten up to see if Nick was coming; now, as Nick reappeared with a very shaken Laurel Stevenson behind him, Brian dropped back into his seat. "You'll feel a little giddy . . . swimmy in the head . . . then, nothing." He glanced at Nick. "Until we all wake up."

"Right!" Nick said cheerily. "And who knows? I may still be right here. Bad pennies have a way of turning up, you know. Don't they, Brian?"

"Anything's possible, I guess," Brian said. He pushed the

throttle forward slightly. The sky was growing bright again. The rip lay dead ahead. "Sit down, folks. Nick, right up here beside me. I'm going to show you what to do . . . and when to do it."

"One second, please," Laurel said. She had regained some of her color and self-possession. She stood on tiptoe and planted a kiss on Nick's mouth.

"Thank you," Nick said gravely.

"You were going to quit it. You'd made up your mind. And if he won't listen, I'm to remind him of the day you brought the daisies. Have I got it right?"

He grinned. "Letter-perfect, my love. Letter-perfect." He encircled her with his left arm and kissed her again, long and hard. When he let her go, there was a gentle, thoughtful smile on his mouth. "That's the one to go on," he said. "Right enough."

27

Three minutes later, Brian opened the intercom. "I'm starting to decrease pressure now. Check your belts, everyone."

They did so. Albert waited tensely for some sound—the hiss of escaping air, perhaps—but there was only the steady, droning mumble of the jet engines. He felt more wide awake than ever.

"Albert?" Bethany said in a small, scared voice. "Would you hold me, please?"

"Yes," Albert said. "If you'll hold me."

Behind them, Rudy Warwick was telling his rosary again. Across the aisle, Laurel Stevenson gripped the arms of her seat. She could still feel the warm print of Nick Hopewell's lips on her mouth. She raised her head, looked at the overhead compartment, and began to take deep, slow breaths. She was waiting for the masks to fall . . . and ninety seconds or so later, they did.

Remember about the day in Belfast, too, she thought. *Behind the church. An act of atonement, he said. An act . . .*

In the middle of that thought, her mind drifted away.

28

"You know . . . what to do?" Brian asked again. He spoke in a dreamy, furry voice. Ahead of them, the time-rip was once more swelling in the cockpit windows, spreading across the sky. It was now lit with dawn, and a fantastic new array of colors coiled, swam, and then streamed away into its queer depths.

"I know," Nick said. He was standing beside Brian and his words were muffled by the oxygen mask he wore. Above the rubber seal, his eyes were calm and clear. "No fear, Brian. All's safe as houses. Off to sleep you go. Sweet dreams, and all that."

Brian was fading now. He could feel himself going . . . and yet he hung on, staring at the vast fault in the fabric of reality. It seemed to be swelling toward the cockpit windows, reaching for the plane. *It's so beautiful,* he thought. *God, it's so beautiful!*

He felt that invisible hand seize the plane and draw it forward again. No turning back this time.

"Nick," he said. It now took a tremendous effort to speak; he felt as if his mouth was a hundred miles away from his brain. He held his hand up. It seemed to stretch away from him at the end of a long taffy arm.

"Go to sleep," Nick said, taking his hand. "Don't fight it, unless you want to go with me. It won't be long now."

"I just wanted to say . . . thank you."

Nick smiled and gave Brian's hand a squeeze. "You're welcome, mate. It's been a flight to remember. Even without the movie and the free mimosas."

Brian looked back into the rip. A river of gorgeous colors

flowed into it now. They spiralled . . . mixed . . . and seemed to form words before his dazed, wondering eyes:

SHOOTING STARS ONLY

"Is that . . . what we are?" he asked curiously, and now his voice came to him from some distant universe.

The darkness swallowed him.

29

Nick was alone now; the only person awake on Flight 29 was a man who had once gunned down three boys behind a church in Belfast, three boys who had been chucking potatoes painted dark gray to look like grenades. Why had they done such a thing? Had it been some mad sort of dare? He had never found out.

He was not afraid, but an intense loneliness filled him. The feeling wasn't a new one. This was not the first watch he had stood alone, with the lives of others in his hands.

Ahead of him, the rip neared. He dropped his hand to the rheostat which controlled the cabin pressure.

It's gorgeous, he thought. It seemed to him that the colors that now blazed out of the rip were the antithesis of everything which they had experienced in the last few hours; he was looking into a crucible of new life and new motion.

Why shouldn't it be beautiful? This is the place where life—all life, maybe—begins. The place where life is freshly minted every second of every day; the cradle of creation and the wellspring of time. No langoliers allowed beyond this point.

Colors ran across his cheeks and brows in a fountain-spray of hues: jungle green was overthrown by lava orange; lava orange was replaced by yellow-white tropical sunshine; sunshine was supplanted by the chilly blue of Northern oceans. The roar of the jet engines seemed muted and distant; he looked down and was not surprised to see that Brian Engle's slumped, sleeping form was being consumed by color, his form and features overthrown in an ever-changing kaleidoscope of brightness. He had become a fabulous ghost.

Nor was Nick surprised to see that his own hands and arms were as colorless as clay. *Brian's not the ghost; I am.*

The rip loomed.

Now the sound of the jets was lost entirely in a new sound; the 767 seemed to be rushing through a windtunnel filled with feathers. Suddenly, directly ahead of the airliner's nose, a vast nova of light exploded like a heavenly firework; in it, Nick Hopewell saw colors no man had ever imagined. It did not just fill the time-rip; it filled his mind, his nerves, his muscles, his very bones in a gigantic, coruscating fireflash.

"*Oh my God, SO BEAUTIFUL!*" he cried, and as Flight 29 plunged into the rip, he twisted the cabin-pressure rheostat back up to full.

A split-second later the fillings from Nick's teeth pattered onto the cockpit floor. There was a small thump as the Teflon disc which had been in his knee—souvenir of a conflict marginally more honorable than the one in Northern Ireland— joined them. That was all.

Nick Hopewell had ceased to exist.

30

The first things Brian was aware of were that his shirt was wet and his headache had returned.

He sat up slowly in his seat, wincing at the bolt of pain in his head, and tried to remember who he was, where he was, and why he felt such a vast and urgent need to wake up quickly. What had he been doing that was so important?

The leak, his mind whispered. *There's a leak in the main cabin, and if it isn't stabilized, there's going to be big tr—*

No, that wasn't right. The leak *had* been stabilized—or had in some mysterious way stabilized itself—and he had landed Flight 7 safely at LAX. Then the man in the green blazer had come, and—

It's Anne's funeral! My God, I've overslept!

His eyes flew open, but he was in neither a motel room nor the spare bedroom at Anne's brother's house in Revere. He was looking through a cockpit window at a sky filled with stars.

Suddenly it came back to him . . . everything.

He sat up all the way, too quickly. His head screamed a sickly hungover protest. Blood flew from his nose and splattered on the center control console. He looked down and saw the front of his shirt was soaked with it. There had been a leak, all right. In *him*.

Of course, he thought. *Depressurization often does that. I should have warned the passengers . . . How many passengers do I have left, by the way?*

He couldn't remember. His head was filled with fog.

He looked at his fuel indicators, saw that their situation was rapidly approaching the critical point, and then checked the INS. They were exactly where they should be, descending rapidly toward L.A., and at any moment they might wander into someone else's airspace while the someone else was still there.

Someone else had been sharing *his* airspace just before he passed out . . . who?

He fumbled, and it came. Nick, of course. Nick Hopewell. Nick was gone. He hadn't been such a bad penny after all, it seemed. But he must have done his job, or Brian wouldn't be awake now.

He got on the radio, fast.

"LAX ground control, this is American Pride Flight—" He stopped. What flight *were* they? He couldn't remember. The fog was in the way.

"Twenty-nine, aren't we?" a dazed, unsteady voice said from behind him.

"Thank you, Laurel." Brian didn't turn around. "Now go back and belt up. I may have to make this plane do some tricks."

He spoke into his mike again.

"American Pride Flight 29, repeat, two-niner. Mayday, ground control, I am declaring an emergency here. Please clear everything in front of me, I am coming in on heading 85 and I have no fuel. Get a foam truck out and—"

"Oh, quit it," Laurel said dully from behind him. "Just quit it."

Brian wheeled around then, ignoring the fresh bolt of pain through his head and the fresh spray of blood which flew from his nose. "Sit *down,* goddammit!" he snarled. "We're coming in unannounced into heavy traffic. If you don't want to break your neck—"

"There's no heavy traffic down there," Laurel said in the same dull voice. "No heavy traffic, no foam trucks. Nick died for nothing, and I'll never get a chance to deliver his message. Look for yourself."

Brian did. And, although they were now over the outlying suburbs of Los Angeles, he saw nothing but darkness.

There was no one down there, it seemed.

No one at all.

Behind him, Laurel Stevenson burst into harsh, raging sobs of terror and frustration.

31

A long white passenger jet cruised slowly above the ground sixteen miles east of Los Angeles International Airport. 767 was printed on its tail in large, proud numerals. Along the fuselage, the words AMERICAN PRIDE were written in letters which had been raked backward to indicate speed. On both sides of the nose was a large red eagle, its wings spangled with blue stars. Like the airliner it decorated, the eagle appeared to be coming in for a landing.

The plane printed no shadow on the deserted grid of streets as it passed above them; dawn was still an hour away. Below it, no car moved, no streetlight glowed. Below it, all was silent and moveless. Ahead of it, no runway lights gleamed.

The plane's belly slid open. The undercarriage dropped down and spread out. The landing gear locked in place.

American Pride Flight 29 slipped down the chute toward L.A. It banked slightly to the right as it came; Brian was now able to correct his course visually, and he did so. They passed over a cluster of airport motels, and for a moment Brian could see the monument that stood near the center of the terminal complex, a graceful tripod with curved legs and a restaurant in its center. They passed over a short strip of dead grass and then concrete runway was unrolling thirty feet below the plane.

There was no time to baby the 767 in this time; Brian's fuel indicators read zeros across and the bird was about to turn into a bitch. He brought it in hard, like a sled filled with bricks. There was a thud that rattled his teeth and started his nose bleeding again. His chest harness locked. Laurel, who was in the co-pilot's seat, cried out.

Then he had the flaps up and was applying reverse thrusters at full. The plane began to slow. They were doing a little over a hundred miles an hour when two of the thrusters cut out and the red ENGINE SHUTDOWN lights flashed on. He grabbed for the intercom switch.

"Hang on! We're going in hard! Hang on!"

Thrusters two and four kept running a few moments longer, and then they were gone, too. Flight 29 rushed down the runway in ghastly silence, with only the flaps to slow her now. Brian watched helplessly as the concrete ran away beneath the plane and the crisscross tangle of taxiways loomed. And there, dead ahead, sat the carcass of a Pacific Airways commuter jet.

The 767 was still doing at least sixty-five. Brian horsed it to the right, leaning into the dead steering yoke with every ounce of his strength. The plane responded soupily, and he skated by the parked jet with only six feet to spare. Its windows flashed past like a row of blind eyes.

Then they were rolling toward the United terminal, where at least a dozen planes were parked at extended jetways like nursing infants. The 767's speed was down to just over thirty now.

"Brace yourselves!" Brian shouted into the intercom, momentarily forgetting that his own plane was now as dead as the rest of them and the intercom was useless. *"Brace yourselves for a collision! Bra—"* American Pride 29 crashed into Gate 29 of the United Airlines terminal at roughly twenty-nine miles an hour. There was a loud, hollow bang followed by the sound of crumpling metal and breaking glass. Brian was thrown into his harness again, then snapped back into his seat. He sat there for a moment, stiff, waiting for the explosion . . . and then remembered there was nothing left in the tanks to explode.

He flicked all the switches on the control panel off—the panel was dead, but the habit ran deep—and then turned to check on Laurel. She looked at him with dull, apathetic eyes.

"That was about as close as I'd ever want to cut it," Brian said unsteadily.

"You should have let us crash. Everything we tried . . . Dinah . . . Nick . . . all for nothing. It's just the same here. Just the same."

Brian unbuckled his harness and got shakily to his feet. He took his handkerchief out of his back pocket and handed it to her. "Wipe your nose. It's bleeding."

She took the handkerchief and then only looked at it, as if she had never seen one before in her life.

Brian passed her and plodded slowly into the main cabin. He stood in the doorway, counting noses. His passengers—those few still remaining, that was—seemed all right. Bethany's head was pressed against Albert's chest and she was sobbing hard. Rudy Warwick unbuckled his seatbelt, got up, rapped his head on the overhead bin, and sat down again. He looked at

Brian with dazed, uncomprehending eyes. Brian found himself wondering if Rudy was still hungry. He guessed not.

"Let's get off the plane," Brian said.

Bethany raised her head. "When do they come?" she asked him hysterically. "How long will it be before they come this time? Can anyone hear them yet?"

Fresh pain stroked Brian's head and he rocked on his feet, suddenly quite sure he was going to faint.

A steadying arm slipped around his waist and he looked around, surprised. It was Laurel.

"Captain Engle's right," she said quietly. "Let's get off the plane. Maybe it's not as bad as it looks."

Bethany uttered a hysterical bark of laughter. "How bad *can* it look?" she demanded. "Just how bad *can* it—"

"Something's different," Albert said suddenly. He was looking out the window. "Something's changed. I can't tell what it is . . . but it's not the same." He looked first at Bethany, then at Brian and Laurel. "It's just not the same."

Brian bent down next to Bob Jenkins and looked out the window. He could see nothing very different from BIA—there were more planes, of course, but they were just as deserted, just as dead—yet he felt that Albert might be onto something, just the same. It was *feeling* more than seeing. Some essential difference which he could not quite grasp. It danced just beyond his reach, as the name of his ex-wife's perfume had done.

It's L'Envoi, darling. It's what I've always worn, don't you remember?

Don't you remember?

"Come on," he said. "This time we use the cockpit exit."

32

Brian opened the trapdoor which lay below the jut of the instrument panel and tried to remember why he hadn't used it to offload his passengers at Bangor International; it was a hell of a lot easier to use than the slide. There didn't seem to *be* a why. He just hadn't thought of it, probably because he was trained to think of the escape slide before anything else in an emergency.

He dropped down into the forward-hold area, ducked below a cluster of electrical cables, and undogged the hatch in the floor of the 767's nose. Albert joined him and helped Bethany down. Brian helped Laurel, and then he and Albert helped Rudy, who moved as if his bones had turned to glass. Rudy was still clutching his rosary tight in one hand. The space below the cockpit was now very cramped, and Bob Jenkins waited for them above, propped on his hands and peering down at them through the trapdoor.

Brian pulled the ladder out of its storage clips, secured it in place, and then, one by one, they descended to the tarmac, Brian first, Bob last.

As Brian's feet touched down, he felt a mad urge to place his hand over his heart and cry out: *I claim this land of rancid milk and sour honey for the survivors of Flight 29 . . . at least until the langoliers arrive!*

He said nothing. He only stood there with the others below the loom of the jetliner's nose, feeling a light breeze against one cheek and looking around. In the distance he heard a sound. It was not the chewing, crunching sound of which they had gradually become aware in Bangor—nothing like it—but he couldn't decide exactly what it *did* sound like.

"What's that?" Bethany asked. "What's that humming? It sounds like electricity."

"No, it doesn't," Bob said thoughtfully. "It sounds like . . ." He shook his head.

"It doesn't sound like anything *I've* ever heard before," Brian said, but he wasn't sure if that was true. Again he was haunted by the sense that something he knew or should know was dancing just beyond his mental grasp.

"It's them, isn't it?" Bethany asked half-hysterically. "It's them, coming. It's the langoliers Dinah told us about."

"I don't think so. It doesn't sound the same at all." But he felt the fear begin in his belly just the same.

"Now what?" Rudy asked. His voice was as harsh as a crow's. "Do we start all over again?"

"Well, we won't need the conveyor belt, and that's a start," Brian said. "The jetway service door is open." He stepped out from beneath the 767's nose and pointed. The force of their arrival at Gate 29 had knocked the rolling ladder away from the door, but it would be easy enough to slip it back into position. "Come on."

They walked toward the ladder.

"Albert?" Brian said. "Help me with the lad—"

"Wait," Bob said.

Brian turned his head and saw Bob looking around with cautious wonder. And the expression in his previously dazed eyes . . . was that hope?

"What? What is it, Bob? What do you see?"

"Just another deserted airport. It's what I *feel.*" He raised a hand to his cheek . . . then simply held it out in the air, like a man trying to flag a ride.

Brian started to ask him what he meant, and realized that he knew. Hadn't he noticed it himself while they had been standing under the liner's nose? Noticed it and then dismissed it?

There was a breeze blowing against his face. Not much of a breeze, hardly more than a puff, but it *was* a breeze. *The air was in motion.*

"Holy crow," Albert said. He popped a finger into his mouth, wetting it, and held it up. An unbelieving grin touched his face.

"That isn't all, either," Laurel said. "Listen!"

She dashed from where they were standing down toward the 767's wing. Then she ran back to them again, her hair streaming out behind her. The high heels she was wearing clicked crisply on the concrete.

"Did you hear it?" she asked them. "Did you *hear* it?"

They had heard. The flat, muffled quality was gone. Now, just listening to Laurel speak, Brian realized that in Bangor they had all sounded as if they had been talking with their heads poked inside bells which had been cast from some dulling metal—brass, or maybe lead.

Bethany raised her hands and rapidly clapped out the backbeat of the old Routers instrumental, "Let's Go." Each clap was as clean and clear as the pop of a track-starter's pistol. A delighted grin broke over her face.

"What does it m—" Rudy began.

"The plane!" Albert shouted in a high-pitched, gleeful voice, and for a moment Brian was absurdly reminded of the little guy on that old TV show, *Fantasy Island.* He almost laughed out loud. "I know what's different! Look at the plane! *Now it's the same as all the others!"*

They turned and looked. No one said anything for a long moment; perhaps no one was capable of speech. The Delta 727 standing next to the American Pride jetliner in Bangor had looked dull and dingy, somehow less real than the 767. Now all the aircraft—Flight 29 and the United planes lined up along the extended jetways behind it—looked equally bright, equally new. Even in the dark, their paintwork and trademark logos appeared to gleam.

"What does it mean?" Rudy asked, speaking to Bob. "What does it mean? If things have really gone back to normal, where's the electricity? Where are the *people?"*

"And what's that noise?" Albert put in.

The sound was already closer, already clearer. It was a humming sound, as Bethany had said, but there was nothing electrical about it. It sounded like wind blowing across an open pipe, or an inhuman choir which was uttering the same openthroated syllable in unison: *aaaaaaa . . .*

Bob shook his head. "I don't know," he said, turning away. "Let's push that ladder back into position and go in—"

Laurel grabbed his shoulder.

"You know something!" she said. Her voice was strained and tense. "I can see that you do. Let the rest of us in on it, why don't you?"

He hesitated for a moment before shaking his head. "I'm not prepared to say right now, Laurel. I want to go inside and look around first."

With that they had to be content. Brian and Albert pushed the ladder back into position. One of the supporting struts had buckled slightly, and Brian held it as they ascended one by one. He himself came last, walking on the side of the ladder away from the buckled strut. The others had waited for him, and they walked up the jetway and into the terminal together.

They found themselves in a large, round room with boarding gates located at intervals along the single curving wall. The rows of seats stood ghostly and deserted, the overhead fluorescents were dark squares, but here Albert thought he could almost *smell* other people . . . as if they had all trooped out only seconds before the Flight 29 survivors emerged from the jetway.

From outside, that choral humming continued to swell, approaching like a slow invisible wave: —*aaaaaaaaaaaaaa*—

"Come with me," Bob Jenkins said, taking effortless charge of the group. "Quickly, please."

He set off toward the concourse and the others fell into line behind him, Albert and Bethany walking together with arms linked about each other's waists. Once off the carpeted surface of the United boarding lounge and in the concourse itself, their heels clicked and echoed, as if there were two dozen of them instead of only six. They passed dim, dark advertising posters on the walls: Watch CNN, Smoke Marlboros, Drive Hertz, Read *Newsweek,* See Disneyland.

And that sound, that open-throated choral humming sound, continued to grow. Outside, Laurel had been convinced the sound had been approaching them from the west. Now it

seemed to be right in here with them, as though the singers—
if they *were* singers—had already arrived. The sound did not
frighten her, exactly, but it made the flesh of her arms and back
prickle with awe.

They reached a cafeteria-style restaurant, and Bob led them
inside. Without pausing, he went around the counter and
took a wrapped pastry from a pile of them on the counter. He
tried to tear it open with his teeth . . . then realized his teeth
were back on the plane. He made a small, disgusted sound and
tossed it over the counter to Albert.

"You do it," he said. His eyes were glowing now. "Quickly,
Albert! Quickly!"

"Quick, Watson, the game's afoot!" Albert said, and laughed
crazily. He tore open the cellophane and looked at Bob, who
nodded. Albert took out the pastry and bit into it. Cream and
raspberry jam squirted out the sides. Albert grinned. "Ith delicious!" he said in a muffled voice, spraying crumbs as he spoke.
"*Delicious!*" He offered it to Bethany, who took an even larger
bite.

Laurel could smell the raspberry filling, and her stomach
made a goinging, boinging sound. She laughed. Suddenly
she felt giddy, joyful, almost stoned. The cobwebs from the
depressurization experience were entirely gone; her head felt
like an upstairs room after a fresh sea breeze had blown in on a
hot and horribly muggy afternoon. She thought of Nick, who
wasn't here, who had died so the rest of them *could* be here,
and thought that Nick would not have minded her feeling
this way.

The choral sound continued to swell, a sound with no direction at all, a sourceless, singing sigh that existed all around
them:

—AAAAAAAAAAAAAA—

Bob Jenkins raced back around the counter, cutting the corner by the cash register so tightly that his feet almost flew out
from beneath him and he had to grab the condiments trolley

to keep from falling. He stayed up but the stainless-steel trolley fell over with a gorgeous, resounding crash, spraying plastic cutlery and little packets of mustard, ketchup, and relish everywhere.

"Quickly!" he cried. "We can't be here! It's going to happen soon—at any moment, I believe—and we can't be here when it does! I don't think it's safe!"

"*What* isn't sa—" Bethany began, but then Albert put his arm around her shoulders and hustled her after Bob, a lunatic tour-guide who had already bolted for the cafeteria door.

They ran out, following him as he dashed for the United boarding lobby again. Now the echoing rattle of their footfalls was almost lost in the powerful hum which filled the deserted terminal, echoing and reechoing in the many throats of its spoked corridors.

Brian could hear that single vast note beginning to break up. It was not shattering, not even really changing, he thought, but *focussing*, the way the sound of the langoliers had focussed as they approached Bangor.

As they re-entered the boarding lounge, he saw an ethereal light begin to skate over the empty chairs, the dark ARRIVALS and DEPARTURES TV monitors, and the boarding desks. Red followed blue; yellow followed red; green followed yellow. Some rich and exotic expectation seemed to fill the air. A shiver chased through him; he felt all his body-hair stir and try to stand up. A clear assurance filled him like a morning sunray: *We are on the verge of something—some great and amazing thing.*

"Over here!" Bob shouted. He led them toward the wall beside the jetway through which they had entered. This was a passengers-only area, guarded by a red velvet rope. Bob jumped it as easily as the high-school hurdler he might once have been. "Against the wall!"

"Up against the wall, motherfuckers!" Albert cried through a spasm of sudden, uncontrollable laughter.

He and the rest joined Bob, pressing against the wall like

suspects in a police line-up. In the deserted circular lounge which now lay before them, the colors flared for a moment . . . and then began to fade out. The sound, however, continued to deepen and become more real. Brian thought he could now hear voices in that sound, and footsteps, even a few fussing babies.

"I don't know what it is, but it's *wonderful*!" Laurel cried. She was half-laughing, half-weeping. "I *love* it!"

"I hope we're safe here," Bob said. He had to raise his voice to be heard. "I think we will be. We're out of the main traffic areas."

"What's going to happen?" Brian asked. "What do you know?"

"When we went through the time-rip headed east, we travelled back in time!" Bob shouted. "We went into the *past*! Perhaps as little as fifteen minutes . . . do you remember me telling you that?"

Brian nodded, and Albert's face suddenly lit up.

"This time it brought us into the future!" Albert cried. "That's it, isn't it? *This time the rip brought us into the future!"*

"I believe so, yes!" Bob yelled back. He was grinning helplessly. "And instead of arriving in a dead world—a world which had moved on without us—*we have arrived in a world waiting to be born*! A world as fresh and new as a rose on the verge of opening! *That* is what is happening now, I believe. *That* is what we hear, and what we sense . . . what has filled us with such marvellous, helpless joy. I believe we are about to see and experience something which no living man or woman has ever witnessed before. We have seen the death of the world; now I believe we are going to see it born. I believe that the present is on the verge of catching up to us."

As the colors had flared and faded, so now the deep, reverberating quality of the sound suddenly dropped. At the same time, the voices which had been within it grew louder, clearer. Laurel realized she could make out words, even whole phrases.

"—have to call her before she decides—"

"—I really don't think the option is a viable—"

"—home and dry if we can just turn this thing over to the parent company—"

That one passed directly before them through the emptiness on the other side of the velvet rope.

Brian Engle felt a kind of ecstasy rise within him, suffusing him in a glow of wonder and happiness. He took Laurel's hand and grinned at her as she clasped it and then squeezed it fiercely. Beside them, Albert suddenly hugged Bethany, and she began to shower kisses all over his face, laughing as she did it. Bob and Rudy grinned at each other delightedly, like long-lost friends who have met by chance in one of the world's more absurd backwaters.

Overhead, the fluorescent squares in the ceiling began to flash on. They went sequentially, racing out from the center of the room in an expanding circle of light that flowed down the concourse, chasing the night-shadows before it like a flock of black sheep.

Smells suddenly struck Brian with a bang: sweat, perfume, aftershave, cologne, cigarette smoke, leather, soap, industrial cleaner.

For a moment longer the wide circle of the boarding lounge remained deserted, a place haunted by the voices and footsteps of the not-quite-living. And Brian thought: *I am going to see it happen; I am going to see the moving present lock onto this stationary future and pull it along, the way hooks on moving express trains used to snatch bags of mail from the Postal Service poles standing by the tracks in sleepy little towns down south and out west. I am going to see time itself open like a rose on a summer morning.*

"Brace yourselves," Bob murmured. "There may be a jerk."

A bare second later Brian felt a thud—not just in his feet, but all through his body. At the same instant he felt as if an invisible hand had given him a strong push, directly in the center of his back. He rocked forward and felt Laurel rock forward with him. Albert had to grab Rudy to keep him from falling over. Rudy didn't seem to mind; a huge, goony smile split his face.

"Look!" Laurel gasped. "Oh, Brian—look!"

He looked . . . and felt his breath stop in his throat.

The boarding lounge was full of ghosts.

Ethereal, transparent figures crossed and crisscrossed the large central area: men in business suits toting briefcases, women in smart travelling dresses, teenagers in Levi's and tee-shirts with rock-group logos printed on them. He saw a ghost-father leading two small ghost-children, and through them he could see more ghosts sitting in the chairs, reading transparent copies of *Cosmopolitan* and *Esquire* and *U.S. News & World Report.* Then color dove into the shapes in a series of cometary flickers, solidifying them, and the echoing voices resolved themselves into the prosaic stereo swarm of real human voices.

Shooting stars, Brian thought wonderingly. *Shooting stars only.*

The two children were the only ones who happened to be looking directly at the survivors of Flight 29 when the change took place; the children were the only ones who saw four men and two women appear in a place where there had only been a wall the second before.

"Daddy!" the little boy exclaimed, tugging his father's right hand.

"Dad!" the little girl demanded, tugging his left.

"What?" he asked, tossing them an impatient glance. "I'm looking for your mother!"

"New people!" the little girl said, pointing at Brian and his bedraggled quintet of passengers. "Look at the new people!"

The man glanced at Brian and the others for a moment, and his mouth tightened nervously. It was the blood, Brian supposed. He, Laurel, and Bethany had all suffered nosebleeds. The man tightened his grip on their hands and began to pull them away fast. "Yes, great. Now help me look for your mother. What a mess *this* turned out to be."

"But they weren't there *before!*" the little boy protested. "They—"

Then they were gone into the hurrying crowds.

Brian glanced up at the monitors and noted the time as 4:17 A.M.

Too many people here, he thought, *and I bet I know why.*

As if to confirm this, the overhead speaker blared: "*All eastbound flights out of Los Angeles International Airport continue to be delayed because of unusual weather patterns over the Mojave Desert. We are sorry for this inconvenience, but ask for your patience and understanding while this safety precaution is in force. Repeat: all eastbound flights . . .*"

Unusual weather patterns, Brian thought. *Oh yeah. Strangest goddam weather patterns ever.*

Laurel turned to Brian and looked up into his face. Tears streamed down her cheeks, and she made no effort to wipe them away. "Did you hear her? Did you hear what that little girl said?"

"Yes."

"Is that what we are, Brian? The new people? Do you think that's what we are?"

"I don't know," he said, "but that's what it feels like."

"That was wonderful," Albert said. "My God, that was the most wonderful thing."

"*Totally tubular!*" Bethany yelled happily, and then began to clap out "Let's Go" again.

"What do we do now, Brian?" Bob asked. "Any ideas?"

Brian glanced around at the choked boarding area and said, "I think I want to go outside. Breathe some fresh air. And look at the sky."

"Shouldn't we inform the authorities of what—"

"We will," Brian said. "But the sky first."

"And maybe something to eat on the way?" Rudy asked hopefully.

Brian laughed. "Why not?"

"My watch has stopped," Bethany said.

Brian looked down at his wrist and saw that his watch had also stopped. *All* their watches had stopped.

Brian took his off, dropped it indifferently to the floor, and put his arm around Laurel's waist. "Let's blow this joint," he said. "Unless any of you want to wait for the next flight east?"

"Not today," Laurel said, "but soon. All the way to England. There's a man I have to see in . . ." For one horrible moment the name wouldn't come to her . . . and then it did. "Fluting," she said. "Ask anyone along the High Street. The old folks still just call him the gaffer."

"What are you talking about?" Albert asked.

"Daisies," she said, and laughed. "I'm talking about daisies. Come on—let's go."

Bob grinned widely, exposing baby-pink gums. "As for me, I think that the next time I have to go to Boston, I'll take the train."

Laurel toed Brian's watch and asked, "Are you sure you don't want that? It looks expensive."

Brian grinned, shook his head, and kissed her forehead. The smell of her hair was amazingly sweet. He felt more than good; he felt reborn, every inch of him new and fresh and unmarked by the world. He felt, in fact, that if he spread his arms, he would be able to fly without the aid of engines. "Not at all," he said. "I know what time it is."

"Oh? And what time is that?"

"It's half past *now*."

Albert clapped him on the back.

They left the boarding lounge in a group, weaving their way through the disgruntled clots of delayed passengers. A good many of these looked curiously after them, and not just because some of them appeared to have recently suffered nosebleeds, or because they were laughing their way through so many angry, inconvenienced people.

They looked because the six people seemed somehow *brighter* than anyone else in the crowded lounge.

More actual.

More *there.*

Shooting stars only, Brian thought, and suddenly remembered that there was one passenger still back on the plane—the man with the black beard. *This is one hangover that guy will* never *forget,* Brian thought, grinning. He swept Laurel into a run. She laughed and hugged him.

The six of them ran down the concourse together toward the escalators and all the outside world beyond.